THE FIRST TIME

"Yes, I'm John White Owl."

She looked up into a sun-browned face and it seemed to her that her heart stumbled and then accelerated its pace. A coal black braid of hair over either shoulder. Firmly molded lips, decisive chin, high cheekbones, eyes a color she had never seen before.

He stepped forward, nodding. There was a spare grace in the supple movement that reminded her of a bobcat.

An Indian? Papa wouldn't like that. But she held out her hand.

"My friends call me Rowdy," she was horrified to hear herself say with a catch in her voice. The boy, the young man, took her hand.

"My pleasure, Miss Rowdy," he said formally, but the pressure of his hand was not formal, the spark in his eyes was not formal. Rowdy felt herself tremble.

WestWind
Wild
CAROLYN
VAUGHTER

AVON
PUBLISHERS OF BARD, CAMELOT, DISCUS AND FLARE BOOKS

WEST WIND WILD is an original publication of Avon Books. This work has never before appeared in book form.

AVON BOOKS
A division of
The Hearst Corporation
959 Eighth Avenue
New York, New York 10019

First Avon Printing, November, 1981

AVON TRADEMARK REG. U.S. PAT. OFF. AND IN OTHER COUNTRIES, MARCA REGISTRADA, HECHO EN U.S.A.

Printed in the U.S.A.

WFH 10 9 8 7 6 5 4 3 2 1

To Paul

1.

The Indians came while he was helping Ma weed the garden. Out of the corner of his eye, Davey caught the ripple of motion in the loblolly pines and turned to squint, hoping it was one of the spring fawns.

He caught just a glimpse as men and horses melted back into the trees. There were three of them. And big! He reckoned they were big as Goliath, in the Bible. Quiet, though. Even their horses were soundless as shadows. For some reason, the silence gave him a funny feeling in his belly.

"Ma," he said, voice lowered, "there's Injuns in the forest."

Martha Royal straightened, and he saw that beneath her sunbonnet, her face had paled. But she did not glance toward the trees. "Get to the cabin, Davey," she whispered. "Fast!"

"Pa says Injuns are mostly all right," Davey offered hopefully.

"Your pa says a lot of things," she answered. "Come on! Hurry!"

His eight-year-old legs bent and straightened, keeping up with her as she moved across the clearing. He wished he hadn't mentioned Pa. He hated for Ma to get that pinched look and sound so cross.

They reached the cabin, hurried in, shoved the door to, and Ma shot the bolt. Then she leaned against it, drawing a deep breath.

I wish Pa was here, Davey thought. He guessed maybe it was like Ma said; he was never there when you needed him.

"Bring me the rifle, son." Ma interrupted his thoughts.

He fetched the Enfield, the cartridges and percussion caps. Ma loaded, moved near the window, knelt, motioning for him to do the same.

1

There was silence outside, silence that somehow made you hold your breath. Davey stole a quick peek out the window.

"Keep your head down," Ma ordered sharply.

"Maybe they're just passin' through," the boy whispered.

"Maybe." But she kept her grip on the rifle.

They waited for what seemed a long time, and the silence was so acute, it seemed like pressure on his ears.

Then, without warning, there was a hammering on the door. Davey froze as Ma put a finger to her lips. The knocking came once more, twice, then stopped. Again there was silence, then a deafening thud that shook the door and made the whole cabin rattle.

"They're trying to batter their way in." Ma's face was as white as it had been that time he broke his arm.

"I'll take care of you," he quavered.

"I know you will, son; you're a good boy."

There were two more thunderclaps of sound that shook the house. Silence again. Davey felt his eyes stinging. Maybe God had told the Injuns to go away. Maybe He was protecting them like—like those men in the fiery furnace.

It was Ma who stole a glance out the window this time. "Oh, God, no!" She spoke in a rush. "They're gonna torch the cabin, Davey. We'll have to make a run for it!" But she hesitated a moment, put a hand on the boy's head, lifted her face to heaven.

"Father, I pray You to protect my child. Thou dost know I have consecrated him to Thy service." She stood up, well away from the window. "All right, Davey," she said, voice steady. "I'm going to open the door and go first. Maybe I can bring one of them down. You keep close to me as you can. But whatever happens, you keep running. You hear?"

The child nodded, and she stooped to give him one of her rare kisses. "You are in God's keeping," she breathed, and flung the door wide. They darted out, and for a minute or two Davey thought the men had disappeared. Then, just as they reached the first of the trees, a shot sounded.

Ma fell forward. He saw the blood appear beneath her left shoulder blade, saw its rapid spread. "Ma!" he screamed. "Ma!" He tried to lift her, tug her to the safety of the trees. With visible effort she turned her head. "Run, Davey!" she commanded. "I love you."

He tugged at her again, sobbing with frustration because he couldn't pull her along. He heard the sound of hooves as the horses were spurred forward, looked up to see the men bearing down on him.

Blindly, he loosed his hold on his mother and ran. He was sobbing for breath, crashing into trees until he was knocked half senseless. The woods were too dense here for a horse, but he knew Injuns were noiseless on foot.

He ran until he fell and was unable to rise. There was a small ravine nearby, and he crawled into it. For a time he kept hearing sounds, and knew the men were searching for him.

The day wore on endlessly. A black mist of sick rage began to build up inside him. He knew for sure Ma was dead. He hated himself for having been unable to save her. He hated the Injuns for what they had done; hated Pa worst of all because he hadn't been there.

Pa! Ma had begged him to stay home. Davey had heard them quarreling about it more than once.

"I can't make a living on this place, Martha. Nothing but sand and loblolly pines."

"Papa managed."

"Papa gave you the bare essentials. I want better for us. If you'd sell out, we could put the money down on a good place . . ."

Ma had snorted. "If I sold this place, the money'd be gone in thirty days, on some harebrained scheme. Then Davey and I wouldn't even have a place to live."

"I'm gonna make it big one of these days."

"I've heard that before."

Davey tensed as something rustled near him; he finally relaxed, deciding it must have been a squirrel. The mole just above his right eyebrow was itching, burning like fire. He clawed at it, forgetting Ma had told him not to touch it. The day was sultry. His legs and arms stung where they'd been torn by branches and underbrush, and his throat ached. He dozed uneasily, dreaming of sparkling water.

When he wakened, he was momentarily disoriented. Then remembrance returned and sobs pushed into his throat. He felt hot, scorching hot like that time when he

3

had typhoid. Thirst was tormenting him, but he was afraid to leave his hiding place.

He alternately woke and dozed during the interminable day. When it got dark, he would try to find some water. But by the time it was fully dark, huddled beneath the branches, he fell into the feverish sleep of exhaustion.

He dreamed of Pa. Of being swooped up on a broad shoulder. Pa laughing and telling him those stories Ma called tall tales. Pa going off again. In his sleep, Davey cried out, begging Pa not to leave.

When morning came, it was overcast, and he woke to the feeling of being alone in the whole world. Tears rose in his eyes and he brushed them away. No time for cryin', Ma would have said.

His mouth was parched; his stomach rumbled with hunger. He had run without thought of direction, and now had no idea where the cabin was.

He pushed aside the branches and stood up. His knees were wobbly as he began to walk.

He found some pine cones, broke off the woodlike petals, hoping to find something edible. There was nothing. He did find some berries. Ma had always told him to be careful; some berries were poison. He wolfed them down, too hungry to care.

He sucked what nectar he could from some wild honeysuckle blossoms. It didn't stop his thirst, but at least now he could swallow. He continued to wander, hoping to see something familiar. The humid air seemed to press down on him.

Once he thought he heard his name called, and his heart seemed to flop over. The Indians had learned who he was and were calling him. Noiselessly, he stepped into a growth of trees so thick, he could scarcely squeeze through.

2.

The Indians' rampage missed the Ellets. Stub and Serena
first heard of it when two townsmen rode out from Bluffton. A cowpoke in town for supplies had brought the news.

The Ellet children were excited as well as frightened.
Serena went pale, her first thought of Martha Royal,
whose man was always gone.

"Stub," she said through dry lips, "the Royals."

The man nodded. They had been his first thought too,
after he'd given a silent prayer of thanks for the safety of
his own family. It was agreed he'd head northwest while
the townsmen fanned out farther east.

When he reached the clearing where the Royals' cabin
had stood, he smelled the smouldering rubble first, and a
moment later saw Martha's body, already beginning to
swell and decompose in the heat. Stub spent a futile moment cursing the Indians, then slid out of the saddle and,
having brought his shovel, began to dig a gravesite.

As he worked, he wondered about the boy. The Indians were on the warpath about something, for sure, and
might well have carried the boy off. On the other hand,
Davey might have escaped and be hiding in the woods.

After the burial, Stub mopped his face and set out
through the woods. The trees were so entangled, it was
hard to push through. He called Davey's name as he
crashed deeper into the maze, thought once he heard a
limb snap and called again. There was no answer.

The sun was high overhead before he gave up the
search. The forest stretched for miles. It would take at
least a dozen men to cover it, with a better than even
chance the tad wasn't even there.

Back at home, he told Serena what had happened. "I
guess that was all you could do," Serena agreed, but as
they went about their chores, both were uneasy. It was

almost sundown when they agreed Stub should go back once more.

It was late afternoon of that second day when Davey stumbled onto the clearing. Ma's old black wash-pot was still there, by the woodpile. Where the cabin had stood, there was a mound of blackened debris. Davey stood as though turned to stone, a lump filling his throat.

He came on the freshly turned ground, recognized it for what it was and knew his last hope was gone. In an agony of sorrow and guilt, he threw himself down on the moist soil. He did not cry. He blamed himself for not having saved her, and the suffering inside him was too deep for tears. He wanted to die and did not know how.

He scarcely knew when he was lifted from the grave.

"Lord's sake, son," Stub said, "I'd about given up on you. Where you been?"

Without speaking, the boy lifted his eyes, and the man gulped. No child should be burdened with such despair.

"Come along, Davey," he said gruffly. "You'll stay with us until your pa comes for you."

The boy's lips twisted in a smile which, Stub was to tell Serena later, made him go cold.

In the three weeks it took Jim Royal to hear of the tragedy and get home, Davey huddled in a corner of the Ellets' cabin. He ate a few bites if Serena held food to his lips. He lay down on the pallet at night. He ignored the two Ellet children when they proposed games, and for all he spoke, he could have been mute. The only sign he gave of having been reached was when Stub gave him the Testament he had taken from Martha's apron pocket. The small fingers closed around it like a vise; his throat worked convulsively.

His thoughts were locked deep inside him. The Testament made him think of when Ma had dedicated him to the Lord. "Take him," she had said, "and use him as you see fit."

Davey had looked at her uncertainly. "You mean God is going to take me away?"

"No, Davey, not now. You will stay here with me, and I'll teach you. You must learn everything you can."

He had been six then. In the two years that followed, he absorbed learning like sandy soil soaks up water. He learned to read and figure, to write and spell. He learned whole chapters of the Bible.

6

When Jim finally arrived, the Ellets were outside. With tears in his eyes, he expressed his appreciation briefly, anxious to see his son. It was dim in the cabin, and momentarily, he did not see the child. Then his eyes adjusted to the dark and he hastened toward him. "There's just us now, son," he said, his voice choked with feeling, and reached out his arms.

Davey stood up. His sunken eyes were alive for the first time since the attack, impaling his father. "Why weren't you there?" he shrieked. And collapsed.

For nearly a month, Jim and the Ellets nursed the stricken child. His temperature rose and fell, with no apparent cause. The doctor came, shook his head, gave them a bottle of bitter red medicine.

Whether it was the medicine, nursing or providence, Davey began to mend. The day came when he could sit up, when he could walk a few steps, go out into the sunshine. Jim was with him constantly, tending, feeding, holding him close.

And when the boy was strong enough, Jim made arrangements for the two of them to move into Katie Graylinger's boardinghouse, in Bluffton. He thanked the Ellets profusely, told them this had caught him a little short but he would never forget his debt to them.

It was during their three weeks together at Katie's that Jim heard the Indians' rampage had been an act of reprisal. White men had raided their camp, killed an old brave, two squaws and a child, then made off with what food they could find. Outlaws headed for the Kiamichis, most likely.

Jim was sick with helpless rage, vowing vengeance against the outlaws. "Like I said, Davey, Injuns generally don't bother nobody if they're left alone. Yore poor ma . . ."

Davey's face was blank.

"It was," Katie Graylinger said later, "as though everything in the lad's life had been blotted out. And no wonder, neither, them nasty Injuns doing what they done."

It was true. Davey had little recollection of anything prior to his stay at the Ellets. There were two remnants. He hated Indians and despised his father. In neither case did he know why.

When, after the third week, Katie told Jim she needed

the money for their keep, Davey's lip curled. "I know it's been hard," Katie said, "losing your wife and all. If you could pay part now . . ."

Jim smiled, his native charm flashing like an aura. "You're absolutely right, Katie—I may call you Katie, mayn't I?—this terrible tragedy has plumb made me lose sight of everyday things." He turned his pockets inside out. "Not a dime," he said wryly, "but I make pretty good when I'm out tradin'; I'm afeared Davey ain't up to travelin' yet. If you could see your way clear to keep him a few weeks, 'till I get my bearin's again . . ."

About to retort tartly that she wasn't running a charitable institution, Katie caught the agony of humiliation on the boy's face. She hesitated. "Guess I could manage that," she said finally.

3.

The next day, Jim Royal was gone. He hugged Davey and promised he'd be back soon; asked what he should bring him. Davey shrugged.

"He won't be able to pay you even if he comes back," he told Katie as his father rode out of sight.

"Now, boy, that ain't no way to talk about your pa," she said.

Davey didn't answer. His lips trembled. "I don't want to stay without earning my keep," he said. "Have you—got any work I can do?"

Katie looked at him thoughtfully. She saw the fear, the stubborn pride, the rigid shoulders. "Reckon we can find work for a pair of willing hands," she agreed, surrendering. "What with the cow and chickens, garden and such."

Davey stayed at the boardinghouse for four years. In that period, his father returned three times, each time as charming and optimistic, and as penniless, as ever. The last time, he had tried to borrow money from his son, and

Davey laughed, a short scraping sound. In the time he'd been at Katie's, he had had in his possession one coin, a dime, which a drummer had given him for filling a wash-tub with hot water so the man could bathe.

"Where would I get money?" he asked.

"You work here. Katie must pay you something."

"She gives me victuals and a place to sleep, which is more'n you do."

Jim's open hand lashed out, caught the boy across the face. "You keep a civil tongue in your head," Jim stormed.

Davey's hand went to his cheek. There were tears of pain and humiliation in his eyes. The mole above his eyebrow flamed. His face was chalky, voice hard.

"Don't you ever lay a hand on me again," he said, and Jim's blustering was silenced. Jim was uneasy at the deadly quality of the tone, even if the boy was still a . . . knobby-kneed kid.

"Don't be gettin' uppity," he muttered, and turned away.

Shortly after that, Davey told Mrs. Graylinger he was leaving. Her florid face pursed. "Land, boy, where you going?" she asked. "And why? Somethin' you're needin'? I might scare up a cartwheel or two."

"No'm," he said, "everything's fine. And I'm obliged. But a man's got to start sometime. You been good to me," he said simply, and sudden tears glinted in Katie's eyes. She forced them away with her knuckles.

"You've earned your keep," she said roughly. "But who else is gonna hire a boy—a man—as young as you?"

"I been talkin' to Sam Hall. He's got some cattle on open range over in Injun Territory. Thinks he can find something to keep me busy."

"He gonna pay you?"

"Five dollars a month and found. 'Course, it'll be more later."

" 'Course."

When Katie came across Sam in town later that week, she gave him the rough edge of her tongue. "That boy Davey. How come you give him a job? He's still a tad, too little for cowpokin'."

Sam shoved back his hat. "Ever seen him handle a horse?" he asked. "Might'a been born in a saddle. But to

9

tell you the truth, he outtalked me. If you can get him to change his mind, I'd be beholden."

Katie shook her head. "He don't talk much, but when he sets his head on somethin', he's stubborner than ary mule."

"I know. He's been after me four, five months."

Katie, who had once heard herself described as a hardhearted old skinflint and deemed it a compliment, said harshly, "You treat him right, you hear, now?" and stumped off so he couldn't see the moisture in her eyes. There were no tears when she told Davey goodbye. She clapped him on the back and, over his protests, shoved a five-dollar bill in his hand.

"I ain't givin' you nothin'," she snorted. "You earned it."

But she watched long after he set out to meet Sam Hall. He was so small. Could he take the rough cowboy work? It'd kill him if he failed.

For several weeks, Sam Hall kept Dave (he wasn't Davey any longer) around the ranch house. "You help the cook, fetch water, chop kindling." Silently, Dave did as he was told, but there came a day when he sought Sam out again.

"Mr. Hall, I reckon I'm ready for something besides house chores. I'm big and strong. I know how to shoot and rope. I'm fifteen, you know." He didn't like lying, but saying he was twelve made him sound too little.

Hall's lips twitched. "Can you dig post holes and string fence?" he asked.

"If someone shows me how."

Sam chuckled. "Is there anything you don't think you can do?" he asked.

Dave considered the question. "I can't think of anything I wouldn't try," he said.

Sam laughed out loud at that. "All right," he said, "we'll give it a try."

The heavy work in the blistering sun taxed Dave's strength to the limit. Bull England, the cowpoke who was in charge, was surly. "Hell, you ain't heavy enough to run a sharpshooter into the ground," he snorted.

" 'Pears like a feller ought to have a chance to show what he can do." Dave's voice was mild, but the mole began to throb and his face flamed.

"OK, buster, you got the business end of it."

He worked Dave mercilessly, snarling when he slowed to wipe the sweat out of his eyes. The boy's shoulders burned beneath the scorching sun. By afternoon, he was trembling from exhaustion. But he kept on until Bull was ready to quit.

"That's enough for one day," the man said. "Knock off and we'll go down to the creek for a swim."

Dave stayed awake long enough to take a plunge in the cool deep water, but back on the bank, he fell, sodden with sleep. Bull's attempt to waken him brought only a groan. At last he pulled Dave far enough from the bank that a water moccasin wouldn't come nosing around and draped the boy's shirt over him.

Dave wakened first the next morning, so sore and stiff that any movement made him groan, but he choked it back. No one was going to hear him whine. He was shivering. Nights were chill enough on the range that you didn't go sleeping naked. He pulled his clothes on. Sore and cold and aching as he was, there was a fierce pride building inside him. He hadn't whimpered or quit.

Stumbling up the bank, he saw Bull was still asleep. A smile touched Dave's lips. He leaned over to shake the older man.

Bull shot up, wild-eyed, .45 in hand and leveled.

"Hey," the boy yelled. "It's me. Dave."

Bull let loose a string of profanity. "Ain't you got no sense at all, boy?" he snarled. "Never creep up on a fellar like that. I thought it was a snake."

"You scared of snakes?"

"Let's just say we ain't exactly friends. But n'mind that. Don't never touch no one sleepin'. You could get your head blowed off."

Dave nodded solemnly. In the following months, there were many other range lessons Bull taught him. And in the bunkhouse, Bull was his defense if the other men got to badgering him. Like when Bo insisted Dave go into town with them one Saturday night.

"Got the purtiest little gal lined up for you," he baited the boy. " 'Bout your size, too. I mean, I reckon your manhood ain't too big yet. But a fella's gotta learn."

Dave's ears had gone a deep crimson. "I got things to do here," he muttered, and the poke laughed.

"What I'm offerin' would be a lot more fun. What's the matter, kid? Scared?"

11

The mole above Dave's eyebrow began to throb. He was sitting on his bunk, one of Sam's books in his hand. Sam had offered him the use of the library the day he noted the boy looking hungrily at the books lining the living room shelves. Dave swallowed, knowing he was no match for his tormentor. He opened the book, felt his chin seized, his head jerked up.

"Pay attention when I'm talkin' to you, boy." Despite Dave's resolve, the black mist of rage propelled him to his feet. He swung. Bo laughed, pushed him back to the bunk with contemptuous ease.

"Gonna have to eat more sowbelly 'fore you can stand up to a man." Tears of rage were in Dave's throat. He had the sudden wild fear that he was going to start bawling.

"How about me, Bo?" a lazy voice asked. Bull was on his feet. Big as Bo was, Bull was easily his equal. And where Bo was carrying blubber, Bull was lean and hard. "Like to take on someone your own size?" Bull asked the silent Bo.

The moon face turned petulant. "Aw, hell, Bull, I was only funnin' with him. Kid's got to learn."

"He don't need you to learn him," Bull said. Bo threw up his hands.

"All right, all right," he muttered. "Folks what can't take a joke . . ."

From that time, Dave knew he had a friend. To a boy who had never known a man's strength and authority, Bull became the father and brother and friend he'd never had.

Along with the other lessons, Bull taught him one thing which was to plague the boy through life. He taught him to swear with the best of them. When he smashed his finger one day, nailing a recalcitrant piece of barbed wire to a fence post, he yowled "Dagnab it!" dropped the hammer and shoved the blackened finger into his mouth.

"Dagnab it!" Bull thundered. "Oh, la dee dah. That's woman talk, Dave. If yore gonna be a man ridin' the range, you gotta talk like a man. What do you think I'd have said if I'd mashed my finger?"

"God damn that goddam hammer to hell and gone again," Dave answered without hesitation.

Bull laughed. "Now you're talkin'," he said.

For a couple of months after that, when Dave had free

12

time, he rode out onto the prairie alone, and there he practiced the curses which seemed to come so easy to the rest of the men.

In the three or four years that followed, though he had not yet gained his full height, his muscles grew hard and strong. The range lessons had become a part of him. He could still outride most of the men; he seemed to have been born knowing how to break and handle a horse.

4.

On Sundays, the hands who had survived Saturday night in good enough shape staged their own competitions roping and tying dogies, wrestling steers, riding the wildly bucking broncos. Those who were not competing made preposterous bets.

"My half of Texas agin' yourn Cal takes a calf down faster'n Dorado."

"My half of Texas's already pledged, but I'll bet you my gold mine in Californy."

On Sundays, too, they did the more serious work of breaking the horses. And there, after a couple of times, no one bet against Dave.

It was with the horse named Mean that Dave wondered if he hadn't met his match. Sam Hall had bought a herd of wild horses. By and large, the wild ponies of the plains were not much more than half as big as their domestic cousins. But the stallion of this herd was a magnificent chestnut, standing almost fifteen hands.

The mares of the herd were being broken with no more than the usual effort. Not the stallion. Proud, wicked and unmanageable, he had earned the sobriquet "Mean." Frank Box, acknowledged best of the cowpokes with horses, had got a crushed leg when the chestnut smashed him against the corral fence.

Dave begged for a chance at him. Bull shook his head. "He's a natural-born killer. You seen what he did to

Frank. Most horses, once they throw you, are satisfied. They'll go on about their own business. This devil will stay and kick you to death."

Dave went about his work, but his thoughts kept returning to the stallion. For days, he tried going by the horse pen, carrying some tidbit, an apple or carrot. The other horses would nudge up to the fence, nibbling. Not Mean. Dave watched the way he moved, the things that spooked him—which was mostly everything, the boy concluded.

The stallion always stood apart, legs braced, head held high in suspicion, eyes rolling. Even the time or two he was in the corral alone, he showed ferocious teeth, and went into a frenzy of kicking at the boy's approach.

Frank saw Dave once offering a treat and grinned sourly. "Think yore gonna tame that bastard, yore crazy," he said.

It was a dazzling day in May when Dave finally tackled the big chestnut.

Frank had been right. The boy's efforts at making friends had been fruitless. The animal had been herded into the corral only because he refused to leave the mares of his brood, and had spent a good bit of the morning trying to kick down the walls of his prison.

By the time the bulldogging started, he was in a frenzy. Foam flecked his mouth, and he was whinnying in helpless rage. Dave studied him as the mares were led out, one by one, to acquaint them with the important part a horse plays in bulldogging a steer.

"Fixin' to ride Mean?" Frank gibed. Dave shrugged.

Mean reared each time the gate was opened and hastily closed. Once his foreleg smashed against the gate, and Dave held his breath, afraid the splendid animal had broken a bone. But he came down sound.

When the last of the mares had been shunted out of the pen, Dave climbed up on the fence. Mean watched, quivering. Dave slid inside like a shadow. The chestnut's ears went back. Slowly, Dave began to circle. The chestnut moved as the boy did. The other waddies watched, scarcely drawing a breath.

Dave inched closer. The horse did not retreat, but his head went down, his legs braced almost in a crouch.

"It's all right, fellow." Dave's voice might have been

14

the whisper of the wind. Mean's teeth showed as Dave came closer. Muscles rippled beneath the enormous withers.

"All right, boy, all right." And then, in one supple, unexpected movement, Dave sprang to the animal's back. For a moment, Mean seemed shocked into immobility. The next instant, he screamed and reared.

In the second of respite, Dave had locked his arms around the powerful neck. The horse came down with a jolt, bucking to dislodge the hateful burden.

"Open the gate," Dave called. It was hastily swung back, but Mean was not yet ready for freedom. He flung himself toward the wall of the corral and began to lunge against it in a frenzy. Dave's leg took the first shock with stunning pain that ran into his groin. Momentarily, the world went gray.

Then, as the horse would have lunged again, Dave kicked its flank with his good leg. Mean snorted in astonished indignation and bolted. Straight through the gate in a dead-out run.

Dave hung on for dear life.

He had never had such a ride—the wind in his face, the freedom. The horse ran more than five miles. Dave was still clinging when Mean began to slow and finally, lathered with sweat, stopped. This would show the pokes, the boy thought.

The horse swung his head as though trying to get a glimpse of his burden. He was blowing, exhausted for the moment, but his head was still held defiantly high, and, quivering with indignity, he shook himself mightily. Dave stuck, but he was beginning to feel a peculiar sensation.

Admiration for the spirit that would not bow to defeat.

Goddammit, he thought helplessly. He was tired of being called "boy." Long minutes passed. When the horse once again moved restively, Dave unlocked his hands and slid to the ground.

Momentarily, Mean stood frozen. Then, in one fluid movement, he turned around until he and the boy were eye to eye. His muscles were quivering, legs poised for flight. But for the instant, he stood.

"Go on," Dave said softly. "You're free."

The chestnut laid back his ears and the next moment was a brownish streak, whinnying triumphantly as he ran.

15

Dave trudged slowly back to the house, hands clasped behind him, head down in thought. He did not understand his own motives. He only knew it was not right for the stallion to be imprisoned.

5.

At sixteen, Dave had decided he was going to be a runt all his life. Then, almost overnight, he began to shoot up. In six months, he grew more than four inches and was taller than any of the other cowboys except Bull. His breadth increased too, and his hands and feet became enormous.

It was a time of confusion to him. He felt like he was stumbling over his own feet most of the time; his voice grew deep except for an occasional squeak; his sleep was troubled with dreams he could never remember.

He considered trying to talk to Bull, ask him if he'd ever felt like this. But what could he say? That he thought he was going daft?

One day, when Bull had sent him over toward Crockett arroya in search of some yearlings, Dave finally figured out what was wrong with him.

He had found the herd in a small ravine, but a bull had found them too and was having himself a splendid time with the virgin heifers.

"You bastard!" Dave shouted, leaping off his horse and slapping his hat against his thigh. "They ain't ready yet. How the hell did you get in here?"

He rushed forward, yelling and waving his arms. Already mounted, the bull ignored him. Dave came to a halt. To try to dislodge the old devil now—well, he had seen it tried once. It hadn't worked. He climbed back on his horse, ready to herd the bull elsewhere once he was disengaged.

As he sat waiting, the boy felt warmth begin to suffuse his body, a stab of pain in his groin. The dreams which

16

had been tantalizing his memory were suddenly vivid. His face grew hot. Perspiration dampened his back and under-arms.

Lord God, he thought, I'm stupid as any jackass. After being around animals all his life, you'd think a fellow would know when he was ready for a woman.

The next time the cowpokes began to dress up, David washed, shaved and got into his own town clothes. He took a lot of chaffing on the way to town.

"Them saloon gals at the Last Chance is used to some choice men, Dave. Reckon you can handle 'em?" Bo asked with a guffaw. "We'll let you have Dotty tonight. She's special."

Dave didn't reply. He had a sinking feeling that he was going to make himself look ridiculous. He didn't feel now as he had out at the arroya. Even conjuring up the bull's performance brought no answering warmth. What if he went up to one of the rooms with a woman and then couldn't . . .

Just how the hell did you turn it on? Right this minute, he'd rather have been back at the bunkhouse, reading a book. Let me get through this without making a fool of myself, he petitioned some unknown deity. But by the time they entered the Last Chance, he was nauseous and bathed in cold sweat.

With the other men, he bellied up to the bar and or-dered a beer. Vaguely, he noted Bo across the room, deep in conversation with one of the women. Bo was sniggering, and the woman's raddled face lighted with malicious amusement, as the cowpoke gestured at Dave. Then the woman was coming straight toward him.

She squeezed in beside him, her breast against his arm. He could smell her talcum. "Haven't seen you before, cowboy," she said. "I'm Dotty. What's your handle?"

"D-Dave Royal, ma'am."

"Well, Dave Royal, like to buy me a beer?"

Dave gulped. "Y-yes, ma'am," he said, "I reckon."

With the mug of beer in her hand, Dotty grimaced. "Awful hot and noisy in here. Like to go up to my room, where it's quiet, and get acquainted?"

Dave ran his tongue over dry lips. Bo had put her up to something, for sure. But if he didn't go, the waddies were going to make life one hell on earth for him.

"All right, ma'am," he squeaked and followed sheepishly as she led the way toward the staircase. His knees felt like water, and he was sure the room was a mile long. Besides, he sure didn't feel any urge.

In the room, door closed behind them, Dotty motioned toward a horsehide settle. "Don't cost nothin' to sit down," she said.

Dave sank onto the chair, sweating. "Thank you, ma'am, for asking me up here," he mumbled. "All the pokes down there, I mean, a pretty lady like you . . ."

Something very nearly like pain flitted across her face, was gone. "Lady," she repeated softly. She had been sitting on the bed. She stood up, turned her back on him, stood there a long while, silent.

"Dave," she said, turning back to face him, "would you like to just sit here and talk awhile? When we go back down, all the fellows will think you, we—been together."

Dave was tempted. He truly was. He mulled it over. "Ma'am . . ." He hesitated, then suddenly was telling her about the bull and the heifers, how much he wanted a woman then. But now . . .

"I know," Dotty said when he broke off. She turned the lamp down so the room was shadowy, came to sit beside him. "Like this chair?" she asked. "I had it built special." He nodded, felt the pressure of her arm against his.

"Lean back and relax, Dave," the woman said. "Leave everything to me."

It was nearly two hours before they went back downstairs. There was a spring in Dave's walk that no man in the room missed, though no one said a word. As they drew closer to the bar, Dotty patted Dave's cheek. "Cowboy," she purred, "you got my personal welcome any time you want to come back."

"I'm obliged to you, ma'am," he said, and his voice was as exuberant as a rooster's crow. He had been established as a man in his own eyes, as well as those of the crew.

6.

At branding time, everyone worked from daybreak to dark. They set up a long way from the house, close by a mesquite thicket, which would furnish welcome shade at day's end. A cook and provisions accompanied them so they could eat as well as sleep where they worked.

A shallow draw lined by more mesquite lay half a mile or so to their east.

The days were filled with the merciless sun, horse flies, which bit viciously, the smell of burning flesh, the bawling of the animals.

The year before, Dave's arms had quivered with exhaustion before the day's work was complete. Not now. He did his share of the work without difficulty.

It was on the third morning, as the men woke, yawning, and made ready for breakfast, that a fawn broke out of the draw, stood frozen momentarily, forming a delicate chiaroscuro against the shadows.

Something moved in Dave's chest. A lump formed in his throat. Had he stopped to think, he might have said the fawn was pretty or, more prudently, said nothing at all. Instead, he blurted out, "Ain't he sweet?"

Three or four of the hands heard and stared at him, Bull among them. There was a moment's astounded silence, and Dave's heart kicked against his rib cage. Then Bull said incredulously, *"Sweet?"* He choked with laughter. *"Sweet!"* he repeated, and a great series of guffaws went up. The word ran around the camp like summer lightning.

Dave felt his ears burn, his insides turn to ice water, the mole begin to throb. He stared blindly at Bull, disbelief on his face. The disbelief changed to such anguish, and then to such helpless rage, that Bull moved uncomfortably.

Then Dave launched himself at the older, stronger man like a catapult. Bull caught the boy's flailing arms and held them easily. "Come on, Dave, it was a joke." Finally, Dave quit struggling and Bull loosed him. "Gotta hurrah you a little," he said, clapping him on the shoulder.

Dave walked away, spat.

Later, some of the men would have twitted him further about calling a critter "sweet," but he turned on them a look so black and implacable, the gibes died in their throats.

In the months that followed, Dave did his work competently. He had always been shy, not given to speaking much, but he'd whistled as he went about his chores. Now, outside the necessities of the job, he said nothing at all.

He did not consciously plan revenge against the man he had considered his friend. He simply knew the time would come when he would even the score. And it did, on his first cattle drive.

The herd was headed toward Wichita, along the Chisholm trail. It was uncommonly hot and dry, and they had insufficient water. Red River, swollen by a cloudburst upstream, ran wider and deeper than usual. The cattle, scenting water, began to bawl and run. The cowpokes sloped in, trying to slow them, prevent a stampede, but the cattle were wild with thirst.

As the first wave of animals reached the riverbank, they stopped to lower their heads but were swept forward by the others and hurled into the swift current. Within minutes, the entire herd was floundering in the depths, and men were yelling and circling them in an attempt to keep them from being swept away.

By chance it happened that Dave was slightly behind Bull. Still helping contain the beeves, he made his horse swim closer to the older man. A forked stick bobbed past, and he snatched it, held it poised as he yet moved nearer.

"Moccasin!" he shouted and jabbed Bull behind the knee. Bull screamed, dropped the reins, grabbed his leg and went tumbling into the roiling water. Dave's face was expressionless as he watched the big man flounder.

"Help!" Bull shouted. "Help!" His head went under, bobbed back up. "Can't swim!" he screamed, and swallowed another great mouthful of dirty water as he went down again.

It was a temptation to leave him, but Dave could not.

He turned his horse, swam back, helped Bull haul himself up.

Bull was white, shaking. "Bastard struck me," he said. Dave said nothing.

They lost nearly forty animals that day. Bull's horse managed to swim ashore on his own, and Dave's roan carried the two men to safety.

Once on the bank, they stopped to rest. The herd was circled in and, winded, was content to graze. Bull all but fell off the horse and jerked up his pants leg.

Dave dismounted slowly and found, despite his years of practice, that he had to make an effort to keep a straight face. Bull was dough-colored, shouting for someone to do something. The cowpokes gathered round as Dave examined the leg. There was a slight redness where Bull had been jabbed. Dave turned to the silent men. "See any puncture marks?" he asked.

One of them squatted and peered closely at the leg. "No sign," he said, looking doubtfully at Bull. "Sure he struck?"

"Hell, yes, I'm sure!" Bull roared. "I got pains runnin' clean up and down the leg. Get a doctor!" He broke off with a moan, and again Dave spoke to the intent men.

"Any of you see a snake?" he demanded. They shook their heads.

Bull snarled at him. "You seen it, Goddammit! You yelled 'moccasin.' I felt it. What're you tryin' to do?"

Dave stood up, dusted off his hands. "Trying to keep you from going off half cocked," he said curtly. "You ain't been bit." He shook his head. "Got to watch that imagination, Bull. You'll be seein' snakes out of bottles next."

"I ain't been bit?"

"That's right."

Bull let the pants leg fall. He was red-faced as, finally convinced, he got up. A burst of relieved laughter rose from the men. Then relief turned to ridicule.

"Hey, Bull," one of them said, grinning, "we'll get you a carriage next time." Bull scowled, and Dave turned away. No emotion showed on his face, but there was a grim satisfaction within him.

It was that same night, after they were bedded down, that two braves rode up. Dave sat up as they approached; saw them stop when the sentries challenged them. The cowpokes were near Apache country, and some said

21

Apaches were the fiercest of the Plains Indians. To Dave, the vicious heathens all looked alike. He hated their guts.

All the men were up now, and one Indian, riding a beautiful paint, spoke. Dave couldn't understand, but one of the cowboys shrugged, turned to Bull. "They want two steers," he said. Dave felt his body tense. His hand moved, seeking his gun. Then, disbelieving, he heard Bull snort. "Tell 'em to take 'em and git."

"How come?" Dave protested when the braves had driven the beeves off.

Bull scowled. "Blackmail," he said laconically.

Dave had no idea why his hackles had risen, why he felt such hatred toward red men. He spat. "I wouldn't have handed 'em over," he said.

"You're big, Dave," Bull growled, "but you ain't very smart. If they hadn't got those steers, we'd'a been plagued with spooked cattle rest of the trip."

"They're no better'n horse thieves."

Bull, who had not forgotten the snake, said sourly, "Reckon that's what they think about us."

With a snort, Dave turned away.

7.

When he turned twenty-one, Dave decided it was time he saw more of the world than the ranch, the trail and Wichita. He thanked Sam Hall for the job, and especially for the use of his books, stood the cowpokes an evening of drinking and entertainment at the Last Chance and headed north.

He had some money put away, a good horse and saddle and a nebulous desire for excitement. In Abilene, he fell in with a group of happy-go-lucky fellows of his own age, hellbent on having a good time. They worked a few days at whatever they could when they were low on cash. They laughed a lot, drank a lot and, when they could afford it, would visit a bawdy house.

They left Abilene hurriedly, one night, when a man they'd had a fracas with went to the sheriff. With no destination, they rode hard across the plains, drifted into Missouri, wound up in St. Louis.

To Dave, the city was exciting but too big. One evening, when they had, in sheer high spirits, shot up a saloon and the keeper sent for the law, Dave suggested they head for Pequot.

"Heard it's wide open," he told them; "let's ride."

There was instant agreement. They were all groggy to the point at which a man is either amenable to any suggestion or belligerent and ready to fight.

There were three saloons in Pequot, two brothels and a barnlike building called the Games of Chance. They hit the saloons first, were too drunk to want a woman, so turned to the gambling hall.

The saloons had been bright and noisy. The Games of Chance was dimly lit. There was an almost cathedrallike silence there. The click of dice, the low-pitched call of the roulette croupier, the spin of the wheel, the susurration of cards were the only sounds.

Every head in the place swung round as Dave and his crew entered, raucous and sportful. They quickly quieted under the gaze of all those eyes.

"Reckon we ought to mosey on?" one suggested.

"Why?" Dave demanded.

They went in, found places to stand and watch. Dave wound up blinking at a game of five-card draw, realized vaguely he was drunk as a hoot owl. After a couple of hands, one of the players left, and the dealer raised his eyebrows at Dave. "Want to sit in, cowboy?" he asked.

"I'll watch a spell longer."

The man's lip curled. "Hayseed all you got in your pocket?" he asked. One of the other men sniggered. Dave felt his temper rising, the black mist clouding his mind.

"I could manage a buck or two if the company was right," he drawled.

"Something wrong with our company, hayseed?"

"Not to say your *company*. First deck I ever saw, though, where the bottom card was always an ace."

The man came to his feet, shoving back his chair, which crashed to the floor. "You accusin' me of bottom dealin'?" he asked, voice dangerously soft.

Dave shrugged. "If the shoe fits . . ."

The dealer went for his gun. Dave was faster. There were two shots, but as Dave pulled the trigger, he lunged to the right, escaped unscathed. A hole appeared between the other man's eyes. He toppled across the table, sending chips, drinks and cash flying.

The three other men at the table were up, reaching for their guns. Staring death in the face, Dave was instantly completely sober. The shots had stopped all activity in the building. There was an ominous silence. Dave's buddies, weapons in hand, moved to his side.

"Get the hell out of here," one of them hissed in Dave's ear. "We'll handle these dandies."

Dave shook his head. He wasn't leaving other men to finish what he'd begun. With a sudden unexpected movement, he kicked the table over, sending two of the poker players down with it. One of Dave's gang took a shot at the lantern that hung overhead. The metal base punctured. Flaming coal oil appeared briefly. Then the lantern exploded, flinging burning debris throughout the room.

As though that had been a signal, the crowd erupted into a brawling, screaming, cursing mass. The single man left at the poker table didn't attack, but watched the melee, and especially Dave, with a sardonic expression.

"Hope you know what you're doin', buckaroo," he said. "That man you dusted was Dalton kin. 'Sides, the law out of St. Louis keeps an eye on this town when it comes to murder. They're gonna be after you, boy. You're gonna be stretchin' a rope."

"He drew down on me," Dave snapped.

"That ain't gonna matter a tinker's damn to the Daltons," the man assured him. One of his friends at Dave's side suggested they get the hell out of there. Dave decided it was prudent to agree.

Outside, mounted on their horses, one of them said, "We better split up. You take first choice, Dave. You're the one they're gonna be most interested in. Each of us heads a different way, it ought to confuse 'em some if they get up a posse."

"Or if the Daltons show," another contributed soberly.

Dave thought fast; knew they were mostly Texans and would favor familiar territory. "I'll head east," was his decision. "Good luck!"

He spurred his horse and took off. When he passed near St. Louis and saw no sign that he was being pursued, he caught a paddle-wheeler on the Mississippi and headed downriver.

8.

He disembarked the next morning with a thumping pain in his head and a sickness in his gullet. To have killed a man over a card game was unbelievable. His guilt rode him like an albatross.

He made his way slowly across Illinois, into Kentucky and then into the mountains of Tennessee. He avoided towns as much as possible, stopping only to buy a few supplies.

In the mountains, he brewed dye from the bark of a walnut tree, applied it to his unruly blond mop and facial hair. He hid out for three or four months, fishing and killing small game for food. But eventually he grew weary of his own company, packed his scant belongings into his saddlebags and headed his horse, Whiskey, again south by east. "We're gonna be world travelers before this is over," he told the roan.

He again avoided towns, circling when he could see smoke or hear the screech of a train grinding to a stop. But he came on one village, Millet, without warning and decided he might as well buy a little coffee and sugar. He was unkempt enough to look like any saddle bum.

It was as he was leaving the town that he got the jolt. The "Wanted" poster had been tacked to a black-walnut tree, and his own name leaped out at him. Two-hundred-dollar reward, dead or alive. Someone had drawn a picture, but it could have resembled a thousand men. Still, Dave felt a rabbit run across his grave. With a quick glance behind him, he leaned over in the saddle, snatched the poster and shoved it into his pocket.

And as soon as he cleared the town, he pushed Whiskey to his limit. Did the law and/or the Daltons figure he was in the east, or did those posters go out all over the country? He didn't know. He turned back into the mountains.

It was three days out of Millet that he came on the brush arbor meeting. I'm not much of a churchgoer, he thought wryly, but at the moment he hankered for company.

"Be not deceived; God is not mocked, and whatsoever a man soweth, that shall he also reap," the circuit rider was saying as Dave removed his hat and sat down on one of the rough benches. The old preacher, who called himself Brother Roberts, spoke of an eye for an eye, a tooth for a tooth, and Dave felt his troubled conscience begin to smart.

He thought of walking out but decided he'd made enough noise coming in late. Almost against his will, he listened as the old man continued. Then realized he wasn't talking about hell and damnation, but about God's forgiving grace. Dave began to listen more intently.

As he listened, the memories which had eluded him for so many years began to fill his mind. At first, just a face, floating and ethereal. Then, like turning the pages of a book, the cabin kitchen, the smell of baking bread. Saw her hands reach for the Bible. Remembered the Testament, which he still carried with his gear.

He recalled the last bitter words between her and Pa.

Saw himself kneeling beside her as she prayed, her voice thick with anguish. "Make Jim come to his senses," she had cried out. She had been rigid in her beliefs, yet she had spoken of a God of love, much as the old preacher was doing.

Then he remembered the Indians, again saw his mother fall. Tears began to burn his eyes, and he didn't know whether they were tears of hatred or grief. He held them back with an effort.

After the crowd left, he stayed behind to talk with the old preacher. Afraid that someone might have seen the "Dave Royal" poster, he mumbled "Angus Scofield" when the old man asked his name. Angus Scofield had been the name of his mother's brother.

He told Brother Roberts of the exultation he felt in remembering his mother, dwelt on her wholehearted belief. As he talked, he could not hold back the tears. He continued to pour out the happenings of his life, came finally to the night in Pequot.

"I was drunk," he said simply. "But the man is dead, and there's a price on my head."

"We have to face up to our sins before God," the old man said. His smile was rueful. "God will forgive, but the law ain't so lenient."

Sighing, the younger man leaned forward to scratch aimlessly in the dirt. "I asked God's forgiveness while you were preaching." Unaccustomed to sharing his thoughts, he was embarrassed. He could feel his ears go red, the mole begin to throb.

"You didn't come down to the Mourner's Bench," the old preacher said reprovingly.

"It was kind of a private thing between Him and me." Slowly, he pulled the crumpled paper from his pocket. "You can take me in," he said tonelessly. "Earn yourself an easy two hundred dollars. I'm—my name's not really Angus Scofield. It's—I'm Dave Royal, like it says on the poster."

The old man shook his head. "I'm no law man. You're the one's got to decide whether to give yourself up. One way or another, a man pays for his sins."

"Then why bother about religion?"

"Why, that way, son, a man's got the peace and strength to face up to his punishment without breaking. You want my opinion, I'd say gettin' your neck stretched ain't gonna help anyone. But you owe, no doubt about that. Way I see it, there must be some way you can serve God and other people."

"Ma dedicated me to God's service when I was a tad," Dave mumbled.

"There you are," Brother Roberts said, as though that provided all the answers. "All you got to do is find out what He wants."

Dave never saw the old man again. But in the days that followed, the effects of the meeting stayed with him.

He was restless now, indecisive. But he had decided to call himself Angus Scofield. He drifted back the way he had come, finally reached Wichita. He had by-passed both St. Louis and Pequot. Retaining the change in hair color, he signed on to work the holding pens in Wichita.

Then he marked time, much preoccupied with the things he and the circuit rider had discussed that night. He

27

thought often of his mother, of the comfort of her arms. She had been a stern woman, but loving to him. Religious faith had been her way of life, and doing one's duty an obsession.

At times he bucked against his feelings, the sense of waiting for guidance, telling himself he'd gone soft in the head. Men got killed every day. Their killers didn't mope. They were hanged or they went their way without a backward glance.

When the other men went off on their sprees, he stayed behind in the bunkhouse or rode out into the countryside, alone. He had to decide. Either he must turn himself in to the law or he must put the whole incident behind him and get on about what he was to do next. The old preacher had said he owed. Ma had dedicated him to God's work.

But doing God's work, as he saw it, meant preaching. He didn't even talk a lot or easily, much less preach. The story of Moses came back, just as his mother had read it to him. Moses had said he couldn't talk to Pharaoh because he had a speech defect. God had responded by saying He'd send his brother Aaron along to do the talking. Moses' job was to lead the Israelites out of Egypt.

Angus woke before dawn one morning, with the feeling that someone had touched his shoulder. He looked around the bunkhouse. No one else was stirring. Puzzled, he got his pants and shoes on and went outside.

A cool breeze ruffled his hair. Night shadows were just disappearing; the eastern sky was rose-tinged. Angus walked past the animal pens. Amidst a small grove of trees, he sat down on a log.

He had a sense of expectancy. Reckon the sky's gonna open up and give me orders, he thought, mocking himself. The sky did not open up. No orders came. But he sensed somehow that an answer would soon be given. Then, as he walked back to the bunkhouse, he scoffed at himself.

He'd be seeing things, next.

It was that evening that someone brought a *Kansas City Star* to the bunkhouse. It was three weeks old, but Angus read it anyhow. It wasn't often a newspaper came their way.

It was on the fourth page that the word "Pequot" seemed to leap out at him. It wasn't an important bit of news. Two lines. Pequot had gotten itself a sheriff, Jace

28

Owens, who had promised to drive the rough element out of town.

Pequot. Angus sat with the paper, slowly rolling it tighter and tighter. Was this the answer? Did God move in such a small and apparently haphazard way?

There ought to be some clear-cut recognizable instructions if the Almighty wanted a fellow to do something, Angus grumbled to himself. But he had the disquieting feeling that the word "Pequot" itself was an order. He thought about it for a couple of days, then gathered up his meager possessions and headed back.

9.

The town was typical of its day. Perhaps a little rougher than most because when St. Louis had staged its clean-up on gamblers, pimps and prostitutes a few years back, the center of action had simply switched over to Pequot, from which the big city was easily accessible.

Having reached his destination, Angus could not yet bring himself to surrender to the sheriff. It was dusk when he rode slowly up the dusty main street. The saloons were doing their usual thriving business. There were a lot of horse droppings in the street, but not many people about.

He wondered if any of the Daltons were there. But with a new name and the darkened hair, not to mention the beard and mustache he'd grown, he felt sufficiently disguised.

The town had grown enormously. A couple of dozen houses. Stable and blacksmith shop. Furniture dealer. Boardinghouse. Hotel.

He found accommodations at Ma Benson's boardinghouse. No women, no drunks, no cursing. When he had washed the travel grime off, he sat down in the one chair his room afforded and said sourly, "OK, here I am."

He was given no direct answer, but he had a quickened sense of anticipation, which stayed with him as he rode out in the countryside and as he strolled through the town on foot. There were in Pequot two disparate worlds, he had found. There was the daylight world of law-abiding folks and the after-dark world of painted women and flashy men.

Angus could not feel he fitted into either. But on Sunday he went to church, listened intently, yet was no less confused as to what he was to do. He did hear announced that there would be a fund-raising sociable that evening, and decided to go. He might get some home-cooked food.

He did. The tables were groaning under their loads of chicken, cake, roast pork, a cornucopia of foods. Women buzzed about, tending the tables like a swarm of bright bees. He noted with amusement that a goodly number of the after-dark folks were there. Home cooking apparently drew sinner as well as saint.

He ate bountifully of chicken, potato salad, bread, drank three glasses of lemonade and went back for dessert. Angel food and devil's food cake, ambrosia . . .

"I can recommend the strawberry shortcake," a demure voice said. Angus looked up into dancing eyes, amethyst-colored, and caught his breath. A delicately sculpted face, a cloud of—hair. He gawked at the hair dressed high on the girl's head. Small tendrils had escaped the severe style and curled on her forehead and around her ears. But the color? Fifty years later, the color would be called platinum. But Angus could put no name to it. He only knew it was silky; the girl so lovely, she hardly seemed human.

She put a hand up and touched the strands uncertainly. "Is something wrong?" she asked.

Angus drew a deep breath and shook his head, realizing his gaze had been so steady, it disturbed her. "I'm sorry, ma'am," he said, then blurted out, "You're the prettiest thing I've ever seen."

A flush swept from the curved ivory of her neck to color her face.

"I wasn't aimin' to be disrespectful," he stumbled on as her eyes fell. "I—I'm Angus Scofield."

"Mr. Scofield," she echoed primly. "Could I help you with some dessert?"

"Strawberries'll be fine."

She ladled out an enormous helping, handed it to him, took his money without ever looking up again.

Angus wandered away in a daze. He felt as he had

when he saw the fawn that time, as he did when The Glory seemed caught in a sunrise. He watched the girl as best he could, without appearing to be unseemly. And when a ball came his way, with a boy chasing it, he held the toy a minute and asked the youngster the lady's name.

"Oh, that's Electra Colley." The kid panted, snatched the ball and was gone.

Revival services were held after the sociable. Angus heard nothing of what the preacher said. He was watching the second row, where Electra sat by an older woman. Mother, probably, Angus thought, though they looked nothing alike. He could see the tilt of the girl's head as she joined in singing the hymns, could see the proud thrust of her shoulder, the roundness of her breast.

After service he waited around, was rewarded by the barest flicker of a glance as she walked by him.

He didn't mind waiting in Pequot after that. The Almighty could take just as much time as He liked. He saw Electra—I'll call her Lexie, he decided, when I know her better. He had no doubt at all that he would know her better. Occasionally, he caught a glimpse of her, turning in at the general store or—and this puzzled him—carrying a basket into the sheriff's office.

The revival was to last through the week. He attended each night. Afterward, could have told nothing of what had been said. But he could have described the bluish-violet of one of Lexie's dresses, the perfect curve of her cheek, the silken length of her lashes.

He was becoming impatient again. Not, this time, for The Answer, but to be properly introduced to the girl who filled his thoughts by day, his dreams by night.

Finally he broached Ma Benson on the subject. "I keep seeing this young lady go into the sheriff's office. She got folks in jail?"

Ma chuckled. "Not likely. Her ma's so strait-laced, if she had someone in jail, she'd die of shame. No, her ma does the sewing for the town. Electra, she makes the meals for them what's in jail. And I must say, she's had a lot more business since the new sheriff come."

"Tough, is he?"

"Yeah." Ma Benson pinched her lower lip reflectively. "Fact, I ain't sure he don't consider hisself judge and jury as well as sheriff. There's been a mighty lot of lynchings

31

since he took over. Seems like most anyone can bust in the jail and carry off a prisoner. Next you hear of him, he's dancing at the end of a rope or shot, 'trying to escape.' "

"Hm." It gave him much to think about, that conversation. Until now, he realized he had thought that a judge and jury might be lenient. Might understand that men could drink until they didn't know what they were doing. With Sheriff Jace Owens, it would appear that ever getting to stand in front of a judge was decidedly chancy. He thought of the old preacher's words: "You ain't gonna accomplish much for God if yore dead."

Maybe he was supposed to take off and start preaching. Still, there was Lexie. He wanted her. He *ached* for her. Even when he told himself he was a damn fool, he still wanted her.

Indecisive, he picked up a paper in the barbershop one day, glanced at the front page.

And felt like he'd been kicked by a mule.

Sheriff Jace Owens announced today, the paper reported, the arrest of Dave Royal, alleged to be the man who killed Bert Deardorff. The killing occurred in a gambling hall when Royal accused Deardorff of bottom dealing.

"Royal is a drifter," the sheriff was quoted as saying. "He made a mistake, drifting back to Pequot. I'm going to make this town safe for honest folks, whatever it takes."

The prisoner has denied being Dave Royal, the article continued, but has been identified by another man who was present when Deardorff was killed.

Angus put the paper down. He had wanted an answer and gotten one. He couldn't leave an innocent man to take his punishment.

10.

In front of the sheriff's office, he hesitated. His mouth felt dry, and he swallowed. He went inside. Sheriff Owens looked up from beneath shaggy brows.

"You got the wrong man," Angus blurted out. "I'm Dave Royal."

"You drunk or crazy?" Owens scowled.

Angus swallowed again. "Neither, Sheriff."

"Dave Royal's got yeller hair."

"Walnut stain," Angus replied.

Finally, the sheriff rose, the lupine face louring.

"I'm gonna put you in a cell, boy. God help you if you're lying."

God help me because I'm not, Angus thought.

The barred door clanged behind him. "You and the other fellow can both cool your asses 'til I find out what your game is," Owens said, and stalked out.

Angus sat down on the dirty cot, feeling stifled.

"What they got you for?" a man's voice called.

Angus tried to speak, couldn't. Cleared his throat. "Killing a man," he said.

"Me too." The voice was gloomy. "Only, I didn't do it."

"We the only boarders here?" Angus asked, and when the man said they were, knew the voice had to belong to the man mistakenly identified as himself. "You supposed to be Dave Royal?" he asked. "Like I told the sheriff, you can't be Dave Royal. That's—me, my real handle."

"What the hell am I doing here, then? Even that bastard sheriff ort to know there ain't two of us."

"Soon's the stain grows out of my hair," Angus said, "I reckon he'll let you out then."

"If he don't decide to hang both of us, just to be sure. That man's got a streak of vicious a yard wide."

The mole above Angus's eye began to throb. "Let's

33

think on it," he suggested. Then, shyly, "And I'm gonna say a prayer."

"Gawd damn," the other man moaned, "don't tell me you're a Holy Joe."

"Holy, I'm not, for sure. Joe neither, for that matter." He heard the reluctant chuckle as he knelt by the cot. "Lord," he began quietly, "whatever You've got in mind for me, I rightly deserve. This other fellow, though, seems to be only fittin' he should be turned loose. Amen."

"Amen!" the other voice echoed fervently.

Angus had forgotten Electra brought meals to the inmates, until the door separating cells and office swung open. An angel, he thought, that's what she looks like.

The girl put the basket down and reached for the ring of keys that hung behind the door. Without glancing up, she began to hand food through the bars.

"Miss Colley," Angus said, and the girl's head jerked up.

"Mr.—Scofield?" she asked falteringly. Her eyes were enormous.

"His name ain't Scofield." The man in the next cell snorted. "He's Dave Royal."

Ignoring the interruption, Angus said to the girl, "I was thinking you looked like an angel."

Electra's bosom began to rise and fall more rapidly. Even in the dimness of the jail, Angus could see the deepening color in her cheeks. "I didn't mean to embarrass you," he said.

"Wh—what are you doing in jail?" Electra asked. "That sheriff . . ."

Sooner or later, she had to know. Deep inside himself, he knew their future was inextricably linked. So as she passed the food to him, he poured out the whole story.

When he had finished, she stood silently until the other prisoner yelled, "And that's why I'm in jail. They think I'm him."

"Doesn't seem right to keep both of you for the same thing," she conceded.

"I'm Dave Royal. I just took the name Angus Scofield."

She looked from one to the other, then back to Angus. "And you were drunk?"

"Yes, ma'am, that's right."

"Do you do that often, drink 'til you don't know what you're doing?"

"That was the only time."

Without further comment, she walked away, shut the door. Angus tried to eat, couldn't swallow a bite. If he'd had a chance before with Miss Electra Colley, he sure didn't have one now.

It was crazy, he knew, feeling like that about a girl he'd seen no more than half a dozen times, but unless he could spend the rest of his life with her, life wouldn't be worth living anyhow. For no reason at all, his spirits lifted.

"Eat up, boy," he said to the other prisoner. "We're gonna come out of this."

"Don't call me boy," the other snarled. "I got a name. Dunc. And how you know we're comin' out of this? Seein' visions?"

"Nope." How to explain to anyone an intangible certainty? Lexie, he thought. She'd understand.

Lexie brought food twice a day, said no more than a cool "good morning" or "good evening" the first couple of days. But Angus caught the fragrance of violet talc. He wanted to *touch* her, even if only her hand, knew he must not.

"Thank you, Miss Lexie," he said.

She flashed him a wary glance. "Electra," she corrected.

"Lexie's *my* name for you," he said so softly that only the two of them could hear.

"Oh." She snatched up the basket and went hurriedly away.

A week went by. Angus wondered what the sheriff was waiting for. Surely his hair was showing yellow at the roots by now. But in a strange way, he felt lighthearted.

"I don't know what yore so goddam happy about," Dunc protested. "He's gonna string up the both of us, sure as shootin'."

"Nope."

"Reckon now you're a goddam prophet."

"Nope," Angus repeated. Dunc snorted and was quiet.

Each time Lexie came during that week, Angus took the opportunity to ask her questions. He wanted to know all he could about the girl he firmly intended to marry. She admitted to being nineteen, virtually an old maid.

35

She had no family except her mother, and her mother had no truck with her, since she refused to marry the furniture dealer.

"He's nearer her age than mine," Lexie said. "But he's right well off." She shivered. "I *can't* marry him," she said. Then, recalling to whom she was talking, blushed. "Law, you're not interested in all that. Ma says I rattle too much."

"I don't think so," Angus said softly. And, while she handed food over to Dunc, looked around desperately for paper to write on. There was a blank sheet in the front of his Testament.

Hoping it wasn't a sacrilege, he tore out the sheet and wrote hurriedly. When she came back past his cell, he handed her the folded note.

Lexie opened it, read it and looked at him, wide-eyed. Then she dropped her eyes; color stained her cheeks. The dying sunlight glinted on a single tear.

"Mr.—Scofield—Royal . . ."

"Scofield."

"I . . ."

"You don't have to answer now," Angus's voice was so low, she had to lean forward to catch his words. "But think on it."

Lexie made an inarticulate gulping sound and fled.

It wasn't exactly the usual way a fellow proposed, Angus thought. He hoped she'd understand.

It was the following day that the sheriff lumbered into the jail. "Yore hair's comin' in yeller, all right," he greeted Angus.

"Then I want out," Dunc said. "Told you you had the wrong man."

"You been identified as Dave Royal, boy." The sheriff grinned, displaying yellow teeth. With a shock, Angus thought, Dunc had it right about this man.

"We ort to know in a few days. If I can hold off that mob. They been mutterin' cause nothin's been done." Still grinning, he went out.

"That bastard's gonna throw us to the mob," Dunc groaned. "Likely he's rilin' 'em up hisself. Let 'em lynch us both, just for the fun of it."

It was the following day that Lexie came later than usual in the evening. It was already dark.

"Thought you'd forgot us," Angus teased her.

"Be quiet and listen." Lexie's voice was strained. "There's Dalton kin in town. The sheriff's drunk, and he's even meaner when he's drunk. He won't try to hold them back."

Angus moved uneasily and Dunc uttered a strangled cry. Lexie went on.

"I got your horses from the livery stable. They're hitched behind the jail." She unlocked both cell doors. Dunc shot out as from a catapult. Angus moved more slowly.

"I don't want to go without you, Lexie," he said.

The girl looked at the floor, then raised her head. "My horse is out there too."

11.

Neither of them was ever to forget that ride. They ran the horses full tilt and were into a wooded area when they heard the pistol shots, the neighing of horses being hurriedly saddled.

"The mob!" Lexie breathed as, above the susurration of their horses' hooves, they heard the heavier pounding of many horses' hooves.

Think, dammit, Angus told himself desperately. The faint wagon trail they were following was dimly visible in the starlight; they couldn't hold the horses to this pace long enough to outdistance the posse.

"Turn left into the trees," Angus called quietly, wheeling Whiskey as he spoke. Lexie followed, and they had gone perhaps half a mile when Lexie's mount stumbled, catapulting the girl over his head. Angus's heart seemed to stop. He was off Whiskey almost in mid-stride.

"Lexie, oh, God, Lexie!"

"I'm all right," she said shakily. "Molly must have stepped in a hole." She tried to rise. Angus swept her up bodily. Molly got to her feet, took an awkward step or two.

"She's pulled up lame," Lexie whispered.

"We'll have to ride double."

"We'll never make it. They're too close. You go on!"

Angus made a fierce sound in his throat. "Not without you. Wait, I've got an idea." He lifted Lexie up behind his saddle, vaulted up himself, grasped Molly's reins and, leading her, guided Whiskey deeper into the trees. In a few moments, he turned the horse about face.

"You're going the wrong way," Lexie said. "We're headed back the way we came."

"Right," he agreed. "It's the last place they'll look for us. They'll ride another three–four miles before they realize they've lost us. By then, we'll be long gone. We'll head west 'stead of south.

Lexie said no more. She clung to him. Another mile or so, and he released Molly. She'd make her way back home. Meantime, they were on their way—where? He chuckled. He'd never had less idea where he was headed nor ever been so happy.

When he judged they were out of danger, Angus slowed Whiskey to an easy trot. Lexie's head rested against his back, and he felt such a swelling of tenderness in his throat, he wondered if it would burst.

"Tired?" he asked.

"Not very." But he knew she was, and began to look for a place for them to rest. If his bearings were correct, they were headed toward the Kansas line, but they wouldn't make it tonight. Tomorrow night either, for that matter.

Angus had stayed away from any semblance of a road, keeping within the cover of trees. But now he began to look for a trail, and perhaps a half hour later, they stepped out onto the prairie.

A straw stack loomed ahead of them, gleaming gold in the pale light.

"Could you sleep in a straw stack?" Angus asked.

"Hm." Lexie's voice was indistinct.

He stopped the weary horse, dismounted, lifted the girl down. She felt boneless and smelled of talcum and sweat and horse and woman.

He scooped out a hollow in the straw and fitted her into it.

"Don't leave me," she whispered drowsily. Her arms were tight around his neck. He tried gently to loose them, could not. Irresistibly he felt his body drawn down onto hers. He felt the softness of her breasts through his thin shirt, the melting eroticism of her thighs.

"Lexie . . ."

"I love you," she whispered, pulled his head down until her lips were against his.

He felt the blood storming through his veins, the accelerated intensity of his breath, felt an arousal so complete, his whole body ached. Even so, there was a vague feeling of—surprise? disappointment? But after all, they were going to be married. . . .

He reached for the fastenings of her bodice and in that moment realized she was trembling, that there were tears on her cheeks. Thoroughly baffled, he pulled away from her.

"What's wrong, Lexie? I wouldn't—I don't—did I scare you?"

She shook her head. "Oh, Angus," she wailed, "please, I want to. . . . If they catch you . . . I want you at least to have tonight. . . ." The sobs grew deeper. "I've ruined everything," she said, weeping, "and I wanted it to be perfect."

Angus's ardor died before his wonder and love. He rolled over to lie beside her, put his arms around her and drew her close. Not in passion now, but in reassurance.

"Funny little girl," he murmured against her hair. "They're not going to catch me. And when I know you as my wife, it's all going to be legal and—and perfect."

Her sobs began to lessen. She gulped and presently, snuggled closer to him. "You don't think I'm a—bad woman?"

"I would never marry a bad woman," Angus said solemnly, and burst into laughter. For a moment he was afraid he had hurt her feelings by his teasing; then, she too began to laugh.

Despite their weariness, neither of them could sleep. After a while, he began to tell her what his future held, about his consciousness that he must preach.

When he had finished, she was silent for what seemed to him an unconscionably long time. His belly tightened. If it came to a choice, Lexie or God, which would he choose?

It would have to be God, he thought. He was bespoken.

But, Lord, he wanted her too.

"Where you going to do this circuit riding?" Lexie asked as matter-of-factly as though he'd said he was going into the banking business.

"I don't know yet," he said, so relieved, he felt weak.

"Mmmm," she murmured, and he realized she was all but asleep. Feeling a contentment he'd never known, Angus slept too.

They were married the next day, and that night Angus led his new bride to a hotel. Grinning impishly, she said, "I was really looking forward to a haystack."

Angus felt his ears go red. "You're the funniest girl I ever met," he said.

Lexie laughed and as suddenly sobered. "Only with you, Angus," she said shyly, and slid her hand into his.

Angus smiled at her, his whole face illumined as though by a sunrise.

Lexie's eyes grew wide. "Angus Scofield," she cried, "you're downright handsome when you smile like that. And here I thought you were only nice." They were in the hotel room, had been scrubbing away some of the travel stains. Hands still wet, she threw her arms around his neck. "You know something? We're going to have beautiful babies."

Angus shook his head. "You do beat the band, Mrs. Scofield," he said, and hugged her until she squealed.

There was a good deal of fumbling and giggling that night. Lexie had had no sexual encounters at all, and Angus's experience had been only with saloon girls. He was terrified lest he hurt her. But, laughing at him, she pulled him down, holding him close.

"I want you so much," he murmured against her hair, "but I don't want to be too rough."

"I'm not all that delicate," she whispered. She did cry out once, but when he made as if to draw away, she clung, holding him as though in a vise, fingers digging into his shoulders.

"Angus, Angus." She kept repeating his name in rhythmic accompaniment to the pulse of their bodies. And the night was filled with a splendor that exploded into a thousand lights.

She slept in his arms, breath warm and fragrant against his face. He lay unmoving, wondering if anyone anywhere had ever known the ineffable joy and contentment he felt

40

that night. Humbly, he thanked his God for having brought Lexie to him.

They jogged on unhurriedly the next few days. Angus had decided they might as well return to Wichita, where he could again work the holding pens until the Almighty handed down another decree.

Lexie could not remember ever having seen her father, and her mother had been a dour, unsmiling woman, determined that her only child would marry a man of substance. Though Angus could remember his home and his mother's love, there always had been the chill of constraint in his home, and tension because of his father's shortcomings.

So the two-room house the young Scofields rented in Wichita seemed to them their first real home, and the two years they spent there were like nothing either of them had ever known. Love was there, and laughter, a sense of belonging, of shared hopes and dreams. Angus would work his stint at the yards, refuse the invitations of the other hands to stop for a beer. He wanted only one thing, to be home with Lexie.

On rare occasions, he thought of his obligation to God. Reckoned when He wanted something, He'd let it be known. Meanwhile, Angus was more than content to hold Lexie in his arms, feel the liveliness of her body and spirit fusing with his.

It was when he saw an Indian brave strolling down the Wichita street one day that his obligation was brought home to him as if he'd been dealt a blow. Even as his hackles rose, he could hear the voice of his inner consciousness. "The Indians need God."

Angus said a short and ugly word, resolutely put the thought from him.

12.

There were no more "instructions," and gradually Angus grew interested in the talk around town about the Unassigned Lands. Lying south of Kansas and adjoining Indian Territory, the area had been set aside for such tribes as might wish to claim them. They were still unoccupied.

A movement of men calling themselves Boomers had originated in Kansas for the sole purpose of laying claim to the area, which they said was the white man's "right." They had made several attempts to move onto the land, only to be driven off by the militia. But since there was no legal penalty for the offense, the would-be settlers were simply conducted to the state line and turned loose, to try another time.

Then rumors had begun that the government was buying up the land from the Indians and that the territory would be opened legally for settlement. For months, there was ever a fresh rumor to whet the appetite. Eastern papers began to pick up the news, describing the area as a veritable Garden of Eden.

It was said that each family would be permitted to homestead a hundred and sixty acres. The thought of having their own farm was like reaching the end of the rainbow, to Lexie.

"Just think, Angus. We could have farm animals, raise crops, plant fruit trees, raise our children—"

"Whoa!" Angus grinned at her, loving her enthusiasm. "Hold on, there, Mrs. Scofield. What children? We haven't got the first one here yet."

She patted her belly complacently. "Almost," she boasted. "Three more months."

Angus frowned. "Even if the rumors are true, honey, that's Injun country."

"The two territories are going to be completely separate," she said quickly. She put a hand on his arm. "Oh, Angus, just *think*. Our own land."

"It's not for sure yet—"

42

"I heard yesterday it could happen any time—"

"That's wild country, Lexie. There are doctors here—"

"Piffle, I don't need a doctor."

Shaking his head, concerned, Angus said, "Let me think on it."

By the time President Harrison signed the proclamation opening the nearly two million acres to settlement, Angus had capitulated to Lexie's pleading.

The thought of the Indians "who needed God" was a sourness in his mind. "You're thinking on gettin' me down there in position," he silently accused the Almighty one night when he couldn't sleep.

He thrashed about for a time, at last said with finality, "Anything but Injuns. Reckon the whites need God too. I'll ride circuit."

The decision having been made to make the "run," Angus sold Whiskey and the saddle for enough money to be able to buy a team of lesser lineage and a covered wagon. The lands were to be opened April 22, 1889. On April tenth, the young Scofields headed for Arkansas City, on the Kansas-Indian Territory border.

It was unseasonably warm for April. Before they reached the campground, the faint sound of voices and activity came to their ears.

Lexie gripped his wrist. "Isn't it exciting?" she demanded. Her eyes were sparkling, her pale hair ruffled by the wind. Her cheeks were pink, and she sat beside him on the spring seat instead of riding in the wagon bed, as he'd suggested.

"Sometimes I don't know if you're nine or nineteen," he teased her, and she giggled.

"I'm twenty-one," she said primly.

There were men and horses and wagons and surreys and buggies as far as eye could see when they reached the wooded section sheltering the encampment.

"There must be a thousand people here already," Angus said thoughtfully, "and it's still early days. Hope there's enough land for everyone."

"There will be." Lexie was confident. "The good Lord's not going to open Paradise and not provide plenty of room."

They found a shaded spot, and Angus guided the team into it. The young couple walked a bit to get the kinks out of their legs; then, at Angus's insistence, Lexie rested

43

for a time. Angus sauntered about, getting acquainted. At a tent where a hand-labeled sign said "Stable," he paused, met four or five men, including Ira Eckroat, the townsman who owned the place. Ira was enormous—not fat, but standing well over six feet and built like a slab of granite.

Beside him stood a wizened little man who was about five foot three. He looked as though the original clay had been moulded and then given an impatient shove. His left shoulder was an inch or two lower than the right, so he seemed to slope. For all that, his chest and shoulders were so muscular that he had a look of impermeable strength. He had a merry face and an engaging confidence that he was the equal of any man, whatever the size.

Angus gave his name, and the other man reciprocated. "Pete Smith," he said, shaking hands. "From Ohio. Pleased to make your acquaintance. You a farmer or businessman?"

Angus hesitated. It sounded so—well, pompous to say he was a preacher. "I'll be farmin'." Then, lest he seemed ashamed of it, added, "And circuit riding."

"A preacher?" Pete slapped his knee. "I'll be damned. My old lady has been worryin' for fear we'd be livin' in the midst of heathen. Alice is shore gonna be glad to hear about you."

Angus smiled his rare smile.

The three stood talking for a time. Other men drifted over. Angus met some from as far away as New York, others from the Carolinas.

"Not many children around," he said.

"Naw," Ira Eckroat told him. "Mostly it's men by themselves. They'll make the run, stake their claim, then go back for their family. Reckon it's gonna be a mite rough, living there at first."

"My wife insisted on coming along," Angus said, and realized he sounded prideful.

"Mine too." Pete chuckled. "She don't trust me, and that's a fact."

"You one for the ladies, Pete?" Angus asked.

"Naw, but I sure like them playin' cards. Alice don't hold with gamblin'. 'Specially when you lose." He grinned ruefully. "Which I generally do," he added.

13.

Within two days, Lexie and Angus had settled into the camp routine, and Lexie had gotten acquainted with a midwife. "Clover Murphy," the girl bubbled to Angus, "is going to make the run. She'll drive her wagon in tandem with us and settle near where we do. Isn't that wonderful, Angus?" She threw her arms around his neck. "I'm so happy, I could just die."

A chill went down Angus's back. "Guess you could show your happiness a better way than that," he said.

"Oh, you old grump. You worry too much."

He put his arms around her. "Reckon you're right." Then, changing the subject, "I just found out we can move to the border of the lands on the nineteenth."

"Three days *before* the run? Wonderful! I can't wait, Angus, to get our own place. I just can't *wait!*" .

Angus caught her hands in his. "Lexie, honey, please don't get so excited," he said soberly.

"I won't," she promised. "Honest, Angus. I'm going to be so—so sedate, I'll be a perfect parson's wife."

He grinned in spite of himself at the long face she drew. "You little idiot," he said. "What am I to do with you?"

Lexie laughed.

She was not laughing when she woke him at three o'clock the next morning. He hurriedly lit the lantern. In its yellow light, he saw how drawn and pallid her face was. She bit her lip. "Maybe you better get Mrs. Murphy," she said. "My—my water broke."

Angus's heart skidded with fear. He jerked his pants on, chills racing up and down his back. It's too soon, Lord, he kept voicing a silent plea. Way too soon. Without thinking of shoes, he ran between the wagons until he found the one Lexie had pointed out to him.

He shouted the woman's name, unmindful of people

sleeping, and, when she answered, shouted at her to hurry. Lexie needed her. Then he dashed back to his own wagon.

Lexie managed a small smile when he came in.

"She'll be here in a minute," Angus panted. "Can I do anything?"

"Just don't leave me."

Mrs. Murphy was there in minutes, carrying a small case. Angus helped the plump little woman into the wagon.

"Reckon you can go now, Mr. Scofield," she wheezed.

Lexie tightened her hold on his hand. "No," she said, and then added, "My husband's a preacher," as though that somehow exempted him from being banished.

It was nearly three hours before the first real pain began. In the meantime, Lexie dozed. Mrs. Murphy made a small fire outside to heat some water, and Angus still sat, holding Lexie's hand.

The girl shivered. "I'm cold," she whipered. Angus rose and got a heavy quilt. Mrs. Murphy spread it over the slight figure, and suddenly Lexie doubled up as though she'd been hit in the belly.

"There we go," Mrs. Murphy said, and Lexie managed a tremulous smile when the spasm had passed. Angus felt a cold hand close around his heart. He continued to sit, feeling Lexie's fingers clamp around his when the pains came, at irregular intervals. It was going on ten o'clock, and the unseasonable April heat began to compress inside the canvas cover.

"You too hot, honey?" Angus asked, sweltering.

She shook her head. "I'm cold."

"Brother Scofield, if you'd like to leave now"—that was Mrs. Murphy—"I think maybe—"

"Don't leave me!" Lexie cried. Shadows had formed beneath her eyes. There were lines of strain on her face.

Angus glanced up at the midwife, who made a shooing motion. He tried to smile at Lexie. "Mrs. Murphy's been trying to get rid of me ever since she came," he said. "Reckon if I don't git, she's not going to bring us a baby."

The icy fingers loosened on his hand. To him, even the touch of the featherbed seemed suffocating, but Lexie's rigors continued though her face was flushed, skin burning hot. Angus leaned forward to brush a cloud of the pale hair off her forehead.

"You're doing fine, honey."

She nodded, but he could see the tracery of blue veins in her fragile wrists, the rapid pulse in her temple. "Our son will look like you," she said, then doubled up as pain took her again.

"You *got* to leave now, Brother Scofield," Mrs. Murphy insisted. "I'll take care of her."

Reluctantly, Angus turned away. "She's two months early, Mrs. Murphy." It was a plea. To the midwife. To God. To someone.

"I know." The woman shifted her weight to her other leg. "You go on, now."

For all the confidence of her words, he saw her frown and bite her lip as she turned back to Lexie. With a feeling of helplessness, he snatched up his hat and swung himself down from the wagon.

14.

She's all I've got, he thought as he moved blindly across the sun-baked earth. Tall, face weathered by sun and wind, carrying himself with the slouching grace of a horseman.

"Missus coming along all right?" Pete Smith's wizened face peered up at him.

"I don't know, Pete; I'm—scared. I should never have let her come."

"Dreadful strong-willed, women is," Pete said consolingly. Then, in an obvious attempt to divert Angus's thoughts: "Did you know there's a game in camp?"

"A game?" Angus repeated blankly.

"Yeah, you know, cards. Poker."

Angus made an effort to concentrate on what was being said. "Oh, cards. And you with gambling fever, huh?"

"Not me!" Pete said virtuously. "Alice says I lose our belongings one more time, she's gonna run me off."

"Reckon she means it?"

"She means it," Pete confirmed gloomily. Then, again changing the subject: "I got a jar of white mule at the stable, preacher. Like a drink?"

"Thanks." Angus refused. "Don't think I could get it down."

They had been walking near the wagons, over to the stable, back again. Ira Eckroat had stepped outside his tent to inquire about Lexie, when suddenly the girl screamed. Angus whirled, headed toward the sound, was caught and held. The black mist of rage closed in around him, and he swung. Ira Eckroat's two hundred fifty pounds rocked from the blow, but he held.

"You'd just be in the way, you fool," Ira said. "That there is woman business."

Lexie screamed again, and the sound ended in a sob. Angus jerked free. "I won't bother them," he panted; went to stand by the tailgate of the wagon in the blistering heat. If only he could give her some of his strength.

He bowed his head and took off his hat before his God. "Now, Lord," he said aloud, "I'm fixin' to pay off my debt to You. But that killin' was my sin. It ain't hardly gentlemanly to punish Lexie for what I did."

Then he was troubled at his temerity. He didn't know the Almighty all that well. "Meanin' no disrespect," he added.

"Preacher, you out there?"

Angus jumped. "I'm here, Mrs. Murphy," he said, over the thudding of his heart.

"I reckon you better come help."

Angus was in the wagon before the words were out.

"I'm gonna have to use the instrument," Mrs. Murphy said. "That baby ain't movin', and she's wearin' out."

Angus's throat tightened. "What do you want me to do?" he asked. Lexie stirred and moaned.

"I give her some whiskey," Mrs. Murphy said. "She's a mite calmer now, but you're going to have to hold her."

Angus thought of restraining Lexie while she writhed in pain, and cold sweat broke out on his forehead. He felt a sickness in the pit of his stomach. "Tell me what to do," he said.

"However you can best hold her still."

Lexie opened her eyes, and in that moment, Angus saw that she had bitten completely through her lower lip. Unshed tears made his throat knot.

"Is the baby here yet?" Lexie whispered.

Unable to speak, Angus shook his head. Then, clearing his throat: "Soon, sweetheart."

Tears and sweat had smudged Lexie's face. Angus reached for a damp cloth and sponged them away.

Mrs. Murphy raised the girl's head and fed her more whiskey. Lexie gagged, but some of it went down. "Now, preacher, get a hold on her," Mrs. Murphy said. "Lexie, you hold still as you can and we'll get us a baby."

She went down on her knees at the end of the bed. Angus tightened his grip on his wife as the forceps gleamed. Lexie clung to his arms. When the instrument was inserted and the baby had been grasped and started down the canal, she gave a scream of agony and went limp.

"She's dead!" Angus cried, and Mrs. Murphy told him tartly to shut up.

"She ain't dead by a long sight, and the baby's moving."

He prayed in that moment as he had never known he could pray. Deeply, agonizingly.

Mrs. Murphy worked slowly but steadily. In her semiconsciousness, Lexie moaned. This had to be hell, Angus thought, this agony of helplessness.

"Push, Lexie," Mrs. Murphy called. Lexie strained until the cords in her neck stood out, Mrs. Murphy pulled and the baby's head appeared, followed within seconds by a tiny red and wrinkled body. Mrs. Murphy lifted it gently, and the tiny mouth opened in a scream of pure rage.

"There, there," Mrs. Murphy soothed, and laid the squalling infant on Lexie's abdomen while she cut the cord. Angus was fighting nausea. No wonder Ira had said this was women's business. Men didn't have the guts for it.

"You can turn her loose now," Mrs. Murphy said drily, and he found himself still clasping Lexie as though she might escape. Sheepishly, he loosed his hold.

The midwife lifted the baby and put it to one side.

"Lexie's all right?" Angus asked. It was a plea.

"If I can get this bleedin' stopped . . ."

Lexie's eyes opened. "Where is he?" she asked. "I want to see my baby."

The baby was still screeching. Mrs. Murphy was work-

49

ing feverishly. "Lift the baby over to her," she snapped at Angus. "I'll bathe it later."

Angus was petrified. "It's too little. . . ." Mrs. Murphy glared at him. "Get that blanket and put it around her."

"Her," he echoed, and heard Lexie draw her breath.

"Her?" Lexie whispered. "It's a little girl?" The baby continued to yell as Angus wrapped her and awkwardly placed her in the curve of Lexie's arm.

"She don't weigh nothin' at all," he said.

Lexie managed a smile. "She weighs enough. Listen to her; look at those arms and legs go." She put a finger on the button nose. "Hello there, Miss Rowdy," she said softly.

"Oh, Gawd," Mrs. Murphy said suddenly. "Oh, Gawd help us all!" And there was a great gush of blood that seemed to cover the entire wagon floor.

Angus saw the light in Lexie's eyes begin to dim, saw the greenish pallor of her face. He stood stricken, impotent, watching as Lexie's life poured out in a scarlet flood.

It was over in a matter of minutes. In the periphery of his mind, he noted the baby had stopped crying, was nuzzling at Lexie's breast.

Mrs. Murphy had risen, tears running down her leathery face. "I done the best I could, Brother Scofield," she said.

Angus was wordless, in shock. Life couldn't be that fragile, to be gone in a space of moments. Lexie had hardly started to live. He saw Mrs. Murphy pull the sheet of flour sacking over his wife's face. "Don't cover her," he said harshly. "She doesn't like the dark."

"All right." Mrs. Murphy's voice was gentle. She lifted the baby and put her on a pillow. "I'll take her with me for the night," she said. As though she had just recognized her loss, the baby began to howl again. "I'll get her quiet and come back to clean up," Mrs. Murphy said. Angus scarcely heard.

15.

A minister came out from Arkansas City to conduct Lexie's funeral. Angus moved like an automaton. He saw the rough pine box lowered into the grave and knew a part of him had died too.

An eye for an eye, a tooth for a tooth, he thought bitterly as he walked back to his wagon. He had killed a man. God had taken Lexie. His face was so remote, so unapproachable, no one so much as spoke to him.

In the wagon, he flung himself down on the bare floor boards and tried to sleep. He was exhausted, but his mind ground on. He tried to plan. No point in homesteading now. Back to trail driving, he supposed.

"Oh, Lexie!" he whispered, and finally the numbness began to wear off. He was sobbing in great anguished gulps, as he had sobbed at his mother's grave.

After a long while, he slept.

The sun was shining when he wakened. He rose, feeling dazed, and began to put their scant belongings in order. He'd have no need of a wagon on the trail. He'd sell it and the team and get a good riding horse and saddle.

Their clothes, his and Lexie's and the baby's, were in a small trunk. He supposed Mrs. Murphy could dispose of that and the small stove, the bedding . . .

Finished with the mental inventory, he made his way to Mrs. Murphy's wagon.

"Mornin', Brother Scofield." Her pleasant, middle-aged face was compassionate. "Thought I wouldn't disturb you tilst you was ready. The little one's doing fine."

"Would you take Lexie's clothes and things?" he asked. "Give them to someone?"

Mrs. Murphy pushed a wisp of hair off her damp forehead. "Yes," she said simply. "Like some coffee?"

He shook his head. "I'll be sellin' the wagon and team,

51

too. Or I'd trade for a riding horse, case you hear of anyone—"

Mrs. Murphy's face mirrored her puzzlement. "Where you gonna carry the baby?" she asked. "In the saddlebag?"

Angus blinked. "We'll have to find someone to take her," he said roughly. "I'll—I'd expect to pay." He had not thought of the child until this minute, but since it had been brought to his attention, he acknowledged the responsibility.

"Take her?" Mrs. Murphy scowled. "Seems to me a baby's entitled to one parent, at the least."

Angus spread his hands, big-knuckled and rough, and thought of them trying to hold that scrap of life. "What would I do with a baby?"

"Don't you even want to see her?"

Truth to tell, he didn't. It would only remind him more forcefully of Lexie, but Mrs. Murphy's expression was almost an order. "All right," he muttered.

The baby slept placidly in the box that had been fitted out for her. There was a sugar tit in her mouth, and one hand rested on her cheek, like a small crumpled flower.

"She needs a name, preacher. Would you want to call her for her—ma?"

Angus shook his head in quick denial. There could be only one Electra Marshall Colley. "Lexie called her Miss Rowdy," he said. "Reckon that's as good as any."

Mrs. Murphy bristled. "That ain't no name for a child."

Angus rubbed the mole. "I guess not." His mind wouldn't work.

"How about your ma's name?"

"Martha? Yeah, that's all right."

The newly named infant, as though conscious she was being discussed, opened her eyes. She shoved the sugar tit away, screwed up her face and began to howl. Angus's blood ran cold. "What's wrong with her?" he cried.

"Wet, more'n likely." Mrs. Murphy changed the small diaper deftly, lifted the baby on the pillow and held her out to Angus. "Want to hold her a spell?"

"Good God, no!" Angus shouted, backing away. "I'd break her, for sure."

"Babies ain't that easy broke."

Angus shoved his hands into his pockets as though afraid the woman would make him take the child. "Could

52

—you take care of her?" he asked. "I'd pay, of course."
He didn't know how he'd pay, but he would.

"I'd like to, Brother Scofield, best in the world," Mrs.
Murphy said, "but I'm going to make the run, prove up
my claim, same as you. My man's dead, and I got my way
to make. I figure to farm so's I can prove it up. Midwifing
will bring in a little cash."

Under his breath, Angus swore, then asked pardon of
the Almighty, wishing once again he could break that
habit.

"She's gonna have to have a wet nurse," the midwife
said. "I been inquiring around, and . . ."

Angus glanced up from his study of the floor boards as
Mrs. Murphy's voice trailed off. "And?" he asked, puzzled at the red that colored her face.

"And I only heard about one nursing mother. I—I'm
not sure . . ." She faltered again, and Angus frowned,
wondering what was wrong with her.

"Just tell me," he suggested bluntly.

"She's black and—and she's got no man."

"Well"—Angus was relieved—"we can't fault her for
that. You've got no man either."

"But I've *had* a man," Mrs. Murphy sputtered. "T'tell
the truth, Brother Scofield, I hear she—she's got some
girls."

"Oh." Angus thought that over. There were two kinds
of girls. The ones men married and the ones they didn't.
Both seemed to him important, particularly in this raw
country, where men went for long months without a
glimpse of a female. But it seemed advisable, he thought
drily, not to express that thought.

"I reckon a fancy lady's better than nothing," he said.
"The baby's got to eat."

Mrs. Murphy sniffed her disapproval but had no better
solution. "I hear they're at the hotel," she said. "Her—
her name's Dove Dubois."

16.

When Angus knocked on Dove Dubois's door, the babble of voices inside the room stopped. There was dead silence. After a minute or so, Angus knocked again and called, "Miss Dubois, I'd like to talk with you."

"You the law?" a woman's voice demanded.

"No, I have a—a business proposition for you."

Footsteps crossed the floor, and the door was opened a crack. Angus's mouth fell open. The face looking at him in inquiry was the color of richly creamed coffee, the features delicately drawn, eyes the soft dark brown of a doe's, with thick, curly lashes. Why would a girl like this sell herself? Saloon girls were usually ugly as mud.

"Yes?" she asked. He swallowed. He could see two or three other faces in the room, all curious.

"Miss Dubois?" he inquired, and at her nod, asked if she could join him downstairs for a few minutes.

"My girls aren't working," she said briefly and would have closed the door, but he put his foot in the crack.

"Please," he blurted out. "I'm—I'm not looking for a girl. I—I've got a baby . . . my wife died . . ."

"I'm sorry," she said, but the words were automatic. He heard the whispers and giggling in the room, was conscious of how ridiculous he looked, standing here like a blushing schoolboy with his first girl.

"If you could just come downstairs . . ." he entreated.

Dove frowned, shrugged. "Soon as I dress," she said. Angus withdrew his foot and the door closed.

Back in the lobby, trying to ignore the curious glances of those around him, he drew two chairs together in a corner. Dove was as good as her word; she was there in five minutes. As they settled into the chairs, she said drily, "Suzette tells me you're a preacher."

"Suzette?" he asked.

"One of my girls. She's been getting out some, spying out the land, you might say, like Joshua."

A Bible-quoting madam was not quite what he had anticipated.

A dimple appeared momentarily in her left cheek. "You're not here to save my soul, are you, preacher?" she asked mockingly. Angus shook his head, aware that she was antagonizing him without his really knowing why. He couldn't afford to upset her, though.

"No," he said. "I—I'm here—Mrs. Murphy tells me you—you have a baby . . ."

"And you thought we could compare notes. . . ." She was openly mocking now.

"Hell, no!" he snapped. "My baby girl needs a wet nurse."

"And I'm the only one around. And being a nigger, naturally I'm gonna fall all over myself to please the white massa. All he has to do is snap his fingers."

The anger within him was growing, coming nearer the surface. He clasped his hands together, mashed them into fists, thrust them between his knees. His inclination was to go stomping out of the place before he punched her. But Mrs. Murphy had said he *had* to get a wet nurse.

"I am asking," he said holding his voice level with an effort, "I am asking not as a white man to a Negro but as one human being to another." Dove had been watching him with the bright interest of a sparrow watching a worm. Now, her eyes dropped.

"I got a low boiling point," she muttered. It was not quite an apology.

"Me too," Angus admitted.

As though regretting her momentary softening, Dove's eyes narrowed. "It'll cost you," she warned. She was on familiar ground, and held all the aces. Still, his fists relaxed. Bargaining was familiar ground for him too.

"How much?" he asked.

Dove paused to light a slim brown cigar she took from her reticule, letting the moment lengthen. "Dollar a day," she said and blew out a small stream of smoke.

Angus gulped. A dollar a day was cowpoke wages. It would take every cent he earned. Maybe he could get a good price for the team and wagon. Maybe there'd be cash left over after he bought a horse.

Anyhow, he had to come up with her price. The baby

had to be fed. He brightened suddenly. Mrs. Murphy could probably find someone before long who wanted a baby. Someone who'd take her and treat her right. Even if he had to pay for keep, it wouldn't be forever. How long did a baby stay at the breast? Two weeks? Six months?

He looked up to see Dove's cool amusement as though she sensed his floundering. She stood up. "What's the answer, preacher?" she asked.

"My baby has to eat," he said. For a moment he thought her face softened, but if it did, it was only for an instant.

Lifting the cerise skirt of her dress just enough that an inch of lacy petticoat showed, she turned and started toward the stairs.

"Bring her over," she said briefly.

Angus took out his handkerchief and mopped his face. He'd rather meet up with a stampede than with a sharp-tongued woman.

Back at Mrs. Murphy's wagon, the midwife had gotten the baby's clothes ready. Rowdy was yelling again, and Angus wondered sourly if she screamed every chance she got. He stood at the tailgate of the wagon, and Mrs. Murphy handed him the baby on her pillow.

"Mind you keep that blanket around her," Mrs. Murphy cautioned.

He tightened his hold grimly on the blanket-wrapped infant and was rewarded with an even louder howl. She's not gonna let herself be mistreated, he thought, for the first time conscious of her as a human being, rather than just a problem.

"Stay in there, Miss Rowdy," he whispered, absurdly pleased at the display of spirit. "If you don't like something, you let it be known." The yells ceased as he loosened his hold, and she settled back in the crook of his arm, sucking on her fist.

17.

Angus had no trouble being admitted to Dove's this time. She opened the door, introduced him to another girl, Suzette, then took the baby, pillow and all, into her arms. A thin wail came from the other side of the room.

Angus started. "What's that?" he demanded.

"I've got a baby too," Dove said coolly, "or I wouldn't be having mother's milk." Suzette was laughing openly, and the betraying dimple appeared in Dove's cheek.

Angus felt his ears go red, the mole begin to throb. "Of course," he stammered. "A—a little girl?" Suzette went to pick the baby up.

"A little boy," she said, as proudly as though he were hers. "Sam, short for Samson, Dubois." Sam, short for Samson, gurgled and Angus gaped. Sam was a roly-poly infant with skin only a shade or two darker than his own.

"His pappy's white." Dove's thoughts seemed to hone in on his own. He went even redder. "Don't let it discombobulate you, preacher," Dove mocked him.

"He should have married you," Angus blurted out. "You're—"

"I'm what? Pretty? Intelligent? Almost good enough for the white massa? I could maybe 'pass' and no one would know the difference? Well let me tell you something, preacher man, I loved that boy, and he may have even loved me. At least, he thought he wanted to marry me. You know what that would have done to him? Even if we'd left New Orleans? He'd have been scared of his shadow. Scared one of his children would be born a pickaninny with kinky hair. And that scaredness would have eaten at him, twisted him, and pretty soon it would have twisted me too, because he wouldn't have had the guts to stand up before the world and say, yes, I love a nigger gal." She was panting as she broke off, glaring at him.

57

Suzette's eyes were wide. "I never heard you talk like that before," she said, and Dove turned on her.

"You're white!" She spat out the words. "That's no way you could ever understand what it's like to be black."

"But you're not all black."

Dove laughed mirthlessly. "That's right," she agreed. "I'm only half black. Ol' Massa's back door was too nigh my mammy's front door. She told me once she felt honored when he visited her. God damn his soul to hell. She felt *honored*."

Her eyes were brilliant with angry tears. Angus wished he were somewhere else.

"I'm not crying because I'm sorrowed," she shouted at him. "I'm crying because I'm so Goddam mad and because there's nothing I can do about it."

"Well," Angus said uncertainly, half afraid she would thrust the baby back into his arms simply because Miss Rowdy was white, "well, reckon I better git."

He turned toward the door, but Dove's words stopped him. Her voice was as calm as though she hadn't been screaming the moment before. "You're still aimin' to make the run?" she said, and Angus thought briefly that she was like a chameleon, changing from one mood to another so fast, you couldn't follow.

He shook his head. "I'll go back on the trail." He had reached the door.

"The owl hoot trail?" Dove asked, and something cold moved down Angus's backbone. He whirled.

"What're you talking about?"

Dove's grin was malicious. "You ain't like no preacher I ever seen. Just wondered if you was wanted someplace, preacher man."

His thoughts rushed to the "Wanted" poster. Had someone seen it? What did this taunting woman know? He took a step toward them, and Suzette backed off. Dove stood her ground.

"Just funnin' you, preacher. You better sit. You look plumb white. Besides, I want to talk to you." She shoved a chair toward him. Angus ignored it.

"What is there to talk about?" he demanded harshly. "I told you I'd pay for the baby—for Miss Rowdy's—keep."

"But, preacher"—Dove was openly derisive again—

58

"we made them terms when you was gonna make the run. When you was gonna be a part of the settlement, preachin' hellfire and damnation. Like a good Christian woman, I figured it was my bounden duty to help out, so's we'd have a minister."

Suddenly, the black rage clouded Angus's mind. He felt he hated this woman as he'd never hated another human being, not even his no-account father. His hands gripped the back of the chair until his knuckles whitened.

"What in the hell does a woman like you want with a preacher in the settlement?" he exploded. "I'd think the more wide open a town is, the better you'd like it. Or maybe you're expecting me to go in and stake a claim for you."

She shook her head. "I've already got a man for that. I'd make the run myself, but it would be too hard on Sam. Thing is, if a town's wide open, with no law and no church, the menfolks don't get near as much fun out of visiting my girls. They like to feel they're devils, for sure, getting by with something."

Angus thought about that briefly, then said, "Reckon there'll be someone there to do the preaching."

"There ain't no other 'man of God' makin' the run. I done inquired." All at once her self-mockery grated on his ear.

"Stop talking like a third-rate slave!" he said furiously. "You can talk as well as I can."

Dove shifted Miss Rowdy to her other arm. "I can talk better than you can, likely," she snapped. "Ol' Massa was so benevolent, he let his nigger bastids take lessons with his real chillun. Ol' Massa was all heart, top to bottom. When the tutor took us as far as he could, Ol' Massa's real chillun were ready for finishing school. I was ready to start scrubbing floors."

Aware of the depths of hurt and helpless rage seething within her, Angus said, "I'm sorry."

Dove's eyes flashed fire. "Don't you be sorry for me, preacher! Don't you never pity me!" Her voice roused Miss Rowdy, who woke and began to yell. Instantly, Dove's voice became soft, with a steely gentleness that made Angus shiver.

"Don't fret yourself," she said. "The white man is gonna pay me for everything he's done to me. Sweet Jesus, is he going to pay me." She broke off, shook her

59

head, spoke again in a perfectly ordinary tone. "If you make the run, stake your claim and make like a parson, I'll take care of your baby for free. If you go back on the trail, you'll have to find someone else to mind her."

Angus swallowed. The welter of emotions, the switching from a deadly hysteria to equally deadly logic, was too much for him. He felt dazed, as though someone had bested him in a fight, kicked him when he was down.

"Who else could I get?" he asked. Dove smiled, teeth white against the brown velvet of her skin.

"That ain't my problem, is it, preacher?"

18.

Still feeling mauled, Angus had almost reached his wagon, when he heard himself hailed. He turned. Ira Eckroat's stable was apparently the meeting place for half the men in camp.

"Come on over and help us celebrate, preacher. The trains are in." That was Pete Smith. "Fifteen engines, I heerd."

"That's right."

Angus hadn't met the man who confirmed Pete's statement. "Vince Turner, preacher," Pete said. "Vince is a railroad man. This here's Angus Scofield, Vince."

Angus shook hands, seeing a man almost his own height, wearing Sunday pants, dress shirt, city shoes. His hands were woman soft. Dandy, Angus thought fleetingly, the kind of man Ma used to describe as *soft,* in a voice of unutterable scorn. But his eyes were like silverfish, darting first here, then there, and shallow as though they had no depth.

"Pleasure," Turner said, and his lips smiled.

"You're going to live in Oklahoma Territory?" Angus asked. Perhaps his incredulity sounded in his voice, because Turner's answer was curt.

"Yes."

"Hear tell Dove Dubois is gonna care for yore little one," Ira said. Angus saw the amused and speculative glances turned on him and hated himself for reddening.

"My baby had to have a wet nurse," he said. "Miss Dubois was kind enough to help."

"Miss Dubois. You mean the *whore?*" Vince Turner smirked. "She's a good little whore, huh, *preacher?*" There were a couple of sniggers.

Angus felt his choler rise. The mole began to throb. Ignore the man, he ordered himself, trying to dissolve the black anger crowding in. The fellow's drunk. "I'll take that as not said, Turner. Soon as you apologize."

"Apologize?" Turner echoed. "If you want your kid raised by a saloon slut, it's all right with me."

The black mist exploded, and Angus hit the man. Turner fell, was instantly back on his feet, a .38 in his hand. The six-inch barrel caught the sunlight, and the crowd scattered. Angus stood steady.

"You've had a couple too many," Angus said. "Why don't you go on and sleep it off?"

"Got some yellow up your back?"

Reluctantly, Angus reached for his own gun. "And to him who would smite you on one cheek, turn the other also." The words insinuated themselves neatly into his mind. Hell, he thought, what a time to remember that verse. Unwillingly, he let his hand fall to his side, empty.

"You'll have to shoot," he said flatly. "I'm not going to draw." His breathing was shallow, his heart pumping double time.

" 'Fraid of dyin', preacher?" Turner jeered.

"Same as any man, I reckon," Angus conceded. "But I don't want you on my conscience."

With a snort of laughter, Turner holstered his gun. "One excuse's good as another," he said, turned and swaggered off. Angus grabbed his shoulder, whirled him around.

"We got some unfinished business," he said. "Miss Dubois is taking care of my baby. *Miss* Dubois." He shook Turner like a rag doll. The man's hat fell off, and his eyes were murderous. Angus released his shoulders, gave him a kick that sent him face down in the dust. The railroad man's hand again darted toward his holster. Angus put his foot on the fingers and Turner screeched in pain.

61

"Miss Dubois is taking care of my daughter," Angus said without inflection.

Turner was almost in tears, whether from pain, rage or humiliation, Angus didn't know. Didn't care. *"Miss Dubois!"* he insisted, and the man snarled, "Miss Dubois, then, and be damned to you."

Angus moved his foot and Turner got up, nursing the bruised fingers. "I'm not forgettin' this," he promised as he left.

The crowd began to break up presently. Pete walked with Angus back to his wagon. "So many folks," Pete remarked fretfully, "makes a fellow wonder if there's going to be enough land."

"There'll be enough," Angus said, unconsciously echoing Lexie.

"Hope the Injuns ain't too upset, seein' their land grabbed."

Angus felt the familiar spurt of rage. "I'm not wasting any sympathy on them," he said, and marched off, leaving Pete open-mouthed. What's he got against Indians? the little man wondered.

19.

Angus's sleep was restless that night, his spirits leaden when he awoke. One more day before they'd leave here, thank God. Dove had him over a barrel; he'd have to make the run, stay in the new territory until he could make other arrangements for the baby.

And dammit, he didn't like to be pushed around.

In no mood for company, he headed out across the prairie alone. His thoughts were somber as he walked, but it was better to be out than to sit in the wagon. At least he could breathe out here. He was thinking of Lexie and the new baby, of Dove Dubois and how perverse she was. She'd enjoyed seeing him squirm. He thought of the fact that he had no idea how a fellow started preaching. He'd never even been in church very much.

"My grace is sufficient for you." The words floated into his mind, and he gave a short bark of laughter. I'm hearing things now, he thought. Next, I'll be seeing things. Hard on that thought, the sun shone blindingly in his eyes, and he raised his head. Lord, it was nearly sundown. He turned back toward the camp, walking briskly.

He had almost reached his wagon, when he saw Mrs. Murphy running toward him with an awkward lope that made him think of a turkey running lopsidedly across a farmyard.

"Preacher!" she panted as she neared him. "Come quick! You're needed!" She whirled and started back the way she had come, as though certain that he'd follow.

With his long strides, he caught up to her without difficulty and hurried along beside her.

"What's wrong?" he demanded.

"The Holtzworthy boy." Mrs. Murphy was having trouble finding enough breath to speak. "Doctor says he's going fast, and his ma's takin' it awful hard."

Angus ran effortlessly, wondering vaguely how Mrs. Murphy knew about so many people. He had not even heard of the Holtzworthys. Mrs. Murphy skidded to a stop in front of a tent, stood back, hands over her heart, gasping for breath.

"Go on in, preacher," she panted. "See what you can do."

Feeling inadequate, Angus lifted the flap and entered. He was conscious of some movement in the dim tent and, as his eyes adjusted, saw two men and a woman working frantically with a threshing boy. They were struggling to get him into a galvanized tub of water, and Angus wondered, for a moment, if they were all loco. The boy's face was colorless, his arms and legs were flailing in a paroxysmal frenzy and his body was bent almost double, shuddering with spasms.

"Convulsions," one of the men snapped over his shoulder. "You the preacher?"

Angus's mouth was dry. "Yes," he managed to say.

"Stay out of the way but don't leave."

Angus backed off, feeling useless. Mrs. Murphy had said the boy was dying. Unexpectedly, an awful pang of sympathy caught him by the throat, and he felt his muscles tense. Too vividly it brought back Lexie's last moment. I can't stay here, he thought, and half turned to escape.

The Lord will not put on you more than you can bear. The words were incandescent in his mind, and he halted where he stood. Head raised heavenward, he swept off his hat. "You got an answer for everything, haven't You?" he muttered sourly.

The boy was finally in the tub, and within a few minutes the convulsions stopped. The doctor lifted and put him back on the cot. The child was breathing deeply, moaning appallingly as he did so, and Angus found his own chest hurting.

It seemed to him that the death throes lasted forever. But at last, for an instant, the child breathed normally and then did not breathe at all. The doctor felt for a pulse, lifted a stethoscope to the chest, shook his head.

"Oh, *God!*" The woman took one step toward her son and crumpled. Angus sprang forward, bent to lift her, but the doctor waved him back, held a bottle of sal volatile beneath her nose.

Tears were running down the father's weatherbeaten cheeks. He lifted his wife's hand, held it in both of his. "It's all right, Sarah," he kept repeating, as though by the saying of it, he could make it so. "It's going to be all right."

The woman turned her head from side to side, trying to escape the sharp fumes of the smelling salts, finally opened her eyes. Briefly, she appeared to be dazed, then Angus saw the awareness, the agony rush through her. She came to her feet in almost a single movement. "He —is—not—dead!" she cried. "I won't let him be dead!" Her voice was piercing. "My baby, my only baby!"

Angus moved toward her, knowing the agony of loss that boiled within her, part grief, part rebellion. The woman snatched the child's body to her breast as though she would force him to live again. She rocked back and forth with him, wailing.

"He's not dead!" Her voice was a screech, and suddenly, from instinct, as he had occasionally done with a panic-stricken horse, Angus flicked a stinging blow across her face. The woman jerked back, glaring at him, wild-eyed but silent. She put a hand to her cheek. Then a semblance of reason began to replace the frenzy. Shivering, she lowered her son to his pillow. And the tears came. A great, releasing flood of tears, without hysteria.

"Why did God take our baby?" she wept. "You're the preacher; tell me why." Never before, except when he saw Lexie's life slip away, had Angus felt so helpless.

"I don't know," he said simply. "And I don't have any pretty words to make it easier, Mrs. Holtzworthy." He recalled the voice of the old brush arbor preacher. "Faith makes it possible for us to endure grief without breaking," he quoted.

"I'm forty-five years old." Her voice was choked. "Zeb's fifty. He—little Zeb—he was like a miracle. Preacher, he wasn't even five years old. . . ." Her body rocked, and Angus feared she was building toward another attack of hysteria. He put his hand on her shoulder.

"Ma'am," he said gently, "should we ask God's help?"

The suggestion, born of desperation, broke through the woman's anguish. She went on her knees in the dust. After a moment's hesitation, Angus knelt beside her. He heard Zeb and the doctor join them in a small circle.

"Lord," Angus said, "we need help. We try not to question Your will, but when death comes, we feel You have forsaken us, that we are being punished for something, without knowing why."

Later, he could not remember all he said. It was as though he had forgotten the others and was pouring out his own anguish, the feeling of having been robbed of all that made life worthwhile.

He was drained when the prayer ended. He stood up, swaying with exhaustion, and thought vaguely that he must eat something.

He was thoughtful as he walked back to his wagon. What could you say when people had had their whole world torn apart? "You mustn't fret." "God's up there someplace, and he knows best." Angus laughed harshly. For a broken heart, you prescribed a poultice?

Yet there was a strange stirring within him. He had felt a kind of strength—was that what it was?—after the prayer. Not acceptance, not peace, but a kind of tentative groping toward peace.

20.

It was well past sunup the next morning when he wakened to the call of "Preacher!" outside his wagon. Heavy
with sleep, he roused himself, managed to stumble to the
flap, open it.

"Mr. Holtzworthy," he mumbled.

"Preacher"—the man seemed oddly embarrassed—"m
—me 'n' Sarah, I reckon we—we may as well go on and
make the run. I mean, staying here ain't gonna bring him
back, is it?"

Angus shook his head, eased himself down off the
wagon. "No, Zeb," he said, "it's not going to bring him
back."

The gnarled fingers were twisting together, and sympathy made Angus's chest ache. "What is it?" he asked.
"Your wife upset again?"

"No, it ain't that. You—you don't think it would look
like we didn't care, if we had the funeral today, went on
toward the border tomorrow?"

"I think it would be exactly the right thing to do."

"Well, then—" Zeb cleared his throat. "If it ain't too
much to ask, knowin' about your wife, and all, we—we
want you to hold the service."

Something inside Angus shrank like wool thrust into
boiling water. "We could get the preacher from town," he
said roughly. "I'm—I've never held a funeral. I—
wouldn't know what to say."

"My wife's set a store by you. Reckon you know a
psalm and a prayer, don't you? It would mean a heap to
both of us."

Angus fought down panic. "All right," he said at last.
"What time?"

There was cold sweat on Angus's face when he looked
out over the hastily dug grave, at the crowd. He quoted
from the twenty-third psalm, then poured out his heart,

66

repeating again that man could not understand the workings of God, could only trust and hold to his faith, ending the brief service with, "Let us pray."

At the last Amen, a woman's voice was lifted in song; "Safe in the arms of Jesus." Other voices joined with hers until the sound floated out like a banner. Angus swallowed past the lump in his throat.

Afterward, many of the people lingered to talk, but the preacher paid his respects to Sarah and Zeb and left. He was wrung out, shaky. Pete caught up with him as he walked toward his wagon.

"You look plumb tuckered out, Angus," he said. "Come on in the stable and have a dram. Medicinally, of course."

Angus's laugh was jerky. "I don't know, Pete; a preacher's s'posed to—"

"Even the Lord Jesus Christ had a nip now and then, I've heerd."

Angus's laugh spurted out, a release after the past hour. "I never heard it put like that," he said, "but yes, he drank wine."

There was a smile in Pete's voice as he said: "I wouldn't want to set myself up as trying to be better than Him."

Mindful that they'd be pulling out the following morning and that he wanted to see Miss Rowdy before he left, Angus made the drink a quick one. Nonetheless, it steadied him, and Pete's company helped too.

As they parted, Pete said shyly he'd heard Mrs. Murphy was gonna drive tandem with the preacher, so he figured him and Alice might as well tag along, and he'd bet the Holtzworthys would like to join them too.

Touched, Angus said gruffly, "It'd be my pleasure, Pete. We'll start our own settlement."

After the little man had gone, Angus rechecked his wagon, the harness, roped the scant furnishings down so they wouldn't jounce and at last, reluctantly, took off to see the baby. He'd almost as soon face a swarm of angry hornets as Dove Dubois.

At the door of her room, he hesitated. Miss Rowdy wouldn't know whether he told her goodbye or not. Still, he reckoned it was what a father should do. He knocked.

Dove came to the door in a trailing peignoir that made Angus blink. Of sheerest pink muslin inset with lace and ribbons, it fell in fluid folds accenting the magnificent curve of breast, smallness of waist, womanly flare of hips. Through it, the creamy skin gleamed like satin.

Unexpectedly, Angus felt a thrust of sexual desire so intense, his loins throbbed with pain; felt the animal heat rushing through his body.

"Hello, preacher," she said, stepping back so he could enter. "Miss Rowdy's asleep, but you can look at her."

Angus stood rooted to the floor, feeling the swelling that betrayed him, astonishment and a burning shame that he could be so easily aroused, with Lexie not yet cold in her grave. "Get some clothes on!" The words burst out of him. His voice was rough.

Dove's eyes widened. Her face became like a cat's, wicked with understanding. Muscles knotted in Angus's cheeks; his hands clenched. Dove sobered.

"Reckon I could speak to one of the girls," she offered, half amused, half sympathetic.

He drew a jagged breath. "I don't want a saloon girl," he said harshly. Enraged with himself, he struck out at her. "You think I'd take you or any of your girls, after I've had a decent woman?"

Dove winced. In the next moment, she spat at him. Full in the face. "Get out of here, you stinking hypocrite," she shouted. "Pretending to be so good, gettin' the hots first time you see a woman. Get!"

Angus felt the familiar black rage. Blindly, he raised a hand as though to strike her. Dove stood unmoving. "Go ahead and hit me, *preacher!* I ain't nothin' but a nigger. And all de white folks knows niggers ain't got no feelin'!"

With an effort, Angus lowered his arm. Still trembling with rage, he wiped the spittle from his cheek. "Slut!" The word was on his lips, but Dove was gone. The door slammed behind her. He leaned against the wall until the rasp of his breath slowed, his pulses quieted.

Once in shaky possession of himself, he strode down the stairs, through the hotel lobby, looking neither right nor left. And back in the wagon, he went down on his knees.

"I got no callin', Lord," he cried silently. "That circuit rider talked me into this. There's others, Lord, who can do a hell of a—who can do a lot better than me. If it had been a decent woman, it might be a little different."

But then, if Dove had been a decent woman, he

thought, she wouldn't have come to the door in a night-gown.

"I got a man's need, Lord," he finished slowly. "Amen."

He was too restless to relax, and the wagon seemed to be smothering him. He wished the night were past, that they were already moving, but it was scarcely dusk. Finally, he ate a few bites of food and struck out for the grove of trees half a mile or so distant.

He had no idea how long he walked or how far. His mind was on Lexie and how she had looked forward to the new land. He thought of Dove, and there was a sourness in his throat. He thought of the baby, Miss Rowdy, and felt trapped by his responsibility. And finally, reluctantly, he faced his own sexuality.

He had not made love to Lexie after the second month of her pregnancy, though she had laughed at him and told him he worried too much. But he had been terrified that he would in some way injure her.

"It's been a long time," he groaned, "an awful long time," and continued to walk until exhaustion dulled his needs.

Turning back toward the camp, he had almost reached his wagon, when he saw the shifting of shadows beneath a tree, heard the sound of retching sobs. Reluctant to intrude, he said softly, "Ho, there." It was a familiar voice that answered, muffled and uneven.

"Preacher?"

"Yes. Is that you, Pete?"

"It's me."

Again, Angus hesitated. "Want company?" he asked.

"Company won't help."

The man sounded so doleful, Angus was alarmed. "Something wrong with the family?" he asked.

"I ain't gonna have no family when Alice finds out what I done." Pete's voice cracked. He got up. "Sorry, preacher; guess I don't feel like company," he said, and started off.

Angus followed. "Pete . . ."

"Just let me alone!" The little man's voice broke; he sobbed, overwhelmed.

Angus took hold of his shoulder. "For God's sake, man, short of death, nothing's that bad."

Pete whirled to face him. "You don't think so?" he blurted out. "I've lost my family. 'Member I told you

69

Alice said if I ever gambled again, she was through? She ain't a woman what takes her word lightly."

"How much did you lose?"

Pete spread his hands. "The whole kit and kaboodle," he said. "Wagon, team, everything. I wisht I was dead. I'd rather *be* dead than face Alice."

"Whoa, there! Maybe we can think of something."

"Preacher . . ."

Angus was aware the man wanted to be alone with his misery, but the torment went so deep, Angus was fearful of leaving him. "Think you were cheated?" he asked.

"If he was cheatin', he was sure slick about it," Pete said mournfully. " 'Sides, why should he? Him bein' a railroad man, and all."

"Vince Turner!" Angus exclaimed.

"Yeah."

"I don't think he's a railroad man any more than you are. Probably a tinhorn gambler."

"Whatever he is, he's holdin' my IOU for a team and wagon."

A spasm of anger shook Angus. "Let's mosey on over, see if we can get it back," he said.

"I ain't got nothin' more to ante," Pete objected. "I shore don't want you to put yore gear on the line."

"I'm not," Angus promised. "But I've got an idea. They playing anything besides poker?"

"He was telling everyone to name his own game."

Angus said, "Hm." As they neared the tent, Pete came to a halt.

"I ain't goin' back in there. I'll go on—"

"Wait for me," Angus insisted; and then, with sudden inspiration: "If it comes to a fight, I might need some help."

"I'll wait," Pete said glumly. "But I'm tellin' you—"

Despite the crystalline air outside, the tent reeked from the fumes of redeye and cheap cigar smoke. There were perhaps a dozen men crowded in, watching. Five sat at the makeshift table. Three had apparently folded on that particular hand. Turner and the fifth man were studying their cards.

Turner looked up. The silverfish eyes darted at Angus incredulously, darted away, then back. His lips twisted in an unpleasant smile. "Look who's here, by God," he said. "You boys want to clean up your language. We got a *preacher* in our midst. I didn't know preachers was allowed to gamble."

Angus kept his face impassive. He would not, must not, permit the black mist of rage to cloud his judgment. Every eye in the tent was on him, ready to make him a laughingstock. His gun touched his hand as though it had reached for him, rather than the other way around. He jerked his hand away.

"Well, preacher?" Turner made no effort to disguise his malice. Angus could almost read his thoughts. In this encounter, Turner would give back a little of the humiliation he had suffered earlier.

"Go on with your game," Angus said mildly. A little sigh, almost of disappointment, ran through the group. They had thought to see some action.

Shaking his head, Turner turned his attention back to his cards. "Man calls himself a preacher, you can't hardly credit what he's apt to do," he said. Angus's hands knotted and a muscle moved in his cheek, but he kept his silence.

"I'll see your five and raise you five," Turner told the one man who was still in the game.

"Too rich for me." The man dropped his cards on the table, shoved back his chair. "I'm gonna call it a night," he said, getting up.

The other players rose too. "Burke's right," one of them said. "Tomorrow's a big day."

Turner scowled at Angus. "You've done busted up a good game, parson. Reckon you kind of owe it to me to take their place."

"What's the game?" Angus asked.

Turner's teeth shone briefly. "You name it," he said.

"You mean I can say the game?"

"That's right, Holy Joe. Any sittin'-down game, that is." He looked around at the circle of faces and was rewarded with a small ripple of laughter.

Angus squirmed, shuffled his feet. "You sayin' any game at all?" he repeated. "Any sittin'-down game?"

Turner snorted. "If you haven't got the stakes, say so," he said, riffling the cards.

Angus took a chair. "Oh, I got the stakes," he said. "Hear you took a team and wagon off a fellow, couple hours ago. I've got a pair of matched bays and a Springfield I'll put against them."

71

Turner blinked, then laughed. "You got a deal," he said. "Name your poison."

"Hand wrestling."

Turner's face tightened. He glared, those strange eyes seeming to glow almost red. "You trying to be funny?" he demanded. "I asked what game you wanted. What card game."

Angus glanced around the circle of onlookers. "Any of you hear him specify a card game?" he asked. "All I heard was that it had to be a sittin'-down game."

A few tentative grins appeared, and then someone laughed aloud. "Looks like he's got you, Turner." The man chuckled again. "You said *any* sittin'-down game."

A thin line of white appeared around Turner's lips. "Think you're pretty goddam smart, don't you?" he hissed at Angus.

"Put up or shut up," Angus said coolly.

Face black as a thundercloud, Turner rose and jerked off his coat, rolled up a shirt sleeve. "I don't want your dirty hands on my clothes," he said.

Angus grinned. "Sit down, fellow. I'm tired of waiting."

They gripped hands. Turner's nails were burnished, fingers white and puny-looking against Angus's sun-browned flesh.

"I swear, your hands are prettier than a woman's," Angus said.

Turner flushed. "Shut up and go!" he snarled, at the same moment giving Angus's hand a vicious wrench, which pushed back the preacher's arm halfway to the table. The gambler pinched his fingers together, trying to shut off the other man's circulation.

Taken off guard, Angus grunted. Then he shoved back, slowly, almost inch by inch, bringing his arm upright again. The cords in Turner's neck stood out as the muscles of Angus's arm knotted and he slowly but inexorably pushed the gambler's arm toward the table. The bastard's stronger than he looks, the preacher thought.

The contest went backward and forward, with first one, then the other, seeming to have the best of it. But at last Angus drew a deep breath, exerted himself to the limit and slammed Turner's arm down with a force that made a sharp thump.

Turner screamed, his face losing color, and Angus released him. The gambler lifted the savaged arm with his other hand.

"You've broke a bone," he screeched, and began to curse.

"Nothing's broken." Angus was calm. "Leastways, not enough that you can't write out a paper saying the team and wagon are mine."

Turner's eyes were venomous, darting this way, then that. But he dared not welsh when others were looking on. At last, reluctantly, he wrote on the paper Angus shoved at him.

"I ain't forgettin' this, preacher," he muttered.

21.

Those who had their own transportation pulled out of Arkansas City the following morning, heading for the border of the Unassigned Lands. Those who were to go by rail were wistful as they watched the exodus. The trains wouldn't leave until the day of the run.

The Holtzworthys had been more than pleased to drive tandem with Angus and the others, although, Zeb had said, they'd probably be homesteading closer to Oklahoma Station than the rest. Sarah had decided to start a school. So the four wagons stayed within shouting distance of one another until they reached the Logan County line.

If Arkansas City had been hectic, this was bedlam. The homesteaders at last could *see* the Promised Land, and the urge to cross over and put their stakes down was nearly irresistible. What stopped them was the knowledge that anyone entering and making a claim sooner than the "run" automatically forfeited his land, if he was found out.

It seemed as though April twenty-second would never arrive. A score or so fistfights broke out for no other reason than that the enforced wait had made everyone edgy.

Even the children were infected by the tense atmosphere and grew quarrelsome. Alice Smith kept her brood in line by promising them that even if only one of them started something, she'd paddle the lot. "She'd do it, too," Pete told Angus fondly. "This way, every one of them younguns is watchin' to see that none of the others step out of line. She believes in kids mindin', Alice does."

It was on the evening of the twenty-first, while checking his gear for maybe the dozenth time, that the ideal solution about what to do with Miss Rowdy struck him. At least, to him it seemed ideal. The Holtzworthys—their losing little Zeb—Good Lord, why hadn't he thought of it before?

Hurriedly, he scrubbed the axle grease off his hands and sought out Sarah and Zeb.

But when he presented the idea to them, Sarah's eyes brimmed with tears, and she went so white, he thought she would faint. "No!" It was almost a scream.

Angus stepped back. "It was just a thought," he said hastily. Sarah put a hand on his arm, tears streaming down her cheeks.

"I couldn't," she said, and her voice broke. "I couldn't risk loving like that again. Anything happened . . ." She shook her head. "No, I'll teach children and love them, too. But at a distance, preacher. Never close again."

22.

The morning of April 22, 1889, dawned bright and clear. Angus was up at daybreak but found the camp already buzzing like a swarm of bees although the go signal would not be given until noon.

The hours dragged. By eleven o'clock, everyone was poised, ready to dash across the border. Angus blinked when he saw one man mounted on a high-wheeled bicycle. A few were on foot, others on horses, which stamped impatiently as though caught up in the excitement.

The trains chugged importantly into the station, and Angus thought they looked like nothing so much as animated pincushions with human pins stuck to them. The coaches of all fifteen were full, and people clung precariously to the sides, sat on the rooftops, and even on the cowcatchers.

Stationed at intervals along the line, US Army men sat on their horses. Finally, at precisely twelve o'clock, they put bugles to their lips. The blasts sounded. Pistol shots echoed the call.

The wagons broke loose, the horses dashed, the trains chugged, men ran on foot. For some, the trip was over almost before it began. They tamped their stakes into quarter sections within sight of the starting line.

Angus and his party kept their horses at a steady pace. The preacher had in mind an area about fifteen miles northwest of Oklahoma Station.

What would later be six counties were opened to settlement that day, close to two million acres, which also included six townsites. Driving roughly parallel with the train tracks, Angus was thinking that they must be reasonably close to Guthrie townsite, when he saw one of the trains begin to slow, and in the next moment, a swirl of skirts tumbled off the cowcatcher.

Good God, a woman had lost her footing. A cold chill touched his neck. Almost without thought, he shouted, "Ho, the wagons!" and began to circle. The other three wagons followed.

As they drew closer to the site, what looked like an inanimate bundle of rags suddenly moved, and a woman stood up, hammer in hand. "There!" she said, dusting off her skirts. Then, seeing people plunging toward her, she dropped the hammer and snatched up a rifle. "This is my claim!" she shouted at them.

Angus and the others who'd piled out of the wagons skidded to a halt. It was one of the kids who giggled first; then the whole assemblage burst into laughter. The woman glared.

"What's so all-fired funny?" she demanded.

"Ma'am—" Angus swept off his hat. "We thought you were hurt, falling off the train like you did."

"Falling off?" She snorted. "I had to bribe the con-sarned engineer to slow down when I signaled."

Hurriedly, Angus introduced himself and the others and said they'd be getting on. The woman's manner thawed as she realized they had no designs on her land.

"Maggie Cruikshank," she introduced herself. "Un-claimed blessing from Massachusetts."

"Lawsy me," Sarah said fretfully, "how're you going to manage in this wild country, with no man?"

Maggie tossed her head. "What do I need with a man?" She sniffed. "I'm strong, and I got ideas of my own. I do take it kindly, though, that you stopped. Where you aimin' to settle?"

They told her. Called hasty invitations to come visiting and headed on.

It was well into the afternoon when the Holtzworthys broke away from the others, heading due south. Angus, the Smiths and Mrs. Murphy continued on their south-west course. A couple of hours later, the Smiths found a place to their liking, and shortly thereafter, Mrs. Murphy stopped her wagon.

Angus went on. He should be nearing Buffalo Creek. It had been marked on the crude map he had. He hoped whoever had penciled it in had been accurate. He sighted a heavy growth of trees such as would line a creek's banks, only to find, when he reached it, a shallow draw. He didn't know whether to swear or cry, in his dis-appointment.

Then, less than a mile farther west, over a small in-cline, he came on another growth and knew in his bones he'd reached his goal. Something quickened in his heart.

There were enormous cottonwoods, black walnuts, birch, elm, a few spruce and cedar. Near at hand he saw a dogwood and redbud growing side by side. It was as though they were a good omen. The dogwood, which re-produced each spring Christ's stigmata, and the redbud, from which tradition said His cross had been fashioned. Angus's mother had told him the legends when he was a child. He had not thought of them again until now.

With a feeling akin to awe, he jumped down from the wagon, bowed his head for a brief prayer of thankfulness and began to unhitch the team.

About twenty yards to the south, on a sloping knoll, was an outcropping of red sandstone. Angus walked to the low summit. It made him think of the rocks Jacob had placed to mark his encounter with God.

"Hey! Whatcha doin' up there?" The angry shout made him whirl about, gun in hand without his consciously having reached for it. "Damn it, put that gun away!" the voice spluttered, and into Angus's view came a grizzled scarecrow of a man.

He could have been anywhere from thirty-five to seventy. His hollowed cheeks were covered with heavy stubble, mouth shrunken over toothless gums. "Whatcha doin' on my claim?" he demanded.

Angus holstered the gun. "Don't see any stakes," he said mildly.

"Stakes." The old man snorted. "What's stakes? I got a crop already growing. Come and see, if you don't believe it."

A grin made Angus's lips twitch as he walked in the direction the old man led. "You a sooner?"

"Sooner, nothin'. This ground's so rich . . . well, you'll see." They came to a large patch that had been tilled. There were two-inch spikes of onions; potatoes were breaking through the soil.

"How long you been here?" Angus asked.

The old man puffed out his lips. "Two, three hours," he said. "This-here ground's so rich, you throw them seeds in, plants pop right back out at you."

Angus laughed, stuck out his hand. "Angus Scofield," he said, "circuit rider."

"Oh, Gawd, you mean I been lyin' to a preacher?"

"That worse than lying to anyone else?" Angus asked, amused.

"Yeah, reckon it is." Almost reluctantly, he put his hand in Angus's big paw, withdrew it quickly. "I'm Tenny," he said. "Reckon this means I gotta move out, seein' I come in illegal."

"Not on my account," Angus said. "I'll move my stake farther down the creek."

Together, they found the government marker, and Tenny put his stake down roughly half a mile from the official line.

"That takes care of it," Angus said. "That side's yours; this side's mine." And was momentarily thankful that the knoll, the dogwood and redbud were his.

Later, he was to learn that most of the disputes that

arose that day, when an estimated hundred thousand people surged onto a raw land, had been settled as amicably. In only one case was there a fight that ended in tragedy. In Oklahoma Station, a man was shot to death in an argument over a town lot.

It was said variously that his killer had been hanged by men who saw the shooting, that he had left the country and that he had quietly slunk away to make a claim elsewhere.

But since there was no organized law in the territory for the first thirteen months after the run, and since apparently no one was sure enough of who the killer was to put in a complaint with the cavalry that sporadically checked the area, no charge was ever brought.

Angus was invited to eat supper with Tenny that evening. There was a fire, hot coffee, beans and sowbelly, sourdough biscuits. "It ain't nothin' fine," Tenny said, "but it'll keep your belly from eatin' up your backbone."

"Tastes good," Angus said. Leaning back against a tree trunk, hands clasped around his bent knees, he stared moodily into the darkness. No moon, no stars, but a scudding of silvery clouds. If Lexie were here, this would be the greatest adventure man ever undertook. He sighed.

"You got no woman?" Tenny asked.

"My wife died in Ark City."

"Oh, hell, there I go, puttin' my foot in it again. You a drinking man, preacher?"

"I've been known to take a nip," Angus admitted. "But I reckon I'm not. Folks wouldn't hold with a parson indulging."

"Folks," Tenny mimicked, digging a jug out from under the wagon, "wouldn't know nothin' about it."

"But I would," Angus said. "You go ahead."

He was not a drinking man in the sense that alcohol was a problem for him, but he knew a moment's pang when Tenny tilted the jug and the whiskey gurgled. It would be good to get drunk tonight, blot out thoughts and memories. Pretty soon he'd be bawling like a new calf, he thought in disgust, and got to his feet.

"Been a long day," he said. "Think I'll turn in. Obliged for the hospitality."

But sleep had to wait awhile longer. He had begun to settle himself on his bedroll, when one of the horses neighed. Angus sat up, head to one side, listening. The faint beat of horses' hooves, almost noiseless in the grass. He got to his feet, gun in hand. Who'd be out this time of night unless he meant mischief?

He strained his eyes, peering to the north, from which the sound seemed to come, and presently, almost ghostly in the darkness, saw horse and rider. His horses, David and Beth, whinnied; the other horse gave an answering snort. Hefting his .45, Angus stood motionless.

"Halloo, the house!" The hail came while man and horse were still shadowy, but Angus breathed a sigh of relief and put down his gun.

"Pete, you old bushwhacker," he yelled. Pete's Lily trotted up, and at the same instant, Tenny appeared over the crest, demanding what was going on.

"Light down a spell," Angus invited Pete, before answering Tenny. Pete swung off the horse, and the two men clapped each other on the back as though they'd been separated for years. Then Angus stepped back.

"Pete, this is Tenny, my next-door neighbor," he said, and the two men shook hands. "Where's your claim?" Angus asked next. "Here, sit down."

Tenny turned. "Reckon this calls for a celebration," he mumbled, and took off. He was back before Angus and Pete had gotten firmly settled against the cottonwood, jug clasped to his chest.

"Man, you are pure-D livin' high on the hog," Pete said as Tenny handed him the jug. He took a long drink, wiped his mouth on the back of his hand. "That's got a wallop like the kick of a mule."

He handed the jug back to Tenny, who held it out to Angus. "Preacher?" And when Angus hesitated, added, "For old times' sake, so to speak."

"Old times' sake." Angus laughed. "What're you talking about, you old coyote?"

Stars had finally made their appearance, and in the dim light, Tenny's toothless grin split his face. "Seems to me you been here a long time already," he explained. "Having to watch my p's and q's around a preacher makes the time seem longer."

Angus shook his head, grinning, accepted the jug and, taking a snort, sputtered.

"Tastes like coal oil and lye water," he gasped when he could speak.

"I take that most kindly," Tenny said. "Made it myself."

As the three men sat talking, Pete and Tenny passed the jug back and forth. Angus refused more of the potent liquid and asked again where Pete's claim was.

" 'Bout three miles to the north and east," Pete said.

"But you are on a creek?" Angus was anxious. "Some of that upland stuff, so I've heard, won't raise good weeds."

"On the creek," Pete assured him. "Soil's black as a storm at midnight."

The men swapped lies for a couple of hours. When Pete got up to leave, Angus asked the little man if he could make it home.

" 'Course I can." He was indignant, then chuckled. "Least aways, Lily can. She didn't have no corn squeezin's."

23.

The following day Angus rode into Guthrie, which had been designated the provisional capital, to record his claim. The cost was a dollar twenty-five. The settler then had to live on the land five years, at which time it became his, free and clear.

He was back home by midafternoon, anxious to get a house started, get really settled in. The outcropping of red sandstone making up the knoll would, when properly hollowed out, make a perfect back wall for the house.

He unsaddled the horse, ate a few mouthfuls of jerky and began work. Although the sandstone at first seemed crumbly to the touch, it was very hard to dig out in any sort of symmetrical way. At times it seemed granite-hard. At others, an entire chunk would give way, going wider or deeper than Angus had planned.

He was swearing under his breath and wiping away

sweat, when Tenny showed up. "You orta have somethin' to blast that sucker out," Tenny said.

Glad to stop a few minutes, Angus walked over to the shade of the cottonwood. "Nope," he said. "Might blast off the top. That's going to be my roof."

Tenny squinted. "Pretty good idee," he conceded. "Hard work, though. I'm fixin' to buy me a tent."

When Angus returned to work, the old man joined him in grubbing.

It took a week's hard labor to get the hollow to Angus's liking. He figured it to be about fourteen by six. He and Tenny then loaded the old man's plow on Angus's wagon and set out for the northeast corner of the quarter section, where there was buffalo grass.

Buffalo-grass roots matted more densely than other growths and would make the best soddy. Angus broke the soil to the depth of half a foot, cut it into fourteen-by-eighteen-inch blocks. Innumerable trips were required to bring enough blocks of sod to the site of the house. The grass had to be used freshly dug, or the ever-present Oklahoma wind dried the dirt so that it crumbled.

Swirling red dust bit into eyes, nostrils, mouth, until finally the two men wetted bandanas in the creek, tied them over the lower half of their faces.

The slabs of sod were laid double so that the walls would be thirty-six inches thick. Six feet of sod extended from the sandstone, so the room was now fourteen by twelve.

"Reckon I'll have to cut some trees to make a roof." Angus was thinking out loud.

Tenny spat. "Hell, preacher, yore runnin' this job into work."

"Take a day off," Angus offered. "Pay'll be the same."

"Naw." Tenny grinned. "Reckon I know the woods better'n you. Now, you take soft wood, pine and such, it's gonna rot on you. What we need is some good old blackjack. Hard as iron, them buggers is. And I got a patch of 'em upland side of my place."

So the next two days were spent chopping and stripping blackjacks, hauling them back to the soddy, levering them into position, from sandstone to front wall.

When the cabin was complete, the two men stood back and admired their handiwork. They had left openings for a door and window, scooped out a hole in the roof for a stovepipe.

Tenny scratched his stubbly chin. "Don't know when I've seen a handsomer house," he said.

"And it's built on rock," Angus added in agreement.

24.

On May first, Angus rode into Oklahoma Station to vote.

Requirements set up by the federal government stated that lots must be registered with town officials, but there were no town officials. So the settlers had decided to elect some.

W. L. Couch, who had once led the Boomers, was chosen temporary mayor within a day or two after the run. At the same time, the May first election was set up.

Men were milling around in the streets when Angus rode into town. A muscle hardened in his cheek and he checked his horse when he saw numbers of Indians in the crowd. Some wore white man's garb; others, buckskin pants and colorful beads.

"Whoa up," he cautioned himself, feeling his choler rise, "this is Injun territory. If you can't stand the sight of them, better head out for some other state."

"Indians need God too!"

"Leave me be, Lord," Angus growled, and shook his head.

Having voted, he inquired for the Holtzworthys and headed Beth in their direction. Sarah was fixing dinner, and he felt his spirits begin to rise when she invited him to come and sit awhile. Zeb came in from the field, wiping the back of his neck with a handkerchief.

"Howdy, parson," he said; "hot!" Angus agreed, and Sarah told them to wash up; dinner was almost ready. As they ate, they spoke of the election. "Hear tell the

Seminoles are supporting Couch; the Kickapoos are agin' him," Zeb said.

"The Seminoles and Kickapoos!" Angus snorted. "What the hell—beg pardon, Sarah—have Injuns got to do with a white man's election?"

"Just rumor," Zeb said mildly. "May be nothin' in it." Sarah, watching Angus thoughtfully, spoke almost the identical words he had said to himself earlier.

"Law, Brother Scofield, this is Indian Territory. You're going to have to expect Indians to have a part in it."

"This is *unassigned* territory, Sarah. The Injuns offered to sell it to the United States government. They've got no more right in it than . . . than . . ." He stopped suddenly, aware that he had backed himself into a corner. The whole country had once belonged to the Indians. "People are afraid of them," he finished lamely. "They're savages, every one of them."

Annoyed with both himself and the Holtzworthys for some obscure reason, Angus left a short time later, stopped off back in town. Some enterprising soul had set up a tent and was selling coffee and johnny cake. The prairie grass had already been beaten down by hundreds of feet, and dust rose in red clouds.

Wandering along main street, Angus noted a tight little knot of men laughing uproariously. Mildly curious, he stopped. In the midst of the circle stood a rawboned woman somewhere in her forties, red-faced with indignation.

"You turkey gobbler, hand over my nickel," she rasped.

"Aw, come on, Mary," the man to whom she had spoken said wheedlingly. "I need another button sewed on. No pay 'til you live up to the contract."

The woman said a short pithy word, and the laughter boomed out even louder.

"What's happening?" Angus asked.

"It's Button Mary," he was told. "For a nickel she'll sew a button on. But this feller wants her to sew one that's missing in an important spot." The speaker slapped his knee, roaring with laughter.

"That's no way to treat a woman," Angus growled, starting to push his way through the crowd. The man he'd been talking with hauled him back.

"Don't you worry about Button Mary none, mister," he said. "She can take care of herself."

There was a fresh burst of laughter, and Angus saw the woman bend. She took the fly of the man's pants between two fingers distastefully, as she might have touched a snake, flicked a button into place and sewed a stitch. "Hold still," she warned.

"Aw, Mary, let me move around just a little . . ." the man began, and in the next instant jumped a foot, letting out a bloodcurdling scream. "Damn it to hell, you stuck me. . . ." He was clutching himself, hopping from one foot to the other, face contorted.

"Told you to hold still," Mary said, straightening. "You want that button sewed on or not?"

"You can take your button and ram it."

"I'll take my dime," the woman said, holding out her hand.

"I ain't payin'. You've likely give me blood pizin."

Mary stood her ground. "We had a contract. Ain't that right, fellers?" She appealed to the crowd. The laughter was directed at the man this time. "She's right, Ed," someone called out. "You-all had a contract. Give her her dime." The man glowered at those in the circle, reached reluctantly into his pocket, found a dime and slapped it into her hand.

Couch was duly elected mayor. He was a simple man, not given to great bouts of oratory, but his brief speech was cheered as wildly as though he'd been the most eloquent of chautauqua speakers.

Angus heard him through, picked up some supplies at the store and headed home, well content.

25.

There was a killer tornado the day Dove arrived with her girls. Angus didn't know which caused the most consternation. The tornado uprooted giant trees and killed some stock. The effect of Dove's presence was less lethal but longer lasting.

As soon as the prairie grapevine spread the word, Angus saddled Beth and rode in to see Miss Rowdy. He'd been so busy, he'd hardly given her a thought until then, but as he rode, he was surprised to realize he was anxious to see her.

He had no trouble spotting Dove's house. It was easily the most imposing in the flat country southwest of Oklahoma Station. Angus grinned. A rough framework for a two-story edifice had been erected; the downstairs was complete. There was a fanlight of stained glass over the front door. The wages of sin might be death, Angus reflected, but at that moment it looked like the wages of sin were a house that other folks might envy.

It was well on toward noon when he arrived, but there were no signs of life. The shades were drawn. Swinging down from Beth's broad back, Angus tied her to the hitching post that had been thoughtfully placed behind the house. His lips twitched at Dove's planning. Her callers would doubtless appreciate her discretion.

He knocked softly at the back dooor. No need to wake the whole house, but with two infants around, someone was bound to be up. The door opened a crack, and a bony black face peered at him.

"You too early, cowboy," the woman said. "Come back tonight." She was about to shut the door, but Angus slipped his boot into the opening.

"I came to see my baby," he said hastily. "I'm . . ." As usual when he was flustered, his tongue almost slipped. "I'm Preacher—er—Scofield."

The face scowled. "Take shame to yourself," she scolded. "Preacher's got no businesss 'round a place like this. Git!"

"You don't understand, Auntie," Angus said desperately. "A *little* baby. Martha. Miss Rowdy."

The door swung open so fast, he almost lost his balance. "Why didn't you say so?" the old woman demanded. "Here—" she pulled out a chair, "seat yo'self and have some coffee whilst I see if Miss Dove is receiving."

It was a good half hour before Dove appeared. "Hello, preacher," she said insolently. "Ain't you afeared for your good name?"

Oh, Lord, she was in one of her moods. He didn't try to answer. His eyes were on the baby she was carrying. "She's grown a foot," he said, getting up. "And—her arms and legs are rounded out. And"—he realized suddenly—"she doesn't have to be carried on a pillow any more."

He lifted Miss Rowdy from Dove's arms, and it seemed to him that the baby recognized him and made an indeterminate sound. "She's trying to talk," Angus exclaimed.

"Shore," Dove said sourly. Her hands went to her hips, and Angus was only too aware of the ominous silence in the room, knew that Dove was spoiling for a fight. He sensed too what the underlying trouble was.

"Dove," he said simply, "why don't you find some good, steady man and get married?"

The woman laughed, and the sound hurt his ears. "You offerin', preacher?" she asked nastily. "Or you just figger I need a bedmate and yore offerin' your lily-white body for that?"

The mole began to throb, and he felt his betraying ears redden. "Dove," he said desperately, "I didn't come here to fight. I want to visit with Miss Rowdy and get the hell out of here before you claw me to slivers."

There was a silence while he adjusted the baby in his arm, sat down and began talking to her. Then, unexpectedly, he heard Dove chuckle.

"You a troublesome man," she said.

"You're not exactly soothing syrup yourself," he retorted. Dove pulled out a chair and seated herself across the table from him. There was another silence, which was not altogether easy, yet was somehow companionable, while he played with the baby.

"Don't you think she's smarter than most?" he asked at last. "Seems like she understands what I say."

Dove got up to refill his coffee cup. "Preacher," she said, "every baby ever born seemed out of the ordinary to his ma and pa."

He shifted the baby so he could hold her at arm's length. "You have to admit she's prettier than most," he said, and Miss Rowdy crowed. "See her laugh at that," he said. "And look at those curls."

"She gonna be a looker," Dove conceded. "But *stubborn*, preacher; you better get you a blacksnake whip. I

86

thought to start her on a little mashed potato. At her age, Samsy gobbled 'em up like a good 'un. But her ladyship wasn't having any. She went more than half a day without eating. Man, she howled."

"You let her go hungry?" Angus demanded indignantly.

"Shhh, you'll wake the house. Your girl child wasn't hurt none. When I gave her the breast, she more than made up for lost time. All I'm telling you, preacher, is that she's got the stubbornness of a mule, and you better be figurin' out how to deal with it."

Angus had settled Miss Rowdy back in the crook of his arm again and, after a bit of shifting that reminded him of nestlings settling in for the night, she had fallen asleep. The feathery eyelashes, lucent skin, the snub nose, gave her a look of cherubic innocence. No human who looked so spun-sugar sweet could be fractious. Dove saw his look of disbelief, and a dimple flashed.

"Don't let her looks fool you, preacher," she said drily. "It's those innocent-looking gals who cause the trouble."

26.

The settlers learned, that first year, that crops have to be planted early, in Oklahoma. The harvest was scanty. The wheat did not make back its seed. The summer heat, when it began, in the latter part of June, was all but unbearable.

Yet strangely enough, Angus heard little grumbling. There had been, even before the run, a goodly number of white men living in Indian Territory, though not in the unassigned area. Some of them had married into the tribes; some were the Irish imported to build the railroad. Some were railroad people, and some looked after the herds, on rented lands.

Most of them had lush gardens, and they shared with the newcomers. A few who had made the run sold out their claims for whatever they could get or, discouraged and unable to sell, abandoned the land and left.

It was in the blistering heat of early July that Angus began the circuit. He would go out King Fisher way, build a brush arbor, stop off at a farmhouse to say there would be a meeting. By and large the settlers were God-fearing people, hungry to hear the word. And, Angus wryly acknowledged to himself as time passed, hungry for entertainment, too, for the sociables that followed the service.

Before he decided on the permanent area he would cover, he sometimes ranged as far away as the Stillwater area, and at those times there were occasionally stolid-faced braves who stood, arms folded, at the back of the gathering, listening impassively.

"Indians need God too."

When that thought intruded in his mind, or even when there were Indians in the crowd, something invariably knotted in Angus's gullet, his hackles rose and it was all he could do to keep his hatred from lashing forth. After such a service, he would find himself covered with sweat, and nauseous from the effort to control himself.

He was many times on his knees when he was alone in the depths of a woods or at home in the sod house. "Let go of me, God!" he cried once. "I hate them! I'd like to wipe out everyone of the bastards!"

There was no answer to that prayer. He soon discontinued the Stillwater loop, telling himself there was plenty to do west of Buffalo Creek. Which was, in fact, true. He was away from home most of the time. Tenny kept an eye on things when he was gone.

Miss Rowdy, still with Dove, had begun to fashion words and was taking her first faltering steps. She was a beautiful child, with a gamine face framed by ringlets, their color as unique as Lexie's hair, their intractable curliness like his own. Her eyes were a clear, cool amethyst unlike any Angus had seen.

He knew a pride in her that was, he thought at times, almost sinful. Perhaps from the Scots blood that ran in his veins, perhaps from the hurt dealt him by Bull about the fawn, he was, in his innermost being, a bitterly lonely man. Only three people had penetrated the fastness of his heart: his mother, his wife, and now his daughter. With the other two dead, love for the child absorbed his whole being.

27.

The year 1890 was, in the words of the tight-lipped settlers, a back-breaker. If the crops had been sparse the year before, this year was so dry, they didn't even sprout. Some tried to water their vegetable gardens, but the creeks and rivers ran low, and well water had to be saved for drinking.

This was the year the younger boys rejoiced because there were no longer Saturday-night baths in the big galvanized tubs. There were a few ponds near the settlements, and people washed as best they could in those or in the muddy creeks.

The railroad had distributed seed to those who had failed to make a crop the year before. Doing so was not altruism. The railroad people wanted the settlers to stay and generate business for them. Vince Turner busied himself around the distribution point, emphasizing that this was a gift, as though he were actually connected with the line. But the settlers ignored him, doggedly kept track of the gifts and made repayment, though in most instances, it took more than a year.

When he was not on the circuit, it pleased Angus to bring Miss Rowdy home with him. She gave him a feeling of family, and of purpose. Old Tenny was fascinated by the child, "never having had a chick of my own," he said, and spent as much time with her as he could.

It was on one of these occasions that Vince Turner rode up in a spring wagon. "Hello, the house!" he called. Angus and Tenny had been at opposite ends of the soddy, Miss Rowdy tottering from one to the other as they held out their arms. Her steps were still unsteady, and frequently she went down on her small bottom, but she was crowing with delight, as proud of herself as Angus was of her.

At Turner's hail, Angus looked up with a scowl. "What's that carpetbagger doing out here?"

Tenny chuckled. "I thought God-people were supposed to love their fellow men."

"I'm a preacher, not a saint," Angus retorted, and, scooping Miss Rowdy up, headed outside. Turner had climbed down from the seat.

"'Mornin', preacher," he said. "What God doesn't provide, the railroad does. I've brought you some seed."

"Who asked for seed?" Angus demanded. At his tone, the baby leaned back to peer into his face, then hid her face against his shoulder. Old Tenny stood silent, shrewd little eyes moving from one man to the other. The antagonism between them was almost tangible, and Tenny's hand slid instinctively toward his holster. Why Angus didn't like the man, he had no idea, but he trusted Angus's judgment, and if there was going to be trouble, he was ready.

Vince smirked. "Come on, now, preacher, you know you didn't make a crop. The railroad wants to help."

"I don't need seed," Angus said mildly, but Tenny saw the muscles knot in his cheeks.

Turner's smile was sleek. "But you have to think of your little girl, don't you?" he asked unctuously. "Children can't be allowed to go hungry because their elders are pigheaded."

Angus's arms tightened around Miss Rowdy, then loosened as she squirmed in protest. "Get out!" Angus said.

Vince's face went a mottled red. For a moment it looked as though he would lunge. Tenny's hand moved again toward his gun. Turner halted, exhaled through his nose with a little snorting sound, shrugged, then wheeled and got into the wagon. As he picked up the reins, the strange silverfish eyes met Angus's dark ones head-on.

"I'm keepin' track, preacher," he said viciously.

"Funny the railroad would hire a wrong un like that," Tenny said as Turner took off.

"I don't think he works for the railroad. Think he claims that so as to appear respectable. It's my notion he's a snollygoster."

"Why'd he drive clean out here to bring you seeds?"

"He thought to see me taking charity," Angus growled.

"No need of that. I got enough for the both of us. As a loan," he added hastily, at the dark look Angus gave him.

The woods were virtually stripped of game that year as men foraged to feed their families. The creeks fell too low to support fish. People became thin. The prairie hay, which had been lush the year before, was no more than brown stubble, which the livestock cropped to the ground.

The big cattlemen had their herds driven back into Texas, but the settlers had no such choice. The animals' ribs began to stand out. Cows ran dry of milk, even for their calves.

As Angus slowly made the circuit, walking most of the way to spare Beth, he was sickened by the sight of cows dead and bloated, half delivered of calves in some instances, too weak to complete the birthing.

Only the buzzards fared well.

During July and August, the temperature hovered around the one-hundred-degree mark. Activity came to a virtual standstill. Some of the settlers whose oxen or horses were still able to plod, made trips to Kansas or Texas and brought back barrels of precious water.

Despite the grueling hardships, most of the settlers stayed. Provisions were shared. Buffalo Creek still held a small amount of brackish water.

On one of his visits to pick up Miss Rowdy, Angus found that Dove had bought up four quarter sections, these from New Englanders unable to endure the heat. Amused, he asked if she were going into cattle ranching.

Two vertical lines appeared between the lynxlike eyes. "No, I ain't goin' into no cattle business," she snapped. As Angus had noted before, when she was angry, she deliberately used the drawl and ungrammatical patois of Negro slaves. "But money speaks pow'ful loud, and ah aims to *shout* at dem white folks."

Her eyes were glittering, and he knew better than to tease. "How'd you make the deals?" he asked curiously.

"Through someone else, a'course, massa. Them whites ain't gonna have no truck with no nigger whore."

There was such bitterness in her that Angus shivered. "Quit beating yourself over the head, Dove," he said soberly, and, tossing Rowdy up on his shoulder, made his retreat before the Negro woman could say more.

28.

Although the federal government paid little attention to the new territory, stories of the near starvation had finally made an impression on some people in Washington. And, after much wrangling in Congress, a trainload of provisions was sent to Oklahoma Station.

Tenny had heard the news somewhere and came panting up the bluff to pass it on.

"Guv'ment's sendin' in victuals," he said, trying to get his breath. "S'posed to be in tomorrow."

Angus was thoughtful. "Guv'ment" had no more reality to him than it did to the majority of the other settlers. "How're folks going to pay for it?" he asked, and Tenny's mouth worked in excitement.

"Ya don't understand, preacher. They're gonna *give* it away. Free. Let's us go git our share."

Angus grew even more thoughtful. There wasn't a mouthful of food in the soddy. Tenny, he knew, would soon be in the same predicament. They had shared a catfish the night before; he had found and eaten a few acorns today. He was almost beyond hunger; but strangely, it was a good, strong cup of coffee that he longed for most. He spoke slowly, almost reluctantly.

"I can't take charity, Tenny." Then, realizing how it sounded, he added quickly, "You go ahead. You're older, more needful."

"This ain't charity. I figger it's a gift from heaven." Tenny was at his most sanctimonious. "I ain't turnin' down nothin' that heaven provides. You go with me? Help with the cart?" Angus agreed.

With Tenny's old mare plodding along, pulling the cart, the two men walked into town the next morning to save her strength. The animal's ribs stuck out; her belly was sunk. It hurt Angus to see her, and he was ruefully aware that he frequently felt greater pity for dumb beasts than he did for humans.

At the railroad station, perhaps half a dozen men were shamefacedly accepting the government food. Tenny joined the line, and Angus leaned back against the building, waiting. Suddenly, there was a tug at his sleeve, and a small barefoot boy whispered, "Miss Dove wants to see you, Brother Scofield. Says to hurry."

Angus's heart slammed against his ribs like a sledgehammer. For a moment he was unable to move, then wheeled and ran. He was dripping wet, gasping for breath as he pounded at the door of the big house. Auntie Po let him in.

"What's wrong?" he shouted at her. "Miss Rowdy . . ."

The wrinkled old face creased even more. "Don' fret yo'self, Brother Scofield. She jes' fine. Miss Dove needs talk to you. I'll fetch her."

The trembling began after the old woman had left the room. It started in his legs, spread to his trunk, his arms. For an instant, the room tilted and everything went black. Angus managed to pull out a chair, sink into it, bury his face in his hands. He was nauseous and, at the same time, relieved, and he felt drained.

He didn't hear Dove come into the room, didn't see her until she was on her knees beside him.

"What's wrong, Angus?" she cried. "Auntie Po said you were in a taking. Are you sick? Not getting enough to eat? Lord God, man, you're white as a sheet. What is it?"

He shook his head, slowly sat up and was dumbfounded to see the glint of tears in the amber eyes. Without thinking—needing, in that moment, human warmth—he reached out and touched a long curling eyelash with a shaky finger.

Dove flinched and shot to her feet. "Auntie Po, get Angus some coffee," she said roughly. "Tot of brandy in it, plenty of sugar."

The old woman slip-slapped around the room, doing as she was told, and Dove slid into a chair. With the coffee, Auntie Po brought mounds of crusty bread, butter, jelly.

"You eat up, now," she instructed; "I made that jelly myself."

His hands, thank God, had quit trembling, but he still felt weak as though from a high fever, and his voice was squeaky as he began to butter a piece of bread. "I thought Rowdy . . ."

"I'm truly sorry, preacher," Dove said. "I never thought of scaring you." Her tone became brisk. "Now, here's what I want you to do. Them folks out there is mostly so proud, they're not going to take charity." She pulled a roll of bills out of her pocket.

"I want you to buy those provisions and turn 'em over to Stafford. He's gonna let word get around that folks can buy on credit at his store. I think they'll go for that. They know it's got to rain sometime, and they can pay up."

Angus had been trying to eat, though his throat still felt so tight, he was having difficulty. Now he laid down the piece of bread he was holding and sat, considering her words. A never-ending surprise, Dove was.

"Thought you hated whites," he said finally, tentatively.

Dove's lips curled. "Don't go gettin' no wrong ideas," she warned. "I ain't doin' this out of no goodness of heart. If the settlers leave, I'm out of business. I'm lookin' out for myself."

Feeling slow-witted compared to her sharpness, Angus began again to munch on the bread. "Why not let Stafford buy them?" he asked.

"Don't be so stupid!" she snapped. "The government people aren't going to sell them to a grocer. In fact, from what I hear tell, there's no legal way they can sell them at all. But after folks turn them down, you could get the government man's ear and make a deal. You can let him think you're gonna dole the stuff out to folks. He ain't gonna doubt, what with you bein' a preacher and all. He'll stick the money in his pocket and report back to Washington he's done like he was supposed to."

Angus gave a long whistle. "You know something?" he demanded. "You're a conniving woman."

"You know something?" she mimicked. "I've had to be."

"You're asking me to lie, to conspire to cheat the government and, even worse, to deceive the people."

The impudent dimple flashed. "That's right, Brother Scofield," she said cheerfully.

Angus laughed aloud, the smile illuminating his face. Dove blinked. "You ought to smile more," she said harshly.

94

That reminded him of Lexie, and his good humor died. His face took on its usual dour expression. He stood up. "I'll see to the groceries," he said somberly, and took the money.

By the time he got back to the train station, the small knot of men had disappeared. The two government agents were the picture of frustration.

"Folks out here must be crazy," one of them exploded as Angus approached. "Starvin' but won't take free food."

"Not crazy," Angus told him mildly. "Just proud."

"What are we gonna do with all this junk?"

"I might be able to help," Angus said.

The deal was quickly struck, and Angus walked over to see Stafford, at the grocery store. He then rounded up Tenny and Pete Smith and swore them to secrecy. After dark, the four settlers and the two government men moved the food from the train to the grocery store.

Angus was dead-tired when he finally got to bed that night, but too high-strung to sleep. Lexie having been so vividly called to mind by Dove's remark had torn open the old wound.

It was not only that he missed her gentleness and humor, her essence, but that he missed her sexually, too.

Prior to the time hunger for food had weakened him, he had been fighting for months an all but irresistible sexual hunger. Had managed to deny its existence by exhausting physical labor, felling trees, chopping wood, stretching fence.

Now as he lay in the dark, for the first time he faced the problem openly. He felt guilty, unfaithful to Lexie's memory; but the truth of it was, he knew that when he was once again able to eat regularly, the compulsion was going to return, probably the more forcible for the time lapse.

He had, of course, considered the big white house. Dove herself didn't oblige. He couldn't have made carnal use of her anyhow; she was—well, she was *Dove*. Still, she would have provided him with a girl and thought none the worse of him for it. But he'd long since had experience with the prairie grapevine. The news would have flashed around the countryside before he'd gotten his pants rebuttoned.

In the darkness, he groaned. "Lord," he said, "I can't cut down all the trees in Oklahoma."

With nothing resolved, he turned on his side, resolutely turned his thoughts to building a barn and finally slept.

29.

The rains held off until September. When they did start, it seemed they would never stop. For three days and nights, with hardly a letup, there was a deluge. The cracked earth soaked up the water like a dry sponge, the first couple of days, but by the third day, the ground would absorb no more. The ponds, creeks and rivers began to fill to overflowing. Buffalo Creek was out of its banks and emptying in a never-ending freshet into the Cottonwood. The water was red and roily, and the townfolk of Guthrie watched uneasily as it snaked toward the townsite.

At home, Angus kept careful vigil. The soddy was high enough to be out of danger. But Tenny's land was mostly under water. He and Angus moved the older man's belongings to the bluff to keep them from being swept away.

"Well, I wanted bottom land," he mourned philosophically.

At first the skies had been black and green, with a sickish yellow overcast that presaged hail. The wind slashed so, that to step out in the downpour was to be battered as though the sky were raining rocks. The lightning was forked, wicked-looking and so constant that one snarl of thunder would scarcely be completed before another ripped across the plain. Gradually, the sky turned leaden; gradually, the wind ceased, as though exhausted. But the rain continued, heavy, cold and endless.

Then, around noon of the third day, it stopped as quickly as it had started. The sun, blistering hot, reappeared. From the white men who had been living on Indian land over the years, the '89ers learned that the only crop likely to come up this late was turnips.

Again, the railroad furnished seed. Again, the settlers kept careful track of what was to be repaid. They sowed turnips in every available spot, and the crop grew and flourished. They planted winter wheat too, when the time came, and it somehow justified their eternal faith in the soil when it put out the first green shoots.

The food which had been available at Stafford's was long since gone, but the turnips were doing well. The settlers ate turnips and turnip greens and turnips again. Fried in a bit of precious lard. Boiled. Baked. Even the animals were fed turnips, so the milk started again but tasted strong and bitter. Nonetheless, the children drank it and made few complaints. It helped fill their bellies.

And as Angus rode his circuit, on every hand he was asked to conduct a service of thanksgiving. Looking out over the bowed heads, he wondered at their indomitable spirit. They would not fail, simply because they refused to fail. It was, Angus realized, their faith in God, their willingness to undergo hardship, their unchanging belief that the year ahead would be better, that made them stay. He came away from these services moved and humbled.

30.

Not until the gardens began to produce the next spring, and he once more had enough to eat, did the sexual urge begin to torment Angus again.

He grew short-tempered, shouting at his animals and snapping at Tenny, until the old man asked sourly who'd put a burr under his tail. When he stood up to preach, he felt little of the love of God flowing through him. Was tempted, rather, to condemn the whole human race as hopeless, himself included, and take off for Patagonia, wherever that was.

He even tried to pick a fight with Dove at the end of

the circuit, telling her that her house was getting very notorious. There were whispers that her girls were diseased; that one man had been murdered for the gold he was improvidently carrying.

Instead of exploding, as would have been expected, Dove's eyes narrowed and her face grew thoughtful. "You're makin' that up to be aggravatin'," she said absently. And then: "Angus, you ever think of marrying again?"

"Hell, no!" He slammed his fist down on the table with such force, the sugar bowl turned over; and both Rowdy and Samsy, who were in the kitchen with them, began to howl.

Dove jumped to her feet. "Damn it!" she snapped. "You've scared the kids half to death."

Reaching for Miss Rowdy, Angus began to mumble an apology, but Dove swept both children before her, into the other room. When she came back, she was glowering.

"Take pride in acting like a jackass, do you?" she demanded. But the scowl was fading, and her face grew thoughtful again. "Tho' iffen you was a mule 'stead of a jackass, reckon there wouldn't be no problem. Ain't that right?"

Angus felt blood surging into his face like a tidal wave. The mole began to throb. "You . . . you . . ."

"Vixen?" Dove supplied.

And in the next instant, both of them were laughing helplessly. "Oh, Angus," Dove gasped, "if you could have seen your face . . ."

"It's not funny, damn it," he said, his laughter rueful now.

Dove sobered. "I know it isn't. Angus, why don't you find you a nice clean woman and—and visit her now and then? No man who's as young and—and *male* as you should try to live like a eunuch. It's against nature. No wonder you're cantankerous."

"Catholic priests live celibate, I've heard," Angus mumbled.

"But you're not a Catholic priest," Dove pointed out.

"It's a sin . . ."

"You think acting like a sore-tailed bear's not as bad?" When he didn't answer, she added, "You think on it."

Angus "thought on it" another three or four months but was no nearer a solution.

98

He had no intention of marrying again. He and Lexie had shared a relationship so incomparable that to attempt to replace her would be unthinkable. It wouldn't be fair to any woman to put her up against Lexie. Besides, he had no stomach for marriage just to gratify his sensuality.

Where was this nice clean woman Dove had prescribed? The women he knew were already married or nubile. You didn't spend time with a young woman unless you had marriage in mind, or you were apt to be facing the business end of a shotgun in the hands of an irate father. Besides, he had no desire to seduce a maiden.

There were a few widows about, but, like Mrs. Murphy, they were so fiercely virtuous, the precept still held. To pay them court was tantamount to a declaration of honorable intentions.

Day by day Angus grew more glum. He had forced himself to stop "acting like a sore-tailed bear," as Dove put it, but he could not ward off depression. Too, he became so preoccupied, he sometimes saw people looking at him askance.

On one of his visits to Miss Rowdy, Dove asked delicately if he'd had any luck. Angus shook his head.

Another couple of months passed. On two occasions, Angus's sleep was troubled by dreams so erotic, he was disgusted with himself the next morning.

"Something's got to give, Lord," he said darkly. "I'm going plumb loco. Reckon I ought to be able to control myself better. Wonder how those priest fellows manage it. 'Course, maybe they volunteered. I was more drafted, like, you might say."

The next time he visited the big white house, Dove made no attempt to pry. Perhaps Angus's dejection showed in his face. When he was getting ready to leave, she mentioned casually that if he ever went to Stillwater, she had a favor to ask.

"Go ahead and ask now," he growled. "I got nothing better to do."

"I heard the emporium up there had some velvet, and some of my girls' clothes are getting downright shabby."

"You want *me* to walk in and ask for dress stuff?"

"Sure. Tell 'em it's a surprise for your wife."

Angus grimaced, considered how deep his obligation to Dove was. "All right." He exhaled a long breath. "Tomorrow's good as any. How much of the stuff do you want?"

"I'll make up a list," she promised. "But it can't be tomorrow. Dorsey had to go to Dallas. She'll be back Sunday to say what color she wants. How about Monday?"

Angus nodded dourly and left.

But as the horse jogged toward Stillwater on that Monday morning, Angus's spirits improved. It was one of those dulcet days Oklahoma could produce to make up for her often capricious weather. The sun was a gentle benefice, the breeze cool. Early wild roses were blooming. Angus spotted some red-winged blackbirds among the vernal green of the trees.

This is the day which the Lord has made, Angus thought; I will rejoice and be glad in it.

He was within three or four miles of Stillwater, when he saw the overturned buggy, the horse still trying to extricate itself from the tangle of shafts and reins. Angus put Beth to a gallop. As he drew closer, a woman straightened, pulling a wheel upright and swearing like a trooper.

Angus brought Beth to a stop and sat momentarily, listening. He assumed she saw him, but the words kept right on coming. She knew almost as many curse words as he did.

Despite himself, a grin twitched at the corners of his mouth.

He dismounted, lifted his hat politely. "Can I be of service, ma'am?"

"If you can get that friggin' buggy upright and put this goddammed wheel back on and make that hellion of a horse behave himself . . . Look at me. Axle grease all over, dress ruined . . ."

She broke off, apparently finally conscious that she was addressing a stranger. She blushed. "I was so da— so furious," she explained.

"I judged that," Angus said drily, and managed not to laugh. There was even a streak of grease on her face.

"They don't make these contraptions like they used to," she complained. "Shoddy. I'd like to horsewhip the lot of 'em."

"Well, ma'am"—Angus grinned—"I don't know whether I can come up to your standards or not, but maybe I can make it hold together for now."

"I'd be obliged. I want to get home."

Angus set to work, first getting the frightened horse out of its driving harness. Fortunately, the shafts were intact,

100

the buggy lightweight enough that Angus could get it upright by himself. He could not, however, hold it and manage the wheel at the same time.

"I'm afraid you'll have to help, ma'am," he said, "unless you'd like me to go into town and send the livery man out."

"I'll help," she said. "I couldn't be any worse off than I already am."

It took less than half an hour to get the apparatus back together, but by that time, Angus too was very dirty. "Someone must have had a passel of axle grease to get rid of," he muttered; "it's smeared everywhere. There—" he gave the rim a pat, "think that'll take care of it."

He walked a step or two, leaned over to wipe his hands on the weeds, then pulled a handkerchief from his pocket and tried to clean off more of the grease.

"Good Lord," the woman said, "you're 'most as bad off as I am. Come on up to the house and clean up, Mr. . . ?"

"Scofield," Angus supplied. "That's all right. I'll wash up in town."

"I insist," the woman said. "Got plenty of water and lye soap. 'Sides, reckon I owe you. Think some fresh-baked apple pie and sweet milk might pay?"

After subsisting on his own cooking for nearly a week, apple pie sounded like food for the gods. He hesitated.

"Sure your husband won't misapprehend, Mrs. . . ."

"Lancaster. Pearl Lancaster. And I haven't got a husband. I had one. That was enough." She didn't sound particularly bitter. She did sound determined.

"A piece of pie would be larrupin'," Angus agreed.

There was warm water in a kettle on the cookstove. The woman brought it outside, and the two of them scrubbed up as best they could, Pearl chattering like a magpie.

She was a seamstress and was attempting to establish a business, selling ready-made dresses through mercantile stores in the region. "Some women don't have time to sew; some can't. I figger there's a market for a general line of dresses, if I can get the pigheaded store owners to stock them."

When they had removed as much of the grease as possible, they went into the kitchen, and Pearl brought out a whole pie, a pitcher of cool milk.

Perhaps it was the dressmaker's dummy standing in a

corner and draped sedately in sprigged dimity that afforded a sense of chaperonage. Perhaps it was the kettle singing softly as the water heated, or the kitten rubbing contentedly against Angus's ankles and purring. Perhaps it was the woman herself, completely free of embarrassment at entertaining a strange man when there was no one else in the house. Whatever the reason, Angus had seldom felt so relaxed and comfortable.

He ate two huge pieces of pie, had several glasses of milk. "Mrs. Lancaster, that was—" he began, but she interrupted.

"I don't hold with all this formality. Call me Pearl. What's your front handle?"

"Uh, Angus."

He had never met anyone quite like her. He judged her to be in her early thirties. Her face was pleasant, though not beautiful, and she had the engaging unselfconsciousness of a child.

After he'd had the pie, she showed him around her place. There was a new heifer calf. Her fields looked well tended.

"You don't do all the outside work?" Angus asked.

"No, I've got a hired man lives a couple of sections over. Not overbright in his mind, but he's good with livestock and crops. His folks are glad to have him earn a little money."

As they started back to the house, she took Angus's arm. "Forgot I was wearing town shoes," she grumbled. "Mind if I hang on?"

A tingling sensation ran up and down his arm. "My pleasure," he said.

Back in the house, she showed him half a dozen dresses she'd made, and he complimented her. "So many women never get a boughten dress 'til they're ready for a box," she said bluntly. "I think women ought to have a chance to spruce up a little. They like ribbons and lace and such."

She rattled on, showing Angus the immaculate house, with obvious pride. Her husband had built it. "He was trying to live steadylike, poor thing"—she might have been talking about a pet dog—"but he had itchy feet. Always said his ma had been scared by a band of gypsies. I finally told him it was me or the road. He chose the road."

If this decision distressed her, she gave no sign of it.

"You must get lonesome," Angus suggested.

102

"Only in——" She stopped so abruptly, he looked around at her. She flushed. "Sometimes," she ended lamely. Then, with a quick glance at the clock: "Law, it's way past dinner time."

"I better go. . . ."

"Of course you won't," she said in disagreement. "I don't send good Samaritans away hungry. You just make yourself to home while I whip up some victuals. Won't be anything fancy."

After another half-hearted demur, Angus sat in the big rocker in the kitchen and watched her as she moved deftly about, getting the meal on the table. She talked as she worked, but the sound was not much more than a murmur. At first he tried to listen, but it had a lulling effect like the burbling of a creek in the spring, and he found himself nodding.

"Dinner's ready." Her voice was brisk again, and Angus came to his feet, embarrassed.

"I must have dozed off. . . ."

"That's good," Pearl said. "A body likes to be comfortable." As they sat down, she asked him to say the blessing and held out her hand. Angus's eyebrows were raised in inquiry, and she made as though to draw it back. "I'm sorry," she said. "At home, we always joined hands while grace was said. Guess I forgot you was a stranger. Wouldn't want to upset your wife."

"I don't have a wife," Angus told her, and grasped her hand in his. "A nice custom," he approved, but even as he bowed his head and gave thanks, he was acutely aware of the cool softness of her fingers.

There was beefsteak in a succulent gravy, potatoes roasted in their own jackets, a salad of lettuce and radishes and onions fresh from the garden and a bottle of ruby-red wine, which Pearl said was made by one of her neighbors.

They ate and drank and talked and laughed a great deal. Angus was hardly aware that she slipped away from the table to fetch a second bottle of wine.

His next consciousness was of the warmth of a woman's head against his shoulder, the fragrance of powder, the satiny touch of a woman's flesh.

"Good God!" he cried, and sat up.

Pearl opened her eyes, yawned and stretched. "Angus," she said solemnly, "I'm glad you don't have a wife."

103

Angus's heart gave a sick thud. "Reckon we'll have to get married," he muttered, unable to look her in the face.

"Married?" It was she who yelped this time. "I don't want to get married!" she shouted. "I told you that right off. But you're welcome to visit whenever you like." Her voice sounded smug and sleek and satisfied.

"I'm a preacher." Angus groaned.

"I'm not prejudiced," she assured him. "You're still a man."

Angus groaned again, got up and began to put on his clothes. His head was thumping and the room spun a bit, but he managed to stay upright.

"It's nigh dark," Pearl told him. "No use goin' off in the heat of the day without your blanket, so to speak."

Angus's legs felt shaky. He sat down on a chair.

"You're not a—a loose woman, I'd take my oath. What kind of woman are you?"

"A lonely one," she said with complete candor, "who likes to have a man warm her feet now and again."

Angus shook his head. He had the feeling with her that he had on the rare occasions when Dove was in a particularly good mood. A feeling of ease and companionship, with nothing expected on either side.

"I better head for Stillwater."

"Sure you don't want something else to eat?" He looked up from tying his shoe. Her face was wreathed in grins, and he realized she was teasing him.

"No, ma'am," he said emphatically. "Your meals pack a pow'ful wallop."

When he was ready to leave, she walked to the door with him. " 'Member," she told him, "the welcome mat's always out."

31.

It was in the spring of '93 that Sarah Holtzworthy spoke to Angus about Miss Rowdy. The child was past four now, lively as a cricket, curious about everything and cute as a bug, as Dove expressed it. She had Lexie's tiny build —bird bones, as Angus thought of them.

He kept her with him when he was home, and once had taken her on the circuit. But she was worn out and sick by the time they got back, so he hadn't tried it again. She stayed with Dove.

When Sarah tackled him on the subject, he didn't at first get the drift of her words. That she was embarrassed, he knew. She said firmly, "I must talk to you about something, Brother Angus," and then sat, eyes downcast, fumbling with her apron. He and Sarah and Zeb were having coffee and some of Sarah's gingerbread.

"All right," Angus said mildly, "I'm listening."

"Zeb?" Sarah appealed to her husband, who shook his head and made a great business of pouring his coffee into a saucer and blowing on it. "I already told you, Sarah, it ain't none of our business."

Sarah bristled. "Any child is a part of our business, and Martha's no exception."

Martha? Momentarily, Angus was puzzled. He never thought of the child as anything but Miss Rowdy. His hackles rose. Even Sarah wasn't to criticize his little girl.

"What's wrong with her?" he asked coldly.

"Nothing, with her." Sarah finally met his eyes. "But children notice—things. That—that house . . ." She broke off, flustered.

Angus gave a snort of incredulous laughter. "Good Lord, Sarah," he said, "Miss Rowdy's just a baby. She stays in a different part of the house . . ."

"Preacher!" Having broken the ice, Sarah was confident now. "I've been working with children a long time. Believe me, they know a lot more than you think."

A feeling of helplessness entered Angus's chest.

"I've got no place else to leave her, Sarah."

"We'll keep her," the woman told him. "When you asked before, I—couldn't." Tears filled her eyes, but she cleared her throat and went on. "She's old enough; she could sit in school while I'm teaching. Rest of the time, I'm home."

Angus stared down at his hands. "Sarah." He spoke haltingly. It was humbling to a man to admit he couldn't pay for the keep of one small child. He and Dove had long before worked out a record-keeping system, and in time he'd pay her off, if he had to mortgage his place to do it. The mole began to throb. "Sarah, I—don't see much cash."

"I know she's staying over there on credit," Sarah said briskly, and Angus blinked. How did she know that? Apparently, the grapevine worked in town as well as in the country. "We're not planning to charge, preacher."

Angus's face flamed. "I don't take charity," he said.

Sarah's tone became as uncompromising as his own. "If you're too proud to take a favor from a friend—" she began, but Zeb intervened.

"Now, Sarah, no call to get on your high horse. Reckon we can figure something out. You been sharin' with us, preacher. When folks on the circuit give you monkey grapes or side meat—them grapes shore make tasty jelly —or a jar of honey, we wasn't too proud to take some."

"That was dif—" Angus began, then broke off and grinned sheepishly.

"Reckon you're right," he said. "I'll bring Miss Rowdy over, but on the same arrangement I've got with Dove."

Sarah nodded reluctant approval.

Angus reflected, though, as he rode toward the big white house. It was hard to believe that a little tyke hardly more than a baby would notice goings-on. Still, what did he know about kids? After all, Sarah had been working with children all her life, except when little Zeb came along. She was a good woman, too, not given to gossiping to cause trouble. He sighed.

Then his thoughts turned to Dove. He'd acted awfully hastily and could think of no way to explain his actions to the mulatto woman, other than to tell her the bald truth.

And, Lord God, that was going to cause a ruckus. He tasted the gritty red dirt in his mouth, was irritated by the unrelenting wind, despised the cracker-box buildings that had been put up and was altogether in a thoroughly bad humor by the time he'd reached his destination.

Unconsciously, he squared his shoulders, bracing himself, when Auntie Po let him in.

"I'll bring Miss Rowdy," she said, but he put a detaining hand on her arm.

"I need to talk to Miss Dove first, Auntie."

"Whatever you say, rev'ren'." She shuffled off, and Angus roamed restlessly about the big pleasant kitchen. He looked at the red-checked curtains, bare scrubbed pine table, enormous black cookstove, the rocking chair with its cushion, a bit of knitting in the seat. He didn't hear Dove until she spoke.

"Got a burr under your saddle?" she asked.

Angus swung around. He'd had no inspired ideas about what to say. "I've got to talk to you," he said. He had not intended the words to sound flat and harsh, but realized they did. Great start, he thought.

Dove flung herself into a chair. "Go ahead and talk. The good wives send you to run me out of town?"

Angus shook his head. "Dove, you know how much I appreciate what you've done for Miss Rowdy," he began.

From under his brows he saw her eyes narrow. "So?" she said curtly.

"You kept her from dying. And I—" he swallowed, "I'm beholden to you."

"Get to the point, preacher man."

"Well, Sarah . . . uh, some of the folks in town say, they say children, even—even babies like Rowdy—notice—things." He was conscious of the cold sweat on his forehead, also trickling down his sides from his armpits.

"Notice things?" Dove echoed. "Can't you just say what's on your mind without going all around Callahan's barn?"

"She—they say little kids—well, learn things . . ." he blurted out, and was dumbfounded when Dove threw back her head and laughed. It was a bitter sound but it was a laugh, the last reaction he would have expected. He watched her uncertainly.

Dove sobered. "Sit down, preacher," she commanded.

Angus pulled out one of the cane-back chairs and strad-dled it, facing her.

"All right," he said helplessly. "What's funny?"

"Reckon you are, preacher. Never saw a man so flus-tered. When here, I been thinkin' the same." For an in-stant she was somber, then shrugged. "Kids do notice. I've been trying to figure out what to do about Sam."

"I could ask Sarah if she'd keep them both."

Dove's lip curled. "You know no good white woman's gonna look after no bastard of no nigger whore."

"Quit saying that, damn it!" Angus exploded.

"It's true, ain't it?" She chuckled without mirth and rose. "I'll get her things together," she said.

Angus wiped his forehead.

As they rode toward the Holtzworthys', he explained to Miss Rowdy that she'd be staying with Aunt Sarah and Uncle Zeb awhile; she'd be going to school like a big girl. Learn her ABC's.

"I already know my ABC's," she said with an air of finality.

"There are a lot of other things to learn." She didn't respond.

When they reached the Holtzworthys', the couple came out to meet them. The woman lifted the child off the horse.

"You're going to have to teach Martha to ride side-saddle, Angus," she said. "It's not proper for little ladies to ride astride."

Angus exhaled noisily as he swung off the horse. "Reckon there's a good bit I don't know about little la-dies," he admitted.

In the house Sarah found slate and chalk, and the child sat at the kitchen table, laboriously drawing while her elders talked. They encountered only one problem. When Sarah called her Martha, the little girl didn't re-spond.

"Aunt Sarah's talking to you, honey," Angus prompted. The angel-bright face came up.

"No, Papa," she said, "my name's Miss Rowdy."

Sarah's face was set in firm lines, kind but insistent. "No, dear," she said, "that's your *nickname*. Your real name is Martha."

The baby lips pouted. "My name is Miss Rowdy," she said slowly and distinctly, and turned back to her drawing. Angus's eyes met Sarah's. "I'll take care of it," she said.

Miss Rowdy cried and clung to him when he started to leave, something she'd never done before. He squatted down and put his arms around her.

"Papa will be back," he said. "You'll be going to school." Miss Rowdy wailed louder and clung like a leech. Sarah spoke quietly.

"She'll be all right, Brother Angus, once you're out of sight. Would you like to go out and see the baby chickens, Martha?"

The screams became louder; the arms tightened desperately around his neck. Angus glanced up at Sarah, whose face was still kindly.

"You musn't spoil her, Brother Angus. Children have to be taught to mind."

Momentarily, his head and his heart warred. What he wanted to do was scoop the child up, kiss away her tears and take her home with him. Still, he knew Sarah was right.

Gently, he tugged the small arms loose, stood up. Miss Rowdy drew back as though he'd disclaimed her. Tears were still running down her face, but the look she shot at him from those magnificent eyes was first incredulity, then pure rage. And pride. It was as though, had she put it in words, she would have said, "I won't beg."

Angus ran a finger around his collar. "You sure, Sarah . . ."

"I'm sure. You know the child is going to be treated well."

"I know." He grabbed his hat and hastily retreated, not daring to look back.

32.

The first stop on his circuit rides was in Kingfisher County, at the home of Edith and Ed Graves. At his hail, Ed came out of the house.

"You're an early bird, preacher. Crowd won't be gathering for an hour or so. Come on in and have some flapjacks. Got a surprise for you later."

"Fine. Don't mind if I do."

Inside, the spider griddle was already warming. The platter of victuals Edith set before him presently, would have fed a harvester. Chunk of smoked ham big as his hand, flapjacks, milk cooled in the springhouse, fresh butter, sorghum, coffee.

At home he paid little attention to what he ate, but on the circuit he was fed like a king. Replete, finally, he pushed back his chair. "Probably won't be able to preach, I ate so much," he said, patting his lean belly.

But he did preach, speaking of God's love and forgiveness, his favorite theme. His text was from the eleventh chapter of Second Samuel: David's adultery with Bathsheba, his murder of her husband. (He thought of Pearl Lancaster and knew just how David had felt.) "Yet God forgave him when he repented," he concluded. "As He will forgive us when we ask. Let us pray."

At the conclusion of the brief prayer, Edith Graves lifted her voice in a hymn, and the dozen or so others attending joined in. It was still morning, but the heat was beginning to make itself felt. Angus was sweating and wished that he might forego the "invitation." But it was expected; the people would feel the service incomplete without it.

"If you want to accept God's forgiveness and love for yourself," he said, "come forward and we will pray with you."

One of the rough wooden benches toppled as a man

110

rose. He was unshaven and unkempt, and as he started toward the front, Angus saw that he limped. The man looked vaguely familiar, and Angus wondered if he'd seen him in town once or twice. The preacher put out his hand; the other man grasped it.

"I want to get saved, Brother *Angus*," he said. The emphasis he gave the final word was puzzling. Even as he knelt in the dusty weeds with the old man, even as he prayed, the preacher's mind kept flicking back to that "Angus." There had been something in the timbre of the voice that touched a chord of remembrance.

Angus concluded the prayer and opened his eyes, to meet a faint twinkle, a faint hint of malice, in the old man's gaze.

"Don't know your own father, Davey?" It was just a breath, a whisper, but Angus jumped as though he'd been jabbed with a cattle prod. He shot to his feet, the old hatred of this man he held responsible for his mother's death taking hold of him like a monster. His hands knotted.

"The service is concluded," he said harshly. He knew the congregation would be bewildered, but this was a farce. He could put no trust in anything Jim Royal said.

"Another of your con games?" he demanded under his breath. "What do you want?"

"Davey, we're family," the old voice quavered, and momentarily stirred in Angus something perilously close to pity. He put it aside. How many times had he believed his father's empty promises? How many times had his mother been persuaded that this time Jim had really turned over a new leaf? How many times had Mrs. Graylinger been promised he would pay for the boy's keep?

"Ever pay Mrs. Graylinger?" Angus asked.

The faded blue eyes dropped. "I tried, son, but—"

Angus gave a snort of laughter. And a slow painful flush crept into the old man's cheeks.

Briefly, the preacher had forgotten his congregation, but now he was aware of it again. He could hear the children running and yelling, letting off steam after the past hour's enforced quiet. The adults ostensibly were getting the lunch baskets unpacked, spreading out the tablecloths, but were in reality more interested in what was going on between the two men still in the brush arbor. Puzzled and curious.

111

"How'd you find me?" Angus demanded.

"Your mam's brother's name—they had to be some connection."

"I've got a dollar or two . . ." Angus forced himself to keep his voice low. His father shook his head.

"I ain't got no place to stay, Davey. I been tryin' to work for my keep but I'm tuckered." He had not raised his head, and now slow tears slid down his cheeks and dripped onto his filthy shirt. "I didn't tell them folks you was my son, jest said figgered I might have known you when you was a tad."

So that was the surprise the Graves had spoken of. The black rage within him was making Angus sick to his stomach. He had forced his fists to unknot, had clenched his hands tightly together to keep from striking the old man.

"What do you expect of me?" he asked.

The old eyes came up to meet his, helplessly. "Reckon I got to 'mind you I'm your responsibility, Davey. I'm at the end of my row."

Perhaps no other word he could have used would have moved the younger man. Responsibility. Unable to trust himself any longer, Angus wheeled and strode away, past a woman brandishing a tea towel to fend off the flies. At sight of the food, Angus's gorge rose. Blindly, he made for the creek. The wooded area closed in around him, and he fell down on a log, head in hands, swallowing hard. His stomach was heaving.

"This is just too damned much, Lord," he cried silently.

Honor thy father and thy mother, an inner voice said.

"He didn't honor me, or my mother either. Not by a jugful, he didn't."

In his fury, Angus wanted to scream his curses. "I won't do it! I can't do it! Don't ask it of me!" But after what seemed an interminable time, he drew a deep breath, began trying to accept the grim path of duty he must take. Finally, the convulsion of rage passed, and he was left with only a sense of exhaustion.

It was then that he was conscious of Ed Graves striding toward him. "You all right, preacher?" The plump face was concerned. He was uncomfortable, curious, afraid his intrusion would be resented. Angus moved gingerly, as weak as though he'd been ill.

"Guess I got a touch of sun," he croaked, and the other man's face lit up.

"Sure, I told them women you was all right. But they would have it I come and see about you." He laughed uneasily. "You know women," he concluded.

Angus forced himself to nod, to stand. "We better go back."

As they moved together up the slope, Graves was still ill at ease. "That old man what was saved says he used to know you."

"That's right," the preacher said woodenly.

He cut out the rest of his circuit and, borrowing a horse for Jim, headed home. Not two words were exchanged between them on the ride. Angus was fighting with every breath, to deaden his feelings. He had no idea what his father was thinking. Gloating, probably, that he'd found someone to sponge off for the rest of his life.

Inside the soddy, Angus built a fire, set water to heat, dragged in the galvanized tub. When the water was ready, he filled the tub, found a bar of lye soap.

"Get those filthy clothes off," he ordered, and Jim obediently began to shed them. A stench filled the room, and, remembering how dapper, even dandified, the other man had always been, Angus felt again an unwilling pity. The flaccid skin beneath the clothing was grime-encrusted. Jim wore no socks, and his feet were unbelievably filthy.

"Get in," Angus said briefly, and Jim stepped into the water. He had intended to leave the old man to it, but saw that his left arm moved only with difficulty. Angus grimaced. Was he, for God's sake, going to have to wash him too? Reluctantly, he picked up the soap and wash-cloth.

"Need a scrub brush," he said once, sourly. There was no other conversation. When the old man was as clean as he could be gotten from a single bath, he emerged from the water, red and raw-looking.

"You damn near killed me," he complained but, with a glance at Angus's face, added hastily, "feel better, though."

Angus flung him some of his own clean clothes, and Jim slowly began to dress.

The soddy no longer represented quiet and contentment. Angus emptied the tub and then struck out for Tenny's tent.

113

"You're back early," the old man greeted him.

"Yeah. I—I brought company. Old man I—knew when I was a kid. Down on his luck."

"He gonna stay?"

"More than likely," Angus said glumly.

"Come on in and have coffee. You ort've brought him along."

Angus did not answer, but his face darkened; and Tenny, surprised, began to talk about crop prospects.

The next morning Angus made hoecake, coffee, fried side meat and opened a jar of wild honey. His father ate as though he'd had nothing in his stomach for a month.

"Tastes mighty good, son," he said, wiping his mouth on the back of his hand and belching. Angus looked up, and their eyes collided, Jim's wistful; his own, he knew, were diamond hard.

"Let's just leave it that you're an old man I knew when I was a kid," Angus said.

Jim nodded and got up, flustered, to refill the coffee cups. After breakfast, he insisted he could wash up. "I can use my hand enough to do dishes," he said. "Like to earn my keep."

The younger man's lip curled, and he wondered wearily what his father was up to now. Well, he couldn't do much worse than he had already. Angus's thoughts turned to Miss Rowdy.

"I'm going to ride into Oklahoma Station and see about my little girl," he said.

A dish dropped, and he turned to see the older man's eyes brimming with tears. "You mean I'm a grandfather?" Jim asked.

Angus made a low sound in his throat. "Let's just say you're someone she knew a long time ago too," he suggested.

"What's her name? Where's your wife? Oh, Davey, I missed—"

"Don't try to soft-soap me," Angus warned. "My little girl's name is Miss Rowdy—uh, Martha. My wife is dead."

"Martha! Your mam's name!"

"Yeah." He didn't trust himself to say more. Rising, he thrust back the chair and went out to saddle the mare.

33.

Sarah was guiding her horse into the yard when Angus arrived at the Holtzworthys'. One glance at her face, and he drew a sharp breath.

"What's wrong?" he cried, swung out of the saddle and went to help her dismount.

"Oh, Brother Angus, I'm—so sorry. I tried, I did indeed. I was afraid she was going to make herself sick. She already felt feverish."

"What is it, Sarah?" He had never seen the woman so distraught, except when little Zeb died. His heart seemed to have stopped beating and he was having trouble getting his breath. "Miss Rowdy?" His voice was shaking.

"I—I took her back to—to that woman." Even in her distress, he noted, she could not bring herself to say Dove's name. And in the next instant knew it had cost Sarah a great deal even to go there.

"What happened, Sarah, for God's sake? What's wrong?"

"She cried," Sarah said miserably, her own eyes red and swollen. "She cried from the time you left. Wouldn't eat. Sobbed herself to sleep. Woke up and started crying again until there weren't any tears, only dry heaves. Wouldn't eat." She broke off, weeping.

"You did the best you could," Angus consoled her, weak with relief. He climbed back on Beth as Zeb came out of the house. "Tell her it's all right, Zeb," he implored and took off at a gallop.

"You know what that chile needs?" Dove asked when she opened the door to his pounding. "She needs some peach-tree tea."

"Switch her?" Angus asked blankly. "A baby like that? Do you whip Sam?"

"You bet your bottom dollar," Dove said. Her eyes

115

flashed. "Come on in, preacher. Sam catches it hot and heavy when he's ornery."

"I couldn't do it." He was remembering the woebegone face when he'd left the baby at Sarah's, feeling the imploring pressure of her arms. "When she's older . . ."

Dove snorted.

No matter what any of them said, it didn't matter, Angus thought, as Rowdy came flying into the room, face rapturous, arms outstretched to him. He saw the shadows under her eyes like bruises and thought his heart would break. He scooped her up and held her fast.

"I knew you would come, Papa," the child said. "I knew you wouldn't make me stay there." Her arms were clasped around his neck; her cheek nuzzled against his. "You're scratchy," she said.

At Buffalo Creek, Jim Royal was waiting outside for them. "Glory be!" he shouted. "Who's this? Martha?"

"My name's Miss Rowdy," she said primly as Angus lifted her off the horse.

"Miss Rowdy." Jim had gone down on his knees so that he was face to face with her. Rowdy clutched her father's legs, but Jim made no move to touch her. "You're a mighty pretty little girl, Miss Rowdy," he said.

Suddenly recalling Sarah's words that the child needed to be taught, Angus said, "Say hello, Miss Rowdy."

"Hello," Miss Rowdy repeated, and then, to her father: "Who is he?"

Before Angus could muster a suitable answer, his father, with a quick glance in his direction, said, "You can call me Uncle Jim."

"Like Uncle Zeb and Uncle Pete and Uncle Tenny, Papa?"

"I guess," Angus said. Jim stood up.

"You like corn bread and bumgolly stew?" he asked as they walked into the house. Angus nodded.

"You needn't look so sour about it," Jim grumbled.

"Sorry."

"Tenny shot a rabbit. I fixed up the stuff to go with it." The words tumbled out of Jim. He had, Angus thought, always been a man who liked to talk. A man who liked people around, who was probably at his best in a crowd.

"Tenny's comin' up for supper," the older man went on. "I got baked apples for dessert." When Angus threw his hat on a peg without comment, Jim hurried on. "I'm not helpless, Da—Angus. I mean to earn my keep."

Angus gave a mirthless laugh, and the half-supplicating defiance went out of the wrinkled face. His shoulders slumped. "Yore a hard man," he said.

Even Miss Rowdy seemed to sense the antagonism between them. She drew back to where she could see the faces of both men. There was a crease between the amethyst eyes. "You are silly," she said to them both, and went outside.

Jim swung around to give Angus a sheepish grin. "Out of the mouths of babes, Davey boy."

"Angus." The correction was automatic. He turned and stalked out to join Miss Rowdy. Her hand in his, they walked over the uneven land, Angus pointing out to her the everyday miracles of nature. Thistle, broom weed, the sumac, whose foliage would be a crimson banner, come fall.

"Why does it turn red?" the child demanded.

"God made it that way." He had never talked down to her, even as his mother had never talked down to him, and if Miss Rowdy did not fully understand, she would nod gravely, satisfied.

As the sun began to slide toward the horizon, banks of clouds, blue and red, violet and gray, swirled in to mask it. The golden light shot through the clouds in refracted rays like the glory of God, and Angus's heart lurched with awe.

"That's a little part of God's glory," he said.

"God's sitting right there so we can see part of Him?" Miss Rowdy asked, and Angus made his all but inaudible chuckling sound.

"Reckon you could say that," he agreed.

"Papa," she said, "my throat feels like your face."

"How's that, honey?"

"You know, scratchy."

"Got a mite of cold maybe," Angus said. "Hey, there's Uncle Tenny."

"Evenin', preacher. Evenin', Miss Rowdy," the old man said, joining them.

Angus spoke. Miss Rowdy took hold of Uncle Tenny's hand, and the three of them walked back to the soddy. Jim turned from the heat of the stove, holding an iron spider of cornpone.

"Jest in time. I was fixin' to eat it all myself."

During the meal, Jim talked almost without stopping. Miss Rowdy picked up a spoon, poked at the food on her plate. "It's awful hot in here," she said once, but Angus was absorbed in wondering what he was to do with her. He'd postpone the circuit a few days, try to find someone in Oklahoma Station who had other kids and would be willing to take care of Rowdy. Maybe then she'd be content.

His thoughts were interrupted when Tenny, finished with his meal, asked if Angus would walk partway down the hill with him. Angus pushed back his plate. "Sure," he said.

Miss Rowdy clamored to go along, and he tossed her up on his shoulder. Tenny was silent as they walked toward his place. Angus waited, realizing something was troubling the old man. Finally, Tenny began.

"Brother Angus," he said, "reckon I got me a peck of trouble."

"Oh?" Many people had confided in Angus. He had found that it paid to keep his own words to a minimum. Sometimes, they reached their own solution by talking the problem through. "What is it?" he prompted when Tenny remained silent.

"Angus, I got a feelin' I'm gonna get run off."

"Run off?" Angus repeated, puzzled.

"You know I'm a sooner," Tenny said glumly.

"Sure, I knew." It had been so long since the run, Angus had forgotten Tenny's illegal entry. Surely, the old man had earned his bit of land. "I never mentioned it to anyone else," he added.

Tenny's sigh seemed to come clear from his toes. "No, *you* didn't. I wuz in the saloon one night a while back . . . you know how a feller shoots off his mouth . . . they wuz talkin' about the Boomers and sooners . . . someone said the guv'mint had got rid of all the sooners . . . run 'em out of the Territory . . . guess I wanted to show how smart I wuz . . ." He sighed again.

Dismayed, Angus protested, "But you've already filed and paid your fee."

"Don't make no never mind. The law says no one who come in . . . well, like I did . . . can own prop'ty. This is my home, preacher, first one I ever had." Tenny's voice cracked, and Angus felt his own throat tighten.

"Let's think on it a few days," he suggested. "I'm gonna do some prayin' on it, too, Tenny. You might do the same."

"Me? You think God is gonna listen to an old sinner like me?"

Angus managed a small laugh. "It wouldn't surprise me hardly at all."

He did not pray that night, though, at least not for Tenny.

34.

When the two men parted and Angus walked back toward the soddy, he felt Rowdy's weight heavy in his arms and knew she had fallen asleep. Her face was pressed against his neck, and he was suddenly aware that she was unusually hot. He remembered her complaint that the house was hot, that her throat was scratchy, and was stricken with panic.

"Not her too, God," he cried mutely. "Not my baby."

He reached the house and put the sleeping child on the bed.

"She's wore out," Jim said.

"She's sick. Look at her face," Angus retorted. She was flushed, chest rising and falling with her rapid shallow breaths. As they watched, she began to toss about and moan.

Two other times Angus had known the terror that seized hold of him. Once when he saw his mother struck down, and once when Lexie was birthing. His knees went weak and threatened to buckle.

Jim brought the coal-oil lamp and held it close to the bed. "She's got a fever," he agreed. "Want me to go for the doctor?"

The doctor. Oh, Lord, the doctor was miles away, and Angus had no confidence in Jim Royal. If the old man

119

had a mind to, he might just ride on and forget about the doctor.

"No," he said harshly. "I want you to go for Mrs. Murphy." Quickly, he gave directions to her place. "Ride Beth," he told Jim, "and God help you if you let me down this time. I'll find you and kill you, if it takes the rest of my life."

"Now, Davey boy, is that any way to talk?"

"Damn it!" Angus exploded. "Don't stand there clackin'. Git!"

Jim went. "Go by Tenny's on the way," Angus shouted after him. "Tell him to come up here."

What Tenny could do that he himself could not, Angus had no idea. He was out of his mind with fear, wanted someone standing by. He found a flour-sack towel, dampened it and put it on Rowdy's forehead. The child's skin was burning to the touch, and a great and desperate cry went up from deep within him to his Maker.

When Tenny arrived, he brought castor oil and some herbs he had dried. "Thought maybe they might help," he said. "What's wrong with her?"

"I don't know, Tenny. I purely don't know."

"Think she's bilious? Got a cold, mebbe. They do say grease and a mustard plaster is good for a cold."

"I sent for Mrs. Murphy," Angus said. " 'Til she gets here, we'll just try to keep the temperature down."

He brought the washpan over by the bed, wrung out the cloth and again put it on the little girl's forehead. Miss Rowdy's eyes were half open, glazed. She was muttering incoherently.

It seemed hours before they heard the horse whinny, heard the voices of his father and Mrs. Murphy. They came in together, and Mrs. Murphy came directly to the bed, without stopping to take off her hat. She put her hand on the child's forehead.

"You looked at her throat?" she asked. When Angus said no, Mrs. Murphy took a long-handled spoon from her bag and depressed the little girl's tongue. She made a clucking sound and shook her head. Angus's heart sank further.

"What's wrong with her?" His voice sounded strangled.

Mrs. Murphy straightened.

"Reckon we got us a case of diphtheria," she said. "They's a lot of it around."

All Angus's fear was reborn. "Diphtheria? But that's— that's . . ." He could not get the words out.

"It ain't anything to be taken lightly," Mrs. Murphy agreed. "But we're gonna take care of it, preacher. Now, you just calm down." She straightened and turned to face the three men. "You three, the lot of you, stay away from other folks. Diphtheria's mighty contagious. We don't need an epidemic. And keep an eye on how you feel yourself. If your throat starts botherin' you or you think you're runnin' a fever, be sure to let me know. Now, clear out."

Jim Royal went home with Tenny, but Angus refused to budge. Through the night, he and Mrs. Murphy took turns by Miss Rowdy's side, dampening the cloth to cool her forehead, then another, which Mrs. Murphy placed on her throat. It was four o'clock in the morning when Miss Rowdy began to thrash about, kicking with her legs and throwing out her arms in unconsciousness. Mrs. Murphy's face puckered.

"Get the washtub out, preacher," she said grimly. "Fill it half full of tepid water. Bring the baking sody."

Later, it seemed to Angus he had been in a state of shock throughout the child's illness. Yet, he could remember fetching the tub, filling it with water, dumping in the box of soda.

"Now help me lift her into it. Gently. Gently." They lowered Miss Rowdy into the water, which Mrs. Murphy first tested with her elbow. Rowdy's body jerked when it touched the water, but Mrs. Murphy put first one small foot, then the other, into the tub. She dampened her hand and rubbed it over the small buttocks, the stomach and chest.

"This is gonna feel good now," she said soothingly. "We're gonna let Miss Rowdy take a bath, and it's gonna make her feel a whole lot better."

The child's muttering went on. Mrs. Murphy kept her voice low but distinct. And Angus had the feeling that Miss Rowdy was somehow hearing her. Her head would turn toward Mrs. Murphy when she spoke, and her face would quiver.

"We don't want you to get cold, now, darlin'," Mrs. Murphy crooned. "So we'll lift you out of the nice water and wrap you up all comfy in a soft warm blanket . . ."

It occurred to Angus in his anxiety that Mrs. Murphy was talking to the child as he might talk to a skittish horse. Without being told, he found a blanket. Mrs. Murphy dried the child quickly, tucked the blanket in around her and held her in her arms. The terrifying thrashing had, thank God, stopped.

"Did the fever break?" he asked hoarsely.

Mrs. Murphy shook her head. "Not yet, but we're going to sit here and rock and be cozy."

Rowdy relaxed and snuggled down into Mrs. Murphy's plump arms. After a while, her breathing seemed easier.

"You get some rest," Mrs. Murphy told Angus. "This may take a spell. I'll call you if you're needed."

Angus didn't argue. He didn't know whether Rowdy's illness would involve a day, a week, a month. He knew almost nothing of disease, had never been around a place where anyone was sick. So he flung himself down on the bed, fully dressed, and tried to go off to sleep, but was too tense even to shut his eyes. He moved restlessly several times, turned from one side to the other.

"Get yourself a dram," Mrs. Murphy instructed. "You've got to rest, man." Her voice was low but penetrating. Obediently, Angus rose, dragged out the jug of whisky, poured himself a generous measure and downed it.

He lay down again, letting the waves of alcohol wash through him, over him. He drew a deep sigh, sensed his muscles begin to unknot, felt a sudden stinging of tears in his eyes and fell into unconsciousness as though he'd been sandbagged.

35.

When he woke, there was full daylight coming through the window. Mrs. Murphy still sat in the chair, still held Miss Rowdy in comforting arms. Both woman and child were asleep. When Angus moved, Mrs. Murphy opened her eyes.

"I gave the little one a few drops of your medicine,"

she said in a whisper. She adjusted the blanket so he could see the delicate skin. "She looks better, and her fever's come down some."

Angus rubbed his eyes, ran his hands across her face, got to his feet to peer down at the little girl. She was quiet, relaxed-looking. He touched her forehead. It was almost cool enough to be normal.

"Thank You," he whispered under his breath. "Thank You."

"This ain't over yet," Mrs. Murphy warned. "Tyke's gonna need a heap of nursin'."

"Anything," Angus said. "I can do anything you tell me."

"I got a little time myself," Mrs. Murphy said. "The Brewingtons, out toward Cooper's Corner, she's due 'fore too long. But I'm fixin' to stay here 'til she needs me."

Angus could have howled with relief. Instead, he washed up and busied himself making breakfast.

"Can she eat anything?" he asked.

Mrs. Murphy shook her head. He saw she was half asleep.

"Let me hold her," he said. "You eat and get some rest."

Mrs. Murphy stood up. "She doesn't need holding now," she said, and tucked the little girl into her bed.

The next ten days were a nightmare. Despite all they did, Miss Rowdy's fever could not be kept down. Tenny and Jim came to the door three and four times a day, but did not come in. They carried water, brought eggs; and later in the week, Tenny proudly handed in a couple of quail.

Angus and Mrs. Murphy took turns holding Rowdy when she was restless. It seemed to calm her. And when the fever went too high, they used the soda-water bath. To his horror, Angus noted one day that her hair, delicate as filigree, was falling out by the handful. He called it to Mrs. Murphy's attention.

She nodded. "Lots of folks what runs a high fever loses their hair. It comes back in. Nope, I ain't worried about that. I'm just wishin' the fever would stay down. It's weakenin' to a body."

Angus felt his heart twist again. "Maybe she could eat something more, get some strength."

Mrs. Murphy shook her head. "That little broth I been

givin' her, she's doin' real good to keep that down. I'll try her on a little mashed potato today. But that's as much as I dare try."

To Angus, nothing seemed real any more, except the circumscribed area of the house, the child's painful breathing, Mrs. Murphy's intent face. He was too numb to pray.

On the tenth night of her illness, Angus had taken a healthy drink, was trying to get some sleep, when Miss Rowdy's screams brought him upright and running.

"Papa! Papa! My throat! Papa, help me!" He snatched the child out of Mrs. Murphy's arms, saw she was fighting for breath. Her face had a bluish cast; her arms were flailing.

"Christ Jesus, have mercy!" he shouted mutely. "God Almighty, have pity!"

He never knew why he did what he did then. He only knew his child was strangling. He grasped both her fragile ankles in one hand, gently but quickly upended her. His own breath was rasping in his throat.

"Bring water," he said. "Quick!"

Mrs. Murphy ran to the water bucket, brought back a filled dipper. Angus scooped his free hand into the water, ran it down, across the child's face, found the small mouth and forced it open. He again reached his hand into the water, thrust a finger deep into Rowdy's throat. He felt the plug of mucus lodged there, hooked his finger about it, pulled it out.

"Pat her on the back! Gently, firmly!"

Mrs. Murphy did as she was told. He felt more mucus slide into the throat and extracted it as he had before. At last the child began to retch. The spoonful or two of potatoes she had eaten came back up, but there was also a monstrous outpouring of purulent phlegm. Miss Rowdy was panting for breath, and Angus's chest began to ache as he tried to breathe for her.

Finally, after what seemed an eon, she uttered a little whimper; the retching stopped. Quickly, Angus brought her upright, tucked her into the crook of his arm. The bluish pallor had receded, there was a faint touch of pink in her cheeks, her throat moved convulsively two or three times and then that too stopped and she was breathing normally. Angus let out a great exhalation of relief. He saw Mrs. Murphy looking at him curiously.

"I never saw it done that like before," she said. "How'd you know what to do?"

"I didn't," Angus admitted.

"Then God must have had His arm around you, even if you ain't a Catholic," the plump little woman said, and quickly crossed herself. "I reckon that was the crisis. You can put her down now, let her rest."

The midwife had planned to return home the following morning, but when Jim came up over the bluff as Angus was saddling her horse, he reported that Tenny was delirious, muttering that he couldn't breathe.

Mrs. Murphy's bag was already packed, but when she heard about Tenny, she put her hands on her ample hips. "Who's gonna take care of him?" she demanded.

"We will." The two men spoke together. Mrs. Murphy sniffed. "Preacher, you're gonna be down yourself, 'less you get some rest. Mr. Royal . . ." She looked at him dubiously, finally snorted in resignation, "Never seen a man yet what was any good around a sickroom. Guess the Johnson grass will just have to take my corn."

"I could go over and take care of that," Jim offered humbly. "Reckon we owe you a heap."

"You don't owe me a plugged dime," Mrs. Murphy said. "But if you can do something about my crop, I'd take it kindly. Just hope Mrs. Brewington holds off. Now, I'll see to Tenny."

So for another interminable ten days, the attention of Mrs. Murphy and Jim was focused on Tenny. Jim fetched water down to the tent, carried foodstuffs. When he wasn't there, he was at Mrs. Murphy's place, fighting the Johnson grass, plague of the prairie.

Angus stayed housebound, taking care of Miss Rowdy. He learned to make the broths Mrs. Murphy prescribed. Gradually, the child grew stronger, the hollow cheeks filled out, fine-spun ringlets of hair began to reappear. Angus touched it lovingly; it felt like the soft fluff of a baby chicken.

Mrs. Murphy herself was hollow-eyed by the time Tenny was able to be up and about. Angus suggested she let them take care of her for a few days before she ventured home, but she refused.

"I'll be all right. Jim says the corn has been laid by. And Mrs. Brewington, thank God, must've counted wrong. Now, I got to get home and burn these clothes lest I carry the fever to someone else. Brother Angus, you look after that old man down there. Way he lives like— like a tramp, it's a downright shame. That tent looked like a tornado hit it when I got there. Body couldn't find anything."

"Yes'm," Angus said meekly. His thoughts went back to his conversation with Tenny before Miss Rowdy sickened. "Reckon it doesn't make much difference," he said. "Tenny thinks the Law is fixin' to roust him off his land."

Mrs. Murphy's eyebrows went up questioningly, and Angus, knowing she wouldn't gossip, added, "He's a sooner. Law's trying to get all of them out of the territory."

Mrs. Murphy pursed her lips. "That old fool ain't got a lick of sense," she said, and took off.

36.

For some time, no more was heard about Tenny losing his land. When Miss Rowdy and the old man were once more hale and hearty, Angus went back to the circuit.

On his return home from that trip, he picked up Miss Rowdy and Sam and took them out to the soddy for the time he'd be home.

It had been a scorching day. The wind was strong. Dust was in the air, like gritty fog. After supper, Sam and Miss Rowdy went outside to play. Dishes done, Angus and Jim followed them. The wind was dying down as evening came. The air was cooling.

The men sat on the bench beneath the cottonwood. Angus stretched and yawned.

"Tired?" Jim asked.

"No." The monosyllable was curt. Angus had been trying, while on the circuit, to overcome his feelings about his father. But truth to tell, he'd be a hell of a lot happier if he never saw him again.

"Forgive us our trespasses, as we forgive them that trespass against us," Jim quoted suddenly, and Angus started. It was as though his father had read his thoughts. Then he shrugged. Jim's neglect of his mother, the heartbreak in her eyes, his own yearning for a real father rather than an occasional visitor, these things he could not forget. He would provide for the old man, live up to his obligation. It was the most he could do.

"Miss Rowdy," he called sharply, "you let Sam down from there."

She had cornered the older child in the fork of an elm tree and was keeping him there by punching at him with a sharp stick.

"We're playing sheriff-outlaw," she called back without changing her stance. "Sam just robbed a bank, and I gotta keep him here 'til the posse arrives. Else he'll hightail it for Robber's Cave, and we'll never catch him."

Angus clucked. "Where in the devil did she hear about Robber's Cave?' he wondered.

"No tellin'."

Robber's Cave, in the Kiamichi Mountains, was a hideout for wanted men from all the surrounding states. The whole mountainous area was honeycombed with caves and thick woods and was considered safe only for bobcats, bootleggers . . . and desperadoes.

Where did the child get her wild ideas? Why couldn't she play with dolls, like other little girls? She could ride a horse—astride—skin up a tree and loved to play sheriff-outlaw.

"And what am I going to do about finding a place for her?" Angus fretted, not realizing he spoke aloud. "If she won't stay with Sarah, she's not going to stay with anyone else, other kids or no."

Dusk came, mosquitoes started biting, Sam "escaped" from the tree and the four of them trooped into the house. After they'd had their Bible reading and the children were in bed, Jim said, "Why shouldn't Miss Rowdy stay here?"

Angus gave a scornful snort, and Jim said hurriedly, "I promise you . . ." glanced at his son's steely face and began again. "I know you think I'm not dependable, but look at me, son. I ain't apt to take off, shape I'm in. But I can take care here, make a garden, cook the victuals, look after the child."

From behind her curtain, Miss Rowdy called, "I like Uncle Jim. He talks to me."

Momentarily, Angus felt a pang. Rowdy was his. He shook the thought away. "Let me think on it," he said.

As he lay awake in the darkness, he wished he could place more trust in his father. Maybe Dove would drop by now and then. She'd make damn sure everything was as it should be.

He woke in the morning, still thinking of Dove, and as he lay there for a few minutes, blinking himself awake, he remembered Sam. Dove needed a place for him. If he were out here, she'd probably visit every day.

Excited, he sat on the side of his bed, turning the idea over in his mind and finding no objections to it. Jim stirred, and Angus said, "Think you could take care of two younguns?"

"Huh? Two what?" the older man said groggily; then, rousing himself and rubbing his eyes: "Two younguns? Sure, I could. Two'd probably be easier'n one. I always told your mam . . ." He broke off at Angus's scowl, began again. "Yore meanin' Sam," he guessed, and Angus nodded.

It took a good many trips between the two-story white house and the soddy before the arrangement was finally made. Jim refused payment from Dove. Finally, Angus and Dove settled things between themselves. The cost of Sam's care would be applied to the amount owed for Rowdy's care.

"I'll ride back with you," Angus offered—Dove had come to the soddy to conclude the arrangements—"and bring Sam out here." For a moment, he thought Dove's lips trembled, decided he was mistaken since, when she spoke, her voice was steady, her tone even derisive. "You're gonna carry two younguns in the saddle with you?"

"Sure. Miss Rowdy knows how to ride back of me. She's done it before."

Rowdy grinned proudly, held up her arms to be lifted onto the horse. Angus swung her up.

"Preacher!" Dove's voice was sharp. "You're not letting that girl-chile ride astride? You'll ruin her parts. Besides, it's not ladylike."

Angus grimaced. If two such disparate women as Sarah and Dove insisted the child must ride sidesaddle, then

128

sidesaddle it must be. He'd never thought of harming her "parts."

"Sidesaddle it is," he agreed. "Put both your limbs on one side, Miss Rowdy. That's the way little girls ride."

"No," Rowdy said. Her hands tightened on the saddle and her legs clamped down on Beth's sides. "That's silly," she added.

Angus tried to reason with her. Jim tried to reason with her. But the more they talked, the more mutinous the small face became; the tighter she clung to the saddle. Dove listened impassively. "Now's the time when she needs her bottom blistered," she told Angus finally, and walked away.

Angus was sweating. He felt like a fool, but he could not bring himself to pry loose those white-knuckled fingers. Lexie's eyes watched him from beneath delicately marked brows; the fragile planes of her face were set in lines of consummate sorrow and appeal. She's too little to spank, he thought. Later . . .

He gave in. "Just for this time." Rowdy threw her arms around his neck, pressed her cheek against his. "I love you, Papa," she murmured.

At the house, Samson listened placidly while Dove explained to him that he was going to get to go home with Rowdy, stay at her house awhile. A docile child, Angus thought, and sighed. Rowdy had never had any baby fat, but Samson had, and was just now beginning to lose it. He was a handsome youngster, with the thin lips and patrician nose of a Caesar. A faintly dusky complexion was the only indication of his Negro ancestry.

Auntie Po was snuffling as she got his clothes together. "My baby, my little ol' baby boy," she kept saying until Dove told her fiercely to shut her mouth. When they were ready to leave, Samson clung to Dove desperately but without speaking. Dove pried him loose and gave him a swat on the rear.

"You mind when you're spoken to, now, you hear?" she said fiercely. Sam's eyes filled with tears, but he nodded. "Maman will be out to see you," she added, and her voice cracked on the last word, but she held her head high. "Now, get on out of here," she said harshly. "I got things to do."

Sam gulped, swallowing hard as they rode away. He watched the house as long as he could see it, and Angus felt his heart swelling in pity. "You and Miss Rowdy are going to have fun," he said, and gave the child a hug. Sam leaned against him, sobbing as though his heart would break. Miss Rowdy peered around Angus's back.

"Don't cry, Samsy," she said cajolingly. "You can be my brother. Only, my papa can't be your papa because he can't be anyone's papa but mine."

Attention distracted by this involved reasoning, Samson gulped, hiccoughed, straightened. "Will I really be Rowdy's brother?" he asked. Angus nodded.

"Just like a brother," he reassured him. Sam seemed comforted.

Jim and the two children hit it off from the start. The old man was never too busy to tell them a story or answer questions. Two months passed without incident, but still Angus fretted. Despite all his protestations, one day Jim might decide just to leave, and the children would be untended. Still, he had two safeguards, Dove and Tenny. To Tenny he had explained that Jim wasn't very strong, so it would help if he, Tenny, would look in on Jim and the children now and again.

Samson was no longer allowed to go home, but Dove rode out to see him every other day. At first the little boy cried when she left, but Jim would engage his attention by asking him to help make gingerbread men or fetch some corn cobs and husks to make dolls. For Sam he made soldiers, complete with muskets of twigs; for Rowdy he made baby dolls, complete with moss lace on their skirts. Rowdy thanked him, put them to bed and demanded that he make her animals.

"You like animals better than people?" Jim asked, and she nodded. But when Jim asked why, she had to think a long time; finally, she said slowly, "They're nicer."

Angus had traded for a cow, fenced in a few acres where she could graze. When Miss Rowdy was wanted, Jim had only to head for that pasturage to find the child sitting cross-legged by the cow, talking a blue streak. Daisy was with calf when Angus brought her home, and after Rowdy demanded why she wasn't giving milk, Angus explained that the cow would find a calf before long; then she'd give milk again.

"She'll *find* a calf?" Miss Rowdy repeated. "Where? Could Sam and I find one if we looked?"

Angus took the little girl on his lap; Sam, standing

alongside them, rested his hand on Angus's knee. "No, you couldn't find one," the man answered slowly, and shot his father an appealing glance. Jim rolled his eyes heavenward and shrugged. Finally, though he knew every woman in the settlement would disapprove, Angus decided on the truth.

"Daisy is carrying a little calf in her stomach," he explained awkwardly. "One of these days it will be born. That's what is called finding a calf."

"Oh." Miss Rowdy considered that awhile. "How'd the calf get there?" she asked.

Again Angus's look appealed to his father. The old man's face was scarlet. Angus felt the mole on his forehead begin to throb, knew that his ears were glowing. "Well," he said, "the bull put it there."

Rowdy said, "Oh" again, Sam said, "That was nice of him" and the two children decided to go out and take a look at Daisy, in light of this newly acquired knowledge.

When they had left the house, Jim said indignantly, "That ain't hardly the kind of information to give innocent children."

Angus sighed and got to his feet. "I had to tell them something," he said, "and I'm not going to lie to them."

"Angus," the old man said bluntly, "what that girl-child needs is a mother. And yore a young man with normal wantings. They's a passel of gals in the territory wouldn't mind being courted."

Angus thought of Pearl Lancaster and felt himself begin to redden. Then he reasoned himself out of his guilt feelings. Pearl didn't want to get married any more than he did. He didn't try to excuse himself for his visits to her; he just hoped that God would overlook his human failing.

"Tend to your own business, old man," he said harshly, wheeled and rushed out the door.

37.

It was some months after Miss Rowdy's and Tenny's illness that Angus arrived home from the circuit to find
Tenny at the soddy. He greeted both the older men, gave
Sam a hug and swung Miss Rowdy up in his arms for a
kiss.

The flurry of greetings over, the children ran outside.
The three men sat down to coffee, Jim rattling on about
happenings while Angus had been gone. When he
stopped, Tenny spoke hesitantly. "Preacher?"

"Yeah." Angus yawned and stretched, thinking how
good it was to get home. Then, as his glance fell on
Tenny, he straightened. The old man's face was beet red
and his eyes were on the floor.

"Angus," he said, and swallowed, "reckon you know
what a set of store-boughten teeth cost?"

"I don't have any idea, Tenny," he said in surprise.
"But it wouldn't be hard to find out. You gonna get a
set?"

"Mebbe," Tenny mumbled. "You know that lady what
took care of Miss Rowdy and me when we was sick?"

"Mrs. Murphy. Sure."

"Her front name's Clover," Tenny said, and blushed
more furiously than before. "She's a widder, you know."

Angus nodded, and Tenny went on. "Fine figger of a
woman," he said. Again the preacher nodded.

"I ain't got much to offer," Tenny said humbly. "But I
ain't heerd nothin' more about them takin' my land. I was
thinkin'—if I got some store teeth and—and spruced up a
mite . . ."

Angus finally understood. "It can't hurt to try," he
agreed gravely.

So the courtship of the widow Murphy began. The
store-bought teeth cost ten dollars, cash. Angus and Jim
dug deep in their pockets to add their small hoard to

Tenny's, and the fund was still short two dollars and twenty-three cents. Money wasn't a plentiful commodity in the territory, but the next time Dove came to visit, Angus told her of the predicament. She laughed and supplied the balance.

Tenny got his teeth, mumbled and grumbled, trying to get accustomed to them, trying to keep them from whistling and clacking when he talked. Finally, he conquered them. He bought a new chambray shirt, fifty cents. Angus went through his trunk and found a tie that was salvageable. Tenny washed his best pair of britches, borrowed a sadiron from Jim to press them.

Then he went calling.

Now and again, while he was on his next trip, Angus thought of the couple and wondered how Mrs. Murphy had received the compliment of being wooed.

The circuit that time was without unusual incident, and Angus returned home to find Tenny again at the soddy. His store-bought teeth had been left behind; his clothes were as grubby as they'd been the first time Angus saw him. His face sagged in dejection. She refused him, the preacher thought, and grieved for the old man.

But Tenny's problems had to wait, for the moment. The children demanded Angus's attention first, with stories of what had happened during his absence. Miss Rowdy's eyes were dancing. She had saved the best for last.

"And Daisy found her calf! I helped her because it couldn't get out by itself."

"You *what?*"

"I was out visiting her," Rowdy said primly. "All at once, she laid down. Then I saw two little legs slide out of her back end."

"Good God," Angus said. It was a supplication.

"She was sort of bellerin' and sort of whimperin', and it seemed like she was trying to push the rest of him out. So I took hold of the legs, and the next time she pushed, I pulled. His head and all the rest of him just tumbled right on out."

"Good God!" Angus said again, and sat down.

"She didn't even come get me to help her," Sam reported resentfully.

133

"Where were you?" Angus asked his father.

" 'Tater patch," Jim snapped, red-faced with both embarrassment and anger. "Didn't hear a dem thing 'til she come to tell me the calf was already born. She deserves a good paddlin'."

"Why?" Miss Rowdy demanded.

"Because such as that ain't fittin' for girl-children," Jim grumbled. "Girl-children is s'posed to play with dolls —and such."

"That's silly." Miss Rowdy's tone was tart, and Angus was caught between amusement and horror. "Silly" was the strongest condemnation either of the children could muster. He could share her feeling. She had seen that something needed to be done, had followed her instinct and taken care of it. And very well done, too, he thought with pride. On the other hand, he didn't want his child coming to grips with the uglier aspects of life.

"Papa, it's the prettiest little calf you ever saw." Rowdy seemed to have forgotten Jim and his reprimand. Angus drew a breath of relief. The ugliness of birthing, the pain and blood, Rowdy had apparently disregarded. Her face was radiant as she went on to describe the calf. "I wanted to name him Rusty; then I thought we ought to call him Samson since Samsy didn't get to help."

She ran out of breath, and Angus looked at his father. "It's a male, then," he said. Jim shook his head.

"Heifer," he said gloomily.

Rowdy looked from one to the other. "How can you tell?" she asked. Jim's lips came together in a straight line. "Told you she needed a mother," he growled, and stalked out the door. Tenny also decided it was no place for him and took off to join Jim.

Angus took the children, one on each knee. "Now," he said, "you've seen chickens." They nodded, and he went on. "You know the hen lays eggs; the rooster crows. It's the same with cattle. One's male, one's female. Like you and Sam." He stopped, appalled at where his words had led.

"I know," Rowdy contributed. "Sam's got short hair; mine's long. Papa, I've been wanting to cut my hair. Then it wouldn't have to be combed and combed and combed, and I could wear britches . . . and be a boy," she finished triumphantly.

"God doesn't hold with girls trying to be boys," Angus said sternly. The children had long since learned that when God had spoken, there was no use to argue. "Oh, well," Rowdy said. "But I'd still like short hair."

38.

Angus was sweating. When the children had gone to play, he went out to join the other men.

"Cowards," he said, then suddenly remembered Tenny's dejection. "Noticed you weren't wearing your teeth," he said. "Something wrong?"

"Ain't no use," Tenny mumbled. "I'm losin' my claim, Angus. Lawman rode out today and handed me a piece of paper. I—I didn't have my glasses, so I asked him what it said. I got ten days to get out. I can't never own prop'ty in Oklahoma Territory."

Angus whistled. "What're you going to do, Tenny? You're welcome to stay with us, of course."

He heard Tenny gulp, and when the old man spoke, his voice was unsteady. "That's mighty thoughty of you, preacher. But I reckon you got all you can say grace over. Reckon I'll head out trampin' again. Fellow can pick up a day's work now and again. It—ain't so bad."

Angus lay awake a long while that night. All right, he thought, Tenny broke the law, and the law caught up with him. He recognized its justice, but what was to become of the old man? He'd seen some of the saddle bums who drifted from one place to another; they were eyed with suspicion, unkempt, generally hungry.

Tenny had done a fine job on his quarter section. His land was worked and produced the equal of any in the countryside. Besides, dammit, Angus thought, I like the old rascal. He's a good neighbor. Sighing, he placed the matter before the Final Authority.

The next day was Sunday. It was Angus's custom, when he was home, to hold services in the brush arbor

135

he and Jim and Tenny had put up on the preacher's land.

Pete and Alice Smith were there, as always, with their brood. That in itself, Angus thought, made a congregation. Pete had plenty for the kids to do, though, to keep them out of mischief. He'd sowed the bottom land with cotton, and with the "hands" in his own household could plant, chop, hoe and pick the crop.

Sarah and Zeb Holtzworthy drove out from town. Tenny would be there—wearing both his teeth and a clean shirt this morning, Angus hoped. It wasn't that he minded how the old man looked, but the sprucing up would indicate he was feeling better.

There were others in the community who came occasionally instead of driving into town, but Angus was surprised when Mrs. Murphy drove up in her buggy, and dumbfounded when Maggie Cruikshank showed up. Mrs. Murphy was Catholic and went to church in town. As for Maggie Cruikshank—good Lord, how far was it to her place?

He went about the usual morning services. There were hymns and prayers; he preached and gave the altar call. No one came to the mourner's bench, and he knew that would please the kids. It meant they could eat earlier. Angus suspected their elders felt the same, although they probably also felt sheepish about it.

The last amen had no more than crossed his lips, when Maggie Cruikshank spoke out. "Preacher, could I say a word?" she called out over the heads of the congregation. The children were breaking away, but stopped at the sound of her voice. The grown-ups had stirred but were still in place.

"Guess so, Maggie," Angus said. "Reckon you know what's appropriate in God's house."

"I knew what was appropriate in God's house before you were born," Maggie said tartly, and started toward the front. The crowd laughed. So did Angus.

"This is Miss Maggie Cruikshank, from Massachusetts, folks. She's got a claim up the other side of Guthrie."

Maggie reached the front and turned to face the crowd, fanning herself with a handkerchief.

"I'm not going to talk long," she promised, "but I think church folks are the ones to lead the fight that should have been won long ago." The milling children heard the

136

word "fight" and listened more closely. Maggie went on.

"When God set up the Garden of Eden," she said crisply, "He put people in it. Not all men. Not all women. A man and a woman. Each of them had a job to do. Now, if God hadn't meant them to be equal, he'd have arranged for the race to continue some other way."

There was a shifting of feet in the congregation. Grimly, Maggie continued. "Folks, it's time for women to be treated like American citizens. It's time for women to have the vote! Thank you."

Angus was thunderstruck. He heard a couple of gasps. Women vote? He'd never thought of it. Never heard it mentioned. Women stayed home and raised the kids. 'Course, there were a lot of women who were more level-headed than their men, but . . .

He started toward the back of the arbor, and Mrs. Murphy stopped him. Her cheeks were pink. She was clasping and unclasping her reticule. "Preacher," she said, "reckon . . ." More color flooded her face, and she looked down at her feet.

Angus was puzzled. He'd never seen the plump little woman at a loss for words. "What is it, Mrs. M.?" he asked gently.

The lively blue eyes came up to meet his. "You know Tenny, Tenny's been—been calling on me?"

Angus nodded.

"Well, did you know they're fixin' to take his claim away from him?"

Angus nodded again, puzzled.

Angry tears sparkled in her eyes. "He's such an old fool," she complained. "We—we was s'posed to get married today. Right here. You don't think we're foolish, at our age?" she inserted parenthetically.

"Of course not," Angus assured her. "People need each other whether they're sixteen or sixty."

"Well, then," she went on, "would you believe that old fool has backed out on me?"

"Why?"

"Says since he's losing his land, he's got nothin' to offer. He's crazy, Brother Angus. He could take care of my claim like it ort to be taken care of. I'm not gonna stop midwifin', but I'd still make him a good wife." She was perilously close to tears now. "He's so prideful, preacher. It's a downright sin, that pride of his."

137

Angus didn't know whether to laugh or cry. She was so indignant, and at the same time so unhappy. And perhaps not a little uncertain as to whether Tenny was really backing out for the reason given, or just didn't want to be married.

"I hadn't realized he wasn't here, Clover."

Her lips curved in a smile, making her look like a young girl. "It's nice to hear you call me by my first name," she said. Then: "He said he wasn't coming, but I thought I'd talked him into changing his mind."

Angus put a hand on her shoulder. "Let me see if I can find him, talk some sense into the old scallawag. But wait a minute, you sure you wouldn't rather to go into town to the priest?"

"You believe in God, don't you? I don't think any church has got all of Him sewed up in a little bundle."

Angus chuckled and started off toward Tenny's place. As he passed by where the men were pitching horseshoes, one of them said, "That Maggie woman, she's loco. Next thing, she'll be sayin' women ought to hold office."

They all laughed, and another man said, "Now, that wouldn't be possible 'cause women can't chaw t'baccy."

When he reached Tenny's tent, Angus called out, "Hello, the house." No answer. He opened the flap, stuck his head inside. "Tenny," he called. No answer, but he saw a blurred movement, and then Tenny said, "Have a drink, preacher."

Tenny was sitting at the table. There was a bottle of red-eye and a tin cup in front of him.

"Where'd you get the whiskey?" That was the first thing that popped into Angus's mind.

"Over northeast of here a piece." Tenny's words were slurred, hands unsteady as he reached for the bottle again.

"I've got something to say to you, Tenny."

The old man scowled. "Spit it out. On'y . . . on'y . . ." he held up a forefinger and waggled it, "don't lecture. What the hell diff'rence it make, me being drunk or sober?"

"A lot. When you say 'I do,' I want you to know what you're saying."

Tenny went red as a cockscomb. "I ain't gonna marry that woman," he growled. "I told her I weren't, and I ain't. I don't want no woman remindin' me I come to her empty-handed."

"If you weren't losing your claim, would you want to marry her?"

" 'Course. Asked her, din't I?"

"Clover's a lonely woman," Angus ventured to say. "And as much as she's gone, she needs someone to look after the place proper."

Tenny raised his head, and Angus saw the anguish on his face. "It'd still be her'n. Folks'd say I married her for a place to live." He seized the bottle, tilted his head back and drank, then rubbed his mouth with the back of his hand.

"I'm beholden to you, preacher, for tryin' to help . . ." He gave an enormous hiccough and began to cry.

"Oh, hell," Angus said, "how much of that stuff have you got inside you?"

Without answering, Tenny continued to cry. Angus got up, kindled a fire and made coffee. When it boiled to the proper strength, he doused it well with salt and handed a cupful to the other man. After the first sip, Tenny made a horrified face and spat.

"My Gawd in heaven, whut's thet?" he spluttered.

"Just drink it," Angus snapped, "or I'll pour it down your throat."

Another unwilling swallow, and Tenny gagged. "Yore making me sick to my death. My belly . . ."

"Good!" Angus was ruthless, and the old man finally swallowed enough of the noxious fluid for his stomach to actually rebel. He groped his way out of the tent and retched until Angus wondered if he were going to turn inside out. When the spasms were over, Tenny was almost too weak to stand. Angus got him back inside, washed his face, let him rinse his mouth. Tenny fell into a chair. "You damn nigh killed me," he complained.

"You can't be drunk getting married."

"I done tol' you—"

"Quiet!" Angus thundered. "I've got an idea. I'll draw up a paper that says you don't want any part of Clover's property. I can make it say she doesn't have any claim on your belongings, too, if you want."

Tenny's face was beginning to regain some color. "I'd want to share with her," he growled.

Angus didn't point out that Mrs. Murphy probably felt the same way. He'd pushed Tenny far enough. Quickly, he found a scrap of paper and a pencil stub, drew up the document. When he was finished, he said, "You haven't got your glasses. Want me to read it to you?"

Tenny nodded.

"I, Tenny, hereby state I have no claim to, and want no share of, any possessions Clover Murphy owns."

Tenny frowned. "My proper handle is Reginald Tennyson," he said, "but I'd shore hate for anyone to know it. Reckon that paper's legal like it is?"

Angus managed not to smile. "I'm sure it's legal the way it is. You want to sign it?"

"Shore do!" The change in the old man was incredible. With a bit of effort, he got his name signed, but when he tried to stand, his legs buckled. He fell back in the chair.

"Oh, hell." Angus snorted. He found some honey, a couple of cold biscuits. Alternately threatening and cajoling the older man, Angus got Tenny to eat. At long last, holding Angus's arm, the old man tottered up the bluff.

Dinner was over. The women were cleaning up. Angus called out above the noise of the various groups, "If you'll come back to the arbor, we've got some unfinished business to take care of."

He saw Clover Murphy, beckoned to her. Her face suddenly became radiant. "Tenny's not feeling too peart," he told her quietly as she joined them. "But he can last long enough to say 'I do.'"

Tenny glared at the plump little woman. "I ain't marryin' you for yore land," he said.

"I know that, you old fool."

But Tenny wasn't through. "Preacher's gonna read out the paper," he said, "or there ain't gonna be no weddin'."

Clover nodded, and Angus "read out the paper," then began the wedding service. When it was over, Tenny pecked his wife on the cheek, and the crowd began clapping. Someplace in the back of the congregation, a boy whistled shrilly through his teeth.

Angus grinned, wondering if a wedding ceremony had ever been applauded before.

39.

The months went by more rapidly than Angus would have thought possible.

When the children were six, he began teaching them how to use guns, both rifles and sidearms, and to respect them. He taught them how to handle a lasso. Beth and David were old and placid. If the children wanted to practice by aiming ropes at the horses' necks, the animals would stand patiently awhile before rambling off.

Angus also approached Sarah Holtzworthy about enrolling the children in school.

Sarah was dubious. "Are you sure that—that Sam's mother knows what she's doing?" she asked. "Not that I object, you understand."

"But you think other parents might?"

Sarah bristled. "It's my school; I run it the way I please. Others don't like it, they can send their children to public school." She chuckled. "It's only the snobs who want their children here anyhow, since there is a good free school. They think it gives them a certain cachet."

Angus didn't know the word but understood what she meant.

"No," Sarah went on, "but, speaking frankly, why educate a Negro?"

Angus might not have heard. "If you think it would cause trouble, he's light enough to pass for white."

Sarah looked at him pityingly. "Oh, Brother Angus, you're a good man, but you're not very smart sometimes. There's no one in the territory doesn't know who that boy is and where he comes from. What I meant was, is it wise to educate him above his prospects?"

"It's not going to hurt him to know how to read and figure," Angus said mildly. He didn't tell Sarah that Dove was planning to send the boy east to school when he was older.

141

The years seemed to fly by in earnest after the children started going to school. Angus's work on the circuit grew more demanding. It was, he reflected as he rode slowly toward home one evening, a good life. Even though he'd been conscripted and blackmailed into preaching, he was content with his work, felt himself in compliance with God's will. At home, Miss Rowdy, Sam and Jim gave him a sense of permanence, that he was building something.

The small community of Starling had surprised him with a church building this last trip. Walnut trees had been felled, sawed and planed out by hand. The church wasn't large, but it would comfortably hold the people of the area. The children had proudly showed him the benches they had put together. There was even a small lectern.

Angus had felt his throat tighten when he saw the building, as well as the shy pride of his people, God's people. He had, after gulping for a moment, expressed his pleasure; then, in a special afternoon service, when dinner was over, dedicated the building as best he knew how.

Beth's uneasy whinny disturbed his thoughts. He looked around the heavily wooded area. The towering trees interlaced over his head made a shadowy dimness, but that was nothing new. Still, something had disturbed the horse, and Angus realized the silence was unnatural. Not a leaf stirred; there was no rustling of small animals, no birdsong. He looked up. The little he could see of the sky was midnight black with an overlayer of sickish-looking green.

Tremors had begun to run through the old horse, and Angus patted her withers. "You're right, old girl," he said, "we'd best find us a shelter." A freshet of wind rattled the treetops as Angus slid from the broad back, led the horse after him to a nearby draw. He was looking for a low spot not too close to trees. That was a tornado sky. The lightning in such a storm was often fierce and devastating. Angus had seen more than one tree stripped of its bark by the fury unleashed during a tornado.

He found a spot quickly, but when he tried to get Beth to lie down, she balked. Eyes rolling wildly, she reared, and Angus was finally forced to ground-hobble her and hope for the best. He plunged into his own shelter and, lying on his back, stared upward.

The black of the sky had almost disappeared. The bilious yellow-green presaged hail. The lightning had begun, and its jagged bolts lit up the woods with an eerie glow. Angus heard the crack like a rifle shot as it struck a tree.

The ensuing thunder was like none he'd ever heard. It was not a rumble; it was a roar that sounded as though the beasts of the apocalypse had been let loose. Beth squealed, tried to bolt. "It's all right, old girl!" Angus called. "Easy!"

The wind started then, and a wild spate of rain. The rain barely touched them but the wind bent the sturdy trees like blades of grass. Angus covered his head with his arms when the hail started. More than one death had been caused by those rock-hard chunks.

It seemed to be, thank God, a straight wind, violent, but not the twisting funnel that could scoop up everything in its path. Jim would have the children in the furthermost recess of the house, protected by the bluff.

The hail diminished, and Angus opened his eyes. The trees were once more lashed aside and he saw the sinister outline of the funnel. Erratic in their course as cyclones were, there was no point in running though the vortex of the cone seemed to be whirling directly toward him. Jumping to his feet, he half pulled, half wrestled Beth to the ground. And once the horse was down, she lay quietly enough, though tremors still ran through her body.

Angus rolled close to her, petting her and speaking in a soothing tone. Then he turned on his face and once more put his arms over his head.

The wind increased in intensity, hurling itself through the trees so they bent double. Suddenly, the wind ceased, the hail ceased, the rain ceased and it was as though the universe held its breath.

Then the twister struck. A nearby tree was sucked out of the ground and flung aside. Angus risked a peek. The tree had been uprooted. The roots, big as a man's arm, were raw and nakedly exposed.

Hope the damn storm jumps the draw. Angus had time for that thought before the cone dipped a second time and the trees within twenty feet of him were swept up out of the earth. For a space of time that seemed endless,

143

they swirled in a mad witches' dance. Angus turned his head briefly to one side, arms still protectively raised. He saw the giant cottonwood hurtling toward him, felt the shattering pain as it struck, and then saw and felt nothing.

40.

That morning, when the household chores were finished, before she and Sam headed outdoors, Rowdy paused to get a couple of apples. "Papa'll be home today," she said, rejoicing. "Can we have something special for supper, Uncle Jim?"

"I'll think on it," the old man promised.

When the door closed behind the children, Jim set about making bread. He was certain the kneading would make the crippled left arm as strong as the right, one of these days. After he'd placed a damp cloth over the dough to let it rise, he skimmed cream from the crocks of milk and churned it. Always plenty to do around a farm, he thought, glad to be busy, and thankful he could pull his own weight.

By the time he stepped outside for a breath of air, the sky was a wicked-looking black.

And the children nowhere in sight!

Fretting, he hurried to the highest point of the bluff, looked as far as he could see in each direction. The quarter section rose and dipped in gentle slopes. You couldn't see the whole area. He glanced apprehensively at the sky again. Damn it, those kids *knew* they were supposed to hurry back to the soddy when a storm was brewing.

He gave a piercing whistle designed to bring them running but got no whistle in return.

Fear began to build inside him. They could be in the woods, out in the far pasture, down by the creek, holed up in the hayloft, reading. Not noticing what was happening. In the meantime, the clouds seemed to be getting lower, the black now interspersed with ominous-looking green.

The rustling and chirring of animal life had ceased; even the chickens—surely the most stupid of all God's creatures—were peering around nervously, without making so much as a cheep. Not a leaf stirred.

Jim's fear grew. His heart gave a warning thump, and he massaged the area roughly, as though to scrub away the pain beginning to spread through his chest. Nothing must happen to those little ones. His legs began to tremble, and he found it hard to breathe. What if they were hurt, or if one of them had fallen in the creek? That youngest heifer was old enough to breed. What if a bull had jumped the fence . . .

Jim didn't know which way to turn. Tears began to roll down his cheeks. He loved those damn kids. If anything happened to them . . . Panic flared. Pain was clawing at his chest the way it had that other time. Not now, he thought; I haven't got time now!

Turning, he rushed back to the cabin, grabbed the Winchester, hurried out again. Turning the muzzle to the sky, he pulled the trigger. It seemed to him that in the thick, oppressive air, the sound was so muffled, it couldn't have been heard even five feet. There was no response.

Desperately, he began to lope toward the pasture, scarcely aware of his pain, praying that he was taking the right direction. He had run a couple of hundred feet, when he heard Sam's whistle, saw the children coming over the rise, herding the stock in front of them.

Thank God, oh, thank God! For a moment Jim's knees sagged; tears flooded down his cheeks faster than he could brush them away. He beckoned urgently, pointed to the sky. The children whacked the cows, the horse. The horse began to gallop, but the cows' awkward gait scarcely quickened. Leave the livestock, Jim wanted to scream at them. Hurry! He could not make a sound.

He glanced at the sky again. The clouds were turning, shifting this way and that, though no wind gusts had yet touched earth. The awesome stillness persisted.

After what seemed an eternity, the children had the livestock in the barn, with the door shut. "The chickens!" Rowdy was hurrying Sam. But it was now so dark, the chickens had gone to the roosts of their own accord. Sam closed the door as the first fiery streak of lightning split the sky.

Let the chickens go! Jim wanted to scream at them. For God's sake, get to the cabin! The pain in his chest eased briefly, but he still did not have enough breath to speak. He took a few unsteady steps, stopped, leaned against a fence post.

Rowdy and Sam had rushed to the cabin. Rowdy suddenly glanced back, yelled something at Sam; then both of them were racing back to the old man.

"What's the matter, Uncle Jim?" Rowdy cried.

"Nothin'. Git to the house!" He got the words out somehow. The wind and rain and hail all started at once, and at the same time the thunder exploded like a cannon's roar. The children exchanged a quick glance. Sam took the rifle from him; each of the children grasped one of his arms.

The hail, some of the stones as large as a hen's egg, was bludgeoning them. "Mind yore heads," Jim tried to say, but his voice was no more than a whisper, which the children didn't hear. Half carrying him, they pulled him across the yard and into the house. The wind blew wildly, and it took both the children to close the door against its force.

"Git to the back wall!" Jim gasped.

They took hold of him again, sweeping him along with them. The pain was constant now. His chest felt as though it were on fire, and streaks of pain ran down his left arm.

"Sam, turn the bed back!" Rowdy ordered.

"Just—a—catch," Jim demurred, but was glad enough to lie down. Rowdy knelt and slipped his shoes off. Sam found a candle. He knew not to light the lamp when there was a lightning storm.

By now the wind was howling like some maddened beast, hurling itself at the door, shaking the wall until the window rattled. In the candlelight, Sam's eyes were enormous. "Reckon we're gonna get blown away this time?" he asked, and sounded excited rather than fearful.

Jim tried to shake his head, didn't know whether he had or not.

"I hope Papa's safe," Rowdy said fretfully.

Jim made an effort to sit up, but fell back, and almost instantly dozed restlessly. The children sat silent, and Rowdy thought that if they knew Papa was all right, the

146

storm would be fun, with the lurid lightning, the rampaging wind, the hammering of hail and rumble of thunder, and them so safe and cozy.

"Uncle Angus would have found someplace secure," Sam assured her.

" 'Course he would, Samsy." She tried to reassure herself.

The storm seemed to last a long while, but finally the rain ceased, the wind diminished, the thunder died to a distant mutter. Jim was still asleep. The children headed toward the barn to let the animals out. Without warning, Rowdy skidded in the red mud, her feet flew from under her and she sat down hard.

"Damn!" she said.

Sam stopped. "Your papa'll whip you for that."

She got to her feet, scowling. Her tailbone hurt, and she was thoroughly shaken up. In spite of herself, a couple of tears slid down her cheeks.

"Don't cry," the boy said hastily. "I'm not going to tell."

Rowdy dashed the tears away, leaving mud streaks on her face. "I know you won't," she said, "but just look at me." She sloshed her way back to the cabin, angry and bedraggled. Wish I could wear britches, she thought.

Uncle Jim had woken, gotten up and was sitting in the rocker, but his face was still very white. Rowdy blew out the guttering candle and lit the lamp.

"What happened, child?" Jim rasped.

"Dem mud," Rowdy growled. "I'm wet through." She carried the washpan and a cloth to her corner, jerked the curtain shut, realized suddenly she was wearing her last clean clothes. Tomorrow was wash day. "Damn!" she said again, taking pains to whisper it to herself this time so Uncle Jim wouldn't hear.

She washed, trying to think of something she could wear. She didn't want to put on dirty clothes. She brightened as she thought of Sam's pair of old pants that Dove had pronounced unwearable, the last time she'd been out.

"Patches on patches on patches," Dove had pretended to scold. "You walk on your feet or scoot on your bottom?"

Rowdy rubbed her chin. There ought to be one more wear in them even if they were ragged. She wrapped herself in a quilt and, holding her breath, crept from her corner to Sam's, found the pants and a tattered shirt, slipped back to her own "room" without disturbing Uncle Jim.

His eyes were closed; he was still asleep. She tiptoed to the door and went to hang her sodden garments on the clothesline.

Sam had turned the livestock and chickens out and started back toward the cabin. When he saw the girl, he stopped dead in his tracks.

"You get my clothes off!" he howled.

"Shush, Uncle Jim's asleep."

Without another word, Sam flung himself at her in outrage. Rowdy dropped her soggy clothes and ran. She wasn't afraid to fight, but they'd both land in the mud. . . .

Sam overtook her, jerked her around to face him and began to shake her back and forth. "Get my clothes off!" he yelled again, "or I gonna peel yo' hide!"

He was, she realized, capable of doing just that. Sam didn't get mad often, but when he did, you had better watch out. She wasn't as strong as he, and her head was beginning to feel like it was going to fall off.

"I haven't got any clean clothes!" she screamed at him. The shaking went on. "I—I'll give you my bird nest." His face didn't change. He was very mad. "To keep!" she howled.

The shaking lessened, ceased. She felt her head gingerly, to see if it were still there.

"Your bird nest, for sure?"

"Cross my heart, hope to die, cut my throat if I tell a lie."

Satisfied, Sam released her arms.

Finally, Rowdy got her dress and petticoats pinned to the line. She started back to the house, realized it was getting late. Papa ought to be home.

She had truly forgotten she was wearing britches, when she went into the soddy, but Jim's roar reminded her. "God's sake!" the old man yelled, "what do you think yore up to?"

For an instant she was startled, then alarmed. "Don't get upset, Uncle Jim!" she cried. "It'll make you sick again. I don't have any clean clothes. Besides"—her voice trailed off wistfully—"britches sure are comfortable."

"Comfortable!" Jim snorted, but the effort drained him again. He leaned back, closing his eyes.

Rowdy began supper, but as she worked an uneasy

feeling began to grow in the pit of her stomach. What with the storm, Papa would have been worried about them and would have hurried to get home.

"Wish Papa would get here," she whispered to Sam, who was setting the table.

"He's all right," Sam said stoutly, but his forehead was puckered, and Rowdy knew he was beginning to worry too. The children fixed Uncle Jim a table by his chair, and Rowdy woke him.

"Supper, Uncle Jim."

The old man started and blinked, half awake. "Where's Davey?" Then, realizing what he'd said, corrected himself quickly: "Where's yore papa?"

"Not here yet." Rowdy's voice was studiously casual. "Think I'll ride out a ways and meet him. Sam, you make Uncle Jim behave, y'hear?"

Before either of them could object, she was out the door.

41.

As she galloped west, Rowdy's thoughts were going in two directions. She was sketching out, in her mind, Angus's usual route. Starling, Sweetgum, Mason's Corner, then a straight ride home through the woods.

Simultaneously, she was thinking about Sam's pants, exhilarated by the freedom they gave her. Sensible. No foolishness about riding sidesaddle, or skirts hiking up an inch. No worry about exposing her parts, as Dove had warned her. Besides, britches were easier to iron. Rowdy hated starching and ironing long skirts and the endless petticoats. She hated those sadirons.

Sal had slowed, and although Rowdy's anxiety made her want to push the horse harder, she knew Sal couldn't gallop too long. To the child, it seemed an eternity before they reached Grogan's Woods. And when they finally got there, the woods had never seemed so large. Rowdy could

149

see no path or trail. Papa could be anywhere—that is if he'd gotten this far.

"Sal," she whispered, "what are we going to do?" The horse blew wearily, and Rowdy sat, for a bleak moment, trying to formulate a plan. If you got lost in a woods, she knew, you could start going in circles.

"If I'm facing the sun going in, then it should be at my back when I start the other way," she said aloud. If only the watery sun would stay up long enough.

Evidence of the storm was everywhere. One tree had a charred streak from root to top, where it had been hit by lightning. Branches were thick underfoot. Birds' nests on the ground. Toppled trees.

Dusk began to fall, and Rowdy was frightened. When it got dark, she wouldn't be able to see any landmarks. She could spend the whole night riding aimlessly.

She thought she heard a faint sound and pulled Sal to a stop. Every nerve in her body seemed tensed to catch the sound if it came again. Then Sal lifted her head and neighed. The original sound came again—a nicker so faint, it might have been a whisper of wind.

"Find her, Sal," Rowdy commanded. "Find Beth." Holding her breath, she let the horse have her head. Sal neighed again, and the answering whinny sounded closer.

When she found them, Angus lay, eyes closed, fast against Beth, an enormous tree overlying both. Rowdy's heart seemed to stop. In the murky light Papa looked—dead. She caught her breath and slid from the horse, whispering, "Papa."

Angus didn't respond, but Beth breathed out, struggled to get to her feet, fell back. The tree shifted.

"Oh, Beth, be careful!" Rowdy cried. She went down on her knees beside the man. After what seemed hours, she managed to work the tree free. There was blood on Angus's face, and Rowdy tore a strip from her shirttail to wipe it gently away.

Again Beth moved, and Rowdy turned to put a hand on the horse's withers. "Easy, girl; easy, now." She saw the right foreleg crushed beyond help and felt the hot tears spurt into her eyes. Again the horse tried to stand, and Rowdy cried out in terror, fearful the animal's thrashing would further injure Angus. Rowdy got to her feet, reached for Papa's .45.

"I love you, Beth," she whispered. Tears blurred her

vision. She dashed them away. She cocked the gun, put the muzzle against Beth's head and pulled the trigger.

Then she began to weep in earnest.

Angus opened his eyes to see his daughter standing beside him, holding his gun and crying her eyes out. Momentarily, astonishment kept him from being aware of the pain.

"What're you doing?" His voice was fuzzy.

Rowdy turned. "Her leg was crushed," she sobbed. "I had to shoot her, Papa. Are you—all right?"

"Reckon so." His memory began to return. The storm, the trees slammed about like toothpicks. "I reckon," he repeated a little more strongly and began cautiously to move. His face went even whiter, and he clutched his right shoulder. "May've got bunged up a mite," he said between clenched teeth.

Terror shook the child, but she refused to acknowledge it.

"We've got to get you home, Papa." Her voice trembled. "Do you think if I help, you can get on Ol' Sal?"

"Guess I've got to."

With Rowdy helping, he managed to sit up. The shoulder sent wave after wave of pain riveting through his body, and when he attempted to stand, an equivalent agony made itself felt in his right leg. The world went black, and Angus wavered. Then, digging his teeth into his bottom lip, he countered pain with pain, forced himself to stand.

Rowdy called to Sal, and the horse plodded over. Papa, the little girl saw, was swaying.

"Papa," she shouted, "damn it, don't you dare fall. Get those arms over Sal's back. I'll boost you."

"Don't cuss!" he tried to roar, but it came out a mutter. He attempted to put his arms over the horse's back. The right arm dropped, and he swore.

"Just the left one, then," Rowdy said. "You pull when I push."

It took more than half an hour, and both of them were dripping with sweat, before Angus was finally on the horse.

"Can you lie down, put your head on her mane?" Rowdy asked, but Angus said, "No, this damn shoulder . . ."

"We'll be easy as we can." She took the reins and began to lead the horse carefully. When it appeared Angus would fall off, and she could not rouse him, she was terrified. Stopping Sal, Rowdy put a hand on her father's neck and could breathe again. His pulse was strong. Uncoiling the lariat from the saddle horn, she tied him on securely. "Should have thought of that in the first place," she scolded herself.

It was dark by the time they reached the soddy, and Angus was still unconscious. Sam was outside, watching for them, and helped get the man off the horse and into the house.

Jim was very distressed. Insisting that he felt fine now, he struggled to his feet. When Sam said he'd go for the doctor, the old man agreed. But when Rowdy wanted to help tend her father, he wouldn't hear of it.

"You look plumb tuckered, child." He headed off mutiny by saying hastily that she needn't go to bed; she could sit in the rocker. Sam left, and Rowdy sat down, leaned back, closed her eyes but could still see the flash of the gun, almost feel Angus's suffering when she'd forced him to mount the horse. Slow tears trickled down her cheeks. She put her face in her hands and sobbed bitterly, but without making a sound.

When Angus blearily regained consciousness, Jim dosed him with a liberal slug of white mule. With pain in both the shoulder and leg, Angus wondered vaguely once if there were anyplace he didn't hurt, but thanks to repeated doses of the whiskey, he began to drift in and out of consciousness. Sam returned with Dr. McClung. The young physician made a clucking sound as he explored the shoulder area with cautious fingers.

"This is going to hurt," he warned, and expertly manipulated the arm and the shoulder at the same time but in different directions. There was a slight crunch of bone, a staggering pain and Angus slid off into bottomless darkness. The doctor fashioned a sling.

"With God's help, that ought to do it," he said. "If he starts running a fever, let me know. Now let's see the leg." He folded the cover back, slit the right pants leg. From hip to ankle, there were bruises so ugly, Jim winced and drew back. The leg was swollen, and McClung's swift examination left small imprints on each place he touched. Holding the hip and knee, he moved the leg cautiously; repeated the procedure, holding knee and ankle.

"I don't believe there are any bones broken," he said, "but it's going to take a time for that bruising to heal. I'll leave you some laudanum."

For the first time he noticed Rowdy. His eyebrows shot up. "Boy or girl?" he asked reprovingly.

Miss Rowdy flushed, and glared at him. "Mind your own business," she snapped, bringing a swift reprimand from Uncle Jim.

McClung shook his head and began to gather up his paraphernalia. He left, thinking that children certainly didn't behave now the way he'd had to when he was a kid. He was almost twenty-nine.

42.

It was a week before Rowdy ventured to put on britches again. Angus was able to hobble about a bit, but was grumpy over his confinement. The damn leg seemed to give him more trouble than his shoulder. Sam and Rowdy decided some fish might improve his spirits, and got busy digging worms.

They came back in to fix slices of bread and butter to carry along.

"Just a minute, Sam," Rowdy said, "I want to get my sunbonnet."

She disappeared behind her curtain, came back carrying the bonnet, dressed in Sam's old pants and shirt. The boy's face was caught between disbelief and rage. "It was just for that once—"

Before he could finish, Angus was roaring. "Get out of those clothes!" he shouted.

Rowdy glanced sideways at him. "They're so much more sensible, Papa. Riding a horse, milking, working in the garden, fishing. Don't you see? I'm a lot more—more covered in pants."

Angus's face was brick-red. "Don't argue! Get yourself

back in a dress, young lady, and don't ever let me see you in pants again."

Silently, Jim watched the byplay between the two. Rowdy's eyes grew storm-black; her face was ashen. Hands on hips, she looked her father right in the eye. Angus's lips were set in a straight line.

After a long moment, the girl turned and went behind the curtain. Jim drew a deep breath, let it out noisily. Angus leaned back against the chair, his scowl gradually disappearing.

When Rowdy appeared once more, she was in a dress. "Now you look like Papa's girl," Angus told her.

Rowdy said nothing. She went out the door without looking at either of the men.

When she was safely out of hearing, Angus chuckled. "Knows her own mind."

Jim frowned. "Angus, I think you got more on yore plate than yore going to be able to eat," he said fretfully. "That girl-child is plumb mule stubborn."

"I can handle her," Angus snapped.

But at supper that night, he watched Miss Rowdy sit quietly, eyes downcast, eating not a bite. Jim had made corn bread, her favorite. The sun perch the children had caught were small but tasty. There was polk salad, too.

"Off your feed?" Angus asked, concerned.

She shook her head. "May I be excused?" she asked with elaborate politeness. Angus nodded, and his eyes met Jim's.

"Come here and let Uncle Jim feel yore forehead," the older man said. Rowdy obeyed. "No fever," Jim said. "Stomach sick?"

Rowdy shook her head. "Call me when it's time to do dishes," she said, and went outside. Sam plowed through his meal, but supper was ruined for the two men. It was the children's task to wash up after meals, a job they both hated and got out of as often as possible. Rowdy's biddable reminder to Uncle Jim was unheard of. Angus shifted uneasily.

"Damn shoulder hurts," he complained. This was the first time he'd mentioned it. Jim interpreted the plea correctly.

"She'll be all right," he said. "Give her time to git over the sulks."

Sam finished eating and went outside. Rowdy was sitting on the bench beneath the cottonwood, hands folded demurely in her lap.

"Want to play church?" Sam asked. Rowdy shook her head.

"Sheriff and outlaw?" Again a headshake.

Sam rubbed a bare toe in the dust. "You mad?" he asked.

"No," Rowdy said, "I'm being ladylike."

Sam sniffed. "You're being silly," he corrected, and went off toward the creek. Jim called her in to do dishes, and she did them alone, not demanding Sam's help. When she had finished, she turned up the lamp and sat at the table, doing sums on her slate.

"Learned your multiplication tables yet?" Angus asked.

"Yes, Father."

Angus watched his daughter uneasily. He wanted her to be strong. You needed to be strong-willed to survive. But he didn't want her will directed against him. He hungered for her love, always so freely given, as another man might hunger for power. "Father," she had called him. In a shocked moment, he realized Miss Rowdy was all he had in the world that he loved fiercely and possessively. Three people he had loved. Two of them were dead.

"You understand why you can't wear boys' clothes?" he asked gently, coaxing.

"Yes, Father."

Rage flared in him, the more bitter for being impotent —rage and a kind of fright. You couldn't punish a child for being sweetly biddable. Angus recognized that the sudden gulf between them was all but unbearable to him. But he would not back down. Not on this.

Miss Rowdy sat at the table the next morning and the next evening without touching a bite. The lunch Jim fixed for her came home in the syrup bucket, undisturbed. Even Sam had become infected by the malady of uneasiness that fell over the household.

"You're gonna die if you don't eat," he growled at her.

Rowdy gave him a seraphic smile. "I'm not hungry, Sam."

When the children had left for school on the second day, Rowdy's mush untouched in its bowl, Jim spoke anxiously. "I ain't sure you can outlast her," he said.

Angus snorted. "No kid can get the best of a grown man."

Jim said no more, but both men realized in that moment that they had grown closer than they'd ever been before, in their mutual concern. Angus realized it with a shade of resentment. He thought of his mother and hardened his heart against the older man.

"She'll eat when she gets hungry enough," he finished harshly, and the moment of closeness was shattered.

By that evening, the amethyst eyes, always overlarge in the piquant face, were enormous, with heavy shadows underneath them. The delicate flesh of her face and wrists was transparent, with the blue veining showing beneath the skin. Angus could see Lexie's fragility in her, and his determination weakened.

"Honey, you've got to eat," he said at supper.

Rowdy smiled pensively. "How can I, Father, when I'm not hungry?"

"You've *got* to be hungry," he said. The child shook her head, and Angus looked at Jim as though to implore his help. Jim shrugged. Sam was watching, methodically eating the food heaped on his plate. The contrast between his solid flesh and Rowdy's waiflike thinness was too much for Angus to bear.

"If you had a pair of pants, you could only wear them around here."

"Oh, Papa!" She shot out of her chair and came to cover his face with kisses. "You're the best papa in the whole wide world," she told him. "Besides, Aunt Sarah wouldn't let me wear them to school."

The next time Dove rode out to see Sam, she took one look at the girl and exploded.

"You want to be a damn fool man?" she yelled. "You look plumb disgusting."

"I told her she looked silly, Maman," Sam put in. Rowdy grinned.

"I'm making some velvet ones," she told Dove. "You'll like them better." She and Dove shared a love of the luxurious fabric. Rowdy had laboriously saved the little money she came by, and finally had enough to buy a length of wine-red velvet.

"Velvet!" Dove snorted. "Your Pappy ort to give you a good strappin'. That's what you'd get if you was mine."

Rowdy laughed. "You're even prettier when you're mad," she said. Dove raised her eyes to heaven.

Preoccupied with Rowdy as he had been, Angus had given scant thought to his injuries. With peace restored, he began to chafe at his inactivity. The shoulder appeared to be mending. The swelling had disappeared from the leg, but walking brought torturous pain in the hip.

Angus fretted about the people on his circuit. "They'll think I've deserted them," he growled.

"I could ride out and let them know you're sick," Rowdy offered.

"I'm not sick." Angus snorted. "My leg hurts, that's all. You can't go gallivantin' around the country. It wouldn't be safe or decent."

"I could go with her," Sam volunteered, and Angus all but snarled at him.

"Yore ill-natured as a hornet," Jim said grumpily when the children had gone outside. "Them tykes was tryin' to help."

He racked his brain all day for something to better his son's mood, was half asleep when the answer came. He sat up in bed, planning.

With the children off to school the next morning, he told Angus he needed to ride into Oklahoma Station to take care of some business. "All right if I ride Ol' Sal?" he asked.

"Figuring on coming back?" The question was barbed, as Angus had meant it to be.

Jim flushed, then anger replaced the feeling of guilt. "For a man of God, yore sure full of the devil," he said tartly. And Angus laughed. For a moment, a tenuous thread of intimacy, even of liking, hung between the two.

Angus turned away. "Help yourself," he said.

Outside, Jim headed northeast. He had been horrified when he heard Maggie Cruikshank was breeding horses. Things were pretty bad when women started doing such unseemly things. Still, she was the only one he knew who was in the business of raising horses.

The cottonwoods and native walnut trees were in full leaf. Near the top of an elm, Jim spotted some mistletoe. Mostly, though, his thoughts were on the horse he hoped to get for Angus. Dealing with Maggie Cruikshank, he surmised, was going to be no easy matter. She was a woman with wild ideas. The notion of women *voting* . . . He spat.

He wished he knew someone else to go to. " 'Druther deal with a man every day in the week and twice on Sunday," he muttered. But since she had no man of her own, maybe he could offer to do some work for her—plowing, or something similar.

It was past noon when he found Maggie's place. A couple of dogs big as ponies bounded out to meet him as he opened the gate.

They did not bark but they escorted him, one on either side of the horse, as closely and carefully as though they had been guards shepherding a criminal from one location to another.

Maggie's house was small, built of lumber. The barn was enormous and the corral soundly fenced. Jim had not known exactly what to expect of a woman living by herself. A dugout, maybe. A man could have been proud of Maggie's place.

At the house, Jim called out the customary country greeting, "Hello, the house." There was no answer, and Jim felt the cold sweat begin to trickle down his sides. He didn't like the looks of those dogs at all.

Then he saw the small wiry woman rounding the corner. She wore a sunbonnet, men's gum boots, and her long dress was tucked up around her waist.

" 'Afternoon," she said. Then, with a look at Sal, "You're not figuring on breeding that poor old thing. She'd never carry a colt to term."

Jim's face went red at a woman talking about such things.

"No," he mumbled. "Get those damn dogs away from me, Missus."

"Miss," Maggie corrected. "Come away, Rex. Sukie. Reckon he's harmless."

"I'm Angus Scofield's pa," Jim said.

Maggie's face lit up. The wariness disappeared. "Well,

whyn't you say so, Mr. Scofield?" she demanded. "Light down and sit a spell."

Jim slid to the ground and limped after Maggie as she headed toward the house. At the small porch, smothered in trumpet vine, she stopped. "Sit here," she instructed. "I don't ask men into the house. Folks might talk."

She grinned, and for an instant Jim was reminded of Miss Rowdy. Maggie's mischievous look was similar to hers. He sat down on the steps, thankful to rest. He tired more easily than he used to.

"Coffee?" Maggie asked.

"No, but I could fancy some water."

Maggie disappeared into the house, and Jim decided maybe he should loosen Sal's bellyband, make her comfortable too. The dogs rose as he did. They accompanied him each step as he loosened the girth and watered the horse.

"Damn hounds make me nervous," he complained as Maggie returned.

She chuckled. "You're safe long as I'm around," she told him. "They're good brutes when they know they have to be. Like all males." She handed him the water, and he saw her grin again. Jim felt he should say something sharp in rebuttal, but couldn't think what.

She was a strange one, this woman. Yet there was something about her that made him think over and over again of Miss Rowdy. The word "independent" eluded him. Finally, he consoled himself with the thought that they were both uppity, too big for their britches.

He sighed. He had been supposed to have a way with women when he was younger. It was a long while since he had been stirred sexually. Maybe the stroke had done it to him. But Maggie's self-sufficiency was oddly provocative, though he was well aware that she had no intention of its being so. She was the kind of woman a man would feel almost obligated to dominate.

He sighed again and made his thoughts return to the business at hand. "I come about a horse," he said. "You got any for sellin'?"

Maggie sat down on the top step, smoothing her dress decorously around her ankles. "For riding, or working?"

"Ridin'. Angus's horse got killed in that twister." Then, in the oblique manner of one who wishes to barter: "Fine-lookin' place you got here."

159

"Hm." Thus did Maggie acknowledge the compliment. "Hadn't heard about that." This referred to the news about the preacher. It would have been difficult for a city-bred individual to follow the involuted conversation of the prairie. Neither Jim nor Maggie had any such trouble. "He all right?" she asked.

"Yeah, Angus is comin' along. Shoulder broke, leg banged up some. Gittin' ornery, pinned up so long."

"Maybe Pansy?" Maggie asked, musingly. "She's good and strong. Orion's the sire."

"Yore stallion?"

"One of 'em. Good piece of horseflesh." Maggie might have been communing with herself. "Not too pricey, considering."

Jim moved uneasily. When folks started talking about something not being too pricey, considering, you could bet your bottom dollar it was going to cost an arm and a leg.

"I was thinkin' in terms of maybe doing some work for you," he ventured. Maggie looked him over, and Jim had the uncomfortable feeling that she might have looked at a horse in the same way.

"Don't know I've got need," Maggie said.

"Do yore own plowin' and such?"

"Mostly. Neighbor helps out now and again. Angus needs a good horse for that circuit of his." She took off her sunbonnet and ran her hand through her hair. The heat had made damp curls of the strands that had escaped the tight bun. "Hot for this time of year," she said.

Jim knew when to keep quiet in a trade. He took another sip of water and stared out over the prairie. A hawk circled overhead, and as its shadow swept the farmyard, a hen clucked frantically to her chicks and tucked them under her wing.

"I got a crazy mare out there." Maggie broke the silence. "Belongs to a banker in Guthrie. Wants her bred. She's skittish. Could you manage her while I handle the stallion?"

"Reckon," he muttered without looking at her. Maggie stood up, donned the sunbonnet again.

"Let's go," she said briskly.

Silently, Jim followed her. The mare was shut in the barn, the stallion pacing in the corral. "I tried leaving them together," Maggie explained. "Damn mare went into a convulsion every time the stallion tried to mount her."

160

Jim felt his face getting even redder. Women weren't supposed to curse or use words like "mount." He stared doggedly at the ground.

"Stallion mean?" he asked as they opened the gate.

"No, but this mare's got him a bit upset right now. You stay out here. I'll bring the mare. Back, Sukie, Rex. Get back outside that fence."

The dogs did as they were bid, and Maggie was back in a moment or two with a beautiful sorrel. "First time." Maggie might have been talking to herself. "Probably why she's restive." She handed the rope to Jim. "Figure if we get her in the corner, there, maybe we can work it."

The stallion was already following them, trumpeting. The mare was rolling her eyes. Jim worked her into a corner, and Maggie patted the big stallion. "OK, boy," she said, "we want us a good foal. You just be nice and gentle, now. Don't scare her, you fool!"

The mare was quivering. Jim held the rope tight, allowing no slack. The mare tried to move around, to put the man between herself and Orion. Jim stepped back. He talked quietly to the frightened animal. "It's all right, girl. Just you stand right there. Won't take a minute." He patted her withers.

The stallion trumpeted again, attempted to make the mount. The mare kicked out with her right hind foot and hit the male on his underbelly.

"I'll be switched; never saw the likes of that before." Maggie was screeching with laughter, and in spite of his disapproval of her, Jim found himself laughing too. He felt he was somehow betraying the stallion—males ought to stick together—but he'd never seen anything quite so funny as Orion's obvious bewilderment.

The stallion backed off, pawing the earth. Then, with a mighty heave, he launched himself at the mare, pawed at her until his front feet were up on her back; his enormous organ was outthrust and engorged. Again the mare struggled, flung her head around, trying to nip the interloper. Again Orion attempted to mate, but his member was so stiff, so heavy, he was unable to manipulate it. Expertly, Maggie reached out, lifted, guided it until the two animals were joined.

Jim's jaw sagged. A man might do that if he had to. But a woman? Along with the feeling of stupefaction came an unexpected thrust of sexual desire in his own loins. He felt like a fool. At the same time, he felt a sort of welcoming pride at his maleness. Maybe he wasn't so old after all.

It took a little time for the stallion to deposit his life-giving seed. The mare attempted once more to escape, but when Jim held the rope tight, she planted her legs and stood steady, though the muscles quivered beneath the burnished coat. Finally, the stallion pulled away. Jim loosened the rope and let the mare go. There were beads of perspiration on his upper lip.

"I could go for some of that," he blurted out. "How about you?"

Maggie had started toward the gate, to turn Orion into the pasture. At Jim's words, she paused, head down as though pondering. Thinking he had embarrassed her, Jim felt an unexpected brushing of tenderness. After all, she was a maiden lady. Then Maggie turned and faced him.

"I don't want to," she said calmly, "but I'll hold the horse for you."

She released the stallion, then went to open the yard gate. "Going to stand there all day?" she asked Jim.

Not meeting her eyes, he walked back to where Sal was cropping grass. He felt about as big as a tumblebug, and was sure he'd ruined any chance he might have had for making a deal. It wasn't likely Maggie would even let him on her place again, much less permit him to try to work out the cost of a horse.

He put his foot in the stirrup. The watch fob fell from his pocket as he leaned over, and it dangled before his eyes. The thought came to him that he had a watch to barter. No! It was an inward cry. The watch was his only valuable possession. It was more than a possession. It was a symbol. So long as he had the watch, he wasn't the saddle bum Martha had called him.

A knot pushed itself into his throat, and he swallowed. Maggie had reached the door of her house. He called to her, and his voice squeaked.

She turned. "Yes?"

He could tell nothing from her voice. He supposed she was mad as a wet hen. A bad position from which to start trading. He was at disadvantage. Well, she couldn't do more than say no. He headed back toward the house, reluctantly.

162

"Miz Cruikshank," he said, "I purely do need a horse for Angus. You—you got any need for a man's watch? It's a—good un. Never loses a minute. Case is pure-D gold." He was nervous, talking too much. It wasn't the way to strike a bargain. Sweat trickled down his sides.

Maggie stood hesitantly for a moment, then slowly recrossed the porch. The old man held his breath.

"Angus needs a horse," Maggie said. "And I'm not doing anything Christian. I mean," she explained, brows knitted, "I'm not supporting any missionaries to help convert the heathen. Figured if we took care of our own, they could do the same." Her words conveyed some of her former asperity, and if Jim hadn't been afraid that the sharpness of her tongue might again be directed at him, he might have grinned.

"Reckon I'm owing some," she mused on, "seeing the Almighty's been good as He has to me."

Jim began to take heart. Maybe the old hellcat was going to *give* him the horse. Maggie was far too Yankee for that. "Let me see the watch," she said. And when he had handed it over, she snapped open the case, looked at the dial, opened the back to see the intricate wheels ticking away, pulled out the stem to see that it turned the hands properly.

"It's a good un," Jim repeated with some bitterness.

"I'll take it," Maggie said. "Rest of what the horse is worth is a gift. To Angus, as a man of God."

Suddenly, Jim realized he'd not so much as seen the horse in question. "I got to examine the goods afore it's a deal," he said.

Maggie nodded. "I'll go round her up," she said, and took off for the pasture. When she returned, she was leading a beautiful chestnut. She handed Jim the rope. He pushed the velvet lips apart, looked carefully at her teeth, ran his hands down her legs, paying careful attention to the hocks and fetlocks. Then he lifted each of the legs in turn, to check the condition of the hooves.

It was all for show. Anybody could tell at a glance that the horse was sound as a dollar. He straightened to meet the unmistakable glint of mirth in Maggie's eyes.

"Want her?" the woman asked.

"I reckon." All he really wanted was to get away, never see this female again. Leading the chestnut, Jim walked across the yard, scrambled up on Sal's bony back. Maggie walked out to open the gate for him.

"Nice doing business with you, Mr. Scofield," she said demurely.

44.

At Buffalo Creek, Angus stomped restlessly about in the cabin, wishing the kids were home. Realized with a shock that he was lonely. Even in his most isolated days, as a ranch hand, he'd never felt lonely. Kids strongly affected you. Loving someone made you vulnerable.

He was wondering, too, if Jim would come back. And bring Sal. Of the two, Angus thought sourly, he'd miss the horse more. Then knew it wasn't true. It was another shock. He had grown accustomed to Jim's being there, giving the household a sense of permanence and continuity. He even missed the old man's perpetual chatter. It wasn't affection he felt, he told himself. Not even liking. It was simply that he'd be hard put to take care of the kids if Jim took off again.

Miss Rowdy and Sam arrived punctually from school, hair tossed by the wind, small faces eager and happy. They found joy, Angus thought, in simply being alive.

"Hello, Papa," Miss Rowdy greeted him, giving Angus a kiss. "Where's Uncle Jim?"

Angus felt a pang of something he could not or would not define. "Business somewhere," he said shortly.

The child's face clouded. "And it made you mad?" she asked.

"Not exactly. He's got Ol' Sal, you see, and sometimes, when Uncle Jim takes off, he forgets to come back."

"You mean he's a horse thief?" Sam demanded, wide-eyed. A horse thief was the lowest form of life on the prairies. Far worse than a cattle rustler or bank robber.

Unexpectedly, Angus felt his mood lighten. He laughed and, reaching for the small boy, gave him a hug. Sam squirmed. He had decided, at the age of ten, that he was too grown up for the childishness of kisses and the like. Angus released him.

"No, not a horse thief," he explained. "He . . . he's not very responsible." In his mind, he heard his mother's voice trying to explain to the eight-year-old boy he had been why Pa was gone all the time.

"And a fellow ought to be responsible." Sam had picked up on the unspoken criticism like a ferret after a rat.

Angus nodded. "Everybody should be responsible or people don't trust them."

Sam's brows stitched together. "Is Maman responsible?"

"You bet. When your maman tells you something, you can depend on it."

Sam's brow cleared, and Rowdy, anxious not to be left out, piped up. "I'm a responsible person, aren't I, Papa?"

Angus drew her to him again. "Of course, shitepoke."

They, Sam and Rowdy, knew he used the pet name when they had amused him, but Sam said now, "What is a shitepoke, Uncle Angus?"

"It's an enormous bird which carries off boys and girls who ask too many questions."

Sam looked severe. "You're not being responsible, are you? I mean, that isn't really the truth."

Angus sighed. A very literal child, Sam Dubois. Angus went on to try to define the difference between lying and joking. Sam's face was solemn, and Angus wondered if he'd made it clear. Apparently, there would be no grays in this child's world, only blacks and whites. His mouth twisted wryly. Doubly true, that thought.

"Reckon you're going to have to be a judge, Sam," he said, and could have bitten his tongue off. A Negro judge? "Of course, you wouldn't *want* to be a judge," he said hastily. "Not when you can live on a farm and—and see the—birds, ride horses . . ."

His voice trailed off. There was a glint of puzzlement in the large brown eyes, with their curling lashes, unnaturally clear whites. It was as though the child divined Angus was backtracking, without knowing why. He started to speak again, but Rowdy, always bored when she was not the center of attention, interrupted.

165

"Come on, Sam," she said. "Let's get on our old clothes. I think I know where there's a squirrel nest."

When they headed for their respective corners, Angus pulled out a large handkerchief and mopped his face. At the moment he was almost glad he was gone so much on the circuit. He wondered how Jim managed all the questions.

He did the milking and then began supper, wondering where the hell Jim was. The children played until they could no longer see, then trooped in, starved.

Rowdy set the table, Sam fetched in a pail of water, Angus dished out the food and put it on the table. When grace had been said, Rowdy sat for a moment, chin in her hand. "Why'd they call it johnny cake?" she asked.

"Folks could take it with them to eat on the trail," Angus explained, glad to have his thoughts of Jim interrupted. "At first it was journey cake, and finally that became johnny cake."

Supper over and dishes done, the children studied their sums and some words from their spelling lesson. Angus moped. When bedtime came for the kids, the preacher read them a chapter from Scriptures and heard their prayers.

When both of them were asleep, he stepped out into the fragrant night. Skittering insects made soft brushing sounds among the tree leaves, fireflies twinkled and somewhere a coyote bayed at the moon.

Angus sat down on the bench beneath the cottonwood. He eased his aching leg into a comfortable position and stared bitterly into the darkness. No use expecting Jim now. He was gone, as he had gone so many other times. There wasn't any cure for itching feet, Ma had said.

Angus put his head in his hands. "Oh, Pa," he whispered. "Oh Pa, God damn you, God damn you to hell." Then was horrified at himself. "I didn't mean it, Lord," he cried, lifting his face to the sky. "You know I didn't mean it!"

After a long while, a sour feeling in his belly, he got up and went in.

In bed he lay wide-eyed, unable to sleep. He should have known better than to trust the old man. When he heard the first faint sound of horses' hooves, he sat up in bed.

He heard a horse blow wearily. That had to be Sal. A

few tears burned his eyes. Despite the pain in his hip, he hurriedly swung his feet to the floor, began to pull on his pants.

The door was pulled open, and he heard Jim stumbling about in the dark. "Just a minute and I'll light the lamp," Angus said.

"That you, Davey boy?" The old man's voice sounded near exhaustion.

All at once the black mist of rage swirled up in Angus's brain. His father had stayed out until he was damn good and ready to come home. Thoughtless, as always, of anyone else. "Who'd you expect?" he asked, sarcasm trembling in his voice.

"Well, you, I reckon," the old voice faltered. "I brung you something."

Angus lit the lamp, fitted the chimney into the metal ring, glared at his father.

"Guess it didn't occur to you I might be worrying," he barked. Jim's face fell; his expression was so uncertain, so filled with hurt and sadness, that Angus flushed.

Jim slumped into a chair. "Guess it didn't," he said.

Angus hesitated, at a loss for words. Finally, he said roughly, "Had any grub?"

Jim shook his head. "I ain't hungry. Jest tired."

"Go on to bed," Angus muttered. "I'll take care of Ol' Sal."

He went out into the night again. The moon was high and, together with the millions of stars, furnished enough light for him to see. Sal blew a soft whicker of greeting, and there was another sound. A shifting of feet, a whinny that wasn't Sal's. As Angus's eyes adjusted to the starlight, he saw the chestnut.

"Oh, you beauty," he whispered. "You beautiful, beautiful animal." He put a hand on her neck, and the horse threw up her head, shook it, a blaze of white flashing on her forehead.

Had Jim stolen a horse, for God's sake? They'd be after him with a rope. But of course he hadn't; the old man knew better than that. Maybe he'd found the horse. If that were it, the owner would be combing the countryside to recover such a proud piece of horseflesh. Lord, he thought ruefully, if ever I were going to break the tenth commandment, it'd likely be over a horse like this.

He watered the animals, gave them some oats, turned

them into the pasture and went back to the house. Jim was in bed, his face to the wall.

"Where'd the other horse come from?" Angus asked.

"Traded for it." The words were muffled.

"Traded," Angus echoed. "What'd you have to trade for a horse like that?" He wasn't sarcastic now; he was truly puzzled.

"None of yore damn business," his father snapped. "It's yorn. Go to bed. I'm tuckered out."

Angus wakened early the next morning with a pleasurable feeling. Lord, had he dreamed it? Dressing quickly, he went out into the freshness of the morning, gimped to the pasture.

Sal turned and greeted him with her usual low whinny. Angus stroked her nose. It hadn't been a dream. The new mare was nearby. Pa had said it was his. She was even more beautiful than he had realized last night. The reddish yellow of her coat shimmered. She turned her head, watching him, and he ran a hand down her side. The white of her forehead was her only marking.

"Blaze," he said. "That's a good name for you, girl. And what a beauty you are!"

He gave Sal a swat on the rump, and she took a few sedate turns toward the house. Blaze seemed to take the action as an invitation to frolic. She kicked up her heels and took off at a gallop. Angus watched her, unaware of the grin lighting his face.

He went back to the cabin. "She's been bred," Jim greeted him. He wanted badly to express his pleasure, Angus did, but the long-held resentment against his father warred with the gratitude, tying his tongue.

"Looks like a good animal," he said finally, awkwardly.

"Yeah, I reckon." Jim turned back to the stove.

45.

Angus was still recuperating in mid-June, when school ended. He had consulted the doctor a second time as to why he continued to have trouble with the leg. Dr. Mc-Clung had pushed and probed, said there weren't any broken bones. "Give Nature a chance," he advised.

"Seems like she's sure taking her time about it," Angus grumbled, but, since he could do nothing about it, tried to be patient.

Hot weather had not waited for summer. It was already mercilessly hot, the hard, gritty wind seemed to blow without letup and there was no sign of the sorely needed rain.

It was mid-morning Monday, and already Angus judged the temperature was up past ninety. The field work was in shape for the moment, and the children were picking June peas. Angus eased himself down on the cottonwood bench, reflecting on a conversation he and Jim had had the day before.

They needed more room in the house. Sam and Rowdy had their corners, true, but the two men slept in the open part of the soddy. It was still difficult for Angus to think of Miss Rowdy as anything but an infant. It was Jim who had pointed out that she was getting to be a young lady.

"Not that you and me ain't careful," he had said, "but if Miss Rowdy wants to go to the outhouse at night, she's got to plow right by our bed. Feller kicks the covers off now and again." His voice had trailed away.

"Hm." Long legs extended in front of him, Angus had been wondering how long it would be before he could ride a horse again, without his hip feeling like it was being torn out of the socket. Jim's words finally registered as the old man added, "We need another room."

Angus had begun to give the matter his full attention. "Figured on buying lumber one of these days when I could afford it," he said. "Build a real house. But cash's not exactly plentiful."

"Nothing wrong with the soddy," Jim said stoutly. "I was thinkin' we might cut down some trees, build on a log room." Automatically, he poured coffee for himself and Angus and came to sit across the table, facing his son.

"I can't even fell a damn tree right now," Angus said, fretting.

"I don't mean this minute, boy. Just think on it."

So now, as he watched the kids pick peas, he was thinking on it. It might be a good idea, at that. He realized Miss Rowdy *was* getting to be a young lady. He studied her. In britches and shirt, she was still slim as a boy. The sunbonnet hid her face, but the long pale hair tied in a ponytail reached almost to her waist. She was going to be a beauty, this girl-child of his. Almost as pretty as her mother.

She seemed to feel his eyes on her, glanced up and smiled, the amethyst eyes like enormous violets against the creamy whiteness of her skin. There'd be young men flocking around . . .

Something wrenched at his heart, and he hastily dismissed the thought. That was years and years from now. Sam looked up, saw Rowdy straighten and flex her shoulders.

"Hurry up," he said. "I want to get the chores done and clean up before Maman gets here."

"That's right, this is her day to visit. I'd forgotten."

Sam's snort mingled surprise and indignation. It was as though the girl had said she'd forgotten Christmas.

Angus heard the interchange and rubbed thoughtfully at his chin. He'd never given a great deal of thought to the relationship between Dove and her son. The boy had been so small when he came to stay with them that Angus thought of him in almost the same way as he thought of Rowdy.

And since the child said very little about his mother, Angus would have said Sam considered her as a pretty and pleasant visitor who appeared faithfully once a week to bring goodies and ask both children if they were behaving themselves. She kissed each of them briefly when she arrived and when she left, and Angus had never seen

170

any evidence that Sam wanted, or even thought of having, a closer, warmer relationship with Dove.

But the boy's tone of voice had spoken volumes.

The children finished picking the peas, Rowdy brought them to the cottonwood and she and Angus began to shell them. Sam went inside to wash and put on clean clothes.

"Does Sam ever say much about his mother?" Angus asked.

"No, Papa. Why?"

Jim came out of the soddy, carrying a small crock of golden butter and two half-gallon jars of buttermilk. ". . . put these in the well house; they'll be cool for dinner. Buttermilk and corn bread . . ."

Sam appeared in the doorway in time to hear the old man's words. "Maman's coming today," he cried. "Corn bread and buttermilk, that's not *company* dinner. I could run one of the fryers down and kill it."

Angus's eyes met Jim's. Jim nodded. "All right, Sam," the old man agreed. "You catch us a fryer, and we'll have new peas."

"You don't need to make cookies," Sam told him. "I been saving mine 'til Maman came."

Again the two men exchanged looks, Angus questioning, Jim affirming.

Is he always like this?

Yes, he is.

Angus wondered at his own denseness. There seemed to be so much going on that he didn't see until someone rubbed his nose in it.

The chicken was frying, the peas and polk salad already cooked, Sam's faithfully hoarded cookies on a plate when Dove arrived.

Angus went to help her out of the buggy. "My, you look cool and elegant," he said. Sam reached a skinny arm up to hold her other elbow. Dove grinned.

"Now, that's what I like, a passel of men around. I declare, Samson, you've grown an inch since last week." Watching Sam in light of his newly-acquired knowledge, Angus thought that if the boy had been a puppy, he'd have wriggled with pleasure. As it was, he stubbed his toe in the dirt and said, "Aw."

Dove dropped a kiss on his forehead, looked around for Rowdy and kissed her too. Jim was standing a couple

171

of feet behind them. "Don't I get no kiss?" he complained.

For a minute, Dove's eyes flashed, and Angus held his breath. Unpredictable—you never knew what was going to set her off. He breathed a sigh of relief when she laughed.

"I don't kiss men over ten or under ninety," she said pertly. "You ninety yet?"

Chuckling, Jim shook his head, and they all went in to dinner. After they had eaten and the dishes were cleared, Rowdy was ready to go outside.

"You go on," Sam said. "I'll be along d'rectly."

Dove stretched and yawned. "I declare, Uncle Jim, I get fat as a pig every time I come out here. You sho' do cook up a fine mess of vittles."

Jim flushed with pleasure, and Sam spoke dotingly. "You never get fat, Maman. You're always just right."

Dove rubbed her knuckles against his poll. "You ain't got no kink at all," she said. "Whu'ffo' you been doin', boy? You got some kind of straightener?"

"Naw." He had taken the words as criticism, and said anxiously, "Reckon it'll be kinky when I get bigger."

"It's all right, son," she assured him. "You just leave it the way it is." The boy's liquid brown eyes followed her every move.

Dumb, Angus thought. I've been dumb as Dandy, and blind as a bat. Sam *worships* her. Not that Angus had seen them together too much. He was usually gone when Dove came to visit. But it troubled him now. Sam was already educated better than most whites. And Dove planning to send him east for more education when he was through at Sarah's school . . . no community was going to tolerate an uppity Negro. Unless Dove was planning on his taking over the house. The thought was a sourness inside him.

"Sam," he said, "I need to talk some grown-folks business with your maman. Think you could spare her thirty minutes?"

The radiance faded from Samson's face. He looked to his mother as though hoping the request would be countermanded. Her face was all at once shuttered and inscrutable. The child rose, sighing.

"Guess so," he muttered.

"What's wrong?" Dove asked when he had disappeared.

172

Angus held up a hand. "Now, Dove, don't get mad," he implored. "I'm not meaning to stick my nose into your business."

"Good thing." She had frozen at his words, like a rabbit paralyzed into immobility at the sight of dogs.

"I watched Sam while you-all were talking," Angus went on lamely.

"And?"

"Dove, is it a good idea, educating that boy? I figure you think when he finally goes east, he'll like the treatment he gets there and stay. He won't, Dove. He—he doesn't think the sun can come up in the morning 'til you give it permission. I . . . didn't realize it 'til today."

Dove folded her hands on the table, stared down at them. Angus waited, fearful she was going to explode. When she looked up, there was a glint of tears in her eyes.

"You saying I ought to quit coming out?"

Angus shook his head. "No, Lord, Dove, I don't know exactly what I am saying. Only, I want Sam to be happy, same as I want Miss Rowdy to be happy. And—you know there's not much opportunity . . ." The words petered out.

"Not much opportunity for a nigger," Dove finished bitterly. "That's the truth, for sure."

"Angus didn't want to make you mad," Jim put in.

Dove's face might have been a mask. "I'm not mad," she said. "Leastways, not at you-all." She was silent for a time. Then her eyes squeezed shut, and there were lines in her face that hadn't been there before. "He'll have to stay in the East," she said finally. "He'll get a better shake up there."

"He won't do it, I tell you," Angus repeated. "Not feeling about you like he does."

"Then we'll have to change that, won't we?" she asked, and chills ran down Angus's back.

"I don't believe you can do it," he said.

"Yes, I can do it." There was such savage mockery, and at the same time such resignation, in the statement that Angus winced. He feared to ask her what she had in mind.

"Don't do anything you'll regret," he said finally lamely. And Dove laughed. A laugh as brittle as ice.

"Don't worry about it, preacher man," she said mockingly. "Any fool know a nigger's got no feelin'."

173

46.

At breakfast a couple of mornings later, Jim asked Angus
if he knew Pete Smith's wife was not well.

"Alice?" Angus asked, surprised. "What's wrong with
her? Oh, the new baby here?"

"Yup. A boy. That's the twelfth. But it weren't just the
birthin'. She's taken the childbirth fever. Doc's plumb
worried about her."

"Where do you hear all the news?" Angus asked.

"I asked him that once," Rowdy piped up. "He said if
I'd talk less and listen more, I'd know things too."

"And so you would, miss, so you would," Jim said,
pouring some coffee in his saucer to cool. Then, to Angus:
"I saw Tenny yesterday. Clover's over to the Smiths."

"I ought to go see them," Angus said, but when he
rose, an agonizing spasm of pain reminded him of the
injured hip.

Jim saw him wince and said grimly, "Better take care
of yourself 'til that leg heals."

Angus grimaced, but the hip was kicking up such a row
that he did nothing for the rest of the week and stayed off
it as much as possible. On Friday, Jim rode over to
Tenny's to inquire about Alice and was told she wasn't
any better. If anything, she'd taken a turn for the worse.

Then, on Saturday night, Pete arrived at the soddy,
looking like a wild man. Angus was sitting under the
cottonwood, wondering irritably if he were going to be a
cripple the rest of his life.

"She's goin', Angus!" Pete cried, all but falling off his
horse. "You got to do something. I been readin' the Book.
It says to get the elders, and to pray and to anoint the sick
with oil, and she'll be saved." The words were spilling out
so fast that Angus could scarcely understand them. When
he did, his heart sank.

"That was in those times, Pete," he began, but the little man was tugging at his arm.

"Don't stand there clackin'!" His voice was shrill with hysteria. "Get the elders! Bring some oil! For God's sake, hurry!"

He was up on his horse, racing back toward home, before Angus could catch his breath. Nonplussed, he turned toward the soddy. Jim and the children had come outside at the sound of Pete's voice.

"What is it, Papa?" Rowdy cried. "What's wrong?" But Jim's voice overrode hers. "You got to do something, son."

Angus threw up his hands. "We haven't got any elders. As for oil, all we got is axle grease."

"Elders," Sam said solemnly. "Doesn't that mean folks who're older than kids?" Angus blinked thoughtfully, and Rowdy piped up. "We've got camphorated oil. 'Member you but it on my chest when I had a cold?"

Angus was thoughtful for an instant longer, then went into action. It might not do any good, but maybe it would comfort Pete.

"Jim," he said, "you go round up Tenny and any of the other folks you can reach. Rowdy, you fetch that oil. You and Sam can come with me. Get Blaze up here."

They flew into action as though propelled by slingshots. Angus hurried the children onto Blaze and swung up into the saddle. "Hurry, Jim!" he called and, touching the horse with his heels, took off at a run.

When he reached the Smiths', the children were huddled outside in a forlorn group.

"You gonna pray for Ma?" one of the older boys asked.

"We're all gonna pray for your ma," Angus told him. "God listens to you same as He does to me."

"Then He ain't been listenin' very hard," one of the younger girls said, and burst into tears.

Angus felt unutterably helpless. You could talk about faith as much as you like—what these kids wanted was something tangible. They wanted their ma back on her feet, bustling around the house. He did not tell them that he was holding this session simply because their pa insisted on it.

The prayer of faith, he thought. When it came to direct intercession on the part of the Almighty, Angus's own faith was pretty shaky.

"Give me the camphorated oil," he said to Rowdy.

175

"You kids come on in with me." Pete met him at the door, started to tell the kids to stay outside, but Angus forestalled him.

" 'Til other folks get here, you and those kids get on your knees and start praying," he ordered. At least it would give the man something to do, steady him a bit. Obediently, Pete went down on his knees, right where he was. The younger Smiths clustered in a tight knot around him, along with Sam and Rowdy. Angus went into the sick room. Clover turned from where she stood by the bed. Her face was sad and tired. She nodded without speaking.

"Clover, I'm going to anoint Alice with oil, like the Book says," Angus explained.

"Now you're talking like a priest," she said approvingly. "Has the oil been blessed?"

"Blessed?" Angus was at a loss, then suddenly understood. He bowed his head. "Lord, bless this oil," he prayed, and hoped that took care of the necessities. "Pete asked me to call folks in to pray for Alice," he said as he unstoppered the bottle. The pungent fumes filled the room.

"Never knew a priest to use camphor oil," Clover protested.

"It's all I've got," Angus said. "Reckon if the Lord made one kind of oil, he made all of them."

"I've tried everything the doctor told me and some of my own remedies, bitters 'n such, trying to get the fever down." Clover rubbed her reddened eyes. "She's burning up."

Angus approached the bed, poured a small amount of oil into his hand and began to rub it on the sick woman's forehead. "I anoint thee, my sister, in the name of the Father, Son and Holy Ghost," he said, "and pray that your life may be spared for many additional years."

"Amen," Clover said, and crossed herself. They heard people begin to come into the outer room, heard the soft murmur of prayer as now and then one of them gave voice to his thoughts. In the main, though, the house was hushed. Angus heard the ticking of a clock. Then there was a knock on the sickroom door.

Clover opened it a crack. It was Tenny.

"Pete's boy says his ma is scorched with fever," he said. Angus turned as Clover nodded. "You tried dogwood root?" Tenny whispered.

"Dogwood root," Clover echoed, pinching her lower lip. "Never heard of it. You sure?"

Tenny nodded energetically. "I'm sure. Want me to fetch some?"

His wife drew a deep breath. "It can't hurt," she said. "I've tried everything else. Hurry!"

"Start some water boiling," Tenny ordered, and left. Moments later, above the murmured prayers, Angus heard the tattoo of a horse's hooves. He didn't know much about herbs and roots, but Mrs. Murphy (it was still hard to think of Clover as anything but Mrs. M.) had a wide knowledge of them.

"Hope it's not poison," he said soberly.

"Tenny's no fool when it comes to such as that," the woman said tartly, and bustled off to rake up the fire.

Angus sat down by Alice's bedside. She turned, moaning in her unconsciousness, and he took her hand, hoping that someplace deep within her, she sensed the human contact, the prayers being offered.

He heard more of the settlers arrive and, when Clover whisked back into the sickroom, caught a glimpse of the assemblage. The cabin was full to overflowing. The outside door had been propped open, and in the light that came from the house, he could see others in the yard. Kneeling. Intent. Some lips moved. Some heads were bowed. Some lifted skyward.

Angus felt a fullness in his throat. *Good people!*

Sooner than Angus would have expected, Tenny was back with a huge twisted piece of rootage to which bits of black earth still clung. He stepped cautiously, threading his way among those who knelt, and handed the dogwood to his wife.

"Scrub it, shave off the bark, steep it in hot water. Then give her the tea, little at a time."

"I know how to give someone herb tea, you old fool," she said, but there was a glow of admiration in her eyes that Tenny didn't miss. He grinned sheepishly, and Clover went to make the potion.

She came back presently, carrying a steaming cup and a spoon.

"Now, preacher, you raise her head up a mite. We don't want to scald her, nor strangle her neither." Angus cradled Alice's head in the crook of his arm and held her steady. Clover began to coax her to take the tea.

177

"Come on, now, love," she crooned. "It's good; take it for Clover." She murmured soothingly, in a steady stream, and when Angus lifted his eyebrows, said, "Even when a body's out of her head, sometimes they sense more'n you might think."

A good bit of the tea ran onto the towel Clover had draped under the chin of the unresponsive woman, but some of it went down her throat too. They could see her swallow convulsively. It seemed to Angus that the process took hours, but finally the cup was empty.

"You can put her down now," Mrs. Murphy said, and Angus gently lowered his burden. His arm was cramped, prickling with pins and needles. He rubbed it to bring back the blood flow. Clover was watching the sick woman anxiously.

"All we can do now is wait," she said.

"And pray." The words came out without Angus's volition. Mrs. Murphy nodded. "And pray," she repeated, and sat down on the other side of the bed.

In the outer room, Angus could still hear the occasional murmur. But mainly only the silence, and the monotonous ticking of the clock.

Streaks of coral began to appear in the eastern sky. Noting them, Angus despaired. They had been here all night. He could see no change at all. Alice's breathing was shallow and labored.

"Fight!" he whispered to her. "Alice, fight!" He thought of Pete and the even-dozen children, and tears filled his eyes.

And then Clover spoke, very softly, as though fearful her weariness and her anxiety were playing tricks on her.

"Preacher," she said, "is there—can you see—is her forehead damp?" It was as though she herself were afraid to touch the sick woman for fear it was an illusion. Angus brushed his hand carefully across Alice's brow. His fingers came away wet, and he turned the hand so Clover could see in the lamplight. Their eyes met. There were tears on Clover's cheeks.

"That's it," she whispered; "the fever's broke."

As though the event had given her a newfound strength, she sprang up, brought blankets from a chest, found clean, dry nightclothes. "She'll soak those through in minutes," she explained. "Question now of keeping her dry and warm. You want to step outside, preacher?"

178

Groggily, Angus got to his feet. He was immeasurably tired, yet there was a singing within him. He thought numbly: David must have felt exultant like this when he danced before the Lord.

A crowd of faces lifted to him as he stepped into the other room. Fearful, exhausted, questioning. Pete's face was so filled with terror, Angus wanted to put his arm around the small man to comfort him. Instead, he nodded.

"She's—the fever broke," he said.

There was an instant of dazed silence, and in that interval, Angus noted that three of the younger children had fallen asleep on the floor.

Then a veritable shout went up. "Glory!" a man cried. The two women were laughing and hugging one another. Two of the men were pounding Pete on the back, until Angus feared they would topple him. But it was apparent Pete didn't notice. He came straight to Angus, wrung his hands without words, his face working. "A miracle, preacher," he finally managed to say.

"Well, not exactly a miracle," Angus temporized. "Reckon the Lord used Tenny's knowledge . . ."

"However He wanted to do it, it was a miracle," Pete insisted, and, dropping Angus's hand, went to see if there were anything he could do in the sickroom.

The crowd began to drift away, and Angus was suddenly aware that he was so tired, his legs were trembling. He found Sam and Rowdy, bleary-eyed with fatigue, shook hands with a hundred people, it seemed to him, and, finally having got the kids up on Blaze, swung himself into the saddle.

It was Jim who seemed to appear from nowhere to comment on Angus's ability to move freely. "Leg quit botherin'?" he asked. Angus looked down at the limb in surprise.

After a thoughtful silence, he nodded. "Feels fine," he said, and turned Blaze toward home, wondering.

Months later, in talking with the doctor about the peculiar occurrence, McClung advanced the theory that Angus's hip joint had been minimally dislocated, that when he rode the horse that night, he had been too concerned with Alice to be aware of pain, and the jogging had slipped the joint back into place.

47.

The Organic Act was adopted by the United States government on May 2, 1890, providing for appointment, by the President, of a governor, a secretary and three judges of the territory. It also provided for an elected legislature of two houses and the election of a delegate to the federal Congress.

David A. Harvey was the first elected delegate. In 1892 he introduced a bill in the House of Representatives to make Oklahoma a state. It was defeated. Succeeding delegates continued to introduce similar bills, with the same result.

In 1901, when Rowdy was twelve, the political pot was simmering. Many of the white settlers favored combining Indian Territory and Oklahoma Territory to form a state. A majority of the Indians preferred a separate state.

Interested combines of businessmen had been attempting to have their particular town named the permanent capital since the first territorial legislature met. Guthrie felt it had the edge because it had been named territorial capital by the Organic Act. But Oklahoma City and King Fisher were determined entrants in the race. The political behive of Frisco, near El Reno, kept a low profile, hoping the three larger towns would reach an impasse and it would win as a compromise.

Very little of politics reached into the countryside. The farmers were more interested in the weather and crops than they were in "them city fellers." Angus kept abreast of the political situation as best he could but had little interest in where the capital was to be located. He recognized that the bitter fight was not over which town could best serve the needs of the people, but involved prestige and profit for a relative few.

Nonetheless, when he was home from the circuit, Angus generally made a trip to Oklahoma Station, to catch up on the news. The prairie grapevine could sniff out a romance, know about a birth ten minutes after it happened and tell you who was sick within a radius of thirty miles. Politics were too boring to be passed along.

Angus knew that Vince Turner and several more of his ilk were concerning themselves with the affairs of the territory. That even as early as the first territorial legislative meeting, they had been "commissioned" by various men to act as liaison, see that their town got its share of the political plums.

It was on one of his fact-finding missions, as he called them, that Angus rode into Oklahoma Station one sunny Saturday in May 1901. Ordinarily, Miss Rowdy went with him and loved it. But today the particular madness that affects females in the springtime was upon her.

She had decided to clean house.

Uncle Jim and Sam agreed that they'd like to catch some fish, as soon as they heard her plans. They found their poles, dug worms and headed for the creek. Rowdy sailed into the housework, washing and ironing the new curtains she had laboriously made a few months before, scrubbing the pots and pans with sand to rid them of their smoke-black, polishing the lamp chimneys, filling the bowls with coal oil, scrubbing the wooden floor within an inch of its life, with brush and lye soap.

With everything spotless, she stood, hands on hips, checking every item. The cleaning urge was still strong. Her eyes fell on Angus's battered trunk, shoved into a corner. She had never seen it opened except when Papa got out his long underwear in winter or put them away in spring.

She lifted the lid and clucked in disapproval. Papers and clothes and pictures, a thin dress of sprigged muslin, an ancient horseshoe, all thrown in any which way.

Rowdy sat down on the floor and began to lift out the contents, one by one. The pictures went into a stack; the dress was carefully folded and put at the bottom of the trunk. She knew it must have belonged to her mother, and wondered what she had been like. Papa had told her once that she was her mother's spitting image. She tried to imagine what it would have been like to have a mother but could think of nothing except Dove and Suzette and the other girls.

Still, that was all right. She had Papa.

The papers were a mess. She lifted them into her lap and began to smooth them into a neat pile. There was a deed that, she guessed correctly, meant that Papa owned his quarter section. There was a bill of sale from Joe something that showed Papa had paid ten dollars for a horse.

She picked up a piece of dirty white paper that had been folded, refolded, folded again, and seemed ready to fall to pieces. She opened it, lay it with the other documents, then picked it back up and read it. "Dave Royal," the flyer said. "Wanted for murder. Pequot, Missouri. $200 reward."

A shadow fell across the doorway, and Rowdy looked up. "Safe for a man to come in?" Angus asked.

"Sure," she said. "Papa, why'd you keep this old 'Wanted' circular? Who's Dave Royal?"

Angus's heart lurched. He had always been perfect in the eyes of this child. Though he could not have put it into words, he knew that he circumscribed her world. In a manner of speaking, he was god as well as father.

He hesitated, then said, "I am, Miss Rowdy. Shall I tell you what happened?"

Her face had gone ashen. "You killed a man?" she wailed.

"It wasn't my intention." His mouth was dry. "It—I was drunk." Her eyes never left his face, and he thought inconsequentially that facing judge and jury could never have been this hard. He couldn't trust his voice to offer any more explanation. There was no condemnation in her eyes, but there was disillusionment and a great groping sorrow.

"Maybe I ought to keep this," she said, " 'less you'll let me burn it. It didn't ought to be lying around."

Angus wanted to catch her to him. In her sudden and terrible maturity, he did not dare.

"I don't want it destroyed," he said slowly. "I might sometime need to show—someone what getting likkered up can cause a man to do."

That was a part, but not all, of the truth. The poster was, in a sense, a memento of Lexie, and there were so few things he had that spoke of her. Except this child.

"I'll take care of it, Papa."

"All right."

He went back outdoors. His head was thumping. He

flung himself down beneath the cottonwood; then, too restless to sit, got to his feet and began to walk toward the pasture. Rowdy watched him from the doorway. His head was down, hands clasped behind him.

She did not let the tears fall. She never did let the tears fall over the incident. She swallowed them.

48.

Sarah Holtzworthy had anticipated trouble when she permitted Sam to enroll in her school. For the first several years, though, none developed, possibly because Zeb left all business dealings, both farm and school, to her. And the bargaining she did with the men of the town had earned her the reputation of being hard-nosed.

It was rumored that the wife of one of the ranchers had protested to him about a *Negro* attending school with their little Ellis, and asked him to speak to Sarah.

"You speak to her," was the rancher's curt reply, "and I'll guaran-damn-tee you Ellis will be going to public school."

"She couldn't do that," the wife objected.

"It's her school. She can do anything she pleases."

Until Sam and Rowdy were thirteen, though, no problems came into the open. In that year the J. Harrison Hazelriggs came to Oklahoma Station from Boston. Mr. Hazelrigg, his wife let it be known while they were staying at the Belmont Hotel, was interested in "investments."

"There's simply no opportunity for a moneyed man in Bahston," she murmured in the ear of Mrs. [Banker] Forbes after they'd met at church. "J. Harrison feels the frontier offers so much more *scope*. Though I do find it frightfully primitive."

This was duly reported to Banker Forbes, who'd been permitted to miss church that day because of an impending heavy chest cold. The news wrought a miraculous cure, and Mr. Forbes acompanied his wife to church that evening.

The two couples gravitated toward each other. The Hazelriggs were invited by the Forbeses to partake of a light collation in their home, after services. The repast included fried chicken, sliced ham, potato salad, mounds of bread, butter, pickles, relishes, jellies, lemonade, ice cream and chocolate cake.

At first the Hazelrigg heir, Sterling, and the Forbes' son, Herbert, eyed each other warily. But after each had eaten until his eyes bulged, the two were ordered by their respective parents to go and play. Perforce they became allies.

"Whaddya wanta play?" Herbert asked, only to be met by Sterling's scornful, "Nothin'. They don't want us to hear what they're gonna talk about. Let's listen."

Herbert hesitated. Strangely enough, it was not his parents' displeasure he thought of, but Mrs. Holtzworthy's. She'd skin him alive for such a stunt. On the other hand, if his mother or father caught him, they'd say they didn't know what children were coming to, and later he'd hear them bragging about his being so sharp. But Mrs. Holtzworthy was nowhere around, so Herbert agreed.

At first the adult talk was boring, but the boys' ears pricked up when Mrs. Forbes said, "And of course you'll want Sterling to attend Mrs. Holtzworthy's private school."

Outside the door, Sterling shot an inquiring glance at Herbert and was answered by a vigorous nod.

"Mrs. Holtzworthy is experienced in the more worthwhile qualities?" Mrs. Hazelrigg asked delicately. Mrs. Forbes hesitated, not knowing exactly which qualities the other woman considered more worthwhile. It was Mr. Forbes who answered.

"Mrs. Holtzworthy is the best I've ever seen in teaching the three R's," he said firmly. "She also teaches the kids to mind their manners."

"Oh?" Mrs. Hazelrigg was doubtful. "You—don't mean she—uses corporal punishment to enforce her rules."

Mr. Forbes might have tiptoed around a forthright answer, had he not seen the gleam of approval in the eyes of his male guest. "Paddles their behinds any time they step one inch out of line," he said.

Mrs. Hazelrigg began to fan herself rapidly with a lace

handkerchief. "Oh, dear," she said, "oh, dear me. J. Harrison, I think we really must go."

Sterling and Herbert fled their vantage point, and were playing in Herbert's room when the Hazelriggs called.

Mrs. Forbes had a few pointed remarks to make to her husband after their guests had gone. But if Mrs. Forbes was annoyed, Mrs. Hazelrigg was outraged.

"Walk *ahead* of us, Sterling," she admonished when her son hung back. Dragging his feet, he advanced two or three feet, and Mrs. Forbes said, "Paddle their behinds, indeed. Disgraceful in the presence of ladies. I'm surprised you didn't speak to him, J. Harrison."

"But I did speak to him. I said, 'Good evening.' " J. Harrison was well aware that his wife was a simpleton. Nonetheless, he was fond of her. Or at least, he was fond of her cooking.

"Oh, you," she fumed. "You know I didn't mean speak to him. I meant *speak* to him. And as for striking Sterling, the very thought is abhorrent. He's never been whipped in his life."

"Not for want of needing it, my dear," her husband said placidly. "Now, do be quiet, if you please. I wish to think on a matter proposed by Banker Forbes."

When her husband spoke in that mild manner, it was no time to argue. Lyonette Hazelrigg smouldered in silence. She'd see to it that her son didn't go to that school. That was a certainty.

The next morning, however, it was J. Harrison who was drafted to take Sterling to enroll. Chocolate cake always made Lyonette sick, and she had disposed of three generous slices at the Forbes'. Thus, Monday morning saw her in a darkened room at the hotel, sniffing sal volatile and moaning of the headache that savaged her.

"Sterling must get started in school," she wailed. "Besides, if he stays here, he'll drive me crazy."

So, albeit ungraciously, Hazelrigg bore his son away and enrolled him in Sarah Holtzworthy's school. He paid no attention at all to the dozen or so other children, being anxious to be done with woman business and get on with his own affairs. In the brief time he was at the school, however, he was impressed with Sarah's common sense, and determined his son should attend there, come hell or his wife's temper.

He remained adamant even when his son reported, at

the supper table, that a nigger was a student in the same class. Lyonette, who had recovered from her headache, began to have heart palpitations and had to resort to smelling salts again.

"But Negroes are servants; it says so in the Bible," she said when J. Harrison went ahead eating, ignoring her indisposition.

"That is a fallacy," he said. "We will not discuss it further. The boy stays at Mrs. Holtzworthy's."

Later, when tears, tantrum and threats of her early decline were of no avail, she sank into sullen silence, determined to take the matter into her own hands. She did not quite dare defy her husband by removing Sterling from the school; so obviously, the Negro child would have to go. It was all a matter of *instructing* these simple folks.

Accordingly, the next day she hired a rig and, dressed in her best bombazine, drove to the school. Through the window, Sarah saw her dismount and start toward the school. Since she was acquainted with the other parents, Sarah assumed this must be Mrs. Hazelrigg.

She noted the belligerent set of the woman's shoulders and wondered if it had been decided that Sterling should go to the public school. That would present no problem. She had taken his measurement already, knew it was going to take a good bit of salt to save him.

It was half an hour until closing time, but she dismissed class so she and the woman could talk in private.

The youngsters put away their books and filed out in the orderly manner they had been taught. Once outside, they erupted into the exuberant young animals they were. Whoops and shouts, jostling, running. Mrs. Hazelrigg drew her skirts aside and stalked toward the door, where Sarah stood.

Sterling hung back, smirking, until Mrs. Hazelrigg ordered him to wait in the rig. She glanced with distaste at the lively children.

"Noisy." She sniffed.

Sarah smiled. "Normal," she said.

"I'm Mrs. Hazelrigg."

Inwardly, Sarah bristled at the condescending tone. Outwardly, she remained placid. "I'm Mrs. Holtzworthy," she said. "What can I do for you?"

The woman flushed. "I'd like to come in out of the heat," she snapped.

Sarah stood aside. "Of course, Mrs.—Hazelrigg, wasn't it?"

"Yes. Hazelrigg. My husband is in investments."

Sarah was silent, her face showing only a polite interest. Mrs. Hazelrigg bit her lip. "I realize that this barbaric country is raw and uncultured, but there are certain principles which must be preserved."

"Like freedom of speech, freedom to worship as we choose, freedom from prejudice," Sarah agreed.

"Yes. Well, yes. But of course we must protect ourselves and our progeny from corrupting influence."

"Such as lying, cheating, judging others. I couldn't agree with you more.'

Mrs. Hazelrigg wheezed. Somehow, the conversation wasn't going right. "I am a plainspoken woman, Miss Holtzworthy," she said.

"Mrs. Holtzworthy," Sarah corrected gently. "I believe in plain speaking myself. But you look a bit flustered. Do have a seat. I'll get you a drink."

The woman sat down on one of the wooden benches, her skirts flowing over it.

"A drink would be welcome," she said. "Just a moment." She opened a brocade reticule and fished out a china cup. "If you would use this . . . I understand there is a Negro child attending here. I would not care to drink from the same dipper."

Things had gone so smoothly for so many years, Sarah had quite forgotten that Sam was a different color. A shock of rage whipped through her, so violent, her knees began to tremble.

"Of course." She would not let her voice shake. It came out cello-deep and rusty. "Black germs are infinitely worse than white germs." She filled the cup, brought it back, sat down facing the other woman, watched as she drank.

Mrs. Hazelrigg patted her lips with her handkerchief. I will remain calm, Sarah thought, digging her nails into her palms. I won't give her the satisfaction of quarreling with her. But she was so angered that there was the taste of brass in her mouth.

Mrs. Hazelrigg glared at her. "You are mocking me, Mrs. Holtzworthy. I am not surprised at such a response.

Since you charge a fee, I suppose you would accept even Indian children."

"Certainly. And Catholics and Jews, if they applied."

Mrs. Hazelrigg stood up, put her cup back in the reticule. "I think you will find, as time goes along, that my husband will have an influence in the town."

With great effort, Sarah smiled. "I believe," she said gently, "it would be better if you took your son elsewhere."

Mrs. Hazelrigg's jaw dropped. "You believe . . ." She was stammering, still furious but frightened. Her husband seldom set his foot down. When he did, he was formidable. "I didn't intend . . ." she quavered. "Sterling's father has set his heart . . ." She started fanning herself with the handkerchief. "I do believe I feel heart palpitations . . ."

From beneath lowered lids, she watched Sarah. Sarah's face was pale, but no emotion showed except a polite determination.

Mrs. Hazelrigg's head came up. She felt the red, as a wave of heat moved up from her neck to her face, and put out a hand in supplication. "My husband is most anxious . . . He was impressed by your . . ." She swallowed. "We truly want Sterling to attend . . ." Anxious tears came into her eyes. Sarah sighed.

"He may continue," she said finally, "if you understand fully that I conduct my school as I wish."

"Oh, I do, I do," Mrs. Hazelrigg babbled. "Now, I really must go. So many things to do . . ."

Sarah sat down at her desk after the woman left. She was shaking so hard, she could not stand. She could not remember ever having been so enraged.

49.

The following day, Sarah watched the children carefully, even staying with them outside while they ate lunch. There seemed to be no unusual occurrences. Perhaps she had worried unnecessarily. Nonetheless, she continued a close watch for the next couple of weeks. All remained calm.

Shortly after that, though, in glancing out the window during the noon hour one day, she saw the boys playing Dodge 'em together, the girls jumping rope in another group. All was normal. Sterling Hazelrigg, she noted, was standing under an oak tree, alone. When the ball tossed at the boy in the center of the ring was thrown too hard, it bounced close to Sterling, and he scooped it up.

"Throw it back," one of the boys yelled, but Sterling held on to it.

"Not 'til you tell me why you play with a nigger bastid," he said.

One of the boys, John Morgan, asked curiously, "What's a nigger bastid?"

Sterling grinned and pointed a finger at Sam. "Ma says . . ."

Sarah felt her heart slam against her rib cage, the sickness of rage in the pit of her stomach. Although the lunch hour was but half gone, she snatched up the bell and swung it furiously.

The children scrambled to fall in line. A boy stubbed a bare toe on the stump of a tree, and for the moment all were distracted.

As she began the afternoon's classes, Sarah felt the heavy grief of helplessness. She wondered briefly how Sterling had learned of Sam's difference. Most of the children had forgotten it, if they had ever known.

She could not know that Sterling, intrigued because Sam's skin was slightly duskier than the others, had asked Herbert if the boy were an Indian.

"Nah," Herbert had shrugged, "he's a Negro."

Now that the difference had been made an issue, Sarah thought sadly, it would be like a Wyandotte chick in a hatching of white Leghorns. The white chicks would peck him to death simply because he *was* different.

She'd been a fool.

She tried, that afternoon, to counteract the poison. She talked about each individual being equal in the sight of God. She dwelt eloquently on the fact that each person had a place in God's master plan. She enlarged on the theme that, especially in a frontier country, people had to help one another simply to survive, that there was no room for one person thinking he was better than another.

She talked at length, and the childish faces were serious. When she had done, they sat in silence for a time. It was strong medicine, Sarah thought. Perhaps they were too young for it. But she had to make the effort.

Feet began to shuffle. None of the children looked at one another. Most of them were staring at their hands. Except Sam and Sterling. Sam's eyes were round and brilliant, Sterling's derisive. His mother should be horsewhipped, Sarah thought.

Rowdy's hand went up, and Sarah nodded at her absentmindedly. "My papa says the only good Injun is a dead Injun," Rowdy said.

Oh, Lord, Sarah thought. She was one of the few people who knew the reason for Angus's bitterness toward Indians.

"I suppose we could say the Indians were—savages—in a sense," she began cautiously. "Their customs were, and still are, different from ours. That does not mean that they were wrong, only that they were different."

She prayed silently that Rowdy—Martha—would let it go at that. I should have known better, she thought ruefully as the girl spoke again.

"Papa says Injuns go on the warpath and kill people just for fun. They steal horses, sometimes even little children." The other students moved restively. All of them on the prairie had heard stories of Indian depredations, true or not.

Inspiration came to Sarah. "How many of you have seen an Indian?" she asked. Every child's hand went up. "How many of you have seen an Indian attack anyone?" The hands went down, and the children began to glance around the room. "How many of you have seen an Indian on the warpath? How many of your folks have had a horse stolen by Indians? Or known of a child who was carried off?"

One boy raised a hand. "We lost a bull. Pa thinks probably Injuns stole him."

"But no one saw them?" Sarah questioned gently, and the boy shook his head.

She dropped the discussion there and started the spelling lesson. But Rowdy's—Martha's—face was troubled the whole afternoon. And when school was dismissed, the girl asked Sam to wait outside for her. With a sinking heart, Sarah realized the discussion was not finished.

"Papa didn't make those stories up," Martha said.

"No, of course not, child."

"Then why should we like Injuns?"

Sarah sighed. "Martha, the Indians who killed your grandmother were wrong, dead wrong. Every nationality has its good people and its bad. We white people have bad men, you know. Men who steal and kill."

Martha was silent, amethyst eyes intent on Sarah's face. "You mean they have outlaws too?" she asked. "Like the Dalton Boys and Billy the Kid?"

"That's what I mean," Sarah said, relieved. Sarah had not been told that the killing of Martha Royal was an act of retaliation.

Rowdy was pensive. "That would mean, then, that the Injuns who killed Grandma—well, that doesn't mean all Injuns are bad."

"That's right, dear. Now, you better skedaddle for home before your Uncle Jim starts worrying."

"Yes'm." All of a sudden the child flung her arms around Sarah's waist and hugged her. "You sure are smart," she said and darted toward the door.

50.

For a week or so, Sam was not baited further. Sarah kept a wary eye on the children even when they were outside. And she prayed for wisdom. Would it make Sam more self-conscious if she expelled Sterling? Uncharacteristically, she was ambivalent. If Sterling continued to behave himself, perhaps the whole thing would be forgotten.

She had kept Sterling after school one afternoon and talked with him at some length. The boy had been glib, nodding and smiling and, she knew, meaning not a word of the promises he made her.

Sarah continued her overseeing. At dinner recess one day, she saw the Hazelrigg boy watching Sam, then turn to say something to a couple of the other boys. The three of them sniggered.

Sam was sitting in the shade of a native walnut, reflectively munching on a drumstick. His syrup-can lunch pail was open beside him. He was not a particularly outgoing child, preferring, many times, to be alone, and Sarah had wondered more than once what went on behind that impassive face. Occasionally, he astonished her, coming out of a reverie to ask an unchildlike question. Once he had wanted to know *why* the air expanding after a streak of lightning could cause the noise of thunder.

He did not speak a great deal, but Sarah frequently had the feeling that he was soaking up knowledge like a bee might suck up nectar and store it for honey.

Now, as Sterling and the other boys sidled closer to Sam, she watched apprehensively. She did not want to intervene unless she was forced to. To be dubbed teacher's pet could only bring Sam additional trouble. The Negro child appeared not to notice the boys until they began to circle the tree where he sat. Then he glanced up.

Sterling threw a quick glance toward the school building. Sarah stepped back from the window but could still see. The three boys moved faster, cocked an imaginery gun at Sam, began to chant: "There's a nigger, pull the trigger. BANG! Pull the trigger, kill the nigger. BANG!"

One of them kicked the lunch pail, and it rattled away, cookies and an apple spilling from it. Sam got to his feet. Sarah saw the ineffable sadness in his eyes. Her throat ached. She started for the door.

By now, the other children had noticed the commotion and began to move closer. One of the girls giggled, which incited the boys to bolder action. They began to poke at Sam, prodding him at each repeated "Bang" as they continued to chant.

When she reached the door, Sarah saw outrage and helplessness mirrored on Sam's face. He could not whip three of them, all larger than he, at one time. And there was, perhaps, the almost instinctive knowledge that a Negro who struck a white put himself at risk. Sarah saw him wince when one of the fingers poked him in the back.

She started toward the knot of children, so infuriated, she could not find voice, and in that moment Rowdy rounded the corner of the building at a dead run. Arms flailing, she cut through the group like a knife through butter. She sounded, Sarah was to tell Angus later, like the wrath of God, and looked like the avenging angel.

"Damn you, Sam!" she screamed at him. "Don't let them get away with that!" She swung on Sterling Hazelrigg, caught him on the nose with her fist, and blood spurted.

Momentarily, Sam stood unmoving, then selected his target. He did not flail. He punched. Hard. One of the three boys doubled, clutching his belly. Sterling was holding his nose, screeching. Rowdy kicked Herbert Forbes on the kneecap, and he bent, howling. Before Sarah could reach them, the three tormentors had lost their taste for action and slunk away.

Rowdy was breathing hard. Her eyes blazed, and the silver filigree hair flamed in the sunlight.

"Anyone else want to fight?" she challenged. There were no takers. The crowd began to melt away. "You'd better leave Sam alone," she shouted at the bullies. "He's —he's my brother. Almost."

Sarah felt as though she'd been punched in the stomach herself. Oh, Lord, Angus, that's really going to cause an uproar if it gets repeated at home. She called the children in, put Sterling and Herbert and the third of the trio, Jack Grimes, in front of the class and lectured them all severely.

"Any more teasing or fights," she promised, "and each of you involved will receive a severe thrashing. And you realize that if you get a licking at school, you'll get worse at home." She looked directly at Sterling Hazelrigg. "Anyone stirring up others to fight will be expelled. Their parents will be told the exact reason."

Even the children who had been onlookers squirmed, and Sarah paused long enough for the threat to have its effect. She needed to rebuke Rowdy—Martha—for her unladylike language and scrapping, but there was so much to be straightened out that that would have to wait. She drew a deep breath.

"One other thing we will discuss, class, is Martha saying that Sam is her brother. You understand, of course, that she was not speaking of him as a blood brother." She touched her forehead with a cambric handkerchief, and inspiration came to her. "She was speaking of his being a brother as Jesus spoke of all people being brothers and sisters to Him and to one another."

She tucked the handkerchief back into her sleeve and began the regular afternoon class, hoping that was the end of the matter. But when school was dismissed, she saw Herbert sidle over to Rowdy.

"I didn't know that nigger was your brother," he said.

Rowdy shrugged. "There are a lot of things you don't know," she answered loftily.

Sarah blew out her breath. That remark could only worsen the situation.

Troubled, she put supper together automatically, and when Zeb came in from the field, told him what had happened. Zeb frowned. He folded his gnarled fingers together and, elbows on the table, rested his chin on his hands.

"We better drive out there," he said at last. "Preacher do need to be warned."

When they pulled up at the soddy, Angus came out to greet them. "Howdy, folks," he said. "Come in."

"Thank the Lord you're home," Sarah said as he helped her out of the buggy. The children had been down by the creek but heard the voices and scrambled up the bank.

"Look, Aunt Sarah, I caught a crappie." That was Sam.

"He was using crawdads I caught for bait." That was Rowdy, not to be outdone.

Sarah smiled at them both. "I'm proud of you, working together like that," she praised them. "Now see if you can catch another crappie, or maybe a couple of sun perch. That would be enough for a meal."

"Bet we can," Sam shouted. "Come on, Rowdy."

Sarah sighed as she watched them disappear. "We need to talk to you, Angus," she said, and Zeb shuffled his feet. "Don't think we're tryin' to nose into your business . . ."

"Of course you're not," Angus agreed. "Come on in."

Jim was baking corn pone, and there were cracklings snapping on the back of the range. "Howdy, folks," he greeted them. "I couldn't leave my fixin's."

When the three of them were seated, Sarah began. "You know we both think a lot of you, preacher."

Angus nodded. "Feeling's mutual," he said, and smiled, trying to break the tension.

Sarah's hands were knotted together. She gulped; then the story poured out like a spring thaw. Mrs. Hazelrigg's visit, Sam being taunted, the fight. "Finally"—Sarah flushed—"finally Martha yelled they'd best leave Sam alone, that he was her brother—almost."

Angus gave a great shout of laughter. "Good for her!" he said.

"But don't you see?" Sarah wailed. "People love to gossip—"

"The tongue is a fire, a world of iniquity," Angus quoted, sobering. "I see your point, Sarah, but I don't know what to do about it. I can hardly put an ad in the *Oklahoman*, saying Sam is not my illegitimate son."

"True," Zeb agreed.

"I'll pray on it," Angus told them, tilting his chair back. "Now let's have coffee and leave off worrying."

But in bed that night, he turned the problem over in his mind, more concerned than he'd let on. The people on his circuit meant a great deal to him. He didn't want what little influence he might have, destroyed.

51.

Angus slept badly and was still perturbed when he woke the next morning. He should take some action, but it would be like fighting fog. You could punch it or bat your head against it, but always it closed in again.

He thought of the stacked lumber that he'd gotten in exchange for Blaze's foal. He should start the additional rooms for the cabin, but he was in no mood for painstaking measuring, planning, sawing. He wished there was something to smash.

Maybe he should ride in and see Dove. Hell, he ought to do *something*.

"Need anything from town?" he asked Jim, who was sitting on the cottonwood bench. Jim shook his head.

"If yore gonna take the wagon, I might go along for company."

"I was plannin' to ride Blaze." He was ill-humored,

didn't want to listen to Jim's constant talking. The old man's face fell, but his voice was gentle.

"It's gonna work out all right, son."

Angus raised his eyebrows. The mole began to burn. He rubbed at it. "Did you get direct word?" he asked, saw the old man's face go red. "Sorry," Angus said quickly. "I meant that to be funnin'."

"It's all right." Jim got up and started toward the house.

"What time is it?" Angus called after him, trying to make amends.

Jim paused to look up at the sun. "Ten-thirty, eleven, I'd say."

"Where's your watch?" Angus asked. An almost furtive look came over his father's face.

"It's broke," he said shortly.

"Let me have it; I'll take it in to be fixed."

"Never mind," Jim said. "I'll take it sometime. But thank you, Davey, I take it kindly."

The old man was lying. Angus knew it. He always got flustered when he was lying. But why? Had he lost it, gambled it away? Impossible. He wasn't gone that much from the place. And it was, after all, his watch. He could do as he pleased with it. Nonetheless, Angus was still wondering about the old man's manner as he went to saddle Blaze.

The horse was feisty after a couple of days' rest, and Angus let her have her head. There were times, he thought, when he felt more comfortable on the back of a good horse than anywhere else. It was as though he became one with the animal, with the wind in his face and the sun on his shoulders.

Vaguely, he wondered again what had happened to Jim's watch. Then, with thoughts of the horse in the back of his mind, parts of the puzzle started coming together.

Jim's lengthy absence that day, his gift of Blaze. Angus thought back and was sure he hadn't seen the watch since then. The old buzzard, he thought, and felt his throat tighten. The poor old buzzard.

The animal had to have come from Maggie Cruikshank. She bred the best in the whole territory.

He decided to postpone seeing Dove, pay a visit to Maggie instead.

He found her chasing a sow who'd somehow rooted out

196

of her pen. She was cursing the ungainly animal with every breath she drew. Unlike Pearl, Maggie's swear words were seldom real. But saying her "dagnabs" and "consarns" in an angry tone of voice made them seem like the real thing.

"Come help me get this old fool back where she belongs!" was Maggie's shouted greeting. The sow was waddling in every direction except the right one. And each time the wiry little woman took a step closer to her, the sow snorted and headed elsewhere.

Angus swung off the horse. His long legs scissored past the sow, and the mean little eyes glared at him balefully.

"She'll charge you," Maggie warned, "if she sees a chance."

"Sooooie!" Angus shouted, waving his arms. The hog came to a halt, stoppered between two tormentors. "Gate open?" Angus asked more quietly, and Maggie nodded. He began to advance slowly toward the sow. "Come on, girl," he said, "this way, turn now . . ."

With the hog safely back in her pen, Maggie, slightly winded, thanked him. "A hog is the stupidest animal in the world," she wheezed, " 'less it's a chicken. Neither one of 'em got sense enough to pound sand in a rat hole."

Still grousing, she led the way toward the house and finally remembered the niceties of hospitality. "Come in and sit a spell," she invited. "I made apple dowdy this morning."

"Sounds mighty good," Angus agreed.

Maggie's sideways glance was mischievous. "I don't generally ask men into the house," she said, "but you being a parson, I could say you were taking up an offering."

Angus clicked his tongue. "Tolerable good story," he said. "Want me to ask for a contribution?"

Maggie giggled, sounding like a young girl. "You can ask," she said. "Won't do any good."

She shed her gum boots at the door and padded around, poking up the fire to heat coffee, finding bowls for the pie and bringing thick cream from the pantry.

"Got to build a well house one of these days." She seemed to be thinking aloud rather than inviting conversation, so Angus put his hat on the staghorn rack and sat down at the table. "Need a good cave, too. Put down some eggs in waterglass . . ."

When everything was assembled to her satisfaction, she

197

sat down across the table from Angus and invited him to eat. "Reckon you came to have the mare bred again," she said. "Get a good foal before?"

Angus nodded. "Real beauty. I traded it with a fellow in Oklahoma Station, for a load of lumber. Been needing more house room.

"No, I didn't come to get the mare bred, didn't even think about it," he continued. "But long as I'm here, might be a good idea. What's the going fee?"

"Ten dollars," Maggie said. "Cash."

Angus whistled. "Whew! Reckon I'll have to settle for one of Pete's jacks."

Maggie snorted. "You're going to breed that beautiful piece of horseflesh with a jackass? What do you want with a mule?"

"Poor people have poor ways." Angus's eyes were twinkling as he changed the subject. "What I really came about," he said, "was, did Jim trade you his watch for Blaze . . . the mare?"

Maggie nodded. "For part of the asking price," she corrected. "The rest was a gift, on account of you being a man of God." The words sounded so pious, Angus chuckled.

"Obliged," he said, "but Jim set a store by that watch. I want to buy it back."

"Twenty dollars," Maggie said promptly.

Angus shoved back his empty bowl, stirred his coffee. "Maggie, you know I haven't got that kind of cash. You need any work done, felling trees, wood chopping? Man work. Helping with the harvest . . . ?"

Maggie pursed her lips. "You'll have to excuse me a minute, preacher," she said. "My feet's getting cold." She went into the other room, and Angus felt his lips twitch. Delaying tactics. Think over a deal while the other fellow sweats it out. She was a sharp one, this unclaimed Yankee blessing.

She was wasting her time, though. Cash was always in short supply where he was concerned. Twenty dollars. He gave a little snort. She might as well have said a hundred.

She came back into the room, and he grinned at her. "Figured out how to hornswoggle me? Can't get blood out of a turnip, you know."

Maggie met his grin with one of her own, then scowled ferociously. "Angus, I'll make a deal with you." She pulled a paper from her apron pocket. "Ever hear of Susan B. Anthony?"

"Think I've heard the name but I don't know where."

"She thinks it's time women stopped being second-class citizens. So do I. She thinks women got a right to vote. So do I."

"I remember your speech at the brush arbor," Angus said drily. "The men in my neck of the woods were mad as hops. The women thought you were crazy."

"I know. What I been turning over in my mind is, folks think a heap of you. Way Susan B. Anthony worked, she got up petitions and sent them to the government, in Washington. Women get the vote, they'll put a stop to war. Not to mention the other crimes going on. You know I've been marching up and down in front of the state representatives' meetin' place in Guthrie."

Angus nodded. "Think it helped?" he asked.

"I gave them a petition," Maggie said. "They laughed." Her chin went up. "Folks laughed at Florence Nightingale too. Called her a low woman, everything else they could lay tongue to. She didn't quit. Neither has Susan B. Anthony. She was put in jail when she tried to vote. I'm not quittin' either." Color had come into her cheeks.

"Angus, God made woman to be man's helpmate. The Book never said anything about her being his slave. We had the Civil War to free the blacks. Reckon we're going to have to have another war before women get their rights?"

She was so somber, Angus couldn't resist a bit of teasing. "I heard some women started a town of their own, a ways west of here. Wouldn't let a man put a foot inside it."

"Crackpots," Maggie said tartly. "I'm talking about sensible, responsible women."

"When would women have time to think about politics and such?" Angus asked. " 'Pears to me they've got all they can say grace over now."

Maggie's lips tightened. "They'd make time."

Angus tilted back in his chair, eyes narrowing. "Just what is it you're asking of me?"

"Take this petition with you when you go on the circuit. Explain to folks why women need the vote. Get them to sign it. I'll send it to the federal government."

"Whether I believe in it or not?"

"If you think on it, you'd have to believe it."

Angus picked up his cup, found it empty, put it back down. Maggie went to fetch the coffeepot.

"I'd trade you the watch back for your trouble."

Angus glanced up at her as she refilled his cup. "That's blackmail, Maggie."

The woman chuckled. "Nope, preacher, that's Yankee horse trading."

"I'll have to think on it."

She thrust the paper into his hand. "Take it along," she urged.

"I'm not sure anyone would sign."

"All right." She took the granite coffeepot back to the stove. "You take it and do your best. Whether you get any signatures or not, the watch is yours. Fact, I'll get it for you now."

Still Angus hesitated. His work was preaching. He didn't want anything to interfere with that. He picked up the paper and began to read: "To the Congress of the United States of America: The undersigned persons, being residents of the Territory of Oklahoma, most earnestly petition you to amend the Constitution to grant the women of this country the right to vote."

He looked up. "The Congress can't amend the constitution, Maggie. It has to be voted on by the people."

"I know that, but I figure this might start those dunderheads, up there, thinking about it."

There was more to the petition, and Angus read it through. Still holding it, he got up.

"I'll take it with me," he said. "I'm not sure I'm going to show it to anyone, much less ask them to sign."

The vinegary little woman darted into the other room, came back with Jim's watch. "Here you are, preacher."

Angus shook his head. "Not now, Maggie. Not 'til I make up my mind."

"I insist. Take the watch. I'm that sure you'll see it my way." When he still hesitated, she added, "Might as well breed the mare while you're here. For free."

"You're trying to put me under so much obligation, I can't wriggle out," Angus protested, and, unexpectedly, Maggie's giggle sounded again.

"You're absolutely right, Angus. Now, come on, before common sense makes me change my mind."

52.

Angus was preoccupied as he rode toward home. Jim's watch had been well wrapped and tucked in Angus's saddlebag. Perhaps I shouldn't give it to him until I decide whether I'm going to present the petition, he thought.

But he considered Jim's feeling for the watch. Ma had once said resentfully, "Your pa might trade you and me off, but he'll never turn loose of that watch." That was when Jim had had a chance to trade it for some excellent milk cows and turned down the opportunity.

Angus grimaced, wishing those early memories could be forgotten. He appreciated the care Jim lavished on the children, knew that a home without Jim would have been an impossibility. But there was a barrier between them that he could not breach. The long-standing anger and hurt and disappointment were too firmly entrenched.

On the rare occasions when he felt himself softening toward his father, the memory of an unfulfilled promise or the sadness of his mother's face would flash into Angus's mind, banishing the softness without a trace.

He'd been paying little attention to Blaze, but as his thoughts came back to his surroundings, realized she had circled, as she stopped now and again to snatch a mouthful of grass. They were headed east by north instead of south by west.

"That's what I get for not paying attention," he told her. "We're off course, maybe plumb into Injun land."

As he swung her about, he saw a team and springboard wagon coming toward them at breakneck speed. He thought at first that it was a runaway, but the man handdling the reins seemed in control. Angus wondered who was in such a hurry, and why. Heavy canvas was stretched tightly from side to side over the wagon bed, apparently to protect the load.

Blaze whinnied a greeting, and the bays nickered back.

As the wagon drew closer, Angus saw that Vince Turner was driving. His first impulse was to send Blaze racing in the opposite direction. He rejected the idea. Turner was probably no worse than any other man, he told himself. They'd simply gotten off on the wrong foot with each other. So he reined Blaze to a stop and waited for the wagon's approach.

Turner, who had previously always seemed to want to talk, even if it were only to heckle Angus, appeared today to want nothing so much as to see the last of him. He gave a half-hearted gesture with the whip, then brought it down with a crack, over the horses' backs. The team responded with an extra burst of speed, clouds of dust swirling up behind them.

Turner was up to something! It was obvious from the sudden tension in his body when he recognized Angus, from the backward glances he flicked over his shoulder.

Angus paused another second, then made Blaze wheel and took off in pursuit. Blaze liked nothing better than the chance to run. They caught up with man and team in a matter of minutes.

"Ho, Turner!" Angus shouted. "Ho, the wagon!" Vince shot another glance over his shoulder. His face, Angus saw, was turkey-red. The pupils of his eyes were twice their normal size, the black almost obliterating the strange-colored iris. Man's scared to death, Angus thought. "Ho!" he shouted again.

"Leave be!" Vince shouted back. "In a hurry!" Again, he hit the horses with the whip, and they spurted forward. But few horses in the territory were the equal of Blaze. Angus touched her flanks, and she sped by the team without effort. Angus checked her slightly, shouted, "Whoa!" and grabbed the bridle of the nearest horse. The team skidded to a halt, horses' sides heaving.

"Damn you! What're you doing? Giddup there, you stupid bastards!" Turner raised the whip again. Angus dropped the bridle and grabbed the man's arm. He took the whip, tossed it on the floor. Turner's face was livid.

"I'm in a hurry!" he shrieked, voice squeaking.

"What's the rush?" Angus asked. "Someone dying?"

"Yeah, feller out here in a bad way. I'm takin' him medicine."

"A wagon load?" Angus drawled.

"Picked up a few supplies, groceries and such, while

202

Doc was grinding the pills. Stand aside, preacher. Life-and-death matter."

Angus rubbed thoughtfully at his mole. "I'll go with you; maybe I can help."

"No!" Turner was fighting for control. He grabbed the whip, struck out at Angus.

The tip flicked him high on the right cheek, cut like a knife blade, and he felt blood well into the wound and stream down his face. He reached for his gun. Vince dropped the whip and went for his own holster.

"Don't even think about it." Angus's voice was rusty and low. His .45 was aimed at Vince's breastbone. The man hesitated, then dropped his hands.

"Light down. Let's see what's under that wagon cover," Angus ordered.

"I—jest supplies. What d'ya think I'm carrying?"

"Something you don't want anyone to see." He motioned with the gun, toward the wagon. "Move your shanks."

Turner's face had gone ashen; his shoulders slumped as though the stuffing had been pulled out of him. He got down slowly, loosened the cover, turned it back.

The wagon was crammed with jugs and fruit jars full of colorless liquid.

"Firewater for Injuns," Angus said slowly. "Vince, you're a bigger fool than I thought. You know the law about selling them likker."

The silverfish eyes darted to meet Angus's scowl, looked hastily away, came back. "There's money in it," Turner said shrilly. "I—I'll halve it with you."

In reply, Angus said curtly, "Turn the horses toward Oklahoma Station. We'll pay the marshal a visit."

"Parson," the other man wailed, "I'll give you my word—"

Angus motioned with the gun. "Save your breath."

Turner leaped for the wagon. Angus's finger tightened on the trigger, then loosened again. Firing to frighten Turner would spook the team. In the seconds it took Angus to think, Vince grabbed the reins, brought them down viciously on the horses.

The animals reared in their harness as one, and in the next instant were running at full speed. Turner's hat flew off, his feet went high in the air, the wagon bounced and jolted across the prairie and the horses ran like demons.

Now and again a fruit jar bounced out of the wagon and shattered on the ground.

Angus was tempted to turn his back on the whole business. Even if Turner weren't killed, the wagon was certain to turn over, destroying the evidence. In either event, there'd be nothing to present to the law. Angus sighed in exasperation. Doing what seemed right was a veritable nuisance at times. The death of a skunk like Turner would probably leave the world better off, but Angus didn't quite have the stomach to do it.

He shoved his gun into the holster, started Blaze after the jouncing wagon. By the time he caught up with them again, Vince had lost his grip on the reins, gone on his knees in the wagon bed and was clinging to the seat for dear life. He mouthed something as Angus shot past, but it was lost in the bedlam of pounding hooves, racketing wagon and rattling jars.

"Whoa!" Angus shouted, and reached again for the bridle of the nearer horse. But the bay knew that trick. He tossed his head, out of Angus's reach. Patiently, Angus tried again. Having gone to this much effort, he wasn't going to let the bastard die. Again he reached, and again the horse, eyes rolling wildly, tossed his head.

"All right, Blaze," Angus said, "reckon we got to do it the hard way." He eased the mare even and as close as possible to the runaways, so it seemed almost as if the three horses were running tandem.

"Little closer, old girl," he whispered, poised. Blaze edged fractionally nearer the bay; Angus reached out for the neck collar and sprang. For the space of a heartbeat, he was straddled between the two horses. Then he grasped both neck collar and hame of Turner's horse, pulled himself up and clung. The frantic horse shook his head, trying to rid himself of this new bedevilment. Angus reached for the dragging reins, thinking it was a miracle the horses hadn't gotten entangled in them.

He was able to grasp one; then, finally, the other, and gave a savage tug. His arms were all but jerked out of their sockets, but he held on. The horses reared in midflight, there was a shriek from Turner and the wagon went over in a welter of smashing glass. The horses stopped, covered with sweat and blowing with exhaustion.

Angus swung down cautiously. Ground-hobbling the

team, he turned toward the wagon. Groans and curses were audible, so he supposed sourly that Turner had survived. Straining, he raised a corner of the heavy wagon. Turner glared out at him.

"Reckon yore happy now; you've almost killed me."

Angus ignored him. By unhitching the team and tying the horses' reins to the wagon spokes, he managed to lever the wagon, right side up. Glass shards tinkled. The acrid smell of white lightning stung his nostrils.

Groaning, Turner clambered to his feet. "Feels like you've broke every bone in my body," he whined.

"You'll live," Angus told him, and began to gather up the unbroken containers. "There's enough left for evidence," he grunted.

The marshal at Oklahoma Station was more than happy to take Turner and the rotgut in charge. Some weeks later, Angus heard that Vince had been taken to Arkansas for trial, sentenced and sent to the prison at Leavenworth, Kansas.

53.

The lamp was lit when Angus rode up to his own place, and his heart lifted, as it always did when he got home. He thought again that he had Jim to thank for that. It seemed as if he carried so much bitterness in his heart, though, that he could hardly speak to the old man without saying something to hurt him.

He thought of the watch in his saddlebag and brightened. Maybe it would say what he seemed unable to put into words.

All three members of his family came out to meet him. He dismounted, swung Rowdy up in his arms, pretended to groan.

"You're getting so heavy, I can hardly lift you," he complained. Rowdy nuzzled against his neck, giggling.

"I'm almost all growed up," she agreed.

"Grown," Angus corrected automatically.

"I won, I won!" Sam was so pleased, he was all but dancing. "Rowdy bet me she could slip that 'growed' in without you noticing." He was beside himself with delight. It wasn't often he bested Rowdy. Angus set his daughter back on her feet.

"Aren't you ashamed?" he demanded sternly. "Trying to fool your poor old papa?"

She laughed and grasped his hand. "No, I'm not ashamed. And you're not poor or old."

"I'm not poor, that's for sure, not with that goodly pile of lumber sitting out there. We got to get started on more room, Uncle Jim."

"Any time, son, any time." He sounded so pleased even to be acknowledged, Angus felt his heart move in pity.

"Wait, kids." He disengaged himself. "I brought something for Uncle Jim." He reached into the saddlebag, lifted out the watch, wrapped in rags. "There you are," he said, handing it to the old man.

"Come in the house, where I can see," Jim bade him. Inside, the older man carefully unfolded the material. The chain fell out first, with its bear's-tooth fob. Then the rags fell to the floor as Jim uncovered the watch.

He stood motionless, briefly, as though he couldn't take it in. When he lifted his head, his face was working. "Oh, son," he whispered, and began to cry.

Angus was stunned. It was Sam who moved first, with Rowdy following almost as fast. Both threw their arms around the old man, and Sam turned an indignant face to Angus. "What'd you do to him?" he demanded.

Rowdy was patting Jim, for all the world like a protective mother. "What's wrong, Uncle Jim?"

Then Jim laughed, the sound broke in a hiccoughing sob, and he laughed again. "Nothin', Sam; he didn't do nothin' bad. Nothin's wrong with me, Rowdy girl. I'm . . . just happy."

"You're *crying* because you're happy?" Rowdy asked, and the children exchanged puzzled glances.

54

It was the next day that Dove drove out to visit. Angus had begun to worry again about Miss Rowdy's breezy claim that Sam was her brother. He took care of some of the chores around the farm that Jim couldn't manage, while he attacked the problem the way a dog does a bone.

In midafternoon he finished clearing some underbrush and decided to call it a day. The children had just come from school, and Angus reached the house, as Dove drove up.

"Maman!" Sam climbed into the buggy to throw his arms around his mother. "How long can you stay?"

"Couple of hours," Dove said offhandedly. "Want to help me out of this contraption?"

"Yes'm," and then: "Wish you could stay all the time."

Dove didn't reply, but Angus saw the suspicious brilliance of her eyes and grieved for her.

The five of them sat in the shade of the cottonwood, talking.

"Heard we're gonna be a state before long," Dove told them. "Us and the Indian Territory combined."

"Yeah, we need those Injuns," Angus said.

Dove shrugged. "It was their land first," she reminded him. Angus snorted.

They had some cookies and grape juice and gabbed awhile longer before Angus told the children he and Dove had some grown-folks business to discuss. The kids took off reluctantly, dragging their feet.

"Dove," Angus began when they were out of earshot. Dove didn't answer. He saw that she was watching Sam; her fingers were intertwined so tightly, the knuckles shone white. "Dove," he repeated gently.

She turned back to him. "You know that kid is the only thing in the world that means anything to me," she said harshly. Angus nodded. It was a terrible thing to see a naked human soul.

"Dammit," Dove whispered helplessly. "Oh, God damn everything in this whole rotten world."

"Dove, don't!" he said, putting his hand on her arm. She jerked away from his touch, swallowed with difficulty, turned to face him.

Jim had slipped soundlessly away.

Angus groped for words. "I—don't know whether you heard what happened at school."

"You mean de white folks going to school wid a nigger? I thought that was settled long ago."

"Dove," he said helplessly. "Don't call him a nigger. Don't keep beating yourself over the head."

"I have to keep reminding myself to 'remember my place,'" Dove said angrily. "When I see how some of de white ge'mmun act at my house, it's hard to 'member they're better'n me."

"They aren't better than you." Why did they always get off into these pointless side discussions? he wondered.

Dove laughed, the sound as sharp as a straightedge razor. "I know they're not better. You know they're not better. Maybe even God knows they're not better. But if He does, it's a secret twixt the three of us."

Angus moved uncomfortably. "You're better off than if you'd been born fifty years ago," he began, realized that was scant comfort and continued lamely, "Someday . . ."

Dove's grimace was eloquent. "Leave it be, Angus. You didn't want to talk about the black man's lot in a white man's world. So what in the hell did you want to talk about? Get to the point."

He told her. About Rowdy's words and the havoc they were bound to cause. "I don't know that anything can be done about it," he finished. "But I figured you ought to know. I know you don't . . . you're not . . ." he said, floundering.

"I'm not a prostitute, and Sam ain't the by-blow of a one-night stand?" Her lips twisted. "I'm just a madam, is that what you're trying to say?"

"I don't know," Angus confessed. "I *am* concerned about you, but I'm also concerned about my—my ministry. What little influence I might have." He knew his ears were beet-red, and the mole was burning. He rubbed it roughly, could never remember feeling so discomfited. "Thought you ought to know," he repeated.

"Do you want me to take Sam home?"

"Oh, Lord, no, that would just stir up more talk. Besides, I don't want Sam at your house any more than I want Rowdy there."

Dove was making formless marks in the dust with her foot. "I could send him away, I guess." She looked up, and tears trembled on her lashes. "I'm going to send him away sometime, Angus. You know that. He's light enough to pass. I'll send him to one of those fancy eastern schools, and he'll be somebody. He ain't gonna clean privies for a living." There was a decisiveness in her voice that was all the more chilling for the deadly calm with which she spoke.

He wanted to take her in his arms and comfort her as a father would a child, but he dared not touch her. She was sodden with grief, ready to crumble at a touch.

He had no sexual feeling for Dove, but he had tremendous respect for her, and, knowing the depths of her bitterness, great pity.

"No need to do anything hasty," he temporized. "It'll be years . . ."

Dove brooded a time longer, then changed the subject. "I can take care of the immediate problem," she said.

Momentarily, Angus was lost. "Oh," he said, "you mean the brother business? How?"

Her face was still somber, but her voice held the wicked sparkle that meant she was up to devilment. "Sorry," she said, "can't tell you. You'd never approve."

Angus was concerned. "Don't do anything that will harm *you*," he urged.

Dove rose like a lazy cat getting to its feet. "No sirree, Bob, preacher. Ah ain't nevah gonna do nothin' whut will harm this li'l ol' black hide."

It was pure insolence now, black against white, and he had the swift desire to slap her.

Her dimple flashed as though she could read his thoughts. "Well, I ain't dull, preacher. You do purely appreciate that?"

"Let's call the children," he muttered.

In bed that night, he lay sleepless. He badly needed to get back to the circuit. People would think he'd died or

209

deserted them. The business about Dove needed to be cleared up, though. If ugly rumors had started circulating about Rowdy's "brother," Angus might not have any circuit to go back to. He was reluctant to leave, with the issue still dangling.

Jim groaned in his sleep, and Angus's thoughts turned to him. The old man had become as enduring a part of his adult life as he had been absent in his childhood.

"Lord," he prayed simply, "I really want to be rid of the bitterness toward him. But I don't know how to change. I plumb just don't know how."

At last he slept.

55.

It seemed to Angus that he had no more than closed his eyes, when he heard the rumble of wagon wheels outside. He sat up in bed, heard a second wagon pull up and what sounded like the hoofbeats of a saddle horse. Groggily, he noted the first light of dawn was beginning to thin the darkness.

He slid silently out of bed and pulled on his britches. Barefoot, he padded to the door and opened it. The exquisite coolness of the morning breeze touched his face as he went outside.

"Ho, preacher!" a man called, and, jumping down from the wagon, went around to help his plump wife descend.

"Brother Angus"—she started talking soon as she hit the ground—"Brother Angus, I told this fool man to let you know we was comin'. But he would have it we was to surprise you." She was lifting a basket carefully out of the back of the wagon. Angus went to help her.

"Well, he succeeded," Angus admitted, and saw they were all grinning like a bunch of Cheshire cats. The man on horseback climbed down, unsaddled the roan and went to open the pasture gate. The people in the second wagon were getting out—the Pritchards and their three oldest boys. Another wagon rolled up. The Lunsdorfs.

"Howdy," Angus said to all in general and none in particular, wondering what in God's green earth was going on. Maybe they'd already heard about the "brother" business and decided they didn't want him as their preacher anymore. But—everyone seemed in a festive mood. The Pritchard boys were pulling tools out of the back of the wagon. Saws, hammers, pliers, a bucket of nails.

Another wagon drove up and stopped, two more men on horseback. One of them opened his saddlebag to disclose fruit jars. "My missus is poorly," he explained, "but she made me bring apples and pickles."

Angus stood wordless, at a complete loss to understand what was happening. The door of the cabin opened, and Rowdy, hair still in tangles, came to put her hand in his. "What is it, Papa? Why is everybody here?"

Then, a young man on an enormous white horse galloped up and pulled his mount to a stop. Still in the saddle, he called out, "Ho, the house. Ho, the preacher. We figured you was having to stay home to build your new rooms, so we come to help." He swung out of the saddle, beaming, proud he'd been named to speak for the assemblage, and came to shake Angus's hand. But his eyes were on Rowdy.

"Mornin', miss." He was taking in everything. The unladylike britches, the pale hair, the budding breasts, the amethyst eyes. Angus's heart sank. This was the Benson boy. He was—what, sixteen, seventeen? It was as though he couldn't take his eyes off Rowdy. She's a little girl, Angus wanted to shout at him. Don't look at her like that!

For her part, Rowdy seemed either unaware or disinterested. "Morning," she responded. "Papa, they're going to build the rest of our cabin?"

"Hank forgot the rest of his speech." A man laughed. "We're gonna have a house-raisin' so's you can get back to the circuit. Have it done, come evening.'"

Reassured that Rowdy didn't share the Benson boy's interest, Angus finally took in what was being said and felt his throat tighten. He tried to speak, but no sound came forth. Sam and Jim were dressed and outside by now, wide-eyed and curious.

"People . . ." Angus gulped, and someone in the back of the crowd—there must have been thirty people by this

211

time—called out, "Never seen you at a loss for words before, preacher." Laughter rippled through the group, and Angus joined in.

"Let's get busy," one of the women suggested. "Preacher, you got a plan drawed out, or you want both rooms the same size? And how far out this way? You got a measuring stick?"

Another woman said severely, "Brother Angus, you'd best get some shoes on 'fore you take your death. Children, you unload them wagons and put the food inside."

By the time all had arrived, there were at least fifty people. The Scofield table groaned under the weight of all the food. Angus put on his shoes and socks as though he were in a daze. These are your people, Lord, he thought. Don't let me disappoint them.

They worked through the long morning. Pete and Tenny showed up about noon, grousing because they hadn't heard about the house-raising sooner.

Everyone stopped when the sun was directly overhead, ate to repletion, rested, chatted a bit, then got back to work. By the time the sun was streaking the western sky red and violet and blue and orange, the two rooms were completed. The large parlor and the smaller one, which would be Rowdy's.

"Yore my partner for the first set," Angus heard the Benson boy tell Rowdy.

"What set?" Rowdy asked blankly, and Angus grinned to himself.

He was not surprised when one of the men produced a fiddle from his wagon and struck up a tune; another took up a stance as the caller. A square dance always followed a house- or barn-raising.

"Choose your partners!" the caller boomed, and the Benson boy materialized beside Rowdy as though by magic. He took her hand. Angus moved closer to them.

"Get someone else," Rowdy was saying. "I don't know how to dance."

"I'll teach you. Reckon I've taught half the girls in the countryside."

Rowdy shrugged. "It's your own fault if your toes get stepped on," Angus heard her say, then Mrs. Lunsdorf came to claim the preacher for the first square and the dance began.

Chicken in the bread box, peckin' out dough.
Mama, will the mare go? No, child, no.
Swing your partner and do-si-do.

Angus dipped and whirled, swung first one partner, then another. One of them chuckled. "That Hank Benson's got no eyes for anyone 'cept your girl. Look at that jig dance he's doin' all by hisself."

The square ended, and Rowdy went to sit beside Sam, who had been looking on. "That was fun, Papa," she said as Angus joined them.

Angus had no chance to answer. As though she were a magnet, Rowdy was suddenly surrounded by a cluster of young men. If they were put off by the britches, they gave no sign of it. Rowdy's eyes were dancing as they clamored for the next dance, the one after that.

The music started again, and Rowdy stepped out on the floor with one of the Pritchards. Dancing was second nature to Angus, but as he went automatically through the steps, his thoughts were on the girl-child who seemed suddenly to have become a young lady. If appearances were any indication, she was having the time of her life. Her face was sparkling, her hair bounced and she might have been dancing all her life, as she followed some of the more intricate steps.

Inwardly, he groaned. She was still a *baby*, just turned thirteen.

When the Benson boy claimed her a second time, Angus sat out the square to watch them. The boy was smitten. The signs were unmistakable. Holding her a little tighter than he should have, watching her lively face as though he were mesmerized. People married young in this frontier country. Angus had performed a service or two himself, in which the boys were no older than Hank Benson. The thought left a sour taste in his mouth.

The evening ended early. It had been a long day. Angus tried to say a few words to express his appreciation, but his throat knotted and his eyes misted. "Darn it all," he croaked finally, "th—thank you."

"Yore welcome!" "Hurry back to the circuit!" "It pleasured us!" All answers were called over their shoulders as people left. Only Hank Benson lingered.

"Could I talk to you, preacher?" he asked, and Angus caught the odor of sour mash on his breath.

"What is it, Hank?"

"Let's step outside," the boy muttered, flushing as he saw Rowdy glance in their direction.

"All right."

But once outside, he seemed to have trouble finding his tongue. They walked a dozen steps or so before he drew a deep breath and blurted out, "I'd like to call on yore girl."

"She's only thirteen," Angus protested.

"I'm only sixteen, but reckon I'm almost a man. I can keep up with any of 'em in the field. Yore girl, well, she ain't growed up, but get her into skirts 'stead of them britches, reckon she could more than hold her own."

Angus felt a coldness trickle in around his heart. He supposed the boy was right. But courting, serious courting, meant Rowdy would have a proposal soon. That wasn't what Angus wanted for his child—backbreaking work and childbearing to make her old before she'd had time to be young.

He hesitated, praying for wisdom. Telling himself not to be too possessive. He wanted her to have a good life, a life with a man she loved. But not yet, Lord, not yet.

"What does Miss Rowdy think about you calling on her?" he asked slowly.

"I ain't mentioned it to her yet, preacher, but if you don't mind, I'd shore like to."

Angus cautioned himself not to be upset about the sour mash. He supposed all the boys took a nip now and then to assert their manhood.

"You can ask," he said finally.

Hank Benson gave an exuberant "Yippee!" and darted back into the house. "Miss Rowdy," Angus heard him call, "would you step outside a minute?"

Rowdy had been helping Sam move the table and chairs back where they belonged. She put a chair down and turned around. "What for?" she asked.

Angus, who had followed Hank inside, saw him flush.

"Want to talk to you." The tone was somewhere between a boast and a supplication. It would appear, Angus thought drily, that the boy was accustomed to girls acting more enthusiastic. He was a good-looking youngster, the older man realized with something of a shock. Curly black hair cropped short, eyes the blue of a robin's egg, broad shoulders and the air of bursting vitality shared by the young of so many animals.

"Back in a minute, Sam," Rowdy said, and walked across the room and out the door without looking at any of them. Hank followed, pulled the door to. But it was less than five minutes before the girl came back in. Her face was rose-pink.

"What'd he want?" Sam asked.

"Nothing," Rowdy said shortly. "He's silly."

Later, when they were alone and Angus pressed the matter, he found Hank had told her she would be *his* girl, and that she wasn't to be dancing with other boys.

"I purely would love to go dancing," she wailed. "But no dumb boy is going to boss me around."

Angus said a humble word of thanks.

56.

At the big white house southwest of Oklahoma Station, Dove lost no time in putting her plan into operation. She wrote two short notes, sealed them in envelopes and hailed a youngster who was passing by.

Before school began, they were hand delivered at the homes of their respective designees, Banker Forbes and Mr. J. Harrison Hazelrigg. The notes were identical. They asked that the recipient call on Miss Dove Dubois as soon as convenient, on a matter of importance.

Mr. Forbes turned such an alarming color that his lady asked what was wrong and was snarled at for her trouble. Mr. Hazelrigg was at table, enjoying a breakfast of smoked ham, eggs, biscuits, sorghum, honey, preserves, coffee and apple pie.

Mrs. Hazelrigg sat at the other end of the table and thought how unfair it was. He could eat like a horse and stay thin as a rail, whereas if she so much as nibbled, her waistline expanded another inch. Their heir sat between them, picking at his food and kicking the chair leg.

215

"Sterling, dear, do stop that," Mrs. Hazelrigg murmured to her son, who ignored her. The hired girl brought the note to Mr. Hazelrigg.

"Excuse me," he said in the general direction of his family. (Dear J. Harrison never forgets his manners, Mrs. Hazelrigg had been heard to observe.)

He read the note without a change of expression.

"What'd you get?" Sterling asked. "Lemme see." He reached out a hand, which his father ignored. His mind was working. Damn and blast the woman, what was she up to? If she thought she could blackmail him, she'd find out differently. He'd have her run out of the community, the house closed. Though Lord knew he'd miss that one little piece of sugar candy. Lying with his wife was somewhat like lying with a lump of damp dough.

"What'd you get?" Sterling repeated, and finally got his father's attention.

"Sit up, quit kicking that chair, or leave the table," his sire barked. The boy got up.

"J. Harrison," Mrs. Hazelrigg wailed, "he's scarcely eaten a bite."

The youth shot a malicious grin at his father. Generally, he got his own way because Pa didn't care enough to argue. When Pa did put his foot down, though, Sterling knew he'd better obey. He gritted his teeth as his father rose. Judging from the look on Pa's face, this was one of those times.

"Then let him go hungry," Mr. Hazelrigg said. "And after this, if he doesn't eat at mealtime, he is to do without. No more begging and petting and special dishes."

Lyonette reached for her hankerchief, pressed it to her eyes. Sterling swaggered off toward his room. He was, as a matter of fact, hungry, but he'd get something after the old man left the house.

J. Harrison seemed to read his son's mind. "He is not to have one morsel of food, not a cookie or milk or an apple, until lunch time. Furthermore, all between-meal eating is to be stopped, effective immediately. Every time I see him, he's got his mouth stuffed."

Lyonette whimpered, but knew better than to argue.

Both Mr. Forbes and Mr. Hazelrigg found they had business that took them out into the country that morning. Mr. Forbes was already seated in Dove's parlor when Mr. Hazelrigg arrived. Mr. Forbes had blustered and

216

demanded an explanation, but had been told chillingly to wait for another guest. Meantime, a cup of chicory coffee had been set before him.

He wished he dared ask for some of the woman's excellent brandy, but her face was so grim, he hesitated even to speak. He gave a sigh of relief when Mr. Hazelrigg appeared.

"What's this all about?" Mr. Hazelrigg's voice was crisp. Mr. Forbes silently applauded. That was the tack to take. He'd be businesslike and unflustered himself, next time he spoke to the woman.

"A small matter of business," Dove answered. "I believe you two gentlemen know each other." Mr. Forbes's nod was sheepish. Mr. Hazelrigg glowered.

"Sit down, Mr. Hazelrigg," Dove snapped, and herself sat primly on the edge of a red velvet chair. J. Harrison hesitated, but when the blasted woman showed no sign of speaking, finally sat, putting his fingers together in the shape of a steeple.

"Mr. Angus Scofield's daughter made a remark at school the other day, which could be misinterpreted. She said that my son was her brother, almost. Your sons were among those who heard her. For myself, I don't care. But Mr. Scofield is a circuit rider. I don't want to see his ministry destroyed."

She paused, giving them time to reflect, then went on. "You all know that gossip spreads like wildfire. A word here, an eyebrow lifted there, and the man's reputation would be in shreds. You gentlemen being leaders in the community, I thought you might be able to help with this problem."

The last words held such an appealing helplessness that Mr. Forbes's chest swelled, and he said, "Of course, my dear, of course." Mr. Hazelrigg permitted himself a slight grin and shook his head admiringly.

"You're a very clever young woman," he said. "You know we could have this place shut up."

Dove's dimple flashed. "There's not another House in the Territory," she said. "Life would surely be dull without us, wouldn't it?"

This time Mr. Hazelrigg laughed out loud. "Be damned if I ever want any business dealings with you. All right. Forbes and I will take care of the matter. Just to keep the record straight, is Sam the reverend's boy?"

"No!" Dove snapped. "Not that it's any of your business. Now, may I offer you both a brandy?"

The two men went directly back to their respective homes. Hazelrigg found his wife in their bedroom, frowning at some dresses she'd pulled from the closet. Her eyes widened when she saw him.

"Why J. Harrison . . ." Then she noted the scowl on his face and hastily put clothing out of her mind. "What's wrong?" she faltered.

Hazelrigg ignored the question. "Lyonette," he said with ominous gentleness, "do you enjoy having hired help?"

"H—hired help? Yes, yes of course I do. W—why?"

"I thought perhaps, with so little to do, you had too much idle time. Time with nothing better to do than spread vicious gossip."

Lyonette felt her knees begin to tremble. She put a hand to her heart and sat down on the bed.

"G—gossip? I don't understand."

"One of my friends tells me you have intimated the son of a colored woman here in town was fathered by a white man."

Lyonette paled. "S—some farmer . . ."

J. Harrison raised his eyebrows. "That farmer, my dear"—his voice was almost frighteningly gentle now—"is a circuit rider, and one of the most respected men in the territory. The boy is not his, and it is quite possible I am going to lose an important business deal because of your tittle-tattle. It occurred to me that if we dismissed the hired girl, you'd have less idle time."

"I'm not strong, you know I can't . . . I only mentioned it to Grace Forbes . . . that is, she . . ."

It was true. She had been hoarding the juicy tidbit until the next meeting of the Elocution and Poetry Club.

The man's face was expressionless. "I would suggest you call on Mrs. Forbes at once and set the matter straight."

"I will, J. Harrison. She was the one who . . . Y—you know I'm not one to talk . . ."

J. Harrison permitted himself a tight grin, and his wife colored.

At the Forbes home, the banker was faring rather worse. His good wife was on her knees, dusting the underside of the piano, when he arrived. She looked up and greeted him with: "I declare, help gets more shiftless every day. Look at this dust cloth, after she said she'd done the parlor."

"At least you have a hired girl," her husband reminded her. His palms were damp, and he was hoping his words would remind her of the advantages she had. Instead, she peered up at him in suspicion.

"What have you been up to?"

"Been up to? I—don't know what you mean. Why should I be up to something?" He was stammering and sweating.

She got to her feet. "I can tell when you have a guilty conscience. You haven't been taking money at the bank?"

"Grace!" he cried, genuinely outraged.

She frowned, thinking, remembering some of the things he'd wanted to do in the bedroom, like wanting her to take off her nightgown . . . leaving the lamp burning. She flushed at the thought, and, seeing the hangdog expression on his face, suspicion blossomed into certainty.

"You've been to that House," she accused him, "and someone saw you."

"No one saw me—"

His wife burst into tears. "How could you, Howard?" she sobbed. "I've never refused you."

A sudden and unexpected anger surprised the truth out of Banker Forbes. "You haven't refused," he cried, "but you act like a martyr being dragged to the stake. Dove's girls, well, they're *fun!*"

His wife wailed afresh.

The man sat down on the piano stool. "Grace," he said, his voice tight, "since you know the truth, I don't have to tell you what it could do to the bank if people knew I went to a bawdy house."

She shook her head without speaking, and he went on.

"D—Dove Dubois tells me there's . . . that she's heard someone said her—her boy was fathered by Angus Scofield."

Grace dropped her hands from her face in astonishment. Her eyes were red and, for just an instant, avid. "Was he?"

Forbes swore at her, something he'd never done before. "It's none of your business!" he shouted. "Or mine!

But if that story gets around, Miss Dubois is going to talk. Name names of her—her clients."

Grace thought of the hired girl and put her finger to her lips. In a broken whisper, she said, "Oh, no, Howard. I could never hold my head up again!"

"You and Lyonette Hazelrigg are leaders among the women. You can put a stop to it before it ruins all of us."

Grace fumbled for a handkerchief, found none and thanked her husband when he handed her his.

"All right, Howard," she said. Then, when his expression didn't change, she crept closer to him, put her head on his shoulder. "I'll try to be different, too, about—you know . . ."

"Sex?" he asked bluntly, and though her face flamed, she nodded.

Howard patted her shoulder and hoped she meant it.

Later, the two women talked together and decided on a course of action, should anyone else bring up the matter. At the next quilting session, Mrs. Grimes said hesitantly that she wasn't one to talk but had anyone heard that—that colored boy's father was . . . She glanced up from threading a needle, saw Grace's riveting glare and Lyonette's frigid contempt, stopped and swallowed. "Of course, there's probably nothing to it . . ."

"I believe we have better things to do than gossip," Lyonette said loftily. "And I think we are more intelligent than to give credence to a lie."

Mrs. Grimes flushed, bit off her thread and said hastily, "Of course, Mrs. Hazelrigg. I knew it was just—"

"Shall we have refreshments?" Mrs. Forbes suggested.

57.

Having passed the problem on to the Almighty and Dove, Angus left on his circuit the morning after the house raising. He was so royally welcomed, he grinned and told people he felt like the prodigal son.

At about the midpoint of his trip, one of the regulars suggested a brush arbor revival "at least a week long. There's sinners out on that prairie won't come to a regular Sunday service, but they'd turn up shore enough for a revival."

That, Angus thought wryly, was probably true enough. Sundays were routine, revivals dramatic. There would be tearful conversions at the mourner's bench, shouting, and embraces between people who'd been at odds with one another.

Angus disliked and mistrusted revivals. He himself felt nearest the Majesty when he was alone in the awesome stillness of the woods. But he had learned from experience that most people wanted, perhaps needed, the "stirring up" that revivals afforded.

So he agreed to hold a one-week "meetin'." Crowds did come, there were conversions and shouts, and sometimes the services lasted until midnight or later, complete with tears and hugs and prayers and general rejoicing.

When finally he rode on to his next stop, Angus prayed as he went that the revival's effects would be lasting.

The circuit completed at last, he headed home. He was extremely tired, but happy to have been again among his people—God's people, he corrected himself. Salt of the earth, he thought, and fell to thinking about Matthew 5 and building a sermon around it.

Angus's reunion with his family held a special warmth. "I thought you were never coming home," Rowdy scolded, and Sam told her not to be silly; Uncle Angus always came home as soon as he could.

Jim stood a bit back from the children, a smile of welcome on his face but, as usual, seeming a little uncertain as to how any advances from him would be received. Angus went to shake hands with him, and Jim's eyes brightened. "Good to see you, son," he said.

Each of the three had a dozen things to tell him. The Smiths' baby was walking very well. Oklahoma Station had a new mercantile store. School was getting harder and harder. Sterling Hazelrigg had won the last spelling bee. He was sure a different kid than he had been when he started school, Rowdy said, and Sam added darkly that he'd better stay that way, too, or Aunt Sarah would have the hide off his back.

Jim had papered the parlor with newspapers, and Angus agreed that it was not only handsome, but would also help keep out the winter wind. Dove had brought Rowdy a pane of glass so she could have a window in her room. A braided rag rug was being made for the parlor, with all three of them working on it.

They had supper, and at long last, Angus said that if they didn't get to bed, they'd never get up in the morning, and hauled the family Bible out for the evening reading.

"Uncle Jim," he said, "would you like to make the selection this evening?"

Rowdy and Sam exchanged glances. Both had thought it was their time and been trying to decide what chapter they'd ask for, but it was, after all, only fair that Uncle Jim get a turn, for once. As usual, it was Rowdy who spoke.

"What's your favorite passage, Uncle Jim?"

"Why, I reckon it would be the third chapter of John," the old man said slowly. "Do you know that John was called the disciple that Jesus loved?"

Sam's mouth fell open. "I thought He loved 'em all," he grumbled. Lord, Lord, he's going to be touchy as Dove, Angus thought with dismay. But Jim was coming up with an explanation.

"Of course He loved 'em all, Sam, me man, but John he loved special-like. And you know why? 'Cause John was a lovin' man hisself." Sam's face was still twisted with doubt, and Jim hurried on. "You like lots of folks. Some you like better than others—they're special to you the way John was to the Lord."

"Oh, I see. You don't s'pose John was black, do you?" he asked wistfully.

Jim's face said more plainly than words that he wished he'd never mentioned the subject. Angus chimed in to help Jim.

"No, John wasn't black," he said, "but the man who first took the Christian faith to Africa was. The Bible doesn't give his name, but he was a eunuch of great importance, treasurer for Queen Candace of Ethiopia."

"Sure 'nuf? Africa? Queen Candace of Ethiopia." Sam spoke the words as though they felt pleasant on his tongue. "What's a eunuch?" he asked.

Angus groaned, silently berating himself for introducing the word. "It's a—well, you know what a steer is."

"Sure. It's a bull with his balls cut off."

222

Jim went fiery red and exploded. "Sam!" he yelped, "you didn't ort to talk like that in front of a girl!"

"You certainly shouldn't," Rowdy agreed. "You're supposed to say 'testicles.'"

Angus thought Jim was going to faint. He himself gulped a couple of times. Sam muttered, "Oh, well, testicles, then," and Angus, recovering his breath, said loudly, "The third chapter of John."

So the passage was read and prayers were said. Sam was undressing behind his curtain, when he called out, "I forgot, Uncle Angus. Maman wants to see you while you're home."

"All right, Sam, thank you," Angus said, and hoped to God her news was good.

When the children had gotten off to school the next morning, Angus visited for a time with Jim. He could not, perhaps, ever really accept him as a father, but at least he could express his gratitude for Jim's taking care of Sam and Rowdy, by being friendly. And try little by little to banish the animosity which had been in him from earliest childhood.

Jim, maundering along in his usual fashion, stopped suddenly, in mid-sentence. "I know yore anxious to see Dove," he said. "Go on along. You and me can talk anytime."

"I was listening," Angus protested.

"I know, son. Put it this way. I'm hankerin' to find out what she did, too."

"In that case . . ."

Angus was out and on his way almost before the words left his mouth. Blaze was always ready for a good gallop, and, jogging along, Angus wondered idly what he'd do with the new foal she would bring. Then thought guiltily of Maggie's petition, lying in his drawer at home. He hadn't taken it along on this swing around the circuit. People had been too long without a ministry to be distracted from the main message.

He'd have to take it on the next trip.

As Auntie Po let him in at the back door of the big white house, a thought struck Angus. "Auntie," he asked, "does anyone ever use the front door?"

Her mouth spread in a toothless grin. "You can come in the front any time you wants," she told him. A wicked glint came into her eyes. "Most of Miss Dove's men callers *prefers* the back."

Angus chuckled. "I'll bet they do. Is Miss Dove in?"

"She in, all right," Auntie Poe said darkly. "I'll see is she receiving callers."

Oh, Lord, Angus thought, not another tantrum. But when, minutes later, Dove swept in, resplendent in a negligee of satin and lace and ribbons, she seemed in amiable enough humor.

"Howdy, preacher. You come to see about that little nigger bastid of yours," she greeted him.

"Dove—"

She held up a hand. "All right, all right," she said. "Sit and have some coffee. Auntie Po?"

"Right here, chile. Fresh made."

When it was poured, Dove began. "I called Mr. Forbes and Mr. Hazelrigg into conference." Her face was bright with mischief. "This is how it went."

By the time she had finished, Angus was laughing so hard, he was alternately holding his sides and wiping his eyes.

"Ain't she the beatenest?" Auntie Po asked proudly, and Angus agreed she was all of that and more, but then changed the subject.

"Auntie Po said she'd see if you were receiving, when I got here, which always means there's a problem. Any way I can help?"

Dove's face clouded, and for a moment Angus feared he had gone too far, that she might think he was sticking his nose into her business. But then she shrugged. "Not 'less you can find me a new girl when you're flittin' around over the countryside," she said. "You know what that Suzette has done to me?"

"Suzette? I thought she was sort of your right-hand man, so to speak. She hasn't—gotten too—old?"

Dove shook her head. "She hasn't got sense enough to get wrinkles and look old," she growled. "It's worse than that. Some Texas rancher rode in here a few months back. I guess she pleasured him pretty good. Leastaways, he cottoned to her. He's been comin' back. What she's gonna do, she's gonna get married, if you please."

"Married!" Angus repeated.

"Yes, married," Dove snapped. "Whores do get married sometimes, you know."

224

"Of course they do," Angus agreed hastily. To change the subject, he said the first thing that came into his head. "Auntie Po, where'd you get that name?"

Auntie chuckled. "I din't weigh no more'n a kitten when I was born, and my Mammy never thought to raise me. Even when I kept on livin, she 'spected the angels to come after me any minute. She always called me, 'You po' little pickaninny.' My brothers and sisters started callin' me Po. Even when I married, my man called me that."

"But you have a real name?"

" 'Course I got a real name. You think I'm some kind of stray? My name's Selema."

"Selema," Angus repeated. "That's pretty. Would you rather be called that?"

The old woman shook her grizzled head, pulled a corncob pipe from her apron pocket and got it going before answering. "Naw," she said, "don't reckon I'd know a body was talking to me if they called me anything but Po."

Angus pushed back his chair, got to his feet. "Once more, I'm obliged to you, Dove," he said soberly. "Hope someday I can repay all my debts."

"Don't get mushy," Dove snorted. "By the by, Suzette wants you to tie the knot for her."

"She does? Where?"

"Well, here—where else?" Dove said, flaring up. "This is the only home she's got. And if she's gonna have a service, we're gonna do it up brown. Next Sunday afternoon, preacher." Her face softened momentarily. "Reckon you could bring Jim and the kids along? I don't think they'd see anything in a wedding ceremony to corrupt them."

"Of course I'll bring them," Angus said. "They'll love it."

He took his leave, feeling, as he so often did, that he'd narrowly escaped a volcanic explosion. She was not exactly a soothing woman, this Dove Dubois. But—he chuckled to himself as he rode toward home—as she'd said once before, she wasn't dull.

58.

The discussion about the eunuch had lain shadowy at the back of Angus's mind since the night before. He needed to have a good talk with both Rowdy and Sam—separately, of course. He knew most people thought that the less a kid knew about the facts of life, the better. He didn't agree with that idea.

He remembered Lexie telling him her mother had warned her that if she let a man kiss her, she would have a baby. He didn't want Miss Rowdy and Sam to have any crazy ideas like that.

Nonetheless, he was sweating when, as he and Jim had arranged, the old man took Sam off that evening to catch some fish.

"Sit down, Miss Rowdy," Angus said. "There's something we need to talk about."

"All right, Papa." She had changed her clothes and was headed toward the door. "I was going to see if there were any baby chicks yet. It's time for that first old hen to hatch."

"You can do that later," Angus told her. "This is something I want to discuss while Jim and Sam are gone."

"Oh." Her eyes grew big. "A secret?"

"Sort of." His palms were damp. He sat down at the table, and Rowdy took the chair opposite him.

"You look funny, Papa," she said. "Is something wrong?"

"Miss Rowdy," he said, not knowing where to start, "Miss Rowdy, where did you hear the word 'testicles'?"

"Oh, that. Aunt Sarah told us. She had a separate session for the boys and girls. I think she did it because one of the boys said his little thingy was sore. She said everyone should know the correct name for the parts of the body."

"Oh," Angus said weakly. "But, well, she did tell you

226

not to use any words referring to the private parts of the body around—well, around other people."

"Oh, sure." Rowdy nodded. "But last night we were talking about *animals*. And you-all are my *family*."

"Yes, but"—Angus fumbled for the words—"Uncle Jim is sort of old-fashioned. I think it upset him."

"Really? That's kind of silly, isn't it?" She deliberated a minute. "I'll be careful," she promised.

Angus drew a deep breath. "There's another thing. You—you're going to start being a woman pretty soon now." He sought desperately for some parallel between people and animals. "You know, in the spring, the robins and mockingbirds and sparrows—all the birds build nests," he said.

"Sure."

"Well, God gives them an instinct that tells them to build a nest so they can have babies. With people, it's different. He's arranged it so—well, the nest is carried in the woman's body." He knew he was doing badly when the child's face screwed up in alarm.

"A nest? In my body?"

"Not a nest, exactly," he corrected, floundering. "But God has prepared a certain portion of the woman's body . . . and that's where she carries the baby until it's time for it to be born."

"Really?" Miss Rowdy clasped her hands and leaned forward, enchanted. "When do I get a baby?"

Why had he ever started this discussion? Angus wondered frantically. He should have asked some woman to talk to Rowdy. He had to say something.

"Girls are supposed to have babies after they're married," he said awkwardly. "You must never let a boy—well, touch you or—or *handle* you before you're married—that is, your private parts. You know the Bible says your body is a temple of God."

"My private parts," Rowdy mused. "Does that mean my bosoms, too?"

Bosoms, Angus thought. That had to be a Sarah Holtzworthy word. He nodded. His throat was dry. "Why?" he asked.

"Oh, one of the boys at that dance tried to pinch me."

Angus felt rage begin to form a mist in front of him. "Who was it?" he shouted.

"Don't worry, Papa. I slapped him."

"It wasn't that Hank Benson?"

Miss Rowdy shook her head no. "It was the youngest of the Kirkpatrick boys."

"Nasty little snot!"

"Please, Papa, it isn't important. Was that all you were going to tell me—about being a woman and having babies and such?"

"Guess that's enough for now," Angus croaked.

"Then I'll go see if there are any chicks."

Angus nodded, knew if he lifted his hands from his knees, they'd be shaking.

Miss Rowdy started toward the door, paused, then turned back to drop a kiss on his forehead. "You're a good papa," she said with a tenderness that made his eyes sting. "Thank you for telling me."

59.

On his next circuit trip, Angus introduced Maggie's petition, which was greeted with every reaction from hoots of laughter to thoughtful silence. Mostly, people were incredulous.

Women voting?

Each time he mentioned it, Angus waited until religious services were over. Then he would ask the congregation to wait a minute longer. He told them the exact circumstances of his presenting the petition, of dickering with Maggie and, wryly, of being bested. More than one knee was slapped in hilarity at thought of the little Yankee woman getting the best of the preacher.

Then he told them with equal honesty that he himself had not decided whether to sign the petition. "It's no secret," he would conclude, "that the ladies are smarter than us poor male critters, or we wouldn't be under their thumbs like we are." There would be sheepish grins then. "But whether their kind of smart is the kind for voting or not, well, I'm not sure yet."

One man voiced the thought most of them shared. "Yore joshin', ain't you, preacher?" he called out uncertainly.

"No, I'm not joshin'," Angus said. He went on to tell them of some of the work Susan B. Anthony had done in in the East. One weather-beaten oldster, forgetting he was in church, spat mightily and said that she sounded like a troublemaker to him. "Probably'd like to wear britches, too," he muttered darkly.

Angus repeated that he was not asking them to sign but that he had agreed to present it to them.

From the entire circuit, three women signed. Angus hoped Maggie Cruikshank wouldn't be disappointed.

If she was, she didn't say so when he finally got the petition back to her. "I presented it to my people, Maggie. This is the way it turned out."

Maggie sighed and pulled off her sunbonnet to let the breeze cool her forehead. "That's all right, Brother Angus," she said. "Looks like I've got the cart before the horse. 'Pears I better start trying to show the females why they ought to want to vote."

Having found her outside when he arrived, Angus hadn't dismounted. Now, she seemed to remember her manners. "Come in and sit a spell," she invited him.

Angus started to shake his head, reconsidered, climbed down and followed the wiry little woman into the house.

"Let me see that petition again," he said. Maggie thrust it toward him. Angus reread it, laid it on the kitchen table, dug a pencil out of his pocket and signed his name. "Now," he told her, "you've got one man's name, anyhow."

Maggie sniffed. "It's good to see there's one male critter in the Territory who's got the sense God gave a goose."

60.

The winter of 1902–1903 seemed to Angus unusually severe. He and Blaze floundered through snow drifts up to the horse's belly. Angus wore boots, and through the worst of the drifts, walked beside Blaze, fighting the stinging wind and swirling snow. Jim fretted about and at him.

"Boy, yore gonna get caught in a real blizzard one of these days, and they won't be able to dig you out 'til spring thaw."

"I'll be all right," Angus reassured him. "Think there's plenty of firewood?"

Jim was sure there was. The children couldn't go to school, with the prairie one vast unmarked sea of white, and so were housebound. Angus had planted a thick row of bois d'arc trees on the north boundary of his land, as a windbreak. The original room of the cabin, dug into the sandstone, was snug. But the howling wind made the parlor and Rowdy's room bone-numbingly cold.

"Nothin' 'tween us and the North Pole but a barbed wire fence," Jim grumbled.

The livestock was kept in the barn. Angus still remembered with horror the forty head of stock he'd seen near King Fisher. An unexpected blizzard had struck, and the cattle had huddled against the fence so tightly that many had been smothered.

In January, Angus finally gave up circuit riding. The drifts even around the cabin were so high, he could hardly plow through them. He didn't want Jim or the children to have to go out to milk. Besides, Bluebell was almost due to calve, and it wasn't long until Blaze would foal.

"Guess you got a right to a little rest before you become a mother again," Angus told the mare, running his hand down her velvety nose. Blaze nipped his hand gently, then rubbed her forehead against his shoulder.

Indoors, Miss Rowdy embroidered a tablecloth, while

Sam whittled animals out of pieces of pine. Jim did his cooking and baking. Frequently, when he was finished, he would doze in the rocking chair in front of the cookstove.

It came as a shock to Angus one day to realize that his father was growing frail. He remembered him from childhood as a big hearty man with a thick shock of black hair and a ruddy complexion. Now his hair was almost white, and thinning. His face was sallow, and the arms that had once tossed a small boy into the air were flaccid.

Poor old man, Angus thought, and wondered what his dreams and hopes had been when he was young. Had any of them been realized? Were any man's dreams realized? he wondered, then decided being cooped up was making him morbid and went outside to see about the animals.

He fought his way to the barn through a screaming wind, shielding his eyes from the pellets hammering against him. It was more like ice than snow. Tugging the barn door open almost wrenched Angus's arms out of their sockets. The wind buffeted him first one way, then the other.

The barn seemed exceptionally dark after the dazzling white outdoors, and Angus stood for a minute, catching his breath and letting his eyes adjust. He heard Blaze's harsh breathing and hurried to her stall.

She was lying down and in obvious pain. Her eyes were rolling, and she was breathing in little whinnying snorts. She's not due yet, was his first thought, not for nearly a month. Due or not, it was obvious that she was in labor and in trouble.

"Here, old girl," Angus said. "First, let's clear the barn." He herded Sal, Bluebell and Honeysuckle out into the cowpen, went back to Blaze. Her flanks were heaving wearily, and she was shivering.

"How long you been about this?" Angus questioned. She'd shown no signs that morning when he did the milking, but it was now well into the afternoon.

He fought his way back to the house, got soap, a bucket of water, a pan of lard and slogged his way back to the barn again. The livestock in the cowpen looked at him in mild reproach.

"Soon as possible," he promised. Inside the barn, he shed his coat, rolled up his shirt and long-john sleeves, washed his hands and arms and coated them with lard,

231

spreading it thin as possible. Then he lay down on his belly and, with extreme caution, ran a hand inside the horse. Blaze twitched and neighed, a soft helpless sound that worried Angus. Her first foal had arrived without difficulty.

He moved his hand, exploring gently. The sac containing the waters had not yet ruptured, and he hesitated to puncture it. Maybe something else was wrong with Blaze, and she wasn't in labor. He started to withdraw his arm, thinking he'd wait a few minutes to see what developed. Blaze nickered, made as if to rise, slumped back as a powerful paroxysm caught her.

A heartbeat later, the sac ruptured. A gush of water drenched Angus before he could move. At the same moment, his hand was caught painfully between the unborn foal and the bone of the pelvis. He could not move the hand, and dared not exert force, for fear of tearing the womb.

His hand went numb. The pain rippled upward, expanding into his arm. Already, his teeth were chattering as the cold penetrated his wet clothing, chilling him to the bone.

He felt the struggling movement of the colt, as though it were demanding to be freed. Finally, the spasm of travail subsided, and Angus was able to withdraw his hand, rub some life back into it.

Disregarding the icy clothing clinging to his body, he washed again, recoated both hands and arms with lard. Then he lay back down on his belly, worked first the right, and then the left hand up through the birth canal. Blaze made a small sound, as though too tired to whinny. She strained, the heavy musculature like clamps, and defecated.

"That's what you think of the whole business, is it?" Angus grunted. "Can't say I blame you." He eased his hands, first one and then the other, into the womb itself, felt the folded legs, then the flanks, and gently, ever so gently, grasped the slippery sides, began to tug.

He stopped and rested a moment, giving Blaze a chance to relax, talking to her softly. Then he readjusted his hands around the small animal still sealed in darkness. Little animal? It felt like the little devil was enormous. "That the problem, Blaze, old girl?" he asked. "All right, let me get a good hold, and when I pull, you push."

He knew his arms would be pinioned this time as he tried to draw the foal down into the canal. "Damn you, you little bastard," he growled, "you're going to have to pull in those sides." The spasm of expulsion came then; Angus's forearms were caught as though in a vise, but he felt the colt move fractionally. If I don't break an arm, he thought wryly, we might make it.

The shadows began to deepen within the small barn, and he swore at himself for not having brought a lantern. Outside the door, Honeysuckle bawled plaintively. Her bag must be hurting, he thought; it was past time for her to be milked.

He hoped Jim and the children hadn't heard the cow. That would be the only excuse they needed to come charging out into the blizzard. He was so chilled by now, he felt like a chunk of ice.

Blaze's paroxysm had subsided; she lay so still that Angus was afraid she had stopped breathing. Then he felt the thud of her heart. He lay unmoving. Each time he had to enter the horse, he knew he ran the added risk of tearing the womb. "Rest a minute, girl," he said, "then let's have another go at it."

Time had dissolved and become endless. Angus wondered how much more the mare could endure. He would not think of Lexie. The wind shrieked and rattled the door.

"Let's try again," he whispered, and the movement of his hands brought this convulsion on. Blaze's flanks were taut, contracted. Again, the colt moved. It was almost entirely in the birth canal, and Angus held his breath, hoping its life had not been snuffed out by the pressure. He waited, letting the mare rest, then tugged gently again and felt the downward thrust of the musculature. Not painful for him this time. They had cleared the pelvis.

And now Blaze didn't wait for his movement. She gave a tremendous heave, and the foal seemed to all but explode from the supine body, Angus still clutching its sides.

Blaze gave a great whicker of relief, her eyes closed and she lay motionless, as though too exhausted to make any more effort. Angus had a moment of panic. He had a deep though inarticulate affection for his animals, and Blaze was his in a special sense.

The wind banged at the door as he got stiffly to his feet. A layer of ice had formed in the bucket; Angus broke it to scrub up as best he could. There was no feeling left in either his arms or his legs. He was numb.

The colt lay where he had fallen at birth, but he was breathing. Angus reached under the small animal to help him up. "Small?" he said again, teeth chattering, "You're a monster." He got the foal to rise on its wobbly legs and nudged it up against Blaze. The colt kicked out with his left hind foot, and Angus laughed.

"You little devil," he said admiringly. "You tried to kick me. You're going to be a bad 'un, aren't you?"

The foal was nuzzling at its mother, and after a long and fearful moment, Angus saw Blaze open her eyes. She gave the colt an exploratory skimming lick, and finally, after what seemed an inordinate length of time, staggered awkwardly to her feet. The colt nuzzled again, and Angus turned away with a feeling of accomplishment that was a benediction.

He let the other animals back into the barn, milked Honeysuckle and floundered his way back to the house. Jim was waiting at the front door. "Boy, I thought them animals et you," he said. Angus didn't answer. Exhaustion was closing in around him, and when he reached the warmth of the kitchen and managed to walk what seemed an immeasurable distance to a chair, he folded into it like a collapsing tent.

His last thought was that the heat was painful.

He woke to find his father dressing him in dry long johns. The wet clothing lay in a heap, and Rowdy was demanding from behind her curtain if she could help *now*.

Jim was scolding and grumbling and growling about Angus's staying out like that . . . pneumonia, probably . . . Sam was pushing Angus's arms into a dry flannel shirt, fetching a heavy sweater. Rowdy brought the whiskey, and Jim spooned it into him. The warmth began to penetrate, make his insides glow, and he was growing drowsy.

"We got us a new colt," he said, and wasn't sure whether he spoke aloud or not.

"Can we see him?" Rowdy and Sam spoke together. Rowdy added, "We could really bundle up, coats, boots . . ."

"No, you ain't goin' out," Jim snapped. "One idiot in the family's enough." He brought Angus a mug of steam-

234

ing soup. "Get this down you," he ordered. "I'm makin' coffee."

Sam's face drooped with disappointment, and Angus said groggily, "Maybe tomorrow, Sam."

"You prob'ly ought to get in bed," Miss Rowdy said, sounding exactly like Auntie Po. Angus chuckled. He drank the coffee, had more soup, and felt an overwhelming, irresistible sleepiness.

Dimly, he was aware of the three of them getting him into bed, felt a warm iron tucked in at his feet, blankets wrapped around him. Then he sank into a warm and comforting blackness.

It was almost noon when he wakened the next day, and he sat up with a start, thinking of Honeysuckle. Poor thing would be in agony by now. He began to scramble out of bed, and Jim, chuckling, said he'd missed breakfast, but the older man might be able to scare up a bite of dinner for him.

"Got to get out and take care of the stock," Angus said groggily. "Eat later."

Sam looked up from the game of hully-gully he and Rowdy were playing. "I took care of 'em," he said laconically.

"I wanted to, Papa," Rowdy chimed in. "Sam drew the long straw."

"Give Blaze plenty of water? Milk Honeysuckle?"

"Yes. Fed the chickens, but I left 'em shut in the house. Shoveled some of the snow out of the cowpen so the stock could stay out there awhile. It's stopped snowing." He shook his hands, holding the button acorns behind his back. "Hully-gully, how many?" he asked Rowdy.

But she wasn't thinking of the game. "Papa," she said, "do you think Sam and I could have the new colt to pull our cart? When he gets old enough, that is."

Angus yawned and rubbed his hand over his scratchy face. "I'm afraid that colt isn't going to be a cart horse, Miss Rowdy. I have a feeling we've got a real ornery critter on our hands. He tried to kick me, soon as he was born."

Rowdy burst out laughing, Jim grinned and even Sam chuckled. "That little old piece of nothin' tried to kick you," she said.

"He's not so little for a foal. Fact is, he's the biggest one I've ever seen."

"Shucks," Rowdy said, and Jim gave her a cautioning look.

"Young ladies ort to talk like young ladies, miss," he said.

"Yes, Uncle Jim," Rowdy said docilely, but the impish glance she shot at Angus said plainly that she was humoring the old man. "What are you going to name him, Papa?" she asked.

"How about Kadif?" he asked, and Sam sniffed.

"It don't mean nothin'," he said.

"Samsy, your language," Rowdy reproached him. "Aunt Sarah would skin you alive."

"That's the pure-D truth," Sam agreed. "All right. Uncle Angus, that name doesn't meant anything."

"It doesn't matter," Angus said slowly. He thought of Mean, the wild horse he had loosed so many years ago. "I figure we got us an unusual animal, so he ought to have an unusual name."

61.

During the time they were all housebound, Angus talked to the children about plans for their future.

"Doesn't seem possible," he said, "but you'll finish eighth grade this year. Reckon your maman is making plans for you, Sam. We got to do some thinking about what you're going to do, Miss Rowdy."

Rowdy smiled. "I've already decided," she said, "if we can afford it, I want to go on to the Normal at Edmond."

Jim sniffed, and muttered that she had already had enough schooling.

"Enough if I were going to get married," she agreed. "But I'm going to teach school. There's Prairie Dale and

Hastings and Wheatland. One of them should be needing a new teacher by then."

Silently, Angus rejoiced. He wanted her to get married sometime; of course he did. But not for a long while yet. If she taught school a few years, there'd still be plenty of time for her to think about marrying.

"We'll manage to get the money," he promised.

Sam had apparently been pondering the question. "I might go on to college too. Not that I'd need it to be a cowpuncher, but Maman says no one can have too much education."

Angus concentrated on his food. He knew Sam was waiting for comment, and was at a loss as to how to answer. Finally, he said gently, as he had before, "Reckon that's going to have to be up to your maman."

Spring came early and, as though to make up for the horrendous winter, was magnificent. It was warm and balmy, and the redbuds and dogwoods blossomed before their time. There was no freeze to kill the English peas, as there so often was. On St. Patrick's Day, when they planted Irish potatoes, there was scarcely a breeze. In fact, March, always notable for its winds, not only came in like a lamb, but it went out like one.

"I tell you, son," Jim said fretfully, turning the seed potato over so the eye was uppermost, "it ain't normal, this weather ain't. We're bound to get an April freeze that's gonna kill everything."

"Aunt Sarah says worrying never helped anything," Rowdy said primly. "She said, as a man thinketh in his heart, it's liable to happen to him."

"That's a misquote," Angus told her, and she giggled.

"I know it," she said. "Aunt Sarah said it wasn't meant as a quote. It was meant as common sense."

"You can't fault that," Angus agreed.

Jim humphed.

There was to be a graduation exercise for the six children completing the eighth grade. Each of them had a recitation to give. Students and audience alike would participate in singing the "Star-Spangled Banner" and repeating the Lord's Prayer. There would be an address by the Methodist minister. Sarah had asked Angus, but he'd told her quite honestly that he was afraid he'd choke up.

As the time for the ceremonies drew near, Sam grew

even more thoughtful than usual. Angus believed he knew why, and held off starting on the circuit until Dove made her weekly visit.

His guess had been right. Dove was just unpinning her hat, when Sam began to speak. "Maman," he said, "you haven't ever come to the school to hear me recite, like other parents do. Reckon you could spare the time when we graduate?"

Dove looked frantically at Angus, but, not knowing how to help, he was studying his fingers.

"Let me get my hat off, Samson." She tried to laugh, but her voice broke. "Got a little cold," she said, and coughed to prove it.

"You-all want coffee?" Jim asked.

"You bet." Dove was overly enthusiastic. "And you got any of that good gingerbread? Law, I don't get gingerbread like yours anywhere else. It is the beatenest. Maybe if you give me the recipe, Auntie Po could stir some up now and again.

"Auntie Po's been ailin' lately. I declare, if it ain't one thing, it's another. Samson, straighten those shoulders, chile. You gettin' round as a hoop snake.

"How come you're not out on the circuit, preacher? Your people run you off? Rowdy, if you don't quit wearin' britches, none of the young bucks gonna come callin'. You want to be an old maid?

"Hasn't this weather been somethin'? Not one twister the whole season. Reckon if we get enough rain, the crops are going to produce a treat. Jim, those early peas you give me were pure-D delicious. Don't think anything tastes better than the first mess of green peas.

"One of my girls picked some polk salad. You know what that dummy was gonna do? She was gonna make *salad* out of it. I told her if she didn't cook it and pour off the first water, she'd poison the lot of us. That'd be a fine kettle of fish."

The spate of words ended as though a spring had dried up. Dove sat down, put her hands on the table and, head bowed, looked at them, wiggling each finger separately, as though to see whether they still worked. The others looked at one another uneasily. Angus's eyes swung back to Dove, and he saw two enormous crystalline tears glisten on her cheeks.

The others saw them too, and were stunned. Sam ran

238

to her. "What's the matter, Maman?" he cried. "Did I do something wrong?"

In an unaccustomed display of affection, Dove caught him to her. "You haven't done a thing wrong, Samsy," she whispered. "Little tired, that's all."

"Maman, I don't have to go to school any more. I can get a job and take care of you. You won't have to work. You can cook and embroider, and I can live at home."

The tears increased, and suddenly Dove was sobbing as though her heart would break, head against Sam's shoulder. Jim muttered something about feeding the chickens and took off. Miss Rowdy looked as though she were going to cry too, and Angus felt so utterly helpless, he wished he were a thousand miles away.

Sam was patting his mother's shoulder. Tears shone on his own cheeks, and he gulped. "It's all right, Maman. Truly, it's all right. You don't have to come if you don't want to."

Angus turned his head, thinking, as he had once before, that it was indecent to look when a soul was stripped naked. After what seemed an endless time, Dove's sobs lessened. She raised her head, sniffed, drew a handkerchief from her sleeve, wiped her eyes, blew her nose and gave them all a watery smile.

"Didn't mean to turn on the waterworks," she apologized, and gave Sam a pat on the bottom. "Go 'long 'bout yore rat killin', chile," she said, sounding almost normal.

After a longish interval, Jim poked a cautious head in at the door and, seeing that the situation was normal, came into the house. "Them hens is tryin' theyselves," he said fussily. "I swear, I think every one of 'em is wantin' to set—and that old rooster prancin' around like he was king of the universe."

"That's natural," Dove snapped, "him being a male." Sam had not yet gone about his rat killing; he and the other two males exchanged relieved glances. Dove was herself again.

But Rowdy was still troubled, sensing what she could not understand.

62.

The end of May eventually came. Miss Rowdy had made herself a new dress for the graduation, of powder-blue dimity. The ruffled neck was high around her throat, there were tiny pearl buttons down the front of the bodice, and a sash of blue ribbon. Angus's heart swelled with pride when she was dressed and ready to go.

"I got the prettiest girl in the Territory," he told her. Jim muttered that pretty is as pretty does, but his chest stuck out an inch or two, despite his grumbling.

Samson was wearing his first store-bought suit. He was, Angus thought, a handsome boy. Straight black hair, a firm jaw, lips well cut and sensitive, smooth skin. Only the liquid depths of his dark eyes, with their fringe of curling lashes, spoke of his Negro blood.

Sam had dressed up for Dove the last time she visited the soddy, but Angus wished with all his heart that she could attend the graduation. Out of the children's hearing, he had urged her to reconsider and come to the school. Her reply had been to snort that he knew it was impossible, just as she did. "I'm jes' glad," she added somberly, "that Sam has got his schoolin'. No one gonna mistreat him."

As he hitched the team to the wagon on graduation night, Angus wondered where the years had gone. It seemed like only yesterday that Miss Rowdy was an infant and he was searching frantically for someone to care for her.

It felt like no time at all since he had made the run. Now he had a house, a farm, a family. Enough of his land was clear and fertile to provide a living for them. His well was deep, his animals sleek—Kadif was going to be a winner—and his circuit riding was a comfortable habit that gave him the sense of carrying out God's will in his life.

He was content.

They arrived early at the school. Angus and Jim helped Zeb arrange the benches. The children's offer to help was vetoed, lest they get their clothes mussed.

"Your class," Sarah told them, "must be an example to all the other students. You are the first ones to graduate who started here. Special privilege, special responsibility." Sam and Rowdy nodded respectfully and went to sit well out of the way, repeating their recitations to each other.

The parents arrived in their Sunday best, Angus noted, and well they might. This was a proud night.

Those in the graduating class, all six of them, were to sit in chairs facing the audience. The Forbes and Hazelrigg boys were quiet and subdued. Sarah's no-nonsense disciplining didn't allow fooling around. Most of the children there had felt the sting of her switch when they needed it. Yet, not one of them considered her harsh or unfair. "Mrs. Holtzworthy says . . ." was the be-all and end-all, the final authority.

There was a ferment of excitement, one girl insisting she was going to be sick to her stomach. Overhearing her, Sarah told her briskly to go outside. Apparently, the nausea subsided.

At seven-thirty on the dot, Sarah rang the handbell on her desk and called on Angus to say the invocation. Sitting near the back, Angus rose. The prayer was brief. He petitioned the Almighty in behalf of all children, especially those graduating tonight. He prayed that their lives might be worthy and he thanked God for this land where people could live and worship as they chose.

Then the congregation stood, and he led them in the Lord's Prayer. It was after Sarah had bustled over to the battered piano and begun to play the national anthem that Angus heard a slight commotion outside.

Thinking one of the town dogs might be spooking the horses, he quietly stepped outside, saw Dove climbing out of her buggy. "Hush, you fool," she admonished her horse in a whisper.

"Dove, you *did* come! Hurry, it's just beginning!"

Dove snorted. "Don't be a fool, preacher. Effen I walked in that li'l ol' school buildin', it would empty faster'n if they was a fire. Respectable folks don't have nothin' to do with folks like me."

"Dove—"

Her face softened. "I know you mean it kindly, Angus," she said. "I'm all right. I'll watch through the window. You better get on back."

"I'll let Sam know you're here."

She turned on him like a fury. "You'll do nothing of the kind," she hissed.

Angus was mystified. "Why not, Dove? It would mean so much to him."

"I'm thinking of the future, Angus. Now, go on 'fore I start bawling."

Perforce, Angus went. The Methodist minister spoke movingly on "New Beginnings," mentioning the run, which had brought these children's parents into this land, saying that doubtless the Territory would soon become a new state, and that the children, with their education and the opportunities they'd been given, would be its new leaders.

When he had finished, the recitations began. Despite their trepidations, each of the graduates performed flawlessly, even the girl with the queasy stomach. Sarah's face glowed with quiet pride when she rose to give out the diplomas, which she had made herself.

The ceremonies ended early, but no one seemed to want to leave. Everyone stood around and visited. The graduates were talking about future plans. One girl had already been "spoken for." Her wedding would be in June. Rowdy admitted that she was going on to the teachers' college in Edmond, and was teased about being an old-maid schoolmarm.

The evening was finally over, and Rowdy went to bid Sarah goodbye. "It seems like everything is ending, Aunt Sarah," she said, kissing the withered cheek. Sarah hugged her.

"Why, child, it's only beginning," she said. And then, in mock reproof: "You weren't listening to the minister."

"Yes, Mrs. Holtzworthy," Rowdy said demurely, with a little gulping laugh. "Yes'm, I was listening." And, mischievously, "I'd have been afraid not to, with you around."

Sam's goodbye to the teacher was quieter and, to Angus, infinitely sad. "Thank you, ma'am," he said, and shook hands. He did not know what his future held, and perhaps this night had brought with it the full realization that despite his intelligence and his schooling, he was, and would always be, different.

Possibly, Sarah sensed the same thing, for she patted his shoulder and said gently, "You've been an admirable student, Sam. I shall be expecting great things of you."

Sam's smile held the sorrow of his race and the cynicism of knowledge. "Thank you," he said.

Dove was gone when they went out into the night. A myriad of stars lit the dark, though the moon had not yet risen. Rowdy was still bouncing with excitement. Had she really done all right? Sam's speech had been better than anybody's. Didn't they think the preacher's talk was exciting? She'd bet that Hazelrigg boy would head East the very next day; it was all he ever talked of.

63.

The summer was a busy one. There were tomatoes and corn and green beans and cucumbers to put up. Pete Smith had planted all his bottom land with cotton, and Sam and Rowdy were recruited to help chop it.

Angus and the children decided to build a cellar. The old part of the cabin was safe enough from tornadoes, but storage space was needed for canned goods; potatoes, to be put down in straw; eggs, to be stored in waterglass.

On a visit in mid-August, Dove left word with Jim that she'd like Angus to bring Sam and his belongings in to her, next time he was home.

"Sam gonna move in with you, then?" Jim asked.

Dove's smile might have been a death rictus. "No," she said, and did not elaborate. If Jim wondered why she didn't take the boy when she left, he was cautious enough not to ask. "Don't say anything to Sam 'til it's time for him to go," she warned.

When Angus came in from the circuit, the message was duly relayed. "What's she up to?" he asked. Surely she wasn't planning to send him away this soon. Jim shook his head. "She didn't say, and the way she snapped at me, I didn't dast ask."

Angus grimaced. "Then she must be going to try to get him off to school in the East." He rubbed his hand over the lower part of his face. "What I don't think she realizes is that Sam is just as stubborn as she is. He won't go."

Jim poured a bowl of sliced potatoes into the spider. "Likely there'll be a real dust-up," he agreed.

Angus postponed the trip a couple of days, dreading the confrontation. Dove wasn't accustomed to being opposed.

Finally, though, it could be delayed no longer. Angus, acting as casual as possible, told Sam that his maman wanted him to bring his clothes and come to her. Sam's dark eyes lit up like a Christmas tree.

"I'm goin' home?" he whispered. "I'm goin' home and I'll live with Maman and take care of her, and she won't have to work and be tired and sad any more." His voice grew stronger as he spoke. Angus had never known whether Sam was aware of what went on at the big white house.

Miss Rowdy said almost timidly that she believed she'd come along with them if there were room. She, more than Sam, seemed sensitive to the fact that the move was tantamount to the family circle's breaking up.

"Sure you want to go along?" Angus asked, forebodings still troubling him. Rowdy nodded, and he said slowly that he guessed it would be all right.

Sam was whistling as he got his things together. The others pitched in to help, so he wouldn't forget anything . . . including the bird nest Rowdy had traded him for her first pair of britches.

The conversation on the way to town was fragmentary. Angus was lost in thought. For a time, Miss Rowdy chattered like a magpie, but Sam was so unresponsive, she finally quieted. The boy's face was aglow.

Auntie Po let them in, said Dove would be there in a minute and fled. A bad omen, Angus thought. Sam had brought in his clothes case and set it down near the door.

"I don't know which room is going to be mine," he explained, grinning from ear to ear.

Dove swept in. She was dressed in an elaborate gown of red satin, beaded with black jet, much fringed and betasseled. Her cheeks and lips were painted carmine, her hair sleeked back like a panther's.

Sam saw none of the stage dressing. He ran to meet her, threw his arms around her neck. "I'm home, Maman. I'm home, and now I'm gonna take care of you."

Dove disengaged herself from his arms. "Grow up, boy," she snapped. "Let's go to the parlor. We got business to take care of."

"We'll wait out here," Angus offered. Dove shook her head.

"You all come in," she said fiercely. "You're about as near family as Samson's got."

She jerked open the door and led the way. When they were all seated, she spoke to her son. "Samson, this is a white man's world. You're light enough to pass, and that's what you've got to do. You'll be leaving on the train this afternoon, with a ticket to Pennsylvania. You've been enrolled in school there. There's money enough in the bank in Philadelphia to get you through school."

She had spoken in a rush, the words running together, blurring.

Sam's jaw dropped. "I'm not gonna leave here, Maman. I'm going to stay here with you. I'm strong. I can work."

"Cleaning out stables?" Dove asked scornfully.

Sam's lips were compressed. His eyes narrowed, and his jaw was tight. "It don' matter what I do. I can earn us a living."

Dove drew a deep breath. "You couldn't earn me no livin' like I got here. I'm used to comfort and style, boy."

"Then I'll stay here. I'll work, but"—his lower lip trembled, and he bit down hard on it—"you can keep the House if you want."

So he did know what kind of house it was, Angus thought. He knew and didn't like the idea but would accept it, or anything else that Dove wished.

The woman laughed, and to Angus's ear, sensitized by pity, the sound was a shriek of pain. "Black boy," Dove said, "I don' want no nigger buck 'round here. Bad for business."

Sam's face was slack with shock and disbelief. "We can't afford no high-priced school," he offered uncertainly.

245

"Don't worry about it," Dove said. "Yo'—yo' pappy give me the money for you. Leastaways," she amended, "the man who thought he was yo' pappy."

"Who is my father?" Sam asked, and Angus was reminded of thick ice on a pond in winter. Dove shrugged.

"Who knows?"

"Maman . . ."

The woman drew another long breath, as though exasperated. "Reckon I'm gonna have to flat-out tell you the truth, boy," she said, her voice harsh. "I never wanted you when you was on the way. I jes' didn't know how to get rid of you. You was a mistake I made when I was too young to know better. You never meant nothin' to me but a problem. I'll be glad to be shet of you."

Sam stood up, unfolding in slow motion, dazed. His eyes glittered; there was a green pallor beneath his skin.

"I don't want your money," he said thickly. He started toward the door, and Dove's hand went out, jerked back.

"Figger you ain't smart enough to make it in a white man's school?" she flung at him. "Yore probably right."

Sam halted. Slowly, he turned around. "I'm smart enough," he said.

Dove shrugged, and the blood rose in Sam's face. "My father left me the money? I'll use it."

He turned again, as though sleepwalking, and started toward the outside door. Rowdy had sat, stunned, during the conversation. There were tears running down her cheeks. She jumped up.

"Wait, Samsy, I'll take you to the station," she called, rubbing fiercely at her eyes. She turned on Dove. "You bitch!" she whispered. "You filthy slut!"

Then she was gone to catch up with the boy.

Angus's mouth had fallen open. He got to his feet slowly, appalled at Dove's brutal handling of Sam, at Rowdy's ugly words. In the dead silence he heard Miss Rowdy call "Giddap" to the horse, heard the screaking of the buggy wheel. When the sound had died away, he said, "Surely you didn't have to . . ." and stopped as Dove toppled.

"Dove!" He went on his knees beside her, could detect no breath. "Auntie Po!" he shouted, and the wizened little woman materialized like a genie.

"Oh, Lawdy," she moaned. "Oh, Lawdy me, I was

246

feared of this." Tears were running down her seamy cheeks.

Angus reached for Dove's wrist. "Get her smelling salts," he ordered, but Auntie Po had taken Dove's head in her lap, was rocking and keening.

Angus jumped up, ran to the kitchen for water and towels.

"Let me get her on the couch, Auntie. You start wringing out those towels." He picked up the unconscious woman. She felt weightless as a wisp of fog. It was as though the past hour had decimated her.

Finally Auntie Po roused herself enough to bring the smelling salts. Angus applied the dampened cloths to Dove's forehead and throat, but it seemed to him that he and Po hovered over her an eternity before she opened her eyes. She said nothing, but it appeared to Angus as if something vital within her had died.

He brought a chair, sat down beside her, took her hand. If Dove knew he was there, she gave no sign of it. She was staring at the ceiling, unblinking.

64.

In the buggy, neither of the children spoke. The merciless sun and hot wind had dried Rowdy's tears, but they had also caused the swirling red dirt to stick to her cheeks in runnels.

The children reached the depot, climbed out. Sam took his case; Rowdy brought his books, which he'd strapped together, the high boots he'd been unable to get in the case and the bird nest.

With everything unloaded, she stood with him, waiting for the train, not knowing what to say. Something inside her hurt for his pain, but there were no words. They sat down on the edge of the platform. There was no one else around. Rowdy had no idea when the train was due. Samson seemed partially to rouse from his stupor.

"You might as well go on," he said tonelessly. "Thank you for bringing me." The words were oddly formal. He might have been speaking to a stranger.

"I can wait with you," Rowdy said. For the first time ever, she was unable to intuit his thoughts. She didn't know whether he wanted her here or not. Dimly, she sensed the wound had been worse because she and Papa had witnessed its infliction.

"I'd just as lief be alone," Sam told her, still in a monotone that held neither life nor feeling.

"All right," she said, and rose. Suddenly, she could no longer bear in silence the stricken face. She stooped and flung her arms around him. "Oh, Samsy!" she wailed. "I'm so sorry!" And kissed his cheek.

Samson jerked away, shot to his feet. Face contorted, he turned on her like a madman. "Don't you feel sorry for me, you—you white woman!"

Rowdy drew back, shaken and confused. Tried to speak and could not. Samson was glaring as though he hated her. Legs rubbery, she turned and began to walk toward the buggy. She heard an indeterminate sound, and an object flew by her head, shedding twigs and bits of cotton. It landed on the ground.

The bird nest.

It took Angus some weeks to convince Rowdy that Dove had used the only means she knew of forcing Sam to leave. After that, he and the girl and Uncle Jim visited the mulatto woman as often as possible. Most of the time she lay on the bed, unmoving, not speaking. She was wasted to the point of emaciation.

It was five years before anyone heard from Sam. Then Dove received a transcript of his records. He had graduated with honors.

65.

In September, Miss Rowdy began school at the Normal.
Sarah's teaching had given her a good foundation. She
read a great deal and became interested in the politics of
the new state.

"How's that gonna help you when yore cookin' side
meat and changin' didies?" Jim demanded once, and
Rowdy laughed at him. "No man's gonna ask you," he
prophesied darkly, and Rowdy laughed again.

She could afford to laugh. The lovely child had become
a beauty. The enormous eyes, with their frame of spiky
dark lashes, went from their original amethyst to deepest
violet when she was excited or angry. The pale hair had
been put up in a severe knot atop her head, but Rowdy
could never constrain all the tendrils. She would still have
liked hair as short as Samson's, but had accepted the in-
evitable. For now. Her waist was seventeen inches
around, her curves proportionately alluring.

A number of young men had asked Angus's permission
to call on her. Even Pollard Koontz, the undertaker, who
was older than Angus, asked to pay suit. With his wife not
two weeks in the ground.

Koontz was refused out of hand, but though Miss
Rowdy would have liked an escort to dances, Angus told
her flatly that she must decide on one and forego the
others.

"That's silly," she protested. "How can you know what
a boy's like unless you go out with him?"

"It's the way things are," Angus said sternly. "You
don't want to be called fast."

It was not until she met Jube McConaghie at school
that Rowdy began to "keep company." Jube was a black-
haired, blue-eyed Irishman with an infectious laugh and
spirits light as Rowdy's own. But even as she accepted his
first invitation, she was perfectly candid.

249

"All the girls in school have been making calf eyes at you," she said. "If you're thinking of serious courting, better choose one of them."

"Well, aren't you a catbird?" He grinned. "Don't you know young ladies are supposed to be demure and never, never, never think about serious courting or marriage until they're asked?"

Rowdy made a derisive sound. "I'd like to go dancing," she said. "That's all."

Jube made a mocking salute. "Agreed, madam," he said. "Truth to tell, I feel the same way."

So for nearly six months Rowdy got to dance as much as she wanted. Jube conducted her to church sociables in town and to picnics in the country. Jube had been as honest with Angus as Rowdy had with Jube. "We don't either one want to get married yet, Mr. Scofield, but I promise to treat her with—with all due respect."

Angus had hesitated. It was an unusual arrangement, and he didn't want his child the object of gossip. On the other hand, he wasn't ready to see Rowdy married yet, either. At last he gave his consent.

As the months went past, though, Angus began to wonder, as did the rest of the community. Propinquity was a great matchmaker.

Though she knew it was unseemly, Rowdy enjoyed being made over and, yes, hugged and kissed. But when Jube would have gone further, and she felt her emotions begin to stir, she backed off.

" 'Member," she said lightly, "no serious courting."

The buggy had been pulled up, the horse was contentedly cropping weeds, the moon lent an ethereal enchantment to the countryside.

Jube's usual lightheartedness had deserted him. "Oh, that," he said. "All girls pretend they're not interested. I'm crazy for you, Rowdy. You must feel the same; you've let me kiss you. And you can't tell me you didn't enjoy it."

Rowdy sighed. Papa had told her she musn't kiss a boy unless they were engaged, and added sternly that some fathers held out for no kissing until after marriage "I did enjoy it, Jube," she said honestly. "It—pleasured me."

"I want to marry you." Jube's voice was uneven.

"Oh, Jube, don't. Please don't. I'm not ready to get married."

"Rowdy." He made as if to pull her into his arms, but she drew away.

"We better go home," she said crisply.

That was the end of Jube McConaghie for Rowdy. Three months later, he married someone else.

66.

Samson had been gone more than two years, when Angus, riding Kadif, headed out one day to visit Dove. Kadif had lived up to Angus's prophecy. He had a great streak of wickedness. It had taken Angus longer to break him to the saddle then any horse he'd ever trained. Even now, as they hurtled across the prairie, the horse seemed on the alert for a moment of absentmindedness on the part of the rider.

But he was a magnificent animal, standing seventeen hands high, with the slender legs of his Arabian ancestors, coal black, spirited, tireless. And dangerous, Angus admitted to himself. Dangerous to anyone else, at least. He had finally accepted Angus's mastery.

Jim and Rowdy had never attempted to ride him. Pete Smith had insisted on trying it once and nearly got killed, though he was an excellent horseman. Most horses, when they throw their rider, will trot away. Not Kadif. After throwing Pete, he tried to stomp the little man. Angus had had to resort to a whip to drive Kadif off.

The preacher came back to the present as wings whirred and Kadif shied. A bobwhite flew past them, lurching awkwardly, as though wounded. Angus patted Kadif's neck.

"It's just a quail, old boy," he said soothingly. "See, she's got a nest close by and she's afraid we're going to hurt her nestlings. Watch her now; she'll pretend she's crippled, 'til we get far enough away that her babies are no longer in danger."

He grinned sheepishly to himself, wondering if other men talked to their beasts as though they were human.

At the white house, Auntie Po let him in. The kitchen smelled deliciously of fresh coffee.

"I's glad you come, Brother Angus." Auntie Po was fretting. "I purely is. Miss Dove, she gonna die iffen she don't eat." The old woman began to cry. "I done prayed like the good Book says, but it ain't done no good. She purely *wants* to die. And she's fixin' to do it."

"She's been like this a long time now," Angus comforted her. "She's no worse than she has been, is she?"

"Not to the human eye—" Auntie Po wiped her eyes on her apron, "but I done dreamed about the Black Angel last night."

"You didn't tell Miss Dove that?"

"Naw, suh, I ain't that foolish. But she been gittin' weaker right along. She gonna die, all right. The girls is gittin' real upset, they's such a sadness in the house. Two of 'em already left."

He had believed time would eventually heal, Angus thought as he headed upstairs toward Dove's room. He was troubled now. Ancient blacks like Auntie Po sometimes had an uncanny sense of approaching death.

Dove turned her head toward him as he opened the door. She was lying on the bed, clothed in what must have been pickings from the rag bag. Her face was drawn. She looked almost as old as Auntie Po.

"Hello, Dove," Angus said, pulling up a chair. Dove inclined her head ever so slightly but did not speak. She moistened her lips, but when he asked if she wanted a drink, she shook her head.

Angus was not ordinarily a voluble man, but he began to talk. He told her all the gossip Jim had gathered since Angus's last visit to Dove. He told her Oklahoma City and Guthrie were still fighting over which was to be the capital. He told her a bill had again been introduced in the Washington government to declare Oklahoma a state.

He told her a scandalous story, true or not, about one of Oklahoma City's leading citizens. Two years ago it would have brought a shout of laughter. Now there was no response. Dove looked away from him, staring out the window.

Desperately, he cast about in his mind for something which would rouse her from her lethargy. Auntie Po was right, he thought dismally. The mark of death was on her.

He stood up. "You stupid nigger whore," he said casually, "always have been a crybaby, sniveling because life isn't perfect. Think you're the only one who's ever known grief? You got no guts, lady. Go on, die! Who cares?"

He turned on his heel, walked slowly out of the room. He closed the door behind him, stood in the hallway, holding his breath.

He heard the sobs begin, hardly more than a catch in the throat; then the intensity increased, became wrenching. Still he waited. The sobs mounted, a sweeping storm of sound that raced eerily trough the corridors, making it hard for him to breathe.

Doors were flung open, cautious heads peeked out, Auntie Po shuffled up from the stairwell. He held a finger to his lips, motioned for the girls to close their doors.

Gradually, the sobs lessened, lingered, became hiccoughs, came to an end. He heard her blow her nose, and one final tearing sob. Momentarily, there was silence, then a whisper of sound.

"Bastard!" Dove spit out. "Stupid Bible-thumpin' two-bit hypocrite preacher." A gush of obscenity followed. She cursed him through earth and eternity, but still there was no sound of her having moved. He waited, a hand on Auntie Po's shoulder to restrain her.

Finally, the bed creaked; he heard the sound of a drawer opening, the scrabble of fingers, the clink of metal. The whites of Auntie Po's eyes were showing.

"She mad," the old woman whispered. "You best take yo'self off whilst you can."

Angus shook his head, again enjoined silence. He heard the bedsprings creak again as, apparently, Dove got to her feet. "I'll kill him!" Her voice was low but distinct. "I purely will kill that son of a bitch!" He heard the susurrus of footsteps charging toward the door.

"I'll kill you, Angus Scofield!" Dove screamed. "You hear me? I gonna kill you, it's the last thing I ever do!" The words were thick with the remnant of tears, but the determination was unmistakable.

Angus grinned at Auntie Po. "Time to leave," he said, and streaked down the hallway, was halfway down the steps when Dove's door banged open.

"I know you're there, Angus Scofield!" she shouted,

racing toward the stair. "An' I gonna kill you!" The man flung himself down the balance of the steps as Dove's double-barreled derringer coughed. The bullet gouged a hole in the wall. Angus crossed the kitchen on the run, heard the second bullet whiz by his head, through the open door.

Then he was on Kadif. He put spurs to the sleek sides, and the big horse exploded into a run. As they tore out of the yard, Angus glanced back. Dove was in the doorway, gun still in hand. Even from such a distance, he could see the glitter of rage in her eyes. He sighed.

"We got her on her feet," he told Kadif. "Reckon now it's up to the Almighty."

67.

Thompson B. Ferguson, appointed by President Teddy Roosevelt, was serving as territorial governor in 1903, when Rowdy entered the Normal. He was still governor in 1906, when she began to teach at the Three Oaks school. There were fourteen children making up the eight grades.

Though the weather was unbearably hot, it was necessary to start classes in August so they could be dismissed when it was time to pick cotton, in September and October.

Miss Rowdy found the teaching satisfying. She had grumbled once, to her father and Sarah Holtzworthy, that teaching was about the only job open to women. Sarah had answered briskly that teaching wasn't only a matter of instilling the three R's; it involved molding character, shaping the world. "It's the most important occupation there is," she had concluded, "outside of raising your own children, of course."

"But the hand that rocks the cradle still rules the world?" Rowdy had mocked gently.

"That's right, my girl," Sarah said. "And don't you forget it. Maggie Cruikshank is out agitating again for women to have their rights. Humph. One way or another, women have been running things ever since Eve made Adam an apple pie. Only thing is, they're subtle about it."

Rowdy snorted.

By and large, though, she found it a wonderful world. Riding to school gave her plenty of time to think. She thought of marriage and wondered if there were something wrong with her. Most of the girls her age were long since married. Several had babies.

She thought of Samson, too, and missed him, wondered if he'd "passed." She missed Dove's visits, too, she acknowledged to herself. She was glad Papa had finally gotten Dove on her feet. Both funny and sad, their encounter had been. By the prairie grapevine, which seemed to run from dugout to mansion to saloon to cabin, they had heard that Dove was up and about, that the house once more resounded with music and laughter.

Rowdy missed Dove's acrid humor, and had suggested Papa try to make it up with the black woman, saying she felt a chunk of her life was missing, with both mother and son no longer around.

"Have to wait 'til she gets over her mad," Angus had said wryly. "She'll let us know when that happens."

It was on the evening of June 17, 1906, that Tenny rode over to the soddy, bursting with news. The previous day, President Roosevelt had signed the Enabling Act, passed by Congress to admit the twin territories into the union as one state.

"Statehood!" Tenny gloated. "We're gonna have a say in the guv'ment, same as New York and them other Yankees." Tenny's days of indolence were long gone. He was a prosperous farmer, a staunch Republican, a steady churchman. He was clean, too, and never seen without his store-bought teeth. Over the years, Clover's sobriquet "that old fool," had changed to a prideful "My husband."

"Statehood." Jim rolled the word around in his mouth as though sampling a new wine. He made a face as though it did not quite reach the mark. "Dunno that's gonna make things any different."

"Of course it will, Uncle Jim," Rowdy cried. "It ought

to have been done long ago. Now we'll have regular representatives and senators, instead of a delegate. Why, the delegate couldn't even vote. Congressmen can. And one of these days, so will women."

She executed a little dance step. Uncle Jim and Tenny exchanged glances, and Uncle Jim grimaced. "Missy's gettin' a bit too big for her britches," he said.

"Why, Uncle Jim," Rowdy teased him, "I haven't been wearing my britches to school at all." She saw him begin to color, and said gently, "I wear skirts, Uncle Jim, like any respectable girl."

"Yore a stem-winder, gal," Tenny told her. "Gonna take some lot of man to handle you."

Rowdy giggled, Uncle Jim scowled and the three went on to discuss statehood and what it would mean to Oklahoma. "Wish they'd quit hagglin' and make Oklahoma City the permanent capital," Tenny groused.

"Why?" Rowdy baited him.

"They'd be lots of advantages," Tenny said. "The capital's just naturally gonna have more business, more improvements. They're talkin' already about brickin' some more streets."

"Hard on horse hooves," Uncle Jim said gloomily.

"Keep the dust down, though," Rowdy contributed. "Aunt Sarah says she hates to hang out her wash, the red dust grimes it so."

Tenny pulled out his turnip watch. "Gotta get a high behind," he said, "or Clover'll give me what for. Oh, one more thing. I heerd Vince Turner is out of Leavenworth."

Uncle Jim frowned. "You 'member him, don't you?" Tenny asked, and Jim nodded. Rowdy shook her head.

"No 'count," Tenny said briefly. "Got sent up for sellin' moonshine to Injuns. Well, I got to git." Neither he nor Jim mentioned that Angus had been instrumental in sending Turner to the federal penitentiary.

It was a couple of months later, on a blistering hot day, that Dove showed up, unannounced. Rowdy was making herself a new pair of velvet pants. Jim had finished his morning chores and was sitting under the cottonwood. Angus was doing some fence mending, and refurbishing the scarecrow in the garden. Nearby, a rain crow cawed his derision.

Angus heard the smart clop of horses' hooves, glanced

up, recognized the buggy, grinned a little and went on restuffing the scarecrow's coat. When the buggy pulled to a stop in the yard, he ignored it. Jim went to help Dove alight.

"Yore a sight for sore eyes," Angus heard the old man say as Rowdy ran out of the house.

"Dove!" she cried, and the two women flew into each other's arms. Rowdy shed a couple of tears and began to ask questions. How was Auntie Po? Was Suzette still married to that rancher? Had Dove been to St. Louis to see the new styles? "But come in the house," she interrupted herself. "Uncle Jim must have known you were coming. He made your favorite gingerbread this morning."

"Just a minute," Dove said. "I got to see your pa."

"Oh," Rowdy said. "Sure. Come on, Uncle Jim, you grind the beans and I'll make fresh coffee."

In the garden, Angus went on with his work. He had the coat on now, and was tying a slim length of red cloth around the scarecrow's hat. Not that there was much left in the garden; still, there remained turnips, black-eyed peas and pumpkins. Besides, he didn't want the crows to get in the habit of visiting the patch.

Still ignoring Dove, he hammered a nail hole through two small pieces of tin, ran a cord through them and tied them at the end of each scarecrow "arm."

Dove's steps dragged as she picked her way across the uneven ground. "Looks jes' like you," she offered, affecting pertness. The effect was belied by the uncertainty in her voice.

Angus turned. "Hello, Dove," he said.

Dove shifted her weight from one foot to the other. "You don't seem very glad to see me."

"I wanted first to be sure you weren't totin' iron."

Her skin was light enough that the red showed when she flushed. He watched it creep up from her neck to the roots of her hair, didn't know whether she was embarrassed or angry. She was staring at her feet.

"You always was a mean cuss, and ain't changed a bit," she said sulkily.

"That what you drove out here to tell me?" Angus asked.

She raised her eyes to his. "I—I come to thank you," she muttered. Her lower lip was trembling. "I'm beholden to you," she said grudgingly, and he knew what the acknowledgment had cost her. He put an arm lightly across her shoulders.

"Let's go in and have some coffee," he said.

68.

The year 1907 was an auspicious year for Oklahomans. In addition to the opening run of '89, a number of other parcels of land had been opened to settlement.

The Indians who had advocated two separate states were disappointed. A constitution had been completed by the territorial legislature. President Roosevelt made no bones about the fact that he disliked it, but all provisions of the Enabling Act had been met, and he had no recourse but to accept it.

He proclaimed November sixteenth as the date when the government of the new state would take over. The state, and particularly the city of Guthrie, went into a frenzy of preparations for celebrating statehood.

At the Three Oaks school, Rowdy's pupils went over Oklahoma history, in honor of the big day. Rowdy told them of the territorial governors, the hardships the '89ers had endured.

"God has been very good to this country," she concluded. "We have it easy now, compared with what our folks went through." She told them, too, that she planned to go to Guthrie for the ceremonies and the barbecue, and would be glad to take any of those students whose parents couldn't attend. There were no takers; everyone was going.

Except Angus.

When she asked him what time he'd like to leave, he growled shortly that he had no intention of going.

Rowdy was stunned. "Why, Papa?" she demanded. "You're an Eighty-niner. They'll be honoring you-all especially."

Angus's face was set. "There's going to be a tomfool wedding. Injun squaw, white man." He all but spat, then remembered he was inside the soddy.

"It's symbolic, Papa," Rowdy cried, "Indian Territory and Oklahoma Territory being united into one state."

"Bear's ass," Angus retorted. It was his ultimate expression of disgust. Rowdy had never heard him use it before. She stared in astonishment, saw the stubbornness of his face and said no more.

"I'll go with you, girl," Uncle Jim volunteered.

Scowling at both of them, Angus got up and walked out.

The day dawned fair, as a bridal promise. It was cool, the sun was shining and for once the wind was still. The horse stepped out smartly in front of the buggy. Rowdy had tied a red bow on either side of his bridle.

"I'm so excited, I could just bust," she said.

"Don't do that." Uncle Jim chuckled. "I don't want to have to stop and pick up the pieces."

"Did you know Governor Haskell is going to take the oath of office right there?" she demanded. "And Mr. Owen and Mr. Gore are both going to speak. I do think they'll make fine senators."

"Met 'em, have you?" Uncle Jim teased her.

"No, but I've heard a lot about them. You know something? The flag will have a new star. I hadn't thought of that."

"I know they's gonna be more moonshiners," Uncle Jim grumbled. "Prohibition. Pshaw! What's wrong with a man wettin' his whistle now and again?"

"It won't bother you," Rowdy said. "You don't drink anything to speak of."

"It's the principle of the thing," Jim growled. "They's gonna be drunks a plenty in Guthrie today, missy. They'll be tryin' to finish off all the white lightnin' 'fore prohibition starts at midnight. Mind you stay close to me. Some men get downright ornery when they've had a drink or two."

"Yes, Uncle Jim." Rowdy was at her most demure.

The National Guard had been called out to add a touch of military smartness to the festivities. "Don't you go gettin' sweet on none of them sojers," Uncle Jim admonished, and Rowdy laughed.

As they neared Guthrie, it seemed as if people of half

259

a dozen states were converging there. There were vehicles of every description, people on horseback, people walking. At the outskirts of town, the sound of music could be heard.

A band, of sorts, had been assembled, and was thumping out the national anthem, "Yankee Doodle" and "Dixie" with fine impartiality. Rowdy leaned forward, lips parted, eyes dancing. It was still early, but already there was an enormous crowd.

Rowdy seized Jim's arm. "Isn't it *exciting?*" she demanded, and tapped an impatient toe against the front of the buggy.

Jim let out a roar. "What in tarnation are you doin' with them proud shoes on?" he yelled. "High heels. Ain't you got no sense at all? You can't walk on them pegs!"

Rowdy tossed her head. "I've got on my Sunday dress," she said. "I can't wear workaday shoes with a Sunday dress. Now, if I could have worn pants . . ."

Jim snorted. "That's what comes of havin' two pairs of shoes. I told yore Pa . . ." He broke off as though at a loss for words. Rowdy grinned and hugged him.

"I'll drive up close to the library," Jim said grumpily. "You get out there; I'll go find a place for the buggy."

"Thank you, Uncle Jim."

People were laughing and calling, jugs were being passed around openly, the day shimmered. Uncle Jim maneuvered the horse and buggy through the crowd, mumbling his disgruntlement.

Finally, they were reasonably close to the library, where the speakers would appear. "Mind you wait on the west side," Jim cautioned Rowdy. "I don't like you being out alone . . ." He continued to mutter instructions and dire predictions, and Rowdy nodded and nodded and nodded.

Left alone, she obediently picked her way toward the back of the library. She saw no one she knew. Tinkers were elbowing their way through the crowd, offering everything from drinking water to pins and needles. The air had a lovely crisp warmth to it.

Nearby, Rowdy heard the plink of a banjo, a hoarse voice singing. Curious, She eased her way toward the sound—it wasn't far from where she was to meet Uncle Jim—and saw a medicine wagon set up. The singer finished his tune, danced a jig, and the spieler came to the back of the wagon, holding a single tin box in his hand.

"Anyone here gots aches or pains?" he demanded. "But I don't need ask that. We all get pain, from overwork, too much heat, too much cold, the rheumatiz or too much—indulgence." He paused, significantly rolling his eyes, and the men in the crowd gave sheepish barks of laughter. The women looked down at their feet.

Rowdy was enchanted. She had heard about medicine shows but never seen one. The speaker was going on. "Having saved the life of an Indian chief . . . uh, an Egyptian king, my great-great-great-grandfather was granted the secret of the sacred herb that grows only along the Nile.

"The common folks were not allowed to use this herb. Indeed, it was considered so sacred, they could not even touch it. It was reserved for the use of worship, offered up as a sweet incense and used to cure the ills of the royal household.

"The secret of preparation died with the early Egyptian kings. Today, I alone know that secret. It has been handed down in my family, father to son. And since I have no son, it will die with me."

He paused dramatically. "My friends, I am an old man. This will be the only chance you will ever have to obtain this medication, which has been described by some as having magical properties.

"It will help your backache, your leg ache, bunions and calluses. It can be used to poultice a boil, to ease rheumatiz. Rubbed on the forehead, it is guaranteed to make you feel better the morning after. Rubbed on the stomach, it does away with the bellyache. It is, my friends, even said to ease the pangs of childbirth.

"Now the cost of this wonder salve is fifty cents." Sensing the dropping away of interest, he added hastily, "Fifty cents ordinarily. But today, because this is the grand and glorious celebration of a new state in the union, I'm gonna let each person have one, but only one, for twenty-five cents. That's right, ladies and gentlemen, the fourth part of a dollar."

Rowdy had worked her way to the front of the crowd, and stood gawking with the others. The medicine man's eyes fell on her. "Tell you what else I'm gonna do," he intoned. "Because this little lady, here, is so beautiful, I'm

261

gonna give her a box, not for a quarter, not for a dime, but FREE!"

The boy who had done the singing jumped off the tailgate and brought the box to Rowdy as though offering her jewels. Embarrassed at being singled out, the girl wished she had minded Uncle Jim.

"Open it up, little lady!" the barker shouted. "Let these good people see the salve that will bring them so much relief."

Feeling herself blushing, Rowdy fumbled with the lid. The boy took the tin back from her, lifted the lid, inhaled deeply, rolled his eyes.

"Lawdy, Doctor," he yelled, "I feel better from just taking a sniff. Sure you wanta let folks in on this?"

"Yes, buster, I am," the "doctor" came back. "I've been offered a fabulous sum by pharmaceutical concerns in the East. But this is my gift to my fellow man. It's not for the rich and powerful, as it used to be.

"It's available, my friends, only to you. Now, who'll be the first?"

Rowdy lifted the lid of the "magic" salve, sniffed and made a face. It smelled like horse liniment. She began to try to pick her way back through the crowd, but was wedged in so tightly that she could scarcely move. She noted a number of Indians in the gathering and was glad Papa hadn't come. Uneasily, she hoped Uncle Jim hadn't made it back to the library yet, again tried to ease through the crowd. It was too dense.

Her movement seemed once more to have attracted the attention of the "doctor." She saw a puzzled look come into his funny silverfish eyes. Abruptly, he stopped the sales pitch, announced there'd be another show in an hour and jumped to the ground.

Rowdy knew a moment of panic as he headed in her direction. She thought of all the dire warnings of Papa and Uncle Jim and attempted to move backward. But the doctor was there.

"Do these old eyes deceive me," he asked, "or could this be Miss Martha Scofield?" When she hesitated, puzzled, he added, "It must be. You're the spittin' image of your dear mother."

"You knew my mother?" Rowdy asked.

"I had that honor, my dear young lady, and I know

262

your father, too." He glanced around. "Is he here?" he asked.

Rowdy shook her head. The funny darting eyes put her off a bit, but if he'd known Papa and her mother—he must have, or he'd never have recognized her—he must be all right.

"I'm sorry if I should remember you." It was half apology, half question.

"You would have been too young. I've been away from this beautiful country for several years. Business elsewhere. Ah, the cares of the world. I'm Vince Turner."

The name sounded vaguely familiar. "How do you do," Rowdy murmured, and would have turned away, since the crowd had dispersed, but he took her arm.

"Just a minute, Miss Martha. Here's someone you should meet." Beginning to be annoyed, Rowdy turned, with a sharp word on her lips. Turner had put his other hand on the arm of a young Indian man.

"John White Hawk?" he asked tentatively. Before answering, the Indian stared down at Turner's hand on his arm. The doctor hastily removed it.

"Yes, I'm John White Hawk."

"Miss Martha, may I have the pleasure of presenting Mr. White Hawk? John, this here is Miss Martha Scofield. Seeing' you're both Oklahomans now, I figured you should meet."

The man was gabbling, Rowdy thought, the strange eyes darting around like dragonflies. She wondered if he were a little crazy. Or drunk, maybe. Whatever he was, Uncle Jim was probably waiting by now. And furious.

She looked up into a sun-browned face, and it seemed to her that her heart stumbled, and then accelerated its pace. A coal-black braid of hair over either shoulder. Firmly molded lips, decisive chin, high cheekbones, eyes a color she had never seen before. Tawny, she thought.

He stepped forward, nodding. There was a spare grace in the supple movement, which reminded her of a bobcat.

An Indian? Papa wouldn't like that. But surely he wouldn't want her to be rude. She held out her hand.

"My friends call me Rowdy," she was horrified to hear herself say with a catch in her voice. The boy, the young man, took her hand.

"My pleasure, Miss Rowdy," he said formally, but the pressure of his hand was not formal, the spark in his eyes was not formal. "Could I offer you a cool drink?" he asked, and seemed to have forgotten he still held her hand.

Rowdy's eyelashes dipped. Papa would die, he would surely die, but it seemed of small moment compared with the effervescence beginning to bubble within her. Vince Turner was forgotten. Uncle Jim was forgotten. Papa was forgotten. Her eyelashes swept back up. "Why, yes, Mr. White Hawk," she said demurely, "I think I could fancy a cool drink." It was hard for her even to speak.

He seemed suddenly aware that he still held her hand, and released it, flushing. Rowdy took hold of his arm. "The crowd and all," she explained, thankful that her voice was cool and prim.

"Of course."

His skin, she thought, felt like satin. She shivered.

Forgotten, Vince went off, grinning maliciously to himself and rubbing his hands together. That son of a bitch had put him in the penitentiary. He knew how Angus felt about Indians. To annoy the preacher had been his sole motive in introducing the young people. He had expected no more from it than that someone would report to Angus that his daughter had been talking to a red-face.

But he had seen the flash of wonder in Rowdy's eyes, the startled, almost dazed expression on John's face. Oh, Lord, if they should become really interested in each other, what a wonderful, beautiful, satisfying revenge. "Kee-rist," he whispered, all but hugging himself.

As they made their slow way through the crowd, to the wagon where lemonade was being sold, Rowdy wondered desperately what to say. Her mouth was dry. She, who was never at a loss for words. John hadn't uttered a word. She stole a glance at him. His profile was as sharp as though it had been chiseled out of marble. He seemed to feel her glance, turned and smiled.

"I almost didn't come today," he said. "My father wished for a separate state."

"Papa doesn't approve either. But I'm glad you did come, Mr. White Hawk." If that was being forward—oh, dear, she didn't know whether it was or not. She seemed to have lost her bearings.

The boy laughed, and she was charmed by the sound. "My friends call me John," he said, mimicking her earlier

264

words. Angus had said that Indians never laughed, never even smiled.

"John," she repeated, knew she was going faster than the social amenities allowed. Didn't care. She felt like laughing aloud, yet tears seemed perilously near the surface.

She saw and spoke to the Holtzworthys, saw their smiles go blank, the easy words of greeting break off as they saw her hand resting on John's arm. She introduced him as she would have any other young man. Sarah and Zeb nodded, but Rowdy noted and resented the fact that neither of them offered to shake hands.

"Where are your folks, Martha?" Sarah asked severely.

"Papa's on the circuit. Uncle Jim's gone to take care of the horse and buggy. He'll be along directly." She knew Sarah noted, if Zeb did not, that the color in her cheeks was heightened and that her eyes were shining.

I don't care, she thought. I—do—not—care.

She and John left the older couple and found a tinker selling honey dips. John bought two, and they stood, eating—the sticky sweetness dripping off their fingers—laughing, speaking now and then, but mostly just looking. It was as though, if they probed deeply enough with their eyes, they would know all about each other.

They bought lemonade and carried it over to a shady locust tree, found a place to sit down. "Won't your dress be ruined?" John asked.

"It doesn't matter," she said dreamily.

They sat, they ate, they talked. Although there were hundreds of people around them, they were aware only of each other. Once in a long while, Rowdy remembered Uncle Jim and thought vaguely that she should go and look for him. Then the thought would float away, forgotten in the glory of the moment.

She learned that John was twenty. He was a Cherokee, and his father was a member of the tribal government. John had gone to school near Tahlequah. He had been to Oklahoma City a number of times and was intrigued by the white man's ways, though he could not see himself adapting to them.

For her part, Rowdy told him of her father's ministry.

"My family holds to its ancient beliefs," John said, "but we had a man among us once who called himself a missionary."

265

"It couldn't have been Papa," Rowdy said quickly. "His circuit lies the other way."

The ceremonies, the speeches, and music continued, and finally the "wedding" between Mrs. Leo Bennett, of Muskogee, a beautiful young Cherokee woman, and C. J. Jones was performed.

Rowdy and John might have been marooned on a desert isle. In the late afternoon, great mounds of barbecue and other foods were eaten. Finally, the crowd began to break up. The two were oblivious to it.

The shadows were growing long when Uncle Jim found them. Rowdy had never seen the old man really angry before. He was white-faced with fury. A vein throbbed in his forehead.

"Where in hell have you been?" he shouted.

Rowdy glanced up. "This is John White Hawk, Uncle Jim," she said, as though that were explanation enough.

John got to his feet, helped the girl up. "Miss Rowdy and I were talking," he said.

The old man was speechless. He had worried the hours through, had looked and inquired, and was near the end of his strength. During the long hours of searching, he'd died a thousand deaths. Rowdy was his love, his pride. She gave meaning to his life. To see her here, so calm and unconcerned . . . Relief mingled with his anger, producing a jumble of feelings.

"I was skeered," he said, and, horrified, felt a tear slide down his cheek. He brushed it away with his knuckles, but Rowdy had seen it.

"I'm sorry, Uncle Jim. Truly." She put her arms around him, kissed his cheek where the tear had made a path. "John, this is my grandfather, Mr. Royal. I wouldn't have got to come today if he hadn't brought me." She had long ago associated the Dave Royal of the poster with the old man and had, one way and another, let him know she recognized the relationship between him and her father, though she continued to call him Uncle Jim.

"How do you do, Mr. Royal," John said.

The old man snuffled and reached for a handkerchief. "Yore Injun?" he asked cautiously.

John nodded. "Cherokee."

Jim directed a glance at his granddaughter. "Yore pa . . ."

266

"We'll talk about Papa later," Rowdy interrupted hurriedly. "It was nice meeting you, Mr. . . ." She shot a beseeching glance at the older man. ". . . Johnny," she finished.

"I would like to see you again."

She dared not ask him to her home. She would have to do some missionary work of her own before that could happen. Her inventiveness was not equal to the situation, not with Uncle Jim standing so close by.

"Perhaps we'll run into each other in Oklahoma City," she suggested. "I go there sometimes."

"Yes." Johnny's voice was wooden. "Goodbye, Miss Rowdy."

In the buggy, the girl was silent, heart and head full of Johnny White Hawk. In her mind, she went over the things he had said, smiling to herself. In her heart, she knew already that their lives were inextricably interwoven.

Was this the way other girls had felt? If so, no wonder they talked incessantly about Wilbur or Tom or Reese. Part of her wanted to ask Uncle Jim if he didn't think Johnny was handsome, clever, intelligent. Part of her wanted to hug her secret to her heart. It was so new and fragile, so shining and beautiful.

Uncle Jim had been urging the horse along at a smart clip. "Buttercup's probably bellering her head off to be milked," he said at last, sourly.

Rowdy said "Mmm," and her dreaminess rearoused his anger.

"Yore pa would have a conniption if he found out."

Rowdy seemed to rouse from her reverie. "Don't worry, Uncle Jim," she said gently. "I'm going to tell Papa."

"Gawd Amighty!" the old man breathed. "He'll kill the both of us."

"No. None of it was your fault. I'm going to tell him so." Then, in a cry that came straight from the heart, she whispered, "Uncle Jim, that's the man I want to marry."

"Yore pa . . ."

"I know, it's going to be hard."

"Hard? Girl, it'll be impossible. He's always been easy with you. Reckon yore the one person he really loves. You get his back up, though, you'll see just how bullheaded he can be. Why, in all the years I've lived in his

267

house, he's never acknowledged me as his pa. I don't s'pose he ever will. Guess I deserve it, but just once, it would be nice . . ."

"I appreciate you, and so did Sampson," she assured him. "I know Papa can be stubborn, but he'll have to see it my way when he knows how much I . . . how much John and I . . . He's got to, that's all."

Deeply troubled, Jim was silent.

69.

The next time Angus rode in from the circuit, a cold snap arrived almost on his heels. He and Jim decided to butcher the hog they'd been fattening. The animal was good-sized—corn-fed—and handsome, as pigs go.

It took all day, even with help from Pete and Alice Smith, and Rowdy told herself that Papa was too tired that first night for her to bring up the subject of John White Hawk.

But on the second evening, when she had finished washing the supper dishes, Rowdy asked Angus if he'd like to take a walk. Her heart was thudding so hard against her ribs, she was certain he'd hear it.

"Sure," Angus said. He'd been working on a new frame for one of the windows, which had warped, but laid aside his miter and went to fetch his jacket. He was filled with a special sense of contentment. A snug cabin, a good farm, work he enjoyed and, above all, his daughter. My cup runneth over, he thought.

Outside, Rowdy's hand tucked into the crook of his arm, he headed east. They walked for some time in silence, and gradually Angus became aware of the tension in the almost painful grip of Rowdy's fingers on his arm. He put his hand over hers, and heard her catch her breath.

"Papa, please try to understand." The words stampeded

against themselves, and Angus was alarmed. Something had to be drastically wrong to put Miss Rowdy in this state.

"All right," he said through dry lips.

"The day of the celebration at Guthrie, I—I met a young man." His heart turned over. Quiet, you fool, he told it. This was bound to happen sometime.

"Go on," he said.

"You mustn't blame Uncle Jim. He went to find a place for the buggy. I met this friend of yours. He recognized me because he said I looked so much like—Mother."

"Who was this?"

"Mr. Vince Turner."

Angus felt the spasm as the muscles tightened throughout his entire body. "He's old enough to be your grandfather," he shouted, "and worthless as tits on a boar hog!"

"Not him. I mean, he's not the one. He introduced me to this boy." Her voice was trembling, but Angus heaved a sigh of relief.

"Does this boy have a name?" he asked gently.

"Yes." Her voice was unsteady, her fingers icy. "This is the part you have to understand, Papa. Don't blow up! His name is John White Hawk."

Had she kicked him in the gut, Angus could not have been more shocked. He halted in mid-stride, broke her grip on his arm when he turned to face her. In the faint light, Rowdy met his eyes without wavering, but he could see her desperate anxiety. He felt the fumes of fury rising thick and black.

"An Injun!" he said in a strangled voice.

"He's educated, Papa. He wears regular clothes. His father is one of the tribal leaders. They've learned so much from the white man, his family even had Negro slaves before the war."

If he was aware of the sarcasm in her words, he gave no sign of it. "Curls?" he asked.

Rowdy felt the blood color her face. "Braids," she said.

"Braids," he repeated.

"You'll like him, Papa, I know you will. Papa, he's everything I want. Handsome, intelligent, gentle. You said Indians never laugh. He's got a wonderful sense of humor."

Angus said "No!" turned on his heel and started back

to the cabin, his strides so long Rowdy couldn't keep up with him. He'd been afraid that if he stood any longer, he'd strike her. His daughter, *his* daughter an Injun squaw? Not, by God, while he drew breath.

As they neared the soddy, he stopped and waited for her. She could see the pallor of his face, the febrile glare of his eyes.

"Martha!" he said—and she thought incidentally that it was the only time he'd ever used that name—"Martha, I've been easy with you. Too easy, some said. But by God, this is where I draw the line. You are not to see this —this savage again. I forbid it!" Rowdy took a backward step. He looked like a picture she had once seen of an incensed Moses smashing the tablets of stone.

"Do you understand?" Angus shouted. She could not speak. Angus grasped her shoulders. His fingers felt like clamps gouging into her flesh. "I asked you if you understood?" he roared, shaking her.

"I understand!" Rowdy finally got the words out. There were tears of pain, humiliation, fright, disappointment stinging her eyes, dampening her cheeks. "You're hurting me!" she screamed in outrage.

The shaking stopped. Momentarily, she thought she would fall, dug her teeth savagely into her lower lip. She wouldn't give him the satisfaction. He released her, but spasms of pain still racked her shoulders.

Angus wheeled and headed for the barn. Rowdy forced herself to hold back the tears. He—no one—was going to see her weeping her heart out. With an effort, she composed herself. It was more difficult to control the trembling of her body. At last, though, she felt sufficiently in control to go into the house.

Uncle Jim looked up as she came into the kitchen, a question in his eyes. Rowdy gave him a curt headshake, got a drink and went to her room. She lay down on the bed, wanting to cry now, but the tears had dried up. She wanted to sleep and could not.

She heard Papa come in hours later, was still awake when he got up early the next morning. She heard the sounds of him getting his things together. So he was going back on the circuit, though it was not yet time.

I hope he doesn't come back, she thought bitterly. Then, never one to deceive herself, knew that wasn't true.

She wanted him back as he'd always been. She felt bereft.
Papa had acted as though he hated her.

The tears came then, scalding and debilitating. She bur-
rowed deep into the pillow so Uncle Jim wouldn't hear
her sobs.

70.

Riding Kadif through a wooded area, Angus was heartsick. It was gray and gloomy, a fitting day for the way he
felt. "Papa, he's everything I want." He could almost see
the words hanging in the air, as though written with a finger of fire.

A squaw. Half-breed kids. He snorted aloud, and Kadif, taking the sound as proof that Angus was not concen-
trating, began to run.

"Behave yourself, you mean son of a bitch!" Angus
shouted, glad of something to shout at. He got the horse
to slow its pace. I can't preach, he thought, not with my
daughter gone out of her mind.

When the Biblical injunction to make peace with his
brother came to mind, he told himself sourly that no Injun
heathen was his brother. Injuns were something less than
human. Woman killers. As for preaching to them . . . He
spat.

Angus followed his usual route, though afterward he
could have recalled not one thing about the trip. But
when, after three weeks, he started home, his mood began
to lighten. It was probably all just a pipe dream she'd had,
he told himself, the passing fancy of an inexperienced girl.
Girls did get queer notions, he'd heard. She'd probably
forgotten the whole incident by now.

It never occurred to him that she would disobey his order.

As for Rowdy, though mutinous, she made no attempt
to see Johnny. Even when Uncle Jim went to Oklahoma
City the following Saturday, she stayed home. Jim was

271

worried about the girl. She was eating almost nothing and getting more peaked and big-eyed by the day. And this time he knew the loss of appetite was real. Rowdy wasn't sleeping well, either. Jim could hear her moving around in her room, hear her weeping.

He wished to God Angus would get home. For the first time since he'd come here to stay, he thought about taking off again, but couldn't. He was too concerned about the girl.

"Like two bulls," he muttered to himself. "Heads locked agin each other, horns a gougin', and both of 'em too stubborn to give an inch."

It was Wednesday of the third week after they'd met that Rowdy saw Johnny again. She'd dismissed school at the usual time, listlessly started getting ready to go home.

She loved Papa, of course. He had filled her whole life, until Johnny. When she thought of Johnny, her heart bounced. She couldn't give him up. She slumped into her chair, put her head down on the desk.

She heard the sound of a horse's hooves and sighed. One of the children had forgotten his lunch pail, she supposed. She straightened, brushed back her hair. Like any old maid schoolmarm, she thought, and was angry with herself when her eyes filled.

She was putting books away when the door opened. She turned. Her hand went to her mouth. "Johnny?" she whispered, scarcely daring to believe her eyes, then: "Johnny!" and she ran into his arms as naturally as steel to a magnet. She lifted her face and they kissed, the boy's arms so tight around her that she could hardly breathe. She didn't care.

The world was back in orbit. The sun was shining. The world was beautiful, and her heart was singing.

When they finally drew apart, Johnny said, "I didn't see you in Oklahoma City."

"I—I guess we missed each other," she stammered; then, slowly: "No, that's not true. Sit down, Johnny. I have to tell you something." They sat on the school benches, and she smiled wistfully at the way he dwarfed the seat. He was watching her closely, brows drawn together.

"Is it so bad?" he asked, and the girl nodded miserably. "Worse than bad," she answered. "You see, Papa doesn't like Indians."

His laugh boomed out in the small room. "Is that all?" he asked. "My father doesn't like white people. All my life, I've heard nothing but tales of treachery, broken treaties, the Trail of Tears. That's the past. We, you and I, are the *now*. I respect and honor my father. But you are my Moonlight on Running Water."

Rowdy caught her breath, felt again the sting of tears. "That's beautiful," she whispered.

He laughed again. "Don't look so sad about it," he commanded. And, unexpectedly changing the subject: "You're the only person who ever called me Johnny. I like it."

Rowdy sighed. "Why can't life be simple? Papa would die if he knew I was seeing you. He'd die if I even spoke to you in a crowd. I guess your father feels the same way."

"He does," Johnny agreed. "But we are grown. Blind obedience is for small children. I'll go to your father and tell him I wish to call on you."

"Not yet," Rowdy said, alarmed. "L—let me try—let me see if I can—"

"I don't like hide-in-the-corner games," Johnny warned.

"Neither do I," she said quickly. "But you don't know what he's like when he's mad. I'm afraid he'd—oh, Lord, I don't know what he'd do."

Johnny grinned. "You mean he'd try to boot me out? Let him try." He spoke with the arrogance of the young buck, secure in the knowledge of his own strength.

The girl was too troubled to respond to his lightheartedness. "I just want you-all to get along. I know Papa would like you. Let me—try to get him to—to meet you. He *must*," she finished.

Johnny stood up. "Tomorrow?" he asked.

"He won't be home that soon. He's usually on the circuit for three weeks. I'll talk to him next time he's home."

They kissed again, and it was he who drew away. "I shall have to change your name to Girl who Heats my Blood if I stay longer," he told her, unsmiling. "That is not what I want. I want you for my wife."

The crazy tears were in her throat now. "That's what I want too," she whispered. "To be your wife, bear your children."

He gave her a quick hug, swung about and was gone.

She stared after him, bemused, went home so buoyed up, she felt she could have skimmed over the earth without the horse.

By the time Papa got back from the circuit, he'd have had time to get over his anger. They could talk like reasonable adults. Once Papa realized how important Johnny was to her, he'd see it her way.

Johnny had said nothing about when he'd return, but he was there again the next afternoon. And continued to come to the school each day so they could spend an hour or two together. Rowdy was all but delirious with happiness.

71.

When Angus finally came back to the soddy, he and Rowdy, after a wary glance at each other, embraced and exchanged pecks on the cheek. Angus shook hands with Uncle Jim, said yes, he'd had a good trip, and what had they been up to?

On the surface, the atmosphere was normal. Jim, though, could feel the tension. It was like a pain in his chest. He'd been pleased with the change in Miss Rowdy over the past few days, since he did not know the reason for it. With father and daughter together again had come this constraint. It made him think somehow of coyotes circling a lone ram, fangs bared but still cautious of the ram's strength.

As for Angus, he kept assuring himself everything was all right. Rowdy hadn't been pining, that was for sure. Not with her face glowing as it was, the gaiety bubbling in her voice. It was just as he had thought: that heathen had been a moment's fancy.

Rowdy's strain revealed itself in loquaciousness. She chattered about everything under the sun. The school kids—one had broken out with measles; she hoped the whole class didn't come down with them. She was glad

274

she'd already had them. It was said that when grown-ups got measles, they could be very sick.

She told them of the Christmas program she was rehearsing; that the Smiths were building two more rooms. (It had been Jim who'd told her about the Smiths. He watched his granddaughter, troubled. She was too keyed-up. She sounded feverish.)

Rowdy said nothing, that night, about Johnny. The next evening, though, she fixed chicken and dumplings, made a deep-dish apple pie. One of Angus's favorite meals.

Her lips twisted once when she realized what she had instinctively done. This was what Aunt Sarah meant when she talked about women accomplishing things by being subtle. Pamper a man's stomach, then trick him into your way of thinking.

It was demeaning, Rowdy thought angrily. She hated acting like that. But this was so important, she'd do almost anything.

By the time supper was ready, she was so tense, she could hardly eat. Her talking streak had ended. She was groping in her mind for a way to discuss the problem. What would be the best way to start? Papa, I know you want me to be happy . . . No, he'd say she couldn't be happy as an Indian wife. Papa, times are different now . . . No. She pushed her food around on her plate. Her insides felt knotted.

After supper, Uncle Jim helped her straighten up, then said he thought he'd walk over and see Tenny. Poor old man, she thought, he's feeling the strain too.

Not Papa, she thought resentfully. He was sprawled out in his chair, reading the *St. Louis Post-Dispatch*, which the Holtzworthys saved for him. The lamp was smoking, blackening the chimney.

"That wick needs trimming," Rowdy said. She brought another lamp, lit it, blew out the first one. Using a cloth, she removed the hot chimney, cut the charred bits from the wick with a scissor and relit it.

"You're handy as a pocket on a shirt." Angus smiled at her. He sounded so normal, so Papa-ish and loving, surely this must be the right moment. She sat down.

"Papa," she said, "I *have* to talk to you."

Angus's heart missed a beat. He laid aside the paper. "All right," he said, "talk."

275

"Papa, I love Johnny White Hawk. I want to marry him."

Angus felt as though he'd been gutted.

Sudden inspiration came to the girl. "You said Mother's folks didn't want her to marry you. She had to run off."

Muscles tightened in Angus's cheeks. "Don't mention your mother in the same breath with that bastard!" His face was livid.

"Papa," she cried, "please try to understand."

Angus leaped to his feet. "Understand?" he shouted. "I understand, all right. You're the one who needs to 'understand.' Injuns are animals. When their women gave birth on the trail, they got behind a tree and dropped their baby . . . like a cow dropping a calf. Then they had to run to catch up with the tribe.

"You want to wrap yourself in a blanket, tend the crops while the men loaf and cry over the past? Too damn lazy to work. Too weak-gutted even to take a drink of whiskey without going crazy!" He was panting.

"Quite a speech!" Rowdy's voice was icy. "You don't know one damn thing about Indians. You've heard some wild stories made up of prejudice and ignorance. Papa, there are good Indians and bad Indians, just like there are good and bad white men."

"The only good Injun is a dead Injun," Angus said flatly, and stomped out of the house.

Rowdy sat, benumbed. Her throat ached, and she wished for the relief of tears, but her eyes were dry, gritty as though she'd been in a dust storm. Shakily, she got to her feet.

Uncle Jim had said Papa was bull-headed. She'd always thought he was fair, though—that he'd at least listen to the other person's side.

She stood a full five minutes, thoughts in chaos, until misery gave way to bitterness. She wasn't a child, to be told what she could or couldn't do. She was a grown woman. She earned her own living.

Papa wasn't going to keep her from Johnny! Just let him try!

Jim returned from Tenny's, took one look at Rowdy's brooding face and scurried off to bed. When, hours later, Angus returned—he had been tromping through the night, trying to shake off a sense of impending disaster—Rowdy was in bed, wakeful and coldly determined.

Again, Angus left early for the circuit. Rowdy was glad to see him go, and, truth to tell, Jim thought wryly, so was he. The feeling of tension in the house was unnerving to the old man. The pain in Jim's chest was heavy as a lump of lead.

72.

Rowdy's nerves were stretched to the breaking point by the time Johnny came to the school that Monday afternoon. She rose to meet him, went into his arms and burst into tears.

"Rowdy"—he was alarmed—"what is it? What's wrong?"

"P—Papa won't even—t—talk," she stammered, sobbing against his shirt front. "He's—I hate him!"

"No," Johnny said. "Our parents must be honored. Don't cry. My father also is very angry, but we'll find a way. Here, dry your eyes."

She took his handkerchief, mopped at her face, blew her nose. "I'm sorry," she said, and tried to smile. "Johnny, I—I can't stop seeing you. Maybe it's unladylike, but I'll meet you any time, any place you say. Just so Papa doesn't find out."

"No."

She looked up, unbelieving, saw his brows drawn together in a scowl and again wanted to weep. Maybe he didn't care as much as she did. Johnny drew her down to the bench, sat beside her.

"I do not play hide-in-the-corner games," he said. "I will go to your father. I'm sure he will hear me as an honorable man. My father . . ." He hesitated. "I honor and respect my father, but if he makes me choose between you and my people, you and I will make a life together somewhere else."

"Papa would kill you," Rowdy said simply. "We can see each other—"

He did not argue. He said again, forcefully, "No!"

"I'm sure I can make him see it my way. I need time . . ."

Johnny folded his arms. His face was stern.

Edgy from worry and sleeplessness, Rowdy's temper flared. "Now you're being the great tight-lipped Indian. Damn it, you're just as stubborn as Papa!"

Johnny got to his feet. He walked across the room. He opened the door and went out. He did not look back.

Dumbfounded, Rowdy waited. He wouldn't go off and leave her like that. He'd come back. He loved her, as she loved him. She heard the sound of the horse leaving, and her heart seemed to stop.

He wasn't coming back. Not now, not ever!

She was still holding his handkerchief. She pressed it against her eyes and wept again.

73.

When Angus returned from that trip on the circuit, he was shaken by the sight of Rowdy's face. It was so thin, she seemed all eyes. And Jim was wearing a perpetual frown of worry.

Nevertheless, Angus gave them both a cool greeting. Rowdy had gotten her own way once by refusing to eat, he thought angrily. Not this time, my girl!

Miss Rowdy went to her room as soon as the meal was finished, the kitchen neat. Jim sat down on a straight chair. He hadn't been able to relax and doze in the rocker since all this trouble started. The pain in his chest was growing worse. He wondered if he had a touch of pneumonia.

"Son," he said, "I'm pure-D anxious about that girl. She ain't said half a dozen words since you left. She don't

278

eat, she don't sleep. And if a body says anything to her, half the time she don't hear."

Angus's answer was a snort. Ostentatiously, he picked up a book and began to read.

Rowdy's sleeplessness continued. While he was home that week, Angus could hear her moving quietly around in her room at night. Once or twice when he, equally sleepless, went out into the cold night to walk himself into exhaustion, her lamp shone through the closed curtain. Damn it, he thought, it's for her own good.

All three felt the strain. Jim's chest pain never left him now. Angus and Rowdy spoke only when it was unavoidable. Once, when Angus asked the blessing at table, he raised his head to see the girl watching him sardonically, and flushed. Jim's efforts at conversation, Rowdy appeared not to hear; Angus answered with a curt yes or no when an answer was required.

Rowdy's misery spilled over into her work. Without realizing it, she had become waspish and impatient with the children. When an eight-year-old girl admitted one day that she'd forgotten an assignment, Rowdy spoke so harshly, the child cried and asked why the teacher was mad at them all the time.

Appalled, Rowdy went over to hug the little girl, near tears herself. "I'm sorry, honey," she said. And to the whole class: "I haven't meant to be cross. I've had—a lot on my mind."

A ten-year-old hand, masculine and grubby, went up. "You mean like my papa, when our new baby sister got there before the midwife?" Rowdy laughed through her tears, realized it was the first time she had laughed for days.

"Exactly like that, Joe," she said. "I'll try not to be so cross. All of you will have to help me."

They promised solemnly, given a new importance by this awesome glimpse into adult life. After school was over, though, the room empty, Rowdy sat at her desk, chin in hands, brooding. She was not only wretched herself. She was making Uncle Jim and her school-children wretched. Every time she saw Papa or even thought of him, the outrage and sense of loss ran through her afresh.

Though she had known Johnny only a few weeks, though their "courtship" had been limited to a dozen or so meetings, she had a deep and certain knowledge that

279

their love had been real, that it would have been lifelong. Now he was lost to her. The room grew cold. The shadows were lengthening. Heavy with grief, she headed at last for home.

The chill air seemed to clear her head somewhat as Biscuit carried her across the countryside. She didn't have to live at home. The thought was like a flash of lightning streaking across her mind.

She was independent, a modern woman. Lord, why hadn't she thought of it before? She could move to town, get a room at Ma Cavelli's, do as she pleased. People would talk, and Papa—Papa would raise hell. Her chin went up. Let them talk, and let him raise hell, she thought defiantly. Her only regret was that she hadn't thought of it sooner.

She'd be farther from school, but she had Biscuit. At least, she guessed the horse was hers. Papa had given him to her. She didn't *think* he'd be an Indian giver and take it back.

She winced at the phrase, Indian giver. She had grown up with such expressions, never thought of them before as slurs.

She put the horse to a gallop, more lighthearted than she'd been for weeks. At home, as soon as she'd shed hat and coat, she rushed into the kitchen. "Uncle Jim," she cried, throwing her arms around him, "I'm going to move, soon as I can get a room. I know it's been hard on you, Papa acting like he has. He'll be easier to get along with when I'm gone."

The old man turned slowly from the big cookstove. "You'll get yoreself talked about," he said, fretting. It wasn't what he was really thinking. Rowdy gone? The sun disappearing from its orbit? The pain sharpened in his chest, and he thought vaguely that he must ask the doctor about it one of these days. Dyspepsia, probably.

He said no more, but slow tears began to course down his cheeks. He turned back to the stove and stirred the black-eyed peas violently.

After supper, Rowdy got her clothes together, her books and keepsakes. She found a rag doll Papa had given her, and laid it aside. Silly to let a doll depress her.

When everything was packed, ready to be moved, she went to bed, for the first time in weeks drifted off immediately into dreamless sleep.

She woke to a garbled noise that sounded like her name was being called. Her room was pitch black. She lay for a moment, blinking, decided she had been dreaming and snuggled back down into the blankets.

"Martha!" The sound was still garbled, eerie in the darkness, but she wasn't dreaming it. Heart pounding, she jumped up, ran to the kitchen, lit a lamp. Uncle Jim lay crumpled on the floor, face down.

"Oh, God!" she whispered, running to him. She turned him over. He was in his long johns, and fumbled at himself to be sure he was covered. Torn between tears and laughter at the gesture, Rowdy said gently, "I won't look at you, Uncle Jim."

"Not fittin'." She caught the faint words. And then: "I fell," he said. It was an apology. She saw that the left side of his face was drawn, his mouth fixed in a rictus. But at least he was alive.

"Let me help you," she said. She put an arm around him, supported him to a sitting position. But when, with her help, he attempted to get up, his left leg was useless. Horror came into his face. With his right hand, he began to massage the leg violently, as though by so doing, he could bring back its use. When he looked up, defeat was in his eyes, tears on his cheeks.

"It's all right, Uncle Jim," Rowdy said past the lump in her throat. "Here, let's get you into bed." She all but picked him up and was surprised at how light he was. "We're going to have to fatten you up," she said lightly, hoping to lessen his misery.

Tucking the covers around him, she went to stoke the fire. "I'll get some coffee going," she chattered. "Make you some good hot oatmeal. All you've done for us, it's about time someone did a little something for you."

"It'll go away," the old man quavered. "Tomorrow. The other time, I warn't in bed only a day or two." So he realized he'd had another stroke, she thought, and bit her lip, fearful that this one was more serious. His left side seemed completely useless. He dozed, and she sat by his bed.

When he wakened, she brought water and a washcloth, let him wash himself. Despite Papa's poor opinion of Uncle Jim, she knew the old man had a strange and vulnerable pride. He wouldn't like her treating him like an invalid.

When breakfast was ready, she helped him slide into a chair, draped a blanket around his shoulders. "Soon as we eat," she said, "I'm going to ride over to Clover's for a minute."

"I'll be all right." The words came out in a burble of sound, hard to understand. She noted that the left eyelid did not blink.

"Of course you'll be all right," she said. "I'll tuck you up all snug like you used to tuck me in when I was a little girl. I do need to see Tenny, though."

"School," he mouthed.

She shrugged. "I need a day's vacation, and I don't think the kids will object."

He ate sparingly, got down a cup of coffee, half a bowl of oatmeal, a bite or two of bread. Part of the food dribbled onto his chin, and he swiped at it after a quick glance to be sure she wasn't watching. Rowdy wanted to weep.

When he was again in bed, she put Biscuit to a run and was at Clover and Tenny's in minutes. Rapidly, she told them what had happened, asked Tenny to ride over and dismiss school, telling the children not to come back until they got word. Then, would he please go for the doctor?

"Do you want me to come over and see to him?" Clover asked.

"No, I'll stay." Suddenly, tears overwhelmed her. "Mrs. M.," she sobbed, "it's not only the—stroke. He—he acts embarrassed, like he'd done something he shouldn't and was ashamed."

Clover nodded, hands on hips. "Takes men like that a lot of times. Now, child"—she changed the subject—"I'll go over and keep school for you a few days, if you want. I'm not eddycated like you, but I've got a little book learnin'."

"Could you do that?" Rowdy faltered. "I hate for the kids to miss even a few days. It's so easy for the bigger ones not to start again, once they stop."

And so it was arranged. Tenny would go straight for the doctor; Clover would go to the school. They were good people, the girl thought as she rode back toward home, the people they knew. The Smiths and Holtzworthys, Tenny and Clover, Maggie Cruikshank, the folks on Papa's circuit. She drew back from the thought of Papa, and her heart slid. No chance of moving away now. Uncle Jim had to be cared for.

He was up on his right elbow when she went in; she knew it galled his pride to be in bed. "Think it'd be all right for you to sit up," she told him briskly. "Wait'll I get this coat off."

She maneuvered him into the rocker and got a flour sack. "Now, don't fuss," she scolded before he could protest. "I'm gonna tie this around here, kind of like a support, 'til the doctor sees you."

She saw the poor twisted face go mutinous momentarily, but he said nothing.

When the doctor came, poked and pried, examined the leg and arm, the poor raddled face, he confirmed Jim's suspicions—another stroke. "Which you been doing," he asked, "working too hard or worrying too much?"

Coldness seeped into Rowdy's heart. She'd always thought of a stroke as being strictly physical. She knew Uncle Jim had been troubled about Papa and her. Had her decision to move been the last straw?

Tears came into her eyes. I'll make it up to him, she thought. Somehow. But there was nothing she could do except take care of him and pray that he would regain use of his arm and leg.

Clover tended school and Rowdy stayed home until Angus returned from the circuit. Jim's left side remained unchanged, and Rowdy was heartsick. A thousand times she wished she'd never even thought of moving.

When Angus came home, she greeted him gravely. He said hello without looking at her, then noted the dish towel tied around Jim's waist. His face softened.

"Not feeling well, Uncle Jim?" he asked.

Tears came into the rheumy eyes. "Feel fine," he said. "Jest a little spell. Be back on my feet any day." Angus and Rowdy exchanged glances. The girl made a slight motion of negation.

"It's time you took a rest," Angus told the old man. "You been waitin' on the rest of us long enough."

Tears began to course down the wrinkled cheeks. "Never been nothin' but a nuisance."

"Now, you just hush that," Angus shushed him. "Don't know how I'd'a made out all these years without you to look after the tads."

Perforce, Angus and Rowdy called a truce. With Jim

283

to be cared for, there had to be a measure of cooperation and conversation between them. But neither of them was giving an inch.

Angus shucked his knit cap, fleece-lined jacket. "Cold," he told his father, blowing on his hands. "Doctor been out?"

"Yes. He said it was a stroke. I already knowed that. Warn't no use going to the expense . . ."

"Doc's charge won't make us or break us," Angus said cheerfully. "You just think about getting well."

Over supper that evening, Jim talked, with some effort. As usual, he seemed to know everything that had been going on. When Angus chuckled at some outrageous story about Maggie Cruikshank's latest stunt, plaguing Governor Haskell to declare himself in favor of women voting, Rowdy looked at the old man in wonder.

"Where do you hear all this stuff?"

"Uncle Jim's got ears like a jackrabbit," Angus joked. "He just hoists them, and everything that's said within a ten-mile radius comes hot-footin' in."

Jim laughed, forgetting for the moment his mortification when food trickled out of his mouth. "Aw," he said, "Pete and Tenny's been over."

Momentarily, it seemed to Rowdy that things were as they had always been, pleasant and—and loving. But Papa's glance in her direction was like flint, and her heart sank. No, things were not the same. She doubted they would ever be again.

It was not until Angus had been home two or three days that father and daughter discussed future plans. Jim was asleep for the moment, and the two bundled up and went outside to be sure the old man didn't hear. Rowdy had already decided on her course of action.

"I'll be staying home permanently, soon as the school board can find someone to take over," she said.

Angus shook his head. He had thought the matter over carefully too. He was proud of Rowdy's achievement and ambition, wanted her to continue her work. The second part of his two-pronged reasoning was more self-serving, but perhaps even more cogent. If she had nothing to keep her occupied except the care of one old man, there'd be too much time for her to brood.

"I'm going to give up the circuit," he told her. "Someone's got to tend the plowing and planting, take care of the stock. You can't do all that."

"Maggie does," Rowdy reminded him. "Besides, you've never gotten along with Uncle Jim. I don't know whether you'd . . . well, I know you'd *mean* to treat him right, but you . . . I'm afraid you'd resent him. He'd sense that."

Shocked and wounded, Angus said angrily, "I wouldn't mistreat a fellow when he's sick."

"I know, but I—owe him." She did not tell Angus about her feeling of guilt, but he heard the note of finality in her voice.

"We'll think on it some more," he said. Rowdy returned to the house. Angus stayed outside. He stared up into the winter-bright night, felt in that moment the piercing alienation from his daughter more poignantly than he would have thought possible. It was like a knife in his gut, sundering him.

That red-skinned bastard! Angus squared his shoulders. He wasn't being unreasonable. People looked down on mixed marriages. Half-breed kids. Rowdy was hurt and angry now, but someday she'd thank him.

74.

On Sunday, after breakfast, Jim insisted that Angus and Rowdy go to church. "I don't need no nursemaid," he grumbled. "Reckon I can stay alone an hour or two."

The eyes of father and daughter met, and they shared a thought. It would be good for the old man to feel he need not have constant attendance. Rowdy dropped a kiss on his head.

"Of course you can, Uncle Jim. We're planning to go."

"All right," he muttered, mollified.

So, though she worried about him during the entire trip, heard little of the sermon, Rowdy was glad they had gone. The Holtzworthys were there, the Smiths, with their brood, Tenny and Clover, and many of their other friends. Usually, they stayed on and passed the time of day after the sermon; today, though, both Angus and Rowdy were uneasy, anxious to get home.

They headed for the door but were stopped by first one, then another friend telling them they might drop by that afternoon. "Uncle Jim will be glad to see you," Rowdy said in each instance. "And so will we."

Company began to arrive around two-thirty. Neighbors, the Smiths, Tenny and Clover. The Holtzworthys and two other families from town. The Bensons and Trapps and Stumboes, from Angus's circuit.

They brought food. Canned goods and hams, side meat and bread.

"What's all this for?" Angus asked.

"This is a poundin', preacher," Liz Benson told him. "Pounding" the preacher was an established custom in the country, where ministers were invariably underpaid, if they were paid at all. It had started with each family in the congregation bringing the minister a pound of food, but the pounds had grown to pecks and then to bushels.

"Uncle Jim's always done the cooking," Sarah Holtzworthy said. "We didn't figure you two knew how."

The sick man brightened. "You do know how to pleasure a feller," he told her. "Let's run Zeb off, and you marry me."

So the first hour or so went by in catching up on news from outside the immediate community. Then, though, the visitors became serious. Their plan was simple.

Each of them would take a turn staying with Uncle Jim. Clover had it organized, names written down. In some instances, a woman could stay only half a day, but most had promised a full day.

As Rowdy read the names, her throat tightened. "There are people on here we don't even know," she said.

"We're neighbors," Sarah Holtzworthy pointed out. "When folks heard about the need, they sent word. Most everyone knows of the preacher, and now lots of folks know of the teacher. They pitched in."

Rowdy turned away, feeling the tears filling her eyes. Angus cleared his throat and gruffly thanked them. Uncle Jim was wordless until the discussion had ended.

"It won't be but for a little while," he said then, fiercely. The lone tear he'd not been able to suppress

286

trickled from the inner canthus of his eye, slid down his nose.

"Sure, Jim." Tenny clapped him on the back. "Truth to tell, we're all tryin' to get out of work. Figger if we sit over here a few hours, we can't rightly be accused of loafing."

"Pete'd be here every day if I'd let him get by with it," Alice Smith agreed, and they all laughed. Rubbing his nose, Jim looked up, a wobbly grin touching the good half of his mouth.

75.

With Uncle Jim's care assured, Rowdy's thoughts once more turned to Johnny White Hawk. She *had* to see him again. Her dreams were filled with him, and brought hot blood surging into her cheeks when she thought of them during waking hours. She wondered if other girls fantasized about their lovers in such explicit detail, or if she were wanton.

She knew from snippets of conversation, from headshakings and mutterings about the demands of husbands, and wifely sacrifices on the altar of conjugal relations, that women supposedly had no sexual desires.

Or was that a fraud, too, as was the pretended disinterest in boys, on the part of girls?

For herself, she wanted Johnny's arms about her, his body thrust against hers. She wanted him in her bed. Her face burned when such feelings rose to haunt her, but she could no more ignore them than she could ignore her belly when she was hungry.

How was she to see him again? More important, how was she to convince Papa that Johnny would be a good husband? She was deeply troubled, lost more weight and was scolded by Aunt Sarah for damaging her health, worrying over Uncle Jim.

When Dove Dubois drove out one Sunday afternoon,

however, it was a different matter. Somehow or other, Dove had failed to hear of Jim's stroke for almost a month, was furious at both Angus and Rowdy for not sending her word.

Angus was on the circuit, so missed her wrath. Rowdy, invited out to see the mulatto woman's new buggy, took the full brunt of it. "You know I'd'a been here like a shot, did you let me know," she scolded. "Uncle Jim, he's *family*."

"I'm sorry," Rowdy apologized. "Guess I figured you'd hear about it."

Dove smouldered for a bit, then took a new tack. "All right," she said, "what's wrong with you? You look worse then Uncle Jim."

Rowdy blushed. "I've been—worried . . . Uncle Jim . . ." she said feebly.

Dove snorted. "Cut the bull," she said, deliberately vulgar. "Worry about no uncle never caused a female to go gaunt and puny, then turn bright red like you're doin'. Who're you sweet on?"

The lump that lay leaden in Rowdy's stomach rose to her throat. "Oh, Dove," she wailed. "I—I love a boy— Johnny White Hawk. And Papa . . ."

Dove's mouth fell open. "Good Lord God Almighty, girl," she whispered. "You mean an Injun?"

Rowdy nodded, the tears she seemed always to be fighting, flooding down her cheeks. "He's wonderful," she sobbed, "but Papa . . ."

"Your papa hates Injuns nigh as much as I hate whites," Dove concluded for her.

Rowdy nodded. "I've got to see him, Dove. If—if I can't marry him, I'll die, I purely will die. Could you—"

Dove backed off, spreading her hands, palms down. *"No, ma'am!"* she said emphatically. "I won't have nothin' to do, no time, no how, with that kind of dynamite. I don't want Angus Scofield after me with no shotgun."

"I'm afraid that's what'll happen to Johnny if I see him again." Rowdy gulped. "If you could just know him, Dove, you'd understand."

"Child, child," the other woman counseled, "your papa . . . There's just no future for you and this boy."

"I can't live if I can't have him," Rowdy said, choking on the words.

"Yes, you can live," Dove said somberly. "I loved a

man too. It wouldn't have worked. I gave him up. I gave Samson up too. You can do anything that you *have* to do."

"You've never loved anyone since then, either, have you?"

"No."

"I can't go through life like that. I'm not strong like you."

Dove laughed, and the sound was bitter as quinine. "I'm not strong, girl. I'm tellin' you. When push comes to shove, you do what you have to. I had a few weeks of heaven. Better to remember one wonderful time than have it dragged out 'til it turns to misery. Now, go over to the pump and rinse your face before you come back in the house."

Slowly, Rowdy did as she was told.

Dove's purpose in coming out, she said when they were once more in the cabin, was to offer her services to Uncle Jim. If there were medicines or special foods required, if they needed cash . . .

Uncle Jim's eyes grew moist. "Everyone's been so good," he quavered, "but we don't need nothin', Dove."

"If you *should*, you just let me know. I owe you, Uncle Jim. You never let me pay a dime for Samson's care."

"You saved Miss Rowdy's life," the twisted mouth countered.

"We're beginnin' to sound soupy," Dove said tartly. "I brought some dandelion wine Auntie Po made. She swears it's good tonic for the system."

Uncle Jim brightened. "I'm ready for that," he said.

76.

For Rowdy, the days dragged interminably. She had no idea how to get a message to Johnny. She grew even thinner, and Angus was both worried and angry, reminding himself roughly that there was plenty of food. If she got hungry enough, she'd eat. She was just trying to get his goat.

Such a thought had never entered the girl's head. She was in such a morass of depression, she could scarcely think of anything.

Maybe Johnny hadn't cared as she did. Maybe he'd just been curious, wondering how a white girl would respond. The months seemed to last forever. The winter faded; March came, with its chilly ceaseless winds. April appeared, with the miracle of sprouting seed.

Toward the latter part of that month, Rowdy's students were particularly restive. Equal parts of spring fever and the sulphur and molasses with which they were dosed to thin the blood, Rowdy thought absently. Why not give them a few hours off to get the restlessness out of their systems?

So shortly after they had eaten dinner, she told the class that the afternoon was a holiday, and a whoop of undiluted joy went up. One of the boys hung back as the others trooped out, to say, "Golly whillikers, Miz Scofield, yore shore sumthin'," and then fled, blushing furiously.

Rowdy sat at her desk after they left, exhausted in spirit as well as in body. She wished Johnny would walk through the door, that the two of them could ride away, leaving their problems behind. She did not cry. She was too numb.

After a long while, she got unsteadily to her feet. Maybe if she went out in the sunshine, she could rid herself of her malaise. She locked the school behind her and wandered aimlessly toward a nearby thicket.

When she heard the pounding of hooves, her first thought was of Uncle Jim. Then, when the paint pony was close enough for her to see the rider, she thought she was hallucinating. He drew nearer, pulled to a stop, slid to the ground.

"Johnny?" she whispered, not moving for fear the mirage would disappear.

"I had to come back," he said, and his voice echoed some of her own desperation.

"Oh, Johnny, it *is* you!" They moved toward each other in the same moment, went into each other's arms. Rowdy was both laughing and crying, and Johnny stroked her hair, holding her so close, she could feel the strength of his body. They kissed, and she reached up to touch his face in wonderment.

Her throat was aching with joy. Her body began to

awaken. It was, she thought, like rebirth. Suddenly, the whole of nature was alive and throbbing with beauty.

"Johnny, Johnny, Johnny." She was saying his name over and over in a kind of litany. "I didn't think I'd ever see you again."

"Surely you knew better than that."

"But it was so long . . ."

"I thought you would send me word when you were no longer ashamed to be seen with me."

"*Ashamed?* You thought I was ashamed to be seen with an Indian? Oh, Johnny, you fool! I was afraid of what Papa would do. Truly. Oh, my love . . ."

She broke off, knowing she was babbling.

"Hush, little Moonlight on Running Water," Johnny said. "It doesn't matter now. We're together."

The trunk of a fallen cottonwood was near, and they sat down, the boy's arm around her, her head on his shoulder.

"Tell me what you've—"

They said the words together and burst out laughing. "You first," Johnny said.

"No, you. I'm hungry to hear all about you. Everything. Johnny, I don't know anything about Indian life. You don't go on—buffalo hunts . . . or war parties?"

"There are no more buffaloes to hunt," the boy said, and for a moment his face was somber. "The white buffalo hunters wiped out the herds. And there are no more war parties. Our wise men tell of a time when rival tribes met for battle with bow and arrow. It was a time of—of honor."

In Rowdy's mind, his words called up the jousting on English fields of armor-clad knights who fought to the death. "There is no honor, no skill in fighting with the white man's arms," Johnny went on. "One points a clumsy weapon of wood and metal and pulls the trigger."

"But I've heard that the Indians want to buy guns . . ."

"One must fight fire with fire. Enough." He laughed suddenly, unexpectedly. "I don't know anything about the white man's life. Or the white woman's."

So she told him succinctly of her father's run in '89. The soddy he had built. His ministry. Her own early life. Uncle Jim. "I was going to move to town," she concluded, "so I could see you. But when Uncle Jim got sick, I couldn't leave him."

"No," he agreed, "that would not have been right."

"But now . . ." She broke off suddenly, held her face up. "Kiss me, Johnny," she whispered. "Hold me." And when he complied, she felt the further quickening of her body, like the earth mother breaking forth in spring. There was a visceral stirring low in her abdomen, so intense, so lovely, it was almost painful. Her limbs felt languorous, began to tremble.

"My love," Johnny murmured. His lips touched her eyelids, her cheek, her throat, came back again to meet her lips. Every emotion, every stirring, every need woman had felt since the beginning of time was in Rowdy's kiss.

They stood without words, walked deeper into the thicket, found a bed of pine needles and sank down together, still embracing. The girl took his hand and held it against her breast.

"I love you, Johnny," she whispered.

His hand slid down her side, drew her to him. She stared upward into amber eyes that wanted and demanded and yet asked a question.

"Oh, yes, Johnny," she whispered. "Yes, oh yes. Like that."

The sky beamed its fairest on them, the thicket murmured its music and their bodies met and took and gave and caressed and cared for and loved each other.

After a long while, spent, they lay back against the pine needles, sharing a sense of complete fulfillment. Gravely, Johnny drew one of Rowdy's petticoats over her. "You must not become cold," he said.

"I could never be cold again," she murmured, and, snuggling against him, drifted into a half sleep.

The boy lay frowning thoughtfully at the sky, and when Rowdy stirred, he said, "My father would be very angry if he knew of this."

Suddenly, she was wide awake, stifling hysterical laughter. "*Your* father would be angry." She choked. "Oh, Johnny, m—my father . . ."

The boy sat up, began to adjust his clothing. "Come, my wife," he said. "We must go to your father. He cannot refuse us marriage now."

Stricken, she looked up at him. "You mean you'd *tell* him?"

'If it were necessary to win his agreement."

She shivered. "Johnny, I can't. We—musn't. You don't know him."

His lips were set in a determined line. "You can. We must."

"I'll go away with you," she offered.

"No, I will not run as though our love were shameful. We will go to your father."

He helped her to her feet. She was shaking. She smoothed her clothing, mind working feverishly for some way to dissuade him. It was Papa's day to come home, but she prayed wildly that he had been delayed. That a spring storm would come up so he couldn't get through. That Kadif would throw a shoe. Anything, God, anything at all, she thought. Just don't let him be home.

Johnny was smiling at her. "You don't have to be afraid," he said gently. "I will talk to your father alone, if you wish."

"N—no . . ."

"Then do not look so troubled."

She tilted her chin up, straightened her shoulders. Maybe Johnny was right. Maybe she was worrying for no reason. She didn't want to tell Papa she and Johnny had made love, but if she had to . . . as Johnny said, Papa would have to let them marry if he knew about this afternoon.

"Maybe you're right," she said slowly. And, to herself: God knows I hope you're right.

On the ride home, she forced herself not to think of the next hour or two. Instead, she harked back to the exquisite moments when Johnny had held her in his arms. And ahead to the days when she would be his wife.

77.

As he rode home, Angus was again hoping Miss Rowdy had come to her senses. He missed her affection, the closeness they had shared. That damn Injun. Shooting was too good for him.

Kadif tossed his head, fractious, and Angus growled at him. "I know you need runnin' to get rid of that orneriness, but not through this woods, boy. I'll take you out on the pasture tomorrow and let you run yourself down."

Kadif tossed his head again, and Angus knew he was waiting for only one minute of inattention, to throw his rider and run wild. But the man held the reins tightly, and the horse perforce behaved.

At the soddy, anxious to see Rowdy, Angus turned Kadif into the lot without unsaddling him. But when he let himself into the cabin, he found only Pete and Uncle Jim. Uncle Jim's face brightened.

"Hello, son," he said.

Angus wished heartily he could bring himself to respond with a casual "H'lo, Pa," but the sense of estrangement he'd felt for so many years held him like a vise. He could not break loose and acknowledge the relationship. "Howdy, Uncle Jim," he said, and went to clasp the gnarled hand. "Fine day." he said. "Like to go outside awhile?"

The twisted mouth smiled as best it could. "I shore would."

With Pete and Angus helping, the old man walked to the cottonwood bench. Pete went back and brought out the rocker.

"I've near wore out that chair's bottom—and mine too," Uncle Jim grumbled. "But I do believe, Angus, I'm gettin' some movement back in this cussed arm and leg."

"Sure, you are," Angus said encouragingly. "A few more days . . ."

Pete said he'd better be getting home, accepted their thanks by saying, "Pshaw, glad to get away from the old woman awhile," with a grin that belied the words.

When he was gone, Jim said, "Davey, I been thinkin', if you could put some wheels on a straight chair, I could manage alone. I shore hate being a burden."

"You're not a burden," Angus murmured, then sat up straight, understanding, for the first time, what it must mean to be entirely dependent on others. "That's a great idea," he said. "I'll ride into Oklahoma City tomorrow and pick up some wheels. Those bicycle wheels, now, they're light."

Uncle Jim grinned. "Yeah, I wouldn't want no wagon wheels."

They heard the horses before they saw them. "Sounds like company comin'," Uncle Jim said.

"Miss Rowdy, likely."

Angus stood up, shading his eyes with his hand. He saw that there were two horses, Rowdy's Biscuit and a paint. Rowdy and a man. He couldn't make out the man's features. The two drew nearer. At the lot they stopped, dismounted, tied the horses. Angus walked toward them.

He saw the braids first, and rage made his heart flip over. The couple started toward him. Angus stopped in his tracks. That goddam Indian Rowdy had been mooning over.

The knowledge was a knife in his gut. The black mist of rage engulfed him. He felt himself strangling and gave a great gulp, trying to draw breath.

Miss Rowdy's face seemed to be swimming toward him. His eyes strained in their sockets. Though his daughter looked apprehensive, her face also wore the bemused radiance, the beatific, almost smug, smile of a woman sexually awakened and gratified.

He raped her, Angus thought. That son of a bitch raped her.

Adrenaline pumped into his blood like a dam bursting. His muscles knotted to the point of agony. Yet from someplace deep inside, he summoned a wiliness he had not known he possessed. Keep calm, Goddammit, he instructed himself; forced his clenched fists to unknot, tried to stop the trembling of his body.

The couple came even with him. The happiness in Rowdy's face had been wiped out, leaving only the fear. "P—Papa, this is John White Hawk." Her voice sounded harsh.

Angus looked into eyes that were light brown—*yellow!* Eyes that were confident, unafraid.

"Hello, John," the man said. He would not, by God, allow his voice to betray him.

"Good evening, Mr. Scofield." The Indian's voice was calm. He did not speak as he should have, fearfully, supplicatingly, Angus thought, and his bitterness grew. The young man spoke as to an equal. The taste of bile came into Angus's throat.

"Come up and sit," he said, and met the suspicion in his daughter's glance with a look of innocence he hoped was convincing. The three walked slowly back to where Uncle Jim waited.

"Martha, maybe you could find us something to drink," Angus suggested. The girl relaxed slightly. Maybe Papa wasn't pretending. Maybe he'd recognized at a glance, as she had, that Johnny was—was decent and—wonderful. Well, maybe not wonderful, she amended to herself. Papa wasn't apt to go that far.

She hurried into the house, began to grind the coffee beans.

Outside, Angus repeated his invitation to sit, and John folded himself onto the bench. A silence fell. Angus was fighting to keep himself under control. John was speculating rapidly on what his father had taught him. It is a good idea to establish an accord before getting to difficult business. He didn't fool himself that it wasn't going to be difficult. He had noted the stiffening on the other man's part when he first came in sight. The way his face blanched, followed by the suffusion of red into it.

"Beautiful horse, Mr. Scofield," he said, nodding toward Kadif moving restlessly about the lot.

"Ornery cuss." Angus got the pride-tinged words out on a loud exhalation.

"Fifteen hands?" John asked politely.

"Over sixteen." Suddenly, the solution came to him. "Never saw his like before," he said. "I'm the only one who can control him."

John smiled, teeth white in the sun-browned face. "Almost any horse can be controlled if a person knows how to handle him."

"Not this one," Angus retorted. "He's meaner'n old billy hell. He ain't no paint pony, boy." He saw John's face tighten and went on. "No, sir," he said, "that's a *man's* horse."

John got to his feet. "Would you allow me to ride him?" he asked.

Uncle Jim made a sound of distress. "Horse's a born killer."

John drew himself up. "I haven't seen a horse I couldn't ride," he told them.

Angus shrugged. "You can try," he said, "but don't say I didn't warn you."

John walked to the lot, lightly vaulted the gate. Show-off bastard, Angus scowled under his breath. John approached Kadif, and the horse stopped his unquiet pacing, eyeing him. John spoke easily, a few words.

He told the horse he was a beauty. Slowly, as he talked, he drew closer. The horse nickered. John reached out a hand, waited for the animal to make the first move toward contact. Kadif threw up his head and shook it. The more overtures John made, the more Kadif disdained them.

At last the boy realized there was to be no understanding reached with the magnificent beast. He would have to mount him by surprise, cling like a burr until the horse knew who was master. Suiting action to the thought, he backed off, still watching Kadif move suspiciously, still hoping he might be soothed.

But when Kadif continued to watch him warily, John took one further step back, launched himself, catapulted to the broad back before the startled horse could move. Kadif reared.

Angus held his breath, thinking the horse would go backward. He did not. He came down, with John clinging like a limpet. The horse's eyes were rolling. He headed for a fence post, slammed his side against it, but John jerked the reins, pulling the bit taut.

Kadif danced off, again shaking his head, began to run in crazy circles about the cow lot, gaining speed. When he reached the gate, he gathered his feet together and hurled himself upward. He sailed over the gate as though winged, stretched his leap to his longest stride and thundered away toward the trees.

Angus smiled grimly to himself as horse and man disappeared.

Carrying the coffee, Rowdy stepped out the door as Johnny flung himself into the saddle. The tray fell from her hands, but Angus was too engrossed to notice. As for the girl, her terror was so great, she was paralyzed.

Kadif will kill him! The words circled around in her mind. She tried to move and felt immobilized. Her heart was smashing against her ribs.

As Kadif cleared the gate, she gave a convulsive effort and got out the word: *"Papa!"*

Angus whirled, held out his hand, fingers spread. "I told him not to try it," he said. Rowdy's disbelief and

297

scorn appeared briefly on her face. Then she began to run, untied her horse, mounted it and took off in the direction Kadif had gone.

More slowly, Angus began to walk the same way. Damned if he'd ride that Indian's pony.

Left alone, Uncle Jim was savagely massaging the dead left leg while slow tears slid down his face.

Afterward, Rowdy had no idea how long the nightmare lasted. It seemed an eternity. The woods were dense. Once, she had considered the forest a quiet and lovely place. Now it was menacing.

"Johnny!" She tried to shout the word, but her voice was a whisper. In a frenzy of fear, she kicked her horse to greater speed, oblivious of the branches that tore her face, the tears streaming down her cheeks.

"Johnny," she attempted to call again and choked on the word. She began to feel that she was fated to ride forever without finding him.

Then, a few hundred feet ahead, she saw Kadif, riderless, pawing the earth. An unmoving mound lay nearby.

Rowdy whimpered deep in her throat. Her chest felt as though it had been torn open. She reached the crumpled form, slid from Biscuit's back.

Johnny's head was bloody. She fell on her knees beside him, saw the dreadful indented wounds where the skull had been trampled. Leaned forward and put her ear to his chest. No heartbeat. Her fingers on his wrist found no pulse.

In that moment, the personage who had been Martha Scofield died. There was left a husk that would move and talk and go through the motions of living. She sat down and took the savaged head in her lap, rocking back and forth in agony.

When Angus reached them, breathless from running, she looked up, face stony and wizened as though senescence had overtaken her.

"You killed him," she said.

Angus neither admitted nor denied it. "Go to the house," he told her. "I'll get word to his kin."

"Go to hell," she said.

He made a convulsive movement, hands itching to strike her.

Miss Rowdy's eyes sharpend to dagger points. Waves of hatred emanated from her which were almost palpable.

"Go ahead," she said, and laughed, a terrible retching sound that held no mirth.

Angus stood for a long moment, staring rigidly at his daughter, then wheeled, mounted Kadif and plunged back into the woods.

78.

Rowdy sat cradling her lover's head against her breast until the shadows lengthened into dusk. Shock had stopped her mind from working. The evening star rose. Star light, star bright, first star I see tonight . . . She could not recall the rest of the jingle and presently began to weep. If she could think of it, everything would come right again.

Johnny's body was stiff, and she was still holding him, when Koontz's springboard wagon rumbled into view. He clucked his distress as he jumped down and came to her.

"Terrible thing, Miss Rowdy," he said with professional unction. "Your pa tells me the young fellow got throwed." She didn't answer. She had never liked Koontz, and the thought of his handling Johnny added to her grief. "I brung a box," he said.

He leaned down to lift the body, but Rowdy held on. He put his hand on her back, and she shivered. Oily, she thought, and her stomach felt queasy. "You'll have to turn loose so I can take care of him," the man said, and let his hand slide down her back. Nausea came into the girl's throat.

Angus showed up then, and Koontz jerked his hand away. "Sorry," the preacher said, "had to go by and see to Uncle Jim."

"She's plumb got a death grip on him," the mortician complained.

Angus grunted. "Turn loose, Martha," he said harshly. "I've sent word to his folks."

There was no response. She did not so much as look

299

up. Finally, Angus began to pry the chilled fingers away, one by one. She did not resist.

Rowdy rode back to the soddy on the seat of Koontz's springboard, the two men having agreed she was in no shape to ride a horse.

Inside the house, moving like a sleepwalker, she went to her room. She did not light the lamp. She sat on the side of the bed, staring blindly into the darkness, still in a merciful void. Angus knocked once on her door. When there was no answer, he went back to the kitchen.

He had told Uncle Jim briefly that the Indian was dead. Now he met the question in the faded eyes with a shrug. "She's a mite upset. She'll get over it. What do you want for supper?"

Ignoring the question, the old man said, "I dunno, Angus, she's an awful lot like you. She won't forgive easy."

"I didn't kill the bastard," Angus growled.

"Didn't you, Davey?" Uncle Jim asked. Angus's mouth tightened. Without answering, he began to slam the pots and pans down. When supper was on the table, he got Uncle Jim in place, started toward Rowdy's room again.

"I'd leave her be," Uncle Jim cautioned. "She ain't gonna eat nohow." Angus hesitated, then came to sit down at the table. Neither man spoke during the meal. The air hung heavy with their awareness of the silent girl in the other room.

When dawn came, Rowdy had scarcely moved from her original position. Her eyes burned as though stung by wind-borne grit. There was no strength in her legs, but, having roused herself from her stupor, she felt impelled to move, take some action.

She laid out fresh clothing, chose the green velvet pants she had made along with a white shirtwaist, went to the kitchen for a wash-pan of water. Her father was nowhere to be seen.

"Angus's gone to milk the cows," Uncle Jim told her. She nodded. "You feelin' better?" he asked. When she did not answer, he added, "I'm dreadful sorry about the boy."

"Thank you," she said woodenly, and, taking the pan, went back to her room.

She washed and dressed herself. Combed the fine hair. Moonlight on Running Water, she thought, and the anguish was like an open wound. She tried to cling to the numbness that had protected her during the night, but it was giving way. She was coming to life again, and the pain was unbearable.

Automatonlike, she went to the kitchen and fixed breakfast, levered Uncle Jim into position, sat down at the table.

Angus came in, bringing the bucket of milk. She ignored him. He washed and took his chair. "Mornin'," he said.

"Mornin', Angus," Uncle Jim responded. Miss Rowdy picked up a biscuit and began to shred it, rolling the bits into small pellets. When the men had finished eating, she cleared the table, poured water from the teakettle to wash the dishes.

"I'll strain the milk and all," Angus said. She did not look around. He cleared his throat and spoke again. "Daughter," he said awkwardly, "I'm going to pay for the Injun's funeral."

Her hands stopped in mid-motion. She turned to face him, lips twisted, gimlet-eyed. "That was proper of you," she said viciously, "seeing as I may be carrying his child. I hope I'm carrying his child."

Rage blotted out reason, and Angus slapped her. Rowdy fell. Face ashen, she put a finger to her cheek. The imprint of his hand stood out like a bruise. The girl laughed, and the sound chilled his marrow.

He turned on his heel and walked out.

Uncle Jim was whimpering. Slowly, Rowdy got to her feet. She was trembling with pain and indignity.

"Don't cry, Uncle Jim," she said absently.

"Child, yore pa—"

"Don't make excuses for him," she said, and the old man subsided.

She went to her room, threw clothing into a small case, closed it. She went back to the kitchen, picked up the rifle from its corner. Saw the fear come into Uncle Jim's face and laughed, the sound harsh and flat. "I'm not going to kill your son," she assured him. "He's not worth hanging over."

Carrying case in one hand, rifle in the other, she went outdoors. Angus had turned her horse out to pasture the night before. She struck off in that direction, walking.

From the barn, where he was making a pretense of mending a harness, Angus saw her go. He thought of David's mourning after Absalom's treachery and death. My son, my son Absalom. It seemed to him that he comprehended fully for the first time the depths of David's despair.

I did what was right, he told himself. Not striking Rowdy, no, that hadn't been right. But the other—you couldn't fault a man for protecting his women. So why did he feel guilty?

The pasture land was uneven. Twice Rowdy stumbled, scarcely noted it. Her whole being was focused on one thought. When she found the horses, Biscuit and Kadif were but a few feet apart, cropping grass. Biscuit whinnied a greeting at her approach, but Kadif shied away, head up, distrustful.

Rowdy put the suitcase down. She pumped a shell into the rifle barrel, pulled back the hammer, braced the gun against her shoulder and put her eye to the sight. Poised for flight yet curious, Kadif watched the movement uneasily. Rowdy drew a bead directly between his eyes.

And fired.

The magnificent animal fell, kicked once and lay still.

At sound of the shot, Biscuit had skittered away a short distance. He stopped, turned. When there was no further disturbance, he slowly ambled back to the girl.

Rowdy tossed the rifle aside, picked up her case and scrambled up on his back. Riding bareback, she headed toward town. She had no destination. She had not thought that far ahead. When she reached the first farmhouse, she borrowed a bridle. Turned the horse's head toward Dove's.

79.

When Angus heard the shot, the blood seemed to congeal in his veins. My God, he thought, she's killed herself, and he started to run.

Not my child, he thought; please, not my child!

It is said that a drowning man's life flashes before his

eyes. As he ran, Angus saw Miss Rowdy's life. Remembered the feel of her in his arms when she was a baby, the tenderness he'd felt at seeing her nurse. Her tear-swollen face when he'd left her at Sarah's. The clasp of her arms around his neck. "You're the best papa in the whole wide world."

It seemed a thousand years before he came on the horse.

Momentarily, he thought Kadif was lying down of his own accord, would presently begin to roll from side to side, enjoying the sun-warmed earth. Then, as he came closer, he saw the blood.

Strength deserted him. His knees buckled. It was not the death of the horse that shook him so profoundly, it was his sense that Kadif's death was symbolic. She had wanted to kill the man. At the moment, he wished she had.

He leaned his head against Kadif's unmoving side and wept like a child.

80.

At Dove's door, Rowdy knocked and was greeted by Auntie Po.

"Chile!" the old woman cried, "what's wrong? You sick?" When Rowdy stood shivering, not answering, the old woman lifted her voice in a shout. "Miss Dove, come quick!"

Dove's soft soles whispered as she hurried down the stairs. "What on earth . . . ?" She saw Rowdy, a walking corpse. Only the eyes alive and smouldering in the dead-white face.

"Rowdy!" She went to the girl. "Get the brandy, Auntie Po," she said. "Come and sit, child." She led the girl, unresisting, to a chair. Auntie Po scuttled away, came back with bottle and a glass. Dove poured the fiery liquid, lifted it to Rowdy's lips.

"Drink!" she said. As though in a daze, Rowdy gulped, choked, coughed until there were tears in her eyes.

"Black coffee," Dove snapped. She had her arm around Rowdy's shoulders, supporting her. Auntie Po brought a cup of the chicory brew.

"Drink now," Dove said. "Slowly, it's hot." Rowdy sipped, grimaced, sipped again. When it was cooled and half gone, the Negro woman laced it with a large dollop of the brandy. Finally, she got both the coffee and the alcohol down the girl, saw color begin to tinge the ashen cheeks. Rowdy slowly straightened, and Dove removed her arm.

"Now," she said briskly, "what's wrong? Nothing's happened to Angus . . . ?"

Rowdy put her face in her hands. "He killed Johnny," she said, and began to cry.

"Oh, Lawdy, Lawdy me," Auntie Po moaned, "why for he do that?"

"Hush, Auntie," Dove said. "I'm sorry, child. I purely am."

Rowdy wept only a moment or two longer. The two older women saw her shoulders go back, her head come up. Good, Dove thought, she's getting her spunk back. But she was unprepared for the glitter in those amethyst eyes.

"Dove, do you think I'm pretty?" Rowdy asked.

"Tolerable."

"Pretty enough to come here and work?"

"Miss Rowdy!" Auntie Po was scandalized, and Dove exploded. "Of all the goddam foolishness I ever heard in my whole put-together," she shouted, "that plumb takes the cake! You want to break your pa's heart?"

"Yes," Rowdy said. There were patches of red in her cheeks, and her breath was coming in short hard gasps. "I want to shame him. Will you, Dove? Please let me work for you!"

Dove snorted. "No, you ain' gonna work here!" she said, eyes blazing. "One more word about it, and I'll beat your behind 'til it's got more ridges than a washboard. You pull yourself together and stop feeling sorry for yourself. Think you're the only one ever grieved over a man? Not by a damn sight, you ain't!"

Shaking with anger, Rowdy jumped up. "I hate you,"

she screamed childishly and stormed out the door, slamming it behind her.

Auntie Po was shaking her head. "You mighty rough on that chile, Miss Dove."

"I know," Dove said somberly, "but someone had to bring her to her senses. I hope it worked."

All but strangling with rage, Rowdy mounted Biscuit and headed toward town. She had to find a room. Before Uncle Jim got sick, she had planned on going to Ma Cavelli's. It was said that she kept a respectable place. She laughed mirthlessly. That ought to satisfy Dove.

At the boardinghouse, it was Ma herself who came to the door. She bristled when she saw the velvet britches.

"Yes?" she said.

"I need a place to stay, Mrs. Cavelli," Rowdy said quietly. "I'm Martha Scofield."

The plump woman put her hands on her hips. "I know who you are," she said. News of the Indian boy's death had already swept through the town, and Ma had a pretty fair idea that the girl's disheveled appearance was related to it. She was curious and moderately sympathetic, without knowing the details. But she wouldn't have a female boarder wearing pants.

"You got any woman-type clothes?" she asked tartly. Rowdy nodded. "You'd have to wear 'em while you was around here."

"All right," the girl agreed. The tension of the past hours had drained her. Suddenly, she was all but fainting with fatigue. "Just show me a room," she said.

81.

Angus had no idea how long he sat beside the dead horse. When he was again conscious of time, the sun was high overhead. He rose, walked wearily back to the cabin. Went in, met the accusation in his father's eyes. Got his Bible out and sat slumped in a chair. Jim sat silent, face drawn with misery.

Angus's mind would not concentrate; his eyes would not focus. After a few minutes, he rose and put the Book back on its stand.

"You ort to get back to the circuit," Jim said. "Get yore mind offen—all this."

"I can't preach any more," Angus growled.

"Davey, them folks—"

"I don't want to talk about it!" Angus shouted, and plunged back outdoors.

Miss Rowdy slept the clock around. When she woke, Sunday afternoon, she was, for a few minutes, disoriented. Then, as her mind began to clear, she wished the short sleep had slipped imperceptibly into the final one: Johnny, she grieved, and felt her body was not big enough to hold the pain she felt.

She thought of her father, and her eyes narrowed. Kadif's death had barely begun to even the score, but she'd find a way. An eye for an eye, she thought grimly.

She went to school the next morning, faced the curiosity in the children's eyes without acknowledging it. Her face was a mask so stern and set, none dared mention the incident.

"Sometimes," one of the older girls complained to her mother as the days went on, "it seems like she's not even *there*."

It was a perceptive bit of insight. Rowdy went through the days by rote. The ache for vengeance consumed her, the feeling about her father a substantiation of the awful truth that there is no hatred so bitter as inverted love.

Aunt Sarah, distressed, came to the boardinghouse to reason with her. "You're destroying your father, Martha."

"He destroyed me."

"Aren't you being childish?"

Miss Rowdy's mouth twisted. "I am my father's child," she said bitterly. "Did he ever tell you he plotted six months to get even with a man who had laughed at him?"

Sarah looked down at her hands. "No," she said. "I find it hard to believe." Rowdy didn't mention he'd been in his teens at the time.

"Oh, he's not God, not by a long shot. I could tell you . . ." She broke off, thinking for the first time of the "Wanted" poster.

Sarah was watching her gravely. "We have all done

things we are ashamed of, Martha. Angus has been a good father to you. It wasn't easy, a man left with a newborn infant in a frontier country. Most men would have handed you to someone, anyone, and left the country."

Rowdy scarcely heard her. Her mind was on the "Wanted" poster, and she was eager for Sarah to leave. "Thank you for coming, Aunt Sarah," she said, rising. Not customarily demonstrative, the woman rose and put her arms around the girl, held her briefly.

"You are very dear to us, child," she said, and was gone.

Rowdy immediately started hunting through her possessions. She had forgotten the name of the town. When she finally found the worn and faded sheet, it was in the small "memory box," which also contained an agate pendant Angus had given her on her tenth birthday. She remembered his saying agates were nature's camera. This one reflected a rainbow arc.

She laughed harshly. Walking to the front door, she slung the small stone as far as she could. The balance of the evening she spent composing a letter to the sheriff at Pequot, Missouri.

There were times, as she waited for a reply, when she felt guilty about sending the letter. She didn't want to see Papa hanged. But they wouldn't do that, not after all this time. Maybe they'd put him in prison. She bit her lip, not wanting to think about that either. But she damn well wanted him punished some way or other.

Two weeks went by, and she had no reply. Maybe someone had come down and picked him up. No, she would have heard. It never occurred to her that in the more than twenty years since the incident, hundreds of posters had been printed, or that some sheriff years ago had tired of looking at the mass of papers and swept all of them into the wastebasket.

When a month and a half went by, she knew there would be no answer, and began casting about in her mind for some other means of vengeance.

Leaving Cason's general store one day, she came face to face with a man who looked vaguely familiar but whom she could not place. She nodded, and the man thrust out a hand. "If it ain't Miss Martha," he said. Hesitantly, she put her hand in his.

"I'm sorry," she said, "I'm afraid—"

"You remember me, Miss Martha. At the celebration when Oklahoma became a state. Vincent Turner. I introduced you to a young Indian man."

The peculiar eyes were watching for her reaction. Rowdy felt the sickness churning in her stomach. He knows, she thought. He knows Papa killed Johnny, and he's twisting the knife. She jerked her hand away, then inwardly scolded herself. It's getting so I think ugly things of everyone, she thought, and made herself smile.

"I remember," she said woodenly. Then she thought of Papa's outburst when she'd mentioned Mr. Turner. Worthless as tits on a boar hog, he'd said.

She spoke more warmly. "You live in Oklahoma City, Mr. Turner?"

"At the moment, I have business here," he said smoothly. He did not tell her that his business concerned a certain rancher who distrusted banks and was reputed to be carrying a large sum to consummate a land deal in Cleveland County.

Turner was too solicitous of himself to be a real outlaw. His game was poker. Failing that, though, he was not adverse to passing information to some less timorous friend—notably, Dude Malicote—and being rewarded with what was in effect a finder's fee.

Vince sighed. "Ah, Miss Scofield, business is a terrible taskmaster. It leaves scant time for a man to develop the more tender passions of life, home, wife, children."

Rowdy considered him. She felt a small *frisson* of distaste. But if Papa disliked him . . .

"Perhaps I could introduce you to some of my friends when you're in Oklahoma City," she said demurely.

Vince picked up the note of defiance in her voice and was puzzled. The girl was up to something, but what? He was strongly tempted to advise her not to try to hoodwink a pitchman, but the modestly lowered eyes, the tender pink staining her cheeks disarmed him.

"You are too kind, Miss Martha," he said. "Perhaps I might be so bold as to offer you some refreshment." Vince was not a womanizer. Sex was something you bought and paid for. But the company of a woman whose father was well thought of was not to be despised.

"A cup of coffee would be pleasant, Mr. Turner."

Vince strutted a bit as he ushered her into the Wagon Wheel Café. He was not well known in Oklahoma City.

Most of the petty crooks who had come in with the run of '89, hoping for some easy money, had soon cleared out. The frontiersmen, for the most part, were either too poor or too prudent to make the pickings attractive.

Turner had eventually gravitated toward the eastern part of the state, preying off the Indians as best he could. Now he basked in a kind of mellow cynicism as three or four well-dressed men stopped to pay their respects to the girl and were introduced to her escort.

Mr. Forbes, the banker. Mr. Cason, the grocer. Mr. Koontz, the undertaker. Not to mention Harry O'Neill, who owned the Wagon Wheel. Oh, yes, the news would get back to Angus, all right.

It did. Sarah had it from Mr. Cason within the hour. Not that the grocery man knew Turner's background. His question was why Miss Rowdy had taken up with a man old enough to be her father, when all the young men wanted to court her. Sarah had no answer. She remembered Vince Turner and was troubled.

Leaving the store, she ran into Alice Smith, mentioned Rowdy and Vince and admitted she was concerned. Alice remembered him too, and her lips tightened. Pete had finally told her about the poker session in Arkansas City. "The man's no more'n a tin-horn gambler." She snorted. "I'm afeared that child's askin' for trouble."

She put aside her errands and headed toward the livery stable to get Pete. When she told him about Rowdy and Vince, his leathery face screwed up in distress, like a monkey's.

"We better get word to Angus," he said.

82.

They were silent, both preoccupied with their own thoughts, as Pete urged the horses along.

If Angus killed that boy on purpose, Pete thought, I'm not sure I could fault him. I wouldn't want one of our girls being a squaw.

309

Half of Alice's mind was on Rowdy and Angus. The other half was on her own problem. Pete had sworn there wouldn't be another baby and hadn't shared her bed since she was sick.

She knew he visited Dove's girls when he could afford it; knew, too, women weren't supposed to have sexual feelings, but she did. And though the doctor had warned her not to, she would have gladly risked another pregnancy rather than do without Pete's embraces. It was funny. He was such a little man, yet such a wildcat in bed. She didn't exactly blame him for going to Dove's. He could no more do without a woman than a fish could do without water. She sighed.

When they reached the soddy, Pete told her to go in and keep Jim company. He could see Angus plowing at the far northeast corner of the farm, and headed that way. Seeing him, Angus stopped the horse, wiped the sweat from his face and went to meet him.

"What brings you out so early?" he called; then he saw Pete's somber face, and his belly knotted. "What's wrong?" he asked.

"You ain't gonna like it," Pete warned, "but we figured you ort to know."

"I haven't liked a lot of things lately," Angus said.

"Miss Rowdy was havin' coffee with Vince Turner at the Wagon Wheel this mornin'."

Angus was silent, staring down at the broomweed at his feet as if to memorize its pattern. A horned toad darted past the two men, and its glittering eye reminded him of Vince. He grimaced, as though in pain.

"Thanks for letting me know, Pete. I don't know if I can do anything about it, but I'll try."

Pete was stunned. A man told his kids what to do, until they were married, didn't he? Sometimes even after that. He'd never expected to hear Angus admit he couldn't control his own flesh and blood. Of course, Rowdy was a wild one. Pete felt a terrible pity for the man he had known so long. Angus's shoulders sloped, and his face . . . why, he looked older than Jim.

"Guess I wasn't a very good father, Pete," he said, and Pete could have wept.

"You done all right, Angus," he said gruffly. If he stood there any longer, he probably *was* going to cry. "Got to git," he said. "Alice's waitin'." He headed back to the cabin, wondering if Angus even knew he was leaving. The man looked like death warmed over.

As their wagon rattled toward home, both the Smiths were in low spirits. "Uncle Jim looks awful," Alice burst out, "like a mortal corpse. Hope we don't get none of them scorchers this summer; he'd never live to see the fall."

"Angus don't look no better," Pete told her gloomily.

"Why can't folks get along?" Alice was fretting. "If they'd jes' open their hearts to each other . . ." She broke off, thinking of her own inability to let Pete know she wanted him in her bed. She tried once more to get the words out but felt her face burning and was tongue-tied.

Angus put the plow away, turned the horse to pasture, took care of Jim's needs, told the old man he was going to town, and why.

"Save yoreself the bother, Davey boy," Jim advised. "You've lost the child. Might as well face it."

"You're a hell of a lot of comfort." Angus's temper flared. His nerves were raw. His conscience before his God felt raw too. Sorrow over his girl was tearing him to pieces. I was right, doing what I did, he kept telling himself. I was right!

As he saddled the mare, he grieved for Kadif, too. Blaze could carry him, but it felt like riding a stick horse after being on a wild desert stallion.

At the boardinghouse, he was shown into the parlor while Ma Cavelli went to fetch Rowdy. Pacing up and down as he waited, he was still trying to think what to say.

"You'll get yourself talked about"? She would laugh. "Vince Turner is a cheap crook"? "Schoolmarms have to set an example"? "I can't bear to see you lower yourself"? "People are saying . . ." He had run through the whole gamut without finding an approach he thought would sway her.

When Ma told Rowdy her father was in the parlor, the girl's heart thumped once, hard. A small vengeful inward smile pulled bitterly at the corners of her mouth. Her knees felt wobbly as she walked down the hallway. She opened the door, and when she saw the dear familiar face so heavy with grief, had a sudden all-but-overwhelming desire to fling herself into his arms, to comfort him and to

311

cry the bitterness and sorrow out of her own heart. Then she remembered.

"Hello," she said coolly.

Angus shuffled his feet, ran a finger around his collar. "Let's walk," he said, realized the words came out as a command rather than a suggestion.

Rowdy shrugged. "All right."

In silence they went outside. The trees were beginning to throw long shadows across the boarded walk. "Will you be warm enough?" he asked, voice roughened by the tightness in his throat.

"I believe so," she said drily, "since it must be almost ninety."

He flushed at the mockery, still did not know how to begin. What would reach through the fastness of her anger and outrage? He was silent so long, she finally asked chillingly if this was a social call.

Angus's temper flared. He swallowed, hard. "You've been seen with Vince Turner," he heard himself blurt out.

"Yes."

"He's nothing but a cheap crook, Martha. He's no good."

"But not a murderer," she said with deadly sweetness.

Angus knew complete despair. His words had but reinforced the wall separating them.

"I'll walk you back to the boardinghouse," he growled.

"That won't be necessary," she said curtly, wheeled and left him. Helplessly, Angus watched her go. He wanted to weep. He wanted to curse. He wanted to scream at the darkening sky. He wanted his child back.

83.

It was Tuesday of the following week that Dove sent word to Angus that Auntie Po had died. She wanted him to conduct the funeral.

Angus was already too sorrowful to weep, but a lump

came into his throat. He had been fond of the old woman. And Dove would be desolated.

When he relayed the news to Jim, the old man's eyes brimmed with tears. "We better go over," he quavered, and Angus nodded. It was a country custom to call on the bereaved as soon as one heard of a death. There wouldn't be many calling on Dove. Those who had known and liked Auntie Po wouldn't dare acknowledge it.

At the big white house, a wreath hung on the front door. Out of habit, Angus started to go to the back, then decided to stop in front. He didn't care who saw his horse —had never cared, for that matter.

He got Jim out of the buggy and carried him to the house. It was Dove who answered, chalk-pale in black, which she never wore.

"Come in," she said tonelessly, and stepped back so Angus could desposit Jim in one of the easy chairs. When the old man was comfortable, Angus took Dove's hands. "I'm so sorry," he said.

Dove nodded. "She was a good woman. Why is it the good ones are taken and us miserable sinners are left?"

"We go when our time comes," Angus said awkwardly.

"Maybe it ain't so bad to go," Uncle Jim reflected. "There's bound to be a happier place than this."

Angus and Dove exchanged a look. Neither of them had ever heard the old man sound so morose. Dove went to put an arm around his neck.

"Now, Uncle Jim, don't be talkin' like that," she told him.

Customarily, one stayed but a few minutes, left to make room for other callers. Today, Angus and Jim stayed almost until milking time. Sometime during their visit, Dove asked vaguely if they were hungry.

Usually, in such cases, the table would be groaning under an assortment of food brought in by neighbors and friends. There was not so much as a cold biscuit here, and Angus's sorrow, and his pity for the black woman, made his insides ache.

As though she divined his thoughts, Dove said quietly, "Suzette will be here tomorrow."

"Dove, have you any folks left in New Orleans?" Angus asked gently.

The almond-colored hands, with their shapely nails, were clasped tightly in her lap. "No," she said. "My brother died several years ago; Mammy followed three months later." Her voice had been composed, but now some of the bitterness returned. "I don't think the Dubois family would welcome me with open arms.

"No, Angus, this is my home. Reckon it would dumbfound decent folks to learn that whores are human, that they can love and grieve, cherish a home."

Angus was silent, not knowing what to say.

Presently, she went on, her voice pensive, "Do you think the time will come when whites don't hate blacks, gentiles don't hate Jews, Irish don't hate the English, Catholics don't hate Protestants?"

Angus was ready to answer soothingly, reminding her to look to God's love, that the lion lay down with the lamb, when Dove added, "And the paleface doesn't hate the Indian?"

He felt as thought a fist had been slammed into his belly. Momentarily, he was enraged. Furious words rose to his lips, but as he flung his head back to shout her down, he saw no malice in her face, only a kind of sad thoughtfulness. His words died on his lips. He swallowed, drew a deep breath, noticed his father was watching him.

Everyone thinks I did wrong, he thought, yielding, for the moment, to self-pity. Well, he meditated grimly, a man can only do what he thinks is right. To hell with what others think.

He sprang to his feet. "We better go," he said roughly. "I'll be here in the morning, Dove. That is, if you want me . . . knowing what I did."

She had risen with him, and came to put her hand on his arm. "You did what you thought was right for your girl, same as I did for my boy. Who am I to judge anyone?"

A knot came into Angus's throat. "Dove," he said, "I think sometimes you got more goodness of heart than all the rest—"

"No!" she shouted. "I'm selfish, calculating, greedy, heartless. You got that?" Her eyes were flashing. For a moment, Angus was taken aback; then, unable to help himself, he started laughing. "Oh, Dove, Dove, Dove," he said, shaking his head.

The creamy face began to lose its belligerence; a sheepish smile touched her lips. "Don't feel sorry for me," she warned. "I'll crumble."

Jim spoke up. "Yore cold, greedy 'n' all them things you said," he assured her, "and it's time for us to go home."

Even Dove laughed then, gave the old man a hug. "Now, you're a man what understands me," she said. "Too bad your son didn't inherit some of your brains."

Jim cackled.

84.

Rowdy went to sit with Dove after supper. But she herself was in such an abyss of depression, she knew she was no help. The two women embraced, and Rowdy said Auntie Po had been a kind woman.

"That's true," Dove agreed, "and God knows there's little enough kindness in this world." She drew back from the girl and looked her over critically. "Lord help us, child," she said, "you look like what the cat dragged in and the kittens wouldn't eat."

"Dove," Rowdy said wryly, "you do have a way of cheering a person."

"Yes," Dove agreed, and was suddenly somber again.

"Could I see her?" Rowdy asked.

"If you like." As the two women walked upstairs, Rowdy could hear the scurrying and whispering of Dove's girls in their second-floor rooms.

"Seems like some of them could sit with you so you wouldn't be alone," she said angrily.

"They offered." Dove shrugged. "But they—they're not family."

Tears came into Rowdy's eyes. "Dove, I'll come and stay here if you want. I don't mean, be one of your girls. I mean, just room here. I'd be company."

"Yes, you would." Dove's voice was sad. "It wouldn't do. You'd be ostracized by 'decent' folks."

"I wouldn't care."

"Yes, you'd care. You'd care a lot if you walked into

315

the general store and Mrs. Goody-Two-Shoes held her skirts aside lest they touch yours."

"You're as good as anyone."

"I'm better than a lot of folks," Dove said, "because I don't pretend to be anything but what I am. That doesn't keep me from being treated like dirt. I thank you, though, Rowdy. I take it kindly." She opened the door to Auntie Po's room.

The ancient black woman lay in bed, covers up to her waist. The wrinkled face had smoothed somewhat in death. The arms were crossed on her chest. Rowdy knelt and said a brief prayer for her.

She kissed Dove when she left. "I'll come early in the morning so I can help with chairs or whatever."

She was as good as her word. She had gotten Clover to tend school for her, was dismounting from her horse the next morning shortly after nine, when Angus arrived.

"Miss Rowdy! Rowdy, girl!" The words burst out before he thought. He called "Whoa!" to the horse, and Rowdy turned.

"Hello," she said, then ran to the buggy. "Uncle Jim," she cried, "how are you? You're looking almost peart again. Don't want to hear any stories about you sparkin' the girls."

The old face brightened like the rising sun. "Yore shore a sight for sore eyes," he said, voice breaking. And then: "I miss you, child."

"I miss you too," Rowdy whispered, then stood aside so Angus could lift the old man from the buggy.

Suzette was there, broadened and beaming, accompanied by the massive Texan who was her husband. The men shook hands.

"Told Ivey he needn't come along," Suzette bubbled. "But he would have it."

"Afraid she'd start remembering how easy life was here, compared with bein' a rancher's wife and motherin' two young hellions," Ivey said, grinning.

"We know how worried you are," Suzette twitted him, and Rowdy saw the promises their eyes exchanged. Love and confidence and—and belonging. That's the way Johnny and I would have been, she thought bitterly.

The kitchen table had been brought into the parlor and Auntie Po's box set atop it, open so all could bid their last farewell. Dove's girls were in attendance, dressed in their decorous best and weeping. Suzette and Ivey, Angus, Jim and Rowdy made up the body of mourners, with Dove. Mr. Koontz hovered at the back of the room rubbing his dry hands together. Rowdy wished he had waited outside.

Angus read briefly, spoke of kindliness and loving one's neighbor, emphasized that skin color was of no importance in the sight of God, and caught Miss Rowdy's sardonic lift of the eyebrow. He flushed but went doggedly on. It hadn't been that Indian's color, dammit, he thought. It had been his—his nature. Everyone knew Indians were treacherous murdering devils.

He finished the service with a prayer, trying to overcome his own sense of loss.

85.

It was a couple of weeks after the funeral when Vince Turner called on Rowdy. Ma Cavelli left him standing on the outside stoop and, mouth set in a thin line, went to tell the girl she had a man caller.

"Who?" Rowdy asked, surprised. Most of the men her age were long since married; the others, she'd discouraged.

Ma sniffed. "Called hisself Turner."

"Turner? Good heavens."

"He's on the stoop," Ma growled, and stumped away.

As she walked down the dim hallway, Rowdy wondered why she hadn't simply asked Ma to send the man about his business. She herself didn't like him. She was, she supposed, still trying to "get even." She stepped outside the door, nodded coolly.

Vince had whipped off his black slouch hat when she appeared. "I trust you won't find me bold," he apologized. "I presumed to call without an appointment, in the hope that you would take pity on a lonely man and sup with me at the Wagon Wheel. I arrived in town only this afternoon."

There was something about his manner that rang false.

Still, Rowdy was lonely and restless. In cutting herself off from her family, she felt alienated also from family friends, knowing they disapproved of her actions. She blinked away the threat of tears. Why not have supper with the man? What difference did it make?

"I'll get my hat," she said.

The Wagon Wheel was serving chicken and dumplings. Rowdy picked at her food while Vince Turner talked on and on. She wasn't listening. Occasionally, when he paused, she made what she hoped was an appropriate sound. Her head began to ache in the heat of the room, and she was more bored than if she'd stayed at Ma's. Besides, Mrs. Harry, the proprietor's wife, was watching, her protuberant eyes avid.

Vince was digging into his pie and Rowdy was sipping coffee when Dude Malicote came in. He swaggered to their table, his pearl-gray Stetson set at a jaunty angle, his highly glossed boots reflecting light from the lamps.

"What have we here?" Dude demanded. The huskiness in his voice sounded like it was caused by whiskey drinking, but was not. Someone years ago had chopped him across the Adam's apple when he made a play for a saloon girl already appropriated. Had the blow caught him full on, he would have been killed. As it was, the larynx was permanently damaged.

He had bided his time and later shot the man in an ambush.

Vince looked up. "Thought we was supposed to meet Thursday."

Dude shrugged. "Finished my business in Arkansas sooner'n what I expected. How'd you manage to hook up with a pretty little lady like this-here?"

Turner chose not to hear. "I'll see you tomorrow."

Rowdy was faintly amused. She didn't care one way or the other whether she and this dandy were introduced. But was it possible, even remotely possible, Vince Turner saw himself in the role of a suitor? Did he have that much audacity? If so, his idea had better be nipped in the bud. She tilted her head and allowed herself to meet the arrogant stare of eyes so dark, they looked black. There was a hairline mustache, a petulant mouth. Cheap and flashy, she thought. Aloud, without inflection, she said, "My name is Scofield."

"I'm Dude Malicote," the man said. "Mind if I sit with

318

you-all?" Without waiting for an answer, he pulled out a chair.

Suddenly, Rowdy was disgusted with the whole stupid evening. It was obvious the little pipsqueak thought he'd made a conquest. At that, he might attract some women. The bold black eyes, the single curl allowed to fall theatrically on his forehead, the thin sharp nose, full red lips. Above all, the blatant sexuality.

He's—what was Dove's word?—he's *soft,* Rowdy thought. When she was small, she'd visualized a "soft" man as squishy, had later realized Dove referred to an inner quality. So she summed up Dude as soft, and snubbed him.

"We are leaving," she said haughtily, and stood up. Perforce, Turner rose too. "Yeah, Dude," he mumbled. "See you later."

A dull ugly red blotched Malicote's face as he watched them leave.

At the boardinghouse door, Rowdy bade Vince a chilly good night, stepped inside before he could respond. She hurried to her room, scoured her teeth viciously with salt and soda, then stripped, and scrubbed her flesh until it was all but raw. Nasty little ferrets, she thought. And I didn't hurt anyone but myself.

She was wrong. The news reached Angus two days later, and he rode into town, faunching. In his rage, he all but beat down the boardinghouse door. Ma came on the run.

"What's wrong?" she cried. "Someone hurt?"

Angus's look was as black as a cyclone sky. "Martha!" he snapped. As Ma turned to hurry toward the girl's room, he followed. Ma knocked, but Angus brushed her aside and flung the door open. "Come out here!" he thundered.

Rowdy had been writing. She looked up, wide-eyed.

"On your feet! Outside!" Angus shouted.

Ma backed away, shivering with pleasurable trepidation. For an instant, tension throbbed between father and daughter while Rowdy considered a childish "Try and make me." Then recognized that in his present frame of mind, Angus was perfectly capable of hauling her out bodily.

She rose slowly and, head held high, marched past him. Outside, she turned on him, two spots of scarlet standing

319

out in vivid relief against her cheekbones. The amethyst eyes glittered.

"I hope you're proud of yourself," she said icily,

Angus was in such a black rage, he found it hard to breathe. "I told you to stay away from Vince Turner," he said raspily. "But Dude Malicote, my God in heaven!" He raised a hand as though to strike her, and Rowdy stepped back.

"You're speaking of my friends," she told him curtly.

"Friends? I won't have it, by God. You can behave yourself or I'll carry you home and tie you up. Dude Malicote is a—a despoiler of women."

"Why don't you tell the sheriff?" she asked mockingly.

"I will!" He wheeled away, overflowing with rage, strode off toward the main part of town, forgetting his horse. He was struggling for breath, and his chest ached from the tears he'd held back.

He had managed to get hold of himself by the time he reached the sheriff's office. Garrison was going over some papers, but rose when Angus came in. He thrust out a hand.

"Howdy, preacher," he said. "Good to see you. Sit."

Angus slumped into a chair. "Garry, Dude Malicote's in town."

The sheriff rested his rump against the desk. "I know."

Angus felt his choler rising again, knew he was edgy; with an effort, spoke calmly. "He's an outlaw, man. Lock him up!"

Garrison spread his hands. "He's been behavin' hisself hereabouts; got no wanted poster on him."

"Run him out of town."

"Yore livin' in the old days, Angus," the sheriff chided him. "If I tried that nowadays, he'd get hisself one of them smart-aleck lawyers and sue me."

"On what charge?"

"Who knows?" The other man was gloomy. "That damn legislature is churning up laws like you wouldn't believe. 'Pears they're more interested in seein' outlaws is treated agreeable than that decent folks is protected.

"You take the Kiamichis, now," Garrison expounded, "you know they've allus been a hideout for outlaws. Robber's Cave, especial."

Angus nodded.

"I swear to you, I think every bad-man from the Dakotas to Texas to Californy is holed up there right now. They've had the gall to send word to one of the sheriffs in the area, daring him to come in.

"Was it up to me, what I'd do if I was them legislators sittin' up there on their backsides and drawin' fancy salaries, I'd get a cavalry regiment to clean that cave out, give 'em a trial where they stood, and hang 'em."

In spite of his worries, Angus couldn't keep from chuckling. Garrison glared at him.

"Laugh if you want, but things ain't like they was in the old days, preacher."

Angus sobered. "I'm not on the circuit anymore, Garry. Be obliged if you wouldn't call me preacher."

Garrison's brows drew together. "You didn't quit over that Injun?"

"I quit," Angus said curtly, and began to rise.

"Sit a minute more," the sheriff said thoughtfully. "You ever thought of bein' a lawman?"

For a moment Angus was sorely tempted. He found that facing Jim's silent accusing face every day was getting under his skin.

But the old man had to be cared for. When he'd been preaching, Angus had accepted help from others, feeling, in some way not clearly defined, that it was their offering to the Almighty. If he were to become a law-man, it would be simply because he wanted to escape his responsibility.

He shook his head.

"If ever you change yore mind . . ."

Angus nodded and took his leave.

86.

For Rowdy, the following two days were excruciating. She felt sick when she thought of Papa. Knowing now the lengths to which his temper could drive him especially where she was concerned, she jumped at every sudden noise. She wouldn't put it past him to shoot both Vince and Dude. Then he'd hang.

Not that I care what happens to him, she told herself angrily. It's just the—the scandal. She tried to read, to sew, to work out her lesson plans for the coming fall, but could concentrate on nothing.

After supper on the second day, Ma came again to tell her, sourly, that she had a visitor. "On the front stoop," she snapped, and stalked away. Who now? Rowdy thought. She didn't think Mr. Turner would have the nerve to call again after her curt dismissal. And if it were Papa, Ma wouldn't have been angry. Rowdy shrugged. The quickest way to find out, she told herself, was to quit sulking and go to the door.

She pulled the front door open, and Dude Malicote grinned at her, stroking his mustache. "Been lookin' for you around town," he said, tilting the Stetson back with one finger so the curl looped down. "Thought I'd drop by and see if you was sick."

Alarm tautened Rowdy's nerves. She glanced up and down the street, then stepped out and shut the door. "For your own good, I'm warning you," she said quietly, "Papa's on the rampage. He just might"—her voice trembled —"he just might kill you if you don't stay away from me."

Malicote smirked, thinking he now understood why this woman had pretended she wasn't interested in him.

"I'm not afraid of Papa," he answered disdainfully. "Wouldn't you like some fresh air? I'll hire a rig, and we can find a cozy spot . . ."

Rowdy felt irresolute. She truly was afraid of what Papa might do, whether Mr. Malicote was concerned or not. Still, was she going to let Papa tell her what to do the rest of her life? Who she should associate with? Defiance made her bring her head up sharply.

"A short stroll would be pleasant," she said.

Dude didn't bother to hide his grin. "Certainly, Miss Scofield," he mocked. "Yore wish is my command."

Distaste twisted Rowdy's lips. Then she forced a feeble smile and stepped out to the boardwalk with him. They traversed the distance to the main section of town while he regaled her with some of his conquests. Sometimes that quickened a woman's interest, he thought.

Few of his words penetrated Rowdy's consciousness.

322

She was glancing back over her shoulder to be sure Papa wasn't there. When Malicote asked if she would like coffee, though, adding that he had a small bottle in his pocket to "sweeten" it, she curtly refused.

"I must get back," she said.

Dude put a hand on her shoulder, let it slide down her back. "Aw, come on, Rowdy."

The girl looked up to see Koontz bearing down on them. She flushed, biting her lip, twisted away from the partial embrace.

"Keep your hands to yourself!" she snapped.

"Don't pretend, girlie; you know you like it."

Face flaming, she whirled and headed toward the boardinghouse. Vaguely—it was hardly more than a pinprick—her mind recorded that Mr. Koontz had not tipped his hat.

She walked hurriedly, expecting every minute to hear Malicote's voice or feel his touch. But Dude stood where she had left him. They all liked to play hard to get. Smirking, he touched his tie and decided to spend the evening at Dove's house.

87.

A couple of days after Dude's visit, Rowdy found time hanging heavy on her hands. There was so much to do in the country. . . . Resolutely, she put that thought away. She could make herself a new velvet pants suit. Ma had been tight-lipped and scowling since Dude called, so though it was hot and uncomfortable, the girl kept to her room. Sewing would give her something to do.

Properly attired in hat and gown, she walked to the dry-goods store. The interior seemed cool after the heat of the dazzling sun. At the counter, a woman was studying a pattern book, and Rowdy recognized the pigeon form.

"Good morning, Mrs. Hazelrigg," she said quietly,

and turned toward the bolts of fabric. There was no answer, and Rowdy looked back, thinking she had made a mistake. But no, it was Mrs. Hazelrigg, all right. The small eyes were slate-hard.

"Humph," Mrs. Házelrigg said, and drew her skirts aside. Then she shoved the pattern book back at the proprietor and, nose in the air, sailed out of the store.

Rowdy felt the heat rise to her cheeks. She remembered telling Dove she wouldn't care if she were snubbed, and Dove's somber reply. "You'd care."

The girl realized she *did* care. Her pride had been assailed, the sense of her own worth disturbed. Her eyes met those of the storekeeper, and she saw the gleam of curiosity, the thinly veiled amusement, before he stooped to thrust the book beneath the counter.

It was that same evening that Sarah Holtzworthy again came to visit. When the knock came at her door, Rowdy called "Come in," thinking it was Ma Cavelli.

The girl had been in a curious state. Heartsick, angry, defiant, all but immobilized by the conflicting emotions. She hadn't gone to the table for either dinner or supper. I haven't done anything wrong, she'd kept telling herself. Then she'd remember the way Mrs. Hazelrigg had snubbed her, the storekeeper's amusement, and felt shamed.

When Sarah opened the door, Rowdy jumped to her feet.

"Lordy, Aunt Sarah, I'm glad to see you," she said, and went to hug her. Sarah sighed.

"I'm afraid you're not going to be glad when I tell you why I'm here," she said. Her voice was gentle, but its underlying sadness puzzled and frightened the girl.

"What's wrong?" she cried. "Not Uncle Jim?"

"No. Sit down, child. This isn't going to be easy."

"Not . . . nothing's happened to Papa?"

Sarah shook her head, and Rowdy saw the sheen of tears in her eyes. Sarah, always so strong and calm. Rowdy felt her heart slide to her toes. She sat down, not realizing her face had lost its color.

Sarah sat on the edge of the bed, took the girl's hands in hers. "Martha"—her voice was uneven—"there's no easy way to say this. The school board is fixin' to fire you. I—I thought you'd rather tell them you quit." The older woman burst into tears. "Child, child, what were you thinking of? Vince Turner and Dude Malicote. Didn't you know people would talk?"

"But I didn't do anything wrong," Rowdy wailed. "Supper at the café, a walk to town. I haven't been 'out' with them."

Sarah wiped her streaming eyes. Her face was stern now. "Martha, you know how people are. You know about avoiding the appearance of evil. A young woman getting herself talked about . . ." She broke off, crying again. "You know Zeb and I love you; you're almost like our own. You know too, though, that a woman has to protect her good name. Especially a schoolmarm."

"Yes." The hurt had gone deep. Rowdy was filled with bitterness. It was unfair; she hadn't *done* anything. She felt that if she uttered more than the monosyllable, she would shatter. She stood up and began to move aimlessly around the room, twisting her hands together. She was crying, and the pale hair had slipped from its moorings and hung around her shoulders.

"Maybe if you would apologize . . ." Sarah suggested uncertainly.

"To whom?" Rowdy asked. "Hang a sign in the general store?" She began to laugh, and the tearing sound seemed to Sarah more painful than the tears. The older woman stood up and went to put her arms around the girl. She held Rowdy until the hysteria had finally passed into apathy. Then Rowdy pulled away.

"You can take my resignation to them," she said, and, finding a piece of paper, began to write.

88.

Oklahoma City was an early-to-bed, early-to-rise town. Most houses were dark by nine-thirty, and Ma locked up promptly at ten. Rowdy was still awake well past midnight, when there was a thunderous knocking at the front door. She wondered dully what more had happened.

She heard Ma shuffling down the hall, muttering irritably, "All right, all right, hold your horses." Heard the door open and her own name shouted. "Rowdy! Rowdy! Girlie!"

She froze. "God in heaven," she whispered. Dude!

There was a burst of imbecile giggling. "Come out, come out or I'll come get you. Got a scheme!" His voice trailed off. Rowdy heard the door slam, heard the clamor start up again. Hammering at the door, shouts loud enough to wake the town. Her door was flung open without a knock. Rowdy had just struck a match to the lamp, and saw Ma's face, crimson with anger.

"Get out there and get that fool quietened down!" she ordered. "And in the morning, Miss, you pack up and get out. I run a respectable house. I don't want the likes of you around."

Nausea rose in the girl's throat. For an instant she swayed, righted herself by holding to the bed post. "I didn't know he was coming . . ."

"Them what lays down with dogs gets up with fleas." Ma snorted.

Rowdy threw a dress on over her night clothes. She was trembling so, she could hardly stand as she tried to hurry down the hallway. She opened the door, stepped outside.

"There you are!" Dude shouted, flung his arms around her, jerked her hard against him and gave her a slobbery kiss. Whiskey fumes assailed her, increasing the sickness in her belly. She grimaced and tore herself away from him.

"You fool!" she stormed. "You idiot! What do you mean, coming here, and at this time of night? I could kill you!"

Dude giggled fatuously. "Woman with spunk, I do like a woman with spunk." The words were slurred, and in the faint starlight, his face looked doltish. "We're gonna be rich, you'n'me. Gotta scheme."

Rowdy could endure no more. She slapped him so hard across the face that he staggered backward. The next moment, he grabbed at her again. "Wanna rassle . . . wanna play rough . . ."

Without warning, she felt the strength drain out of her body and went limp. Helpless as a newborn kitten, she clung to the rail of the stoop.

"Please, Mr. Malicote," she whispered. "Please go away."

He didn't move. His mouth was seeking hers, and she felt his hands on her body. "I'll meet you tomorrow," she said, sobbing.

"Please, Mr. Malicote," he said mockingly. "Not so high and mighty now, are we? Please. That do sound better." He drew an inch or two away. "You promise?"

"I promise," she whispered, and forced herself not to struggle. At last Dude released her.

"Wagon Wheel. Dinner." Giggling again, he lurched off.

Rowdy clung to the porch railing while waves of blackness washed over her. She must not faint. The thought penetrated her hazy senses. At last a measure of strength returned to her. She went to her room and lay awake the rest of the night.

When morning came, she washed, dressed in fresh clothing and walked downtown. She needed a job. Cason's Grocery. The Emporium. Keeping books for the lumberyard.

Swallowing her pride, she stopped at each one and asked for work. She tried the bank, the newspaper office. Some of the men were polite. Some acted like they couldn't get rid of her soon enough. No one had a job. Not for her, at any rate.

She hesitated before the undertaker's parlor, took a deep breath and opened the door. Wreaths and sheaves of wax flowers. A dress and a man's suit, hanging dispiritedly on hangers—shrouds. In the corner, a metal casket displaying a sleazy interior. The girl shivered.

Koontz pushed aside the curtain from the back room, rubbing his dry hands together as if he were washing them. "Can I help you . . . ?" She saw recognition come into his face, and something less definable; nonetheless, it made her hunch her shoulders.

"Mr. Koontz," she said crisply, "I'm looking for a job." He sidled toward her, smiling. He had yellowish teeth with a gap between the two front upper ones. Something inside her shriveled.

"Well, now," he said, putting his hand on her arm. "Well, now. You ain't gonna teach no more?"

He knows, she thought, and sickness rose within her.

The bastard knows all about it and is gloating. His hand moved so that it brushed against her breast.

She jerked away from him, banners of red flaming in her cheeks. "You disgusting old toad," she whispered, shocked and horrified that this could be happening to her.

Koontz's face darkened. "You needn't be putting on airs—" he began, but she whirled and ran out of the building. There was an agony of tears behind her eyelids. The heat, the gritty wind and sleepless night had combined to make her eyes burn. Her mouth was dry, and there was a lump in her throat as big as a turkey egg.

A week ago she had been respected. Now she was being treated like a—a fallen woman. Dove had once accused her of biting off her nose to spite her face. Innate honesty made her admit that was what she had done now. In trying to get back at Papa, she had badly damaged herself.

And had no idea how to undo the damage.

It was almost noon. If she didn't show up for dinner, Dude would, she knew, hunt her down and make another scene. Tears blurring her vision, she began to walk slowly toward the Wagon Wheel. The hell of it was, she thought bitterly, she had no one to blame but herself.

She turned into the café and, sitting at a table, ordered coffee. Within five minutes, Dude showed up. He even walks cockily, she thought sourly, watching him from beneath her lashes.

"What's good today?" he demanded, lowering himself into a chair and sweeping off his hat. Rowdy wrinkled her nose with disgust as he laid it on a chair. The sweatband was filthy, and grease had begun to spread on the hat itself.

When the waiter came, Dude said loudly, "Bacon and eggs for me, old timer. Bring the little lady some bumgolly stew and cornbread. Gal with a little meat on her bones, lot more squeezable, ain't she?"

Rowdy felt her face grow hot, felt the trembling begin in her hands. When the waiter had gone, she said with vicious sweetness, "You humiliate me again, I'll kill you."

Dude started to laugh, to make a flip reply, took a look at her stony face and swallowed. "Jest joshin'," he said weakly; "can't you take a joke?"

"No," Rowdy said. "Speak your piece."

Their food came then, and Dude waited until the waiter had put it down and left them. "This idea I've got," he said between mouthfuls, "we need a stake to get us out of this town."

Rowdy listened somberly. She'd like to leave town, all right. It had grown hateful to her. The dining room was filling up, and she caught the sly glances, the lifted eyebrows. Holding her head higher, she asked curtly, "What do you have in mind?"

"They's a bank in Lincoln, little east of Guthrie. Hear tell you could open it with a buttonhook."

Rowdy's face remained impassive. "You think I'm going to rob a bank?" she scoffed.

"No. I'm gonna take care of the bank. Then you'n'me, we'll take off for Kansas City or St. Louis. New Orleans, maybe. Someplace where they's money. Yore a looker. I'll sniff out the men what've got a roll. You get acquainted, invite 'em to yore room, put a couple drops of sweetenin' in their drink. They'll go sleepy-bye and I'll grab their cash. How's that for a idee?"

"Disgusting," Rowdy said.

"I'll get 'em out of yore room," he went on as though she hadn't spoken. "Toss 'em out in the back somewheres. When they wake up, they'll be too discombobulated to make a fuss."

"Don't be ridiculous," Rowdy said. She ached to leave, didn't quite dare. He was perfectly capable of grabbing her and shoving her back into the chair.

The food had begun to offset the effects of his hangover. "Think on it," he urged. Dude Malicote was neither smart nor clever, but he had a kind of feral instinct about people. "You want to be shet of this yokel town," he said slyly. When she didn't answer, he added, "Jest think on it. Let's go."

She got up, knowing every eye in the place was on her, either openly or covertly. Head high, she marched over to where Mrs. Harry stood at the cash register, picking her teeth. She was grossly fat, there were food stains on the front of her black bombazine bosom, and Rowdy had once heard Clover, who had a good word for almost everyone, dismiss her as "shanty Irish, common as dirt."

When Dude stopped to pay the bill, Rowdy was beside him. Mrs. Harry ducked her head. Rowdy flushed, cleared

329

her throat. The woman ducked her head lower, made a great business of selecting the proper change.

The girl's spirit, already tottering from repeated blows, disintegrated. She saw herself with the town's eyes. Accepted their/her values and found herself worthless.

The helpless rage of a trapped animal shook her. "Mrs. Harry," she said loudly, "your neck's dirty."

She whirled and hurried out of the café, looking neither right nor left, Dude behind her, shouting with laughter.

The heat was overpowering. Gusts of wind carrying grit stung her face. She could feel it between her teeth, in her eyes. Dude was still laughing.

"Oh, be quiet!" she snapped. "How soon can we get out of this town?"

"Wellll . . ." he drawled, pleased and complacent. "Figgered you'd come around."

Rowdy shivered. "Malicote," she said, "I'm going with you. I'll help play your game with rich old men who ought to know better. But"—her tone was deadly—"you lay one hand on me, you're going to be looking death right in the eye."

"It wasn't a hand I was aimin' to lay on you." He guffawed.

Rowdy reddened, quickened her pace. "You lay a hand on me," she repeated, "in anger or—or sexually, I'll kill you. I promise."

He was silent, and she slanted a glance at him, coldly amused to see he had stopped laughing and his face had gone red. She had embarrassed him. Apparently, even cheap crooks balked at a woman talking "dirty."

They walked on together, and after a time, he said sulkily, " 'Pears like you've got an orful lot to say about what's gonna be or not gonna be."

Rowdy shrugged. "Take it or leave it. I'm getting out of Oklahoma City. With or without you, makes no difference to me."

It was dusk by the time they had paid for their respective rooms, bought what provisions they could carry and gotten their horses from the livery stable. Rowdy checked the .38 in her reticule and changed into her velvet britches before leaving the boardinghouse. If the citizens of Oklahoma City wanted something to talk about, she'd provide them with it.

When she met Dude, as prearranged, his mouth fell open at sight of her pants. "Females ain't sposed to—" he began, but she touched Biscuit's flanks with her heels and was off at a gallop.

Dude urged his horse up beside her. "Where d'ya think yore goin'?" he yelled.

"To hell!" Rowdy yelled back. "You going along?"

Dude was silent, uneasy. Rowdy's hair had streamed loose from its pins, and floated around her face in a ghostly aura. In the near darkness, he could see her eyes glinting eerily, giving her a look of madness.

Chill touched the back of Dude's neck. Half fearful, half fascinated, he wondered if she were a little crazy. He'd bet she'd be a hell-kitten in bed.

She was ahead of him again, and he shouted at her to swing north. Obediently, she turned Biscuit's head and rode on without breaking stride. After a few miles, the horse slowed, and Rowdy let her select her own gait. Dude caught up with them.

"What's the damn hurry?" he growled. Rowdy ignored the question.

"I never heard of a town called Lincoln," she said.

"It ain't rightly a town," Dude replied. "Bank and grocery store is about all they is—post office in the grocery."

The night had been an illusion, an unreality. Rowdy had thought only of getting away. Now she began to wonder what she was going toward.

Without warning, the black curtain of despair closed in around her again, and she was all but fainting with weariness and depression.

"Next thicket we come to, I'm bedding down for the night," she said, struggling to get the words out. "You can go on if you want."

"I wouldn't leave you out here by yoreself, girlie." His voice was lubricious, and Rowdy felt her stomach heave. She didn't know which she liked less, his shoddy pretense of being a good fellow, or the swaggering bully which was his normal self.

When they reached the next stand of blackjacks, she pulled Biscuit to a halt. Dude stopped too, but was surly. "You don't wanta go sleepin' in blackjacks," he protested. "That's where rattlers nest."

"If a rattler bit me tonight," she said wearily, "it'd be a tossup which one of us died first." Dude shifted uneasily. What kind of talk was that? Rowdy slid off the horse, uncinched the girth strap and lifted off the saddle. Biscuit began to graze.

"Oh, well, if yore set on it," he said, sulking.

Rowdy ignored him. She spread her saddle blanket on the ground, rolled herself up in it and the next moment was dead to the world.

Dude's eyes narrowed. He had half a mind to take her right now. She pretended to be so high and mighty. Nobody who wasn't a tramp would take off alone with a man she hardly knew. He shifted his feet, vaguely apprehensive. No, he decided, he wouldn't take her now.

Rowdy's sleep was troubled by dreams. Johnny beckoned to her. When she reached him, Papa's hand rose, separated them. She saw Mrs. Harry's jowly face and told her she should use lye soap. Uncle Jim was calling to her, and Aunt Sarah's tears were stretched out across the plain in shining crystals.

She moaned and tossed but never thoroughly awakened. It was dawn before she fell into a restful sleep, and the sun was high in the heavens before she was fully conscious once more. Dude was watching her.

"I let you sleep," he said magnanimously.

"It's a good thing," Rowdy snapped. "Find some water?"

"They's a creek down thetaway."

"Water the horses?"

"Naw, they can wait."

"You son of a bitch," Rowdy said equably.

Dude flushed an ugly red. "Don't be callin' me names, you slut."

Unexpectedly, her silver peal of laughter rang out. "Now we've established our respective statuses," she said, and, untying the horses, led them in the direction Dude had indicated. The man stood glowering at her.

She puzzled and confused him, and he didn't like it. Still—he licked his lips—she had class, and there was that nice juicy setup with rich old men to think about.

Rowdy came back presently with the horses, and Dude scowled. She had scrubbed herself and her hair was pulled up neatly, but she still wore the velvet pants.

332

"I didn't bargain for no man-woman," he muttered.

She shrugged. "No one's holding you."

Bitch, he thought as he saddled his horse. One of these days he'd make her pay for all those insults.

They ate breakfast in Guthrie, and Rowdy made a small purchase. Then once more they rode north by east.

89.

Nearly two weeks passed before Jim found out Rowdy was gone. Even then, Angus never knew how the old man learned about it. Friends still visited Jim; Dove drove out now and again. But by tacit consent, they had all agreed it would be best not to mention the girl. Angus's spirits were low enough; it wasn't necessary to sadden Jim too.

In reality, Angus was still in shock. He went about his daily chores with an efficiency born of habit. He took care of his father's needs with a sort of absentminded kindness.

What he had done lay on his conscience like a millstone. He was still convinced that a marriage between Miss Rowdy and "that Injun" would have been disastrous, but, he thought, there must have been some other way to handle it.

Even so, condemned as he felt before God and condemned as he was by his own child, it had never occurred to him but that they would eventually be reconciled. When he learned that she had taken off with Dude Malicote, he suffered a pain so intense, he thought he was dying.

It was Dove who told him. He had walked out to the buggy with her after her visit with Jim. "I thought you'd rather hear it from me," she said, and began to cry.

Angus was stunned, and then the pain began, like wildfire. Sobs racked his body, dredged up, torn out of him.

Dove put her arms around him and held him gently as a mother.

"I'm so sorry," she whispered. "Angus, don't!" Her tears mingled with his. "She'll come back."

Angus never knew how long she held him. The shadows were gathering when he raised his head, wiped his eyes. "Sorry," he said, embarrassed.

"Don't be. You were with me when I was in the pit."

"You think I should go after her?" he asked brokenly.

Dove shook her head. "She's too much like you. She'll have to do the deciding. You might tie her up and carry her back. She'd be gone again, soon as you loosed her."

"I suppose."

"If you're okay, I better be going."

"Yes." He helped her into the buggy, but as she picked up the reins, he burst out, "Dove, I can't endure it if she doesn't come back!"

Dove said, "Whoa," and then to him, somberly: "We can endure, Angus, you and me. We bend but we don't break." She touched the horse with the whip and was gone.

It was three or four days later that Jim brought it up. In the meantime, Angus had made a valiant effort to act normal. But Thursday evening, as he was washing up after supper, Jim said sorrowfully, "My girl-child's gone, ain't she?"

Angus froze. A dish fell from his hands. "W—what makes you think that?" he stammered.

"Aint she?" Jim persisted.

"Yes." Angus didn't look at him.

"With a grifter," Jim said sadly.

"I'm afraid so."

Tears began to plow their way down Jim's thin cheeks. He sat with his head down and made no attempt to wipe them away. As he got the old man ready for bed, Angus said gently, "She'll come back. She's just got to—to work her mad off."

Jim said nothing. In bed, he turned his face to the wall.

Angus got the Bible and sat down to read. "Read over there in the New Testament where it tells about heaven," Jim said.

There were a lot of passages in the New Testament that spoke of heaven, Angus thought, but the old man's voice was weak and tired-sounding, so Angus chose one of his own favorites. "To an inheritance incorruptible . . ."

"Yore man had an inheritance." Jim said, grieving, and slipped into the light sleep of old age. Angus sat with the Bible still open, not reading, his mind on his child. Where was she tonight? Was she sleeping with that spoiler? His muscles knotted.

His Miss Rowdy. Beautiful, proud, spirited. Was she allowing herself to be debased? If so, Angus knew he himself was the one to blame. Inwardly, he groaned. After a time, unable to concentrate on what he was reading, he shut the Bible and went to bed.

His rest was interrupted sometime during the night by the sound of labored breathing. Still half asleep, he remembered a snatch of dream—one of the horses struggling to pull a too-heavy load.

Then he woke more fully. The house was pitch-black. He lay, straining to hear. Had the sound been a dream? He didn't want to disturb Jim by getting up unnecessarily. He turned on his side and the sound came again, stertorous, painful to hear. Angus jumped out of bed, lit the lamp, went to his father.

Jim lay staring up at him, the faded eyes agonized. His skin was mottled, tinged with blue. "Feared . . . I . . . done . . . it . . . again . . . sorry . . ." he apologized, a gap between each laborious word.

A lump formed in Angus's throat.

"Nothing to be sorry about," he said gruffly. "Fellow can't help it if he's sick." It seemed to him the old man was slipping away from him with each passing moment, and he had a sense of panic.

"I'm going for the doctor," he said. "I'll send Clover to stay with you."

"No!" It was a whispered scream. "Don't . . . leave . . . Davey . . . for God's . . . sake, please . . . don't!"

Angus was pulling on a shirt. He stopped and laid it aside. "I won't," he said. "What do you want? A drink? Sip of whiskey? Cough syrup?" He knew he was gabbling, making no sense, but he was frightened. Jim's lips had turned a deep blue, and it seemed to Angus that the old man's eyes were becoming glazed.

"Davey!" It was a scream of animal terror. "Davey . . . I . . . can't . . . breathe!"

335

Angus went on his knees beside the bed, lifted the old man so he was half sitting. "That help?" he asked, knowing his voice was unsteady.

Jim didn't answer. His eyes sought Angus's, and there was a mute appeal in them. Angus felt a lump come into his throat. He sat Jim up straighter.

"There, now," he faltered. "Better?"

"Can't breathe." The words came out on a great exhalation. Again Angus straightened the frail body, attempted to lift the head to make it easier for the old man to breathe.

"Let me hold you, Pa," he said.

The appeal went out of the faded eyes. A faint smile touched the good side of Jim's mouth. "That's a lovin' word," he gasped.

And died.

90.

It was months before Rowdy learned of Jim's death. Vince Turner had drifted into St. Louis and met up with them. "Hear tell the cattlemen are coming here from all around the country," he told Dude. "Reckon the pickin's ort to be right good."

Dude licked his lips. "Don't take all their money." He guffawed. "Leave somethin' for Her Highness, over there." Rowdy, rearranging the silver by her plate, smiled frostily. In one of their frequent clashes, Dude had shouted that she thought she was better than other people, and since then called her Your Highness when he was sulking. Not that she cared.

Their course had been reasonably smooth. Dude had broken a side window of the Lincoln bank while she stood watch. Her purchase in Guthrie had been a short length of velvet, which she cut into strips. While she waited for Dude, she had tied a small velvet bow on the front door of the bank.

"Nothin' to it," he'd bragged as they rode toward the Missouri border. The take had been only slightly over two hundred dollars, but it served them well enough.

They had stopped in Springfield for a few days, but the hotel guests were mostly drummers. Drummers didn't carry much in the way of cash. Rowdy flirted idly with some of the men in the dining room, for practice. Were men so easily attracted? It appeared they were, for several came to her table. Her frosty innocence sent them into flustered and apologetic retreat.

Rowdy despised them. Even more, she despised herself. Dove's girls have more decency than I do, she thought. At least when they take money, they give something in return. Self-loathing was an ever-present sickness in her throat. She had no appetite. The consequent weight loss had given her an appealing fragility.

This time last year, she thought while Vince and Dude talked, I was a teacher. Respected. I had Johnny's love. Johnny!

She glanced around, fearful she had shrieked aloud. But Dude and Vince were chattering away, undisturbed.

St. Louis was different from Springfield. The streets might be paved with horse droppings, but the hotels were ornate, the guests reeking of wealth. And the pretty little lady, as she heard herself described, was a magnet for masculine attention. Dude, decorously dressed—she had made him get rid of the flashy clothes and fake diamond —would escort her to the dining room or lobby and conveniently disappear.

She learned quickly. Eyes met those of the prospective prey and were quickly lowered. The trappings of confusion and embarrassment when someone sent a note by the waiter or approached the table. The "girls" who worked the hotels were, for the most part, hard-faced and bawdy. The Regal's security man gave them short shrift. Rowdy posed him no problem—she could have graced any gathering. Besides, Dude had made a deal with him.

Now, as the three of them, Vince, Dude and Rowdy, sat waiting for the waiter to bring their meal, Rowdy asked Turner if he had been in Oklahoma City recently.

"Stayed there quite a time after you left," he said. "Had a pretty good game going 'til some joker got all tore up about losing. Accused me of dealing off the bottom."

"Were you?" Rowdy asked idly.

Vince sniffed. "Certainly not," he said. Dude guffawed, and Rowdy thought again how distasteful his laugh was.

"Oklahoma City and Guthrie still arguing over which will be the capital?"

"Yeah, King Fisher too. Oh, one other thing, I heerd your uncle passed on."

The color drained from Rowdy's face. She got blindly to her feet and was racing toward the door before either man could move.

"Damn it!" Dude snarled at Vince, "I had a good one lined up for tonight. Now she won't be worth shootin'."

"You're a cold-blooded bastard," Vince retorted, genuinely regretful. "I hadn't ort to've told her so blunt."

In the sanctuary of her room, Rowdy locked the door and flung herself facedown on the bed. She cried until there were no more tears.

When Dude knocked and called to her, she ignored him, lay in a kind of sick apathy. I didn't go to hurt Uncle Jim, she thought.

During the sleepless night, she wished for death. She had thought more than once of taking her own life, but believed firmly that suicide would consign her soul to hell. The hell here on earth was enough for her.

91.

A preacher from Oklahoma City came out to hold Jim's funeral. The house was overflowing, as was the yard. Some of the mourners wept, but Angus sat dry-eyed, wishing to God he had been more kind.

He had dug Jim's grave himself, at the small cemetery just off the division line between Logan and Oklahoma counties; had shed his tears then.

Some of the women exchanged glances when they saw Alice Smith's bulging belly. Despite her genuine tears, Alice had a sense of smug well-being. No one could know she'd had to ply her own husband with alcohol to get him back into her bed. Just enough liquor to make him forget his intentions; not enough to hamper his ability.

As for Pete, she thought fondly, ever since that eventful night, he'd been going around with a silly grin on his face. And making up for lost time.

When finally the crowd dispersed, Angus took care of his animals, milking the cows, bedding down the piglets, bringing oats for the horses.

He tried not to think as he went about his tasks. But the ghosts were there. Miss Rowdy, who was never far from his thoughts. Samson, whom he missed as he would have a son. Now Jim. Tears made his eyes blur. He'd been so hard-nosed with Jim. Never missing a chance to remind him of his failings. Refusing to call him Pa.

A sickness rose in his gullet, a black spasm of self-hatred. "I'm so goddam stupid!" he screamed aloud, and slammed the bucket against the barn door with such force that it was bent double. He flung it down, kicked it with all his might and headed for the house, drawing deep painful breaths.

It was pitch-black; not even a star was out. "That was quite an exhibition," a feminine voice drawled.

Angus started. "Dove?" he said uncertainly.

"Yes, Dove," she said, sounding cross. "What other female would risk her reputation by going to a man's house alone?"

He had never been so glad to see anyone in his life, and put the thought into words.

"You can't see me." Dove seemed determined to be contentious, but his relief was so great, he didn't mind.

"Come on in," he said. "There's enough food in there for an army."

"I brought my own, thank you," Dove snapped, and as she materialized beside him, his eyes having adjusted in the darkness, he could see that she carried a basket.

"All right," he said, "we'll eat yours."

Suddenly, she laughed. "How can I fight with you when you won't fight?" she demanded.

Angus chuckled with her. "Wish I'd known that a long time ago," he said.

"Angus"—her voice was sober now—"you knew I couldn't come to the funeral."

"You could have, far as Jim and I were concerned."

"I know, but your respectable friends would have disappeared. 'Sides, I thought you'd as lief have company tonight, after the others were gone."

"You were right."

They went into the soddy. Dove busied herself making fresh coffee, put out a snowy cloth, napkins. Lifted a bottle of wine out of the basket, a loaf of fresh bread, oranges and apples, a small crock of paté. "Learned to make that in New Orleans," she said.

"You brought enough," Angus said drily.

Dove shrugged, poured wine into one of his thick tumblers. Angus took a sip. "That's French wine," she told him. "I hope you have the palate to appreciate it."

"I dunno about palate, but my stomach likes it fine."

Angus asked the blessing, and they began to eat. There was silence for a time; then Dove spoke sharply. "Stop being a damn fool, Angus; turn loose of your ghosts."

There were equal parts of sympathy and reprimand in her words, and as usual, he felt slow and dull beside her. "Dove," he said helplessly, "you confuse the hell out of me."

"Good." Her laughter pealed out. "That-there's my resolve, confusin' de white folks. Niggers been doin' it for years. Yassuh, Mistuh Jack. Yes'm, Miss Belle. De white folks, dey jes' shake they heads and say, 'Pore ol' Mose, ain't no use 'spectin' nothin' from him. He too ignerant.' Den, when de white folks is out of hearin', dem darkies, dey plumb bust theyselves laughin'." She smiled grimly. "It's our only defense against despair," she said.

Her mood changed. "In New Orleans, we got the best way to mourn. On the walk to the graveyard, the band plays, sad and grievous, and the folks let the weepin' and wailin' rip. When they start home, though, the band strikes up joyous music, and everyone sings and dances, happy. Time they get back, they've had their proper grief, paid their proper respects, and their spirits are perked back up."

Angus agreed that that sounded like a good idea, but his face was still somber. "You knew Jim was my pa?" he asked.

"Of course."

"You didn't know . . . what the trouble was between us?"

340

"No."

"He didn't treat Ma right," Angus burst out. "He went tinkerin' and tradin' all over the countryside. Always going to pull off some big deal instead of staying home, raising crops and such.

"Didn't take care of his responsibilities. Ma drummed it into me from the time I could remember: I was to take care of my responsibilities.

"If Pa had been home, where he belonged, when those Injuns came, he could have saved her life."

"How do you know that?" Dove asked.

"Well . . ."

"What if he'd been workin' out in the field?"

"There wasn't any field," Angus said. "He never cleared one. Just loblolly pines."

"East Texas pine land? That where you're from? Man, that ground wouldn't raise good weeds. Why'd they stay on a farm like that?"

"Ma inherited it," Angus said hotly.

"And I'll bet she wouldn't go anywhere else."

"Hell, no. At least we had a place to live. If we'd gone somewhere else, we wouldn't even have had that."

"How do you know?" Dove asked.

"Pa would have frittered the money away."

"Sounds to me," Dove said thoughtfully, "like your ma was something of a bitch."

Angus's temper flared.

Dove held up a hand. "Ain't gonna do you no good to hit me," she said placidly. "What if your Lexie had been afraid to take a chance on you?"

"I live up to my obligations."

"Sure. Ever think your pa might have too? Did he have the chance? Besides, preacher, don't be so goddam self-righteous. You ain't perfect." Without a pause, she added, "What are you going to do now, go back to the circuit?"

"I can't," Angus said, his face growing sadder. "I don't deserve to preach. But I don't want to stay out here." He had not known until that moment what his exact feelings were. "It's too . . ." He fumbled for a word, and Dove, almost absently, supplied "lonely." He nodded agreement and she rose.

"I'd best go. By now your good name's already mud-

341

died. Do I stay any longer, folks will be saying, not that we went to bed together, but how many times."

Angus reddened and stood up. "You are a shameless woman," he muttered, a grin touching his lips. "I'll see you to the buggy."

92.

After eight months in St. Louis, Dude decided it was time to move on. He reached his decision hurriedly, after he saw a prosperous-looking old gentlemen watching Rowdy speculatively.

The first evening, Dude assumed the old man was trying to get up his nerve; but the second evening, the guest held a long and earnest talk with the room clerk, whose eyes surveyed the room and came to rest on Rowdy.

That was the clincher. Dude settled their bill that night, and they left the next morning. He had Chicago in mind, but Rowdy shook her head. "Too big. Too far."

Insofar as Dude was capable of being good to anyone, he had been good to Rowdy. He had not forced himself on her physically, and humored her when her whims weren't too outrageous. She was valuable to him.

In addition, he had an almost superstitious feeling about her, as though she were somehow unearthly. He had not forgotten that first night out of Oklahoma City, when the cloud of hair and the glittering eyes had given her a look of madness.

"How about Kansas City?" he asked.

She shrugged. "All right." Smiled to herself, wondering if the pudgy old gentleman who'd unnerved Dude had been watching to see if she wore a velvet bow. Dude didn't know about the small velvet bows she stitched inside the coat of each of her "callers." She hoped they went unnoticed until a diligent housewife made ready to give the coat a thorough cleaning.

She despised the men she defrauded, detested her own

part in the charade. Yet somehow, in some way, there lingered the feeling that she was getting even, though by now she did not know whether it was with her father, the people of Oklahoma City or herself. Mainly, she tried not to think at all.

One evening Dude had brought her a bottle of apricot brandy, in the hope that it would make her more receptive to him. It failed. But it had helped her sleep, and now she demanded it.

In Kansas City, they settled in at the Ambassador. Again, Dude sought out the hotel detective and made a mutually beneficial deal. In the meantime, Rowdy found that a sip or two of the brandy before she went down to the lobby also blurred the reality of her exploits.

93.

At Buffalo Creek, Angus had reached an impasse.

He had built, repaired, whitewashed and cleaned his buildings, taken care of his animals with a vengeance, tried to forget. But he was in such a quagmire of depression that he feared he was losing his mind.

He woke one morning, screaming like a bobcat and trembling so, he could scarcely get out of bed. He had to dunk his head repeatedly in cold water and drink half a dozen cups of strong coffee before he gained control of himself two hours later.

"Enough!" he said grimly, and struck out for Oklahoma City on horseback. In town, he went straight to the sheriff's office, found Garrison busy at his desk. The lawman's head came up, his hand went to his holster, as the door creaked.

"Oh, it's you, Angus. Come in. I been a little dauncy, huntin' them polecats. Guess you heard the Babcock gang was in this neck of the woods."

Angus shook his head.

343

"Well, sit down, man," Garrison said. "What brings you to town at this hour of the morning?"

"That deputy job still open?" Angus asked.

"Oh, hell." Garrison snorted. "Bill Coley's boy's taken it."

"He'll make you a good hand," Angus said, and as Garrison frowned, added, "Don't worry about it, man. I'll find something else."

Garrison ran a hand over the stubble on his face. "Wait a minute," he said slowly. "They's a law job open in Okell, down in Kiamichis, but I dunno . . ." He broke off, and Angus was puzzled.

"What's bothering you?" he asked.

"Reckon you know that country. Hills and hollers, mountains, caves, woods so thick, you can't see daylight. Hideout for the outlaws from Missouri to the Pecos. You heard the old sayin': nothing but bobcats and bandits."

Angus turned the sheriff's words over in his mind. "That ought to keep a fellow occupied," he said with a tight smile.

The grimness in Garrison's face didn't lessen. "Then there's them mountain people. They don't cotton to strangers. Lawmen down there is fair game."

"I can handle a gun," Angus said mildly.

"Yeah, in a fair shootout. But mountain folks or outlaws, it don't matter. They're all bushwhackers. They've killed three good lawmen the last year."

Angus's brows knotted. He did not think of himself as uncommonly brave. Neither was he foolhardy. Still, he was hungering to be of some use.

"Fur as I know," Garrison added, "they ain't but one man down there you could count on. Evan Briscoe's got a ranch near Jack Mountain. He wants a lawman there real bad. Other'n him, though, it'd be you agin the whole kit and kaboodle."

Angus's lips twisted in a wry grin. "Think I'll give it a try," he said.

94.

The game went well in Kansas City. So well, in fact, that Dude grew sleek and bored. Sometimes, he thought that if he could possess Rowdy, he'd be content. But her door stayed adamantly locked even though she was drinking more and more apricot brandy.

Dude had found a house not too far from the hotel where the girls were handsome enough and eager to please, but they never completely assuaged his itch. It was Rowdy he meant to have.

Occasionally, he went on a gambling spree, sitting in with the card sharps and suckers alike. But he was neither lucky nor a good player. He had tried double dealing once and almost got himself killed.

Generally, he returned from a three- or four-day stint at the table, hollow-eyed, ill-tempered and broke. Rowdy didn't care. It gave her freedom for a night or two. At such times, she made her velvet bows, read, and drank enough to sleep.

Sometimes, in her dreams, she was a child back at the soddy. Sometimes, Johnny held her in his arms and spoke of his love. But sometimes, Uncle Jim begged piteously for her help, and she couldn't reach him.

They stayed in Kansas City more than a year before Dude began to feel they were pressing their luck.

"We could move around from hotel to hotel in Chicago," he suggested as they sat over coffee one morning. "Sooner or later, one of yore easy marks here is gonna turn nasty."

Rowdy shook her head without speaking.

"They's some nice shops in Chicago," Dude said slyly.

Rowdy grimaced. "You think I get any pleasure out of buying clothes and baubles so some paunchy old man will want to paw me?"

"You like pretty clothes," Dude argued.

Her face was somber. "I like my velvet pants," she said. "If I had my way, I'd wear them all the time."

"That shore would appeal to men," Dude said sarcastically.

She shrugged again. "I'm not going to Chicago," she said. "It's too far from home."

95.

It took Angus less than two days to put his affairs in order. Pete and Alice's eldest son, Mizell, had recently married and Angus had heard the young couple was looking for a place. They were, and jumped at the chance to rent the Buffalo Creek farm.

That taken care of, he packed a few essentials in his saddlebags and resolving neither to look back nor think back, turned his horse's head to the south east.

The town of Okell (one general store, a post office, a two-cell jail, three houses) appealed to Angus from the first. It was so much a part of the scenery as to be hardly noticeable. Nestled at the foot of one of the taller mountains, the buildings had weathered to silver-gray.

Its inhabitants were inbred mountain people who suspiciously eyed anyone from "outside." Even someone from the other side of the mountain was suspect.

Briscoe, the rancher, was, as Garrison had suggested, the only person for miles around who wanted a lawman there. Briscoe loved the wild country and was anxious to see it become respectable.

"She's a bugger," he told Angus candidly, rolling a cigarette. "My men and me, we stand twenty-four-hour guard so we don't get killed in our beds, and I've got a pack of dogs meaner'n any bitch wolf with cubs. My cattle still get rustled regular."

Angus was thoughtful, and Briscoe seemed to anticipate the question forming in his mind. "I don't know why

I stay," he admitted. "It's like being in love with a fascinating whore. You know she'd turn on you without a second thought; still, you can't resist her."

His voice became wistful. "I'd like to see folks be able to settle down and live here. Know what I'm trying to say?"

Angus nodded. "You'd like to see the outlaws run off and the settlers law-abidin'."

Evan grimaced. "I don't expect the impossible. If we can get rid of the pure-D outlaws, we can tolerate a tetch of rustlin' and moon-shinin'. You good with a gun?"

"Tolerable," Angus said. He snaked the .45 from its holster, said, "Second, third and fourth fenceposts" and put a bullet in each.

"Good enough," Briscoe said. "Come in and have a drink."

They were standing halfway up Jack Mountain, in front of Briscoe's rambling ranchhouse. Around and below stretched the prodigality of nature. Trees and mountains, valleys, springs, crystal lakes.

Angus felt his spirits lift, and turned to follow Briscoe into the house. As they entered a cool timbered room, a woman's voice called out, "That you, Evan?"

"Yep, it's me. Come and meet the new sheriff."

Angus's eyes had begun to make the adjustment from the dazzling sun to the shadowy room. The woman who came in, smiling, was almost as tall as Briscoe himself. Angus drew a harsh breath. A *squaw!* The years had put layers of flesh on her bones; she carried herself like a queen. The mole began to burn.

"You are welcome, Mr. . . . ."

"Scofield," Briscoe supplied.

"Mr. Scofield. Will you stay and take supper with us?"

Angus swallowed. "Thank you," he said stiffly. "I best get settled in before dark."

"Another time, perhaps," the woman offered, and turned to leave them. Angus met Briscoe's eyes. Neither man spoke. The rancher went to open the front door. "If you need help, send word," he said curtly, and slammed the door almost before Angus was outside.

Squaw man, Angus thought, and snorted.

The sheriff's office was empty except for a scarred desk, rickety straight chair, battered cot, iron stove. It

347

contained no pillows or blankets. Angus's feet left prints as he walked across the dusty floor. He picked up a "Wanted" poster from the desk and blew on it. Dust swirled up in a cloud, making him cough.

96.

In Kansas City, Dude was becoming increasingly fretful.

"We got to git out of here," he told Rowdy. "The game's gettin' too chancey."

They were lingering over breakfast. She gave him the angelic meaningless smile that both excited and infuriated him. "Where to?" she asked indifferently.

"Chicago. New York. New Orleans. You'd like New Orleans."

"Wichita," she suggested as though he hadn't spoken. "Topeka. Guthrie."

He made a scoffing sound. "No money in them hayseed towns. Think on New Orleans, Rowdy. You never seen anything like it." He would have gone on, but the girl rose and left him.

The faint whisper of lavender sachet lingered in the air. Rowdy had taken to wearing a small velvet bow in her hair, and Dude's fantasies fastened on ripping it off and freeing that fabulous cloud of pale hair. Mentally, he stripped her of every garment so that she stood before him naked, marble flesh gleaming. That hair would engulf them both as he took her.

"More coffee, sir?" the waiter asked. Dude came out of his daydream with a start, shook his head.

Slut, he thought bitterly. She likes to torment me. One of these days . . .

97.

His first day in Okell, Angus bought cleaning supplies at the general store. He was served by a surly slattern, who never lifted her eyes during the entire transaction and spoke only to mutter the amount he owed.

He ferociously scrubbed the office and the cells, thankful to be kept busy.

In the evening, he went back, bought groceries and asked for a quilt. The slattern's mouth fell open. She raised her head, and he saw eyes of blue so faded as to be almost colorless.

"Quilt?" she mouthed, and then mumbled something Angus couldn't understand.

"Yes, a quilt," he repeated.

She mumbled again. "Folks"—he got that much—"mumble, mumble, mumble, quilts." The woman cackled, a hideous soundless laugh that contorted her face.

What had he let himself in for? Angus had hoped to make friends with the mountain people, despite what he'd been told. Perhaps he had even dreamed of resuming, in some small measure, his circuit work, God permitting. If this was a specimen of the mentality . . .

"I didn't understand you," he said.

"Mmm, said, folks don't *buy* quilts. We ain't got none." The last four words came out distinctly, and Angus finally understood. No one bought quilts. They were *made*. At home.

"Iggerant," she added gratuitously when he paid his bill.

Depression settled on him as he made his way back to the office. Finally, he forced his mind away from people. He was here to do a job, and he was going to do it. He didn't have to have companionship.

He had ridden the horse to Okell, traveling light. Later, he would have what few belongings he needed, brought

349

down by a drayman, or perhaps he'd even bring his own wagon. He wished he had his Bible for the nightly reading. Instead, he settled for saying the first Psalm before blowing out the light. He had brought his saddle blanket in for covering, but grew cold during the night, for the mountain air was chilly, and he rose the next morning, stiff and cramped.

Briscoe had said outlaws might be hiding any place in the mountainous area. Jackfork, Winding Stair, Rich Mountain. But Robber's Cave seemed a focal point for them.

Robber's Cave was easy to recognize. That area was honeycombed with caverns, the rocks enormous and treacherous, piled up on one another willy-nilly, like giant blocks stacked up by some petulant child.

Belle Starr was supposed to have taken refuge there at one time, as well as the James and Dalton gangs, Billy the Kid. Angus wanted to get acquainted with all his territory. Robber's Cave might as well be the first place he visited.

Briscoe had drawn him a crude map showing mountains, known caves, crossroads, settlements. Angus headed northeast. He reached the cave at midmorning. Dismounting at a respectable distance, he approached the entrance from the side; then, hand on gun butt, slid gingerly into the cave itself.

No shots greeted him, only an awesome silence. He edged in farther. There was a rustling sound, and he froze, holding his breath. He had worn dark clothing to meld into the blackness. Letting his eyes adjust to the dark, he waited. Then, without a sound, Angus moved deeper into the cave, where light from the entrance was only a faint glow.

He wished for a lantern. The light from the entrance was hardly discernible now. The silence and sense of isolation from the outer world were eerie. He moved again, cautiously. He heard the rustling sound once more—loud in the silence—and jerked his gun free and pulled the trigger. There was a scrabbling of feet as half a dozen small animals fled in panic.

Sheepishly, Angus holstered the .45. "Ol' Sheriff Fast-trigger," he muttered disgustedly. The reverberations seemed to echo back and forth endlessly, and the smell of gunpowder was strong. Feeling like a fool, he left the cave, rode back to his office to study "Wanted" posters.

Dutch Mankin, wanted for killing a U.S. Marshal. Dusty Rhodes, horse thief. Now, there was someone even other outlaws wouldn't take to. They might accept a killer, but never a horse thief. Jobe England, no picture. Specialty: daylight bank holdups. There were a dozen others.

The next morning, he started south. Briscoe had warned him that the mountaineers were a suspicious lot who shot first and asked questions later, so he went about his exploration cautiously.

The terrain was rugged. He went through forests so dense, he was forced to dismount and lead the horse. At times he had to blaze a path.

He looked with awe on the primordial beauty he surveyed, thinking it must be much as God had originally created it. But he remembered to watch too for signs that he might be coming too close to some mountain man's home or still.

Much of the time he felt unseen eyes. He kept a circumspect path, looking to neither right nor left. Where he saw signs of habitation, trees felled, branches broken, a child's cornhusk doll, ashes from a fire, he did not tarry. But he tucked into his memory the small towns (where he was watched with open suspicion), the short cuts, the faintly distinguishable trails.

By the time he had been in Okell seven weeks and explored the surrounding area without anything happening, he was unmercifully bored. He thought of going back to Oklahoma City, but his obstinacy wouldn't let him back away from a job. Something was bound to happen.

So he rode out and around once more. After three days, he came back to find a horse in front of his office, a man squatting at the door.

Angus dismounted. "Howdy, stranger," he said, hand prudently on his holster. The man got slowly to his feet.

"You the sheriff?"

"That's me."

The man fished in his pocket, and Angus's hand tightened on his gun butt. The man grinned nervously, displaying a row of small brown teeth. "Don't shoot," he said. "I'm on yore side." He brought out a metal badge. "Deputy up at Muskogee," he said. "Heerd it was best not to wear a badge, comin' through the mountains."

Angus laughed. "You're bad-mouthing my territory.

351

Howsoever, glad to see you. Come on in." He unlocked the office.

"Jake Cummings," the deputy said as they went inside. "That's me, not the outlaw." He chuckled at his own wit; then, as Angus built a fire: "You heard of the Eastop boys?"

"Can't say I have." Angus added a dollop of coal oil to the kindling and struck a match. The fire blazed up, and he hastily shut the iron door. "What about 'em?"

"Killers. Me, I figger they're loco. Seems to pleasure 'em to kill."

Angus frowned as he threw a handful of coffee into the pot. "Think they're headed this way?"

"Word we got, they're already holed up down here."

"Must be to the north. I just rode the south section."

"Reckon they could'a slipped in behind you?"

Angus shook his head. "Don't think so," he said slowly, reflectively. "This country . . ."—he sought for words to explain what he meant—". . . even when one of Briscoe's men rides out off his ranch, there's a kind of . . . ripple. Long as there's only the mountain folks, it's kind of like a pond, undisturbed, so to speak." He paused, feeling the explanation was inadequate. "Know what I mean?" he asked.

"More a feelin' you get?" Cummings suggested.

"Yeah, that's it, exactly."

"So they must've holed up to the north. Our sheriff figgered Robber's Cave, maybe."

"That one seems to be a kind of favorite, so I hear."

"Can you round up some men to ride with you?"

Angus shook his head.

"There's a couple other fellers at Muskogee the sheriff can get if he needs 'em. Told me to stay here if you wanted."

"Obliged," Angus said. He didn't say it was company he felt more need of than help. But he thought it.

The two men had a meager meal, slept a few hours and were up with the dawn. "Here's how I figure," Angus said. "You fan out toward the east, around Winding Stair and Cavanal. West of here, it's more coal country."

"More folks and less places to hide out," Jake agreed.

"I'll head straight north," Angus went on. "If they're around, between us we ought to pick up the trail."

"Agreeable," Jake said.

"Let's meet at Robber's Cave in three days if we don't run into them before then."

"And if we're both still alive," Jake said. The two men shook hands and rode off.

The sun was high overhead and beginning to feel uncomfortably hot before Angus came on anything unusual. His horse cleared a copse and shied as a tattered figure stepped onto the path, shotgun at his shoulder. Angus pulled up. The man's eyes had almost colorless irises, like those of the girl at the general store.

"Sheriff." Angus's voice was quiet, though his heart had begun to beat faster. This was bound to be one of the mountaineers who asked questions later, shot first. "We got word the Eastop boys were headed this way. Seen any strangers?"

The oldster spat. "Only you," he said, sighting down the barrel.

Angus began to sweat. "You heard of family feuds?" he asked mildly. The old man nodded, one eye still closed. "Lawmen are like families," Angus went on. "One of their kin gets killed, they don't rest easy 'til a couple folks from the other side are six feet under."

The old man appeared to think that over. He let his arm relax without lowering the gun. "Where-at are you sheriff?" he asked suspiciously.

"Okell."

"Girl there at the store, uncommon pretty, ain't she?"

Angus's jaw dropped. "Pretty?" he repeated incredulously. "God Lord, no." His response had been spontaneous. He regretted it as soon as the words were out of his mouth. "I'm sure she's a nice girl," he said, trying to make amends. "Kin of yours?"

The old man lowered the gun, laughing slyly. "Yore right, lawman," he said. "Ugly as a mud fence. Yeah, I do hear they're a couple of strange faces around. Bank robbers, are they?"

"Horse thieves," Angus said, lying.

"Horse thieves! That's the kind of varmint gives the mountains a bad name."

Angus repressed a grin. A sudden thought came to him. He had hoped vaguely for a chance to preach again, unworthy as he knew himself to be. He'd bet these people had no preacher at all. Maybe I'm a little better than nothing, Lord, he thought humbly.

"I do a little preachin' on the side," he said aloud. "Any your folks need to get married or buried, I'd be proud to help out."

There were remnants of suspicion in the old face, but it had unmistakably softened. "You wouldn't be tryin' to get people saved so they'd forget their rightful business?"

"Not without you-all asked it," Angus assured him.

The old man spat out his wad of tobacco, leaned the gun against a tree, wiped his mouth with his hand. "I take that neighborly, sheriff," he said. "Here, have a swig." He handed over a small bottle of whitish liquid from his saddlebag.

Angus drank, expecting the usual gut-blast of moonshine. The drink went down like silk. "Man, that is fine drinking," he blurted out, handing the bottle back.

"Keep it." If the ancient face wasn't smiling, it was considerably less grim. "Thet'll pay fer the first buryin'. McCord's the name. Alleghany McCord."

"Angus Scofield," Angus reciprocated. He did not offer to shake hands. No use pushing it. "Got any idea which way those horse thieves were headed?"

"Rode in over Jackfork, headed up Sansbois way, so I heerd."

Angus touched his hat. "Obliged," he said, and took off. His heart felt full to overflowing as he rode northeast.

As he drew nearer Robber's Cave, he began to ride in circles. There was no point in looking for fresh tracks. The ground that wasn't covered with rocks was covered with trees and underbrush. He found no new broken limbs in the wooded sections. A cave in the Sansbois was still the logical spot for the Eastops to hole up.

He was too impatient to wait for Cummings to join him. He knew that many of the caves were fairly shallow; he knew, too, that a cave-to-cave search would be foolhardy, if not fatal.

At the summit of Sansbois, he got off his horse and, shielding his eyes from the glare of the sun, made a slow circle, looking downward for evidence of movement. Except for a spiraling hawk and a herd of foraging range cattle, nothing stirred.

As he turned, something glinted in the sunlight across the valley, and he wondered idly if there were quartz hereabout. Once, he had run onto what was virtually a mountain of quartz, in the southwest part of the state, on a cattle drive.

Angus's movements slowed as an idea came to him. He examined it carefully, wished for the small mirror back in his office, wavy lines and all. He looked around, hoping for a discarded piece of metal. There was none. He thought of waiting until he met up with Cummings but doubted the deputy would be carrying anything shiny either.

The sun began its descent, throwing up streaks of silver gray, which meant it was pulling water into the clouds. Angus wouldn't have minded a little cooler weather, but if his plan were even to be tried—always supposing he could find that shiny object—he would need strong sunlight the next day.

A cool breeze swept across the mountaintop as it grew dark. Angus ate some jerky and johnnycake, wrapped himself in the horse blanket and lay watching the stars as they began to appear. Something that would reflect the sun . . .

He awoke with a start, an eerie wail ringing in his ears. Gun in hand, he jumped to his feet, looking first one way, then the other. The cry came again, an echo, and he shivered. It sounded like a woman feeling extreme grief or pain.

The sky was pitch-black; neither moon nor stars were visible. Muscles tense, Angus uncertainly walked a few steps, heard the horse whinny and automatically went to calm him.

He found the lantern. He disliked using a light, targeting himself, so to speak, but disliked more the thought of something unknown creeping up on him. He had heard witchcraft was practiced in the mountains, and while he had laughed at the time, it was not amusing now.

Carrying the lantern, he reached Jeru, patted him, felt the quiver of fear rippling along his back. The horse turned his head, the whites of his eyes showing.

"It's all right," Angus whispered soothingly. Then, from far down the mountain, he sensed rather than saw a blurred movement, heard the terrified bellowing of a cow, the bawl of a calf abruptly silenced.

A tremendous wave of relief swept through him. He relaxed, laughing shakily. "Panther," he told the frightened Jeru. "He won't bother us now. He's made his kill."

He had been told a panther's cry sounded like a weeping woman, but he'd never heard one before. And if truth be told, he though wryly, he'd as lief not hear one again. He blew out the lantern, and as he put it to the side, with his other traps, a sickle-shaped sliver of moon appeared from behind a scudding cloud and glinted dimly on the metal.

"Thank you, Lord," Angus said, and went to sleep.

98.

Angus awoke at dawn to a fine day, found some sandstone and scoured the paint off the lantern. Then he rode down the mountain, took cover in a wooded section opposite the first cove he spotted.

He tethered Jeru out of sight, positioned himself behind a tree. He held the lantern, letting it slowly revolve, so it caught the sun, which glinted on the metal in irregular flashes. Angus hoped that if anyone saw it, he'd be curious enough to investigate.

He stayed in position for half an hour or so. Having seen no sign of activity, he moved on, opposite the next cave. It was slow work, and quite possibly pointless, he thought as he continued to move from one place to another.

If the Eastops were holed up around here, they were bound to be jumpy—trigger-happy too, most likely. As the morning wore on, with Angus moving cautiously, the sun banished the coolness. By the time noon came, he was covered with sweat and beginning to think he was crazy.

If the Eastops were in there, apparently they had sense enough to stay put. Nonetheless, Angus continued to squat behind tree trunks and let the lantern send off its flashes.

The sun was well past its zenith, and Angus was thinking of taking a breather, when the first intimation came.

It came and went so quickly, he rubbed his eyes, uncertain whether he'd actually seen anything.

It had been only a shading of movement, like the shifting of shadow patterns. There had been one infinitesimal gleam of light. Too small and too brief to have been a match flare. It could, of course, have been the glitter of an animal's eyes. Or it could have been light striking the metal of a belt buckle. Or a gun.

Slowly, Angus turned the lantern again so the sun's rays struck it. Then he reversed it. If those coyotes were up there, trying to read meaning into the "signals," they must be very confused by now.

He considered trying to bluff the outlaws into the open but decided to wait for Cummings, who would be there the following day. He settled down to keep an eye on the cave.

He slept that night with one eye open, having instructed himself to rouse fully if there should be some movement. The night was clear, the stars brilliant and the cave remained quiet.

Taking a circuitous route, Angus rode back up the Sansbois at dawn, and Cummings arrived soon after. Angus had risked making a small fire, and they had coffee and side meat. As they ate, Cummings said, "Reckon it'd be best to go in after 'em when it gets dark. They spot us agin' the daylight, they're gonna ventilate our hides."

"I've been thinkin'," Angus answered, and outlined the plan he had devised. When he had finished, Cummings slapped his knee.

"Danged if I don't think it will work."

Back near the cave's entrance, they gathered dry wood from the underbrush, then broke off some green boughs, carried them to the cave and cautiously strewed them across the opening. Angus was guessing that the brothers were far enough back in the cave not to see him. That is, supposing they were in there at all. In any event, no shots came. With the wood piled high, he fetched his grass rope from the saddle horn, as well as his blanket.

They tied the rope to scrub growth at either side of the cave, about six inches above ground. When they'd finished, Angus unfolded the blanket, signaled Cummings. They bent to touch a flame to either side of the pile of wood. The dry twigs flared high. As the fire ignited the green boughs, a cloud of smoke arose. Angus tossed Cummings a corner of the blanket, and the two men began to fan the smoke so it backed up into the cave.

"Smoke signals, that's Injun talk." Cummings chuckled. Angus turned on him a face so sour, the deputy immediately sobered. They continued to fan the flames. The smoke grew more dense as more green wood caught and smouldered. After what seemed a long while, they heard someone cough.

The lawmen grinned at each other.

There was a rush of strangled obscenities, and as Angus and Cummings dropped the blanket and drew their guns, two men erupted from the cave, shooting blindly, eyes streaming. They darted through the flames, hit the rope and sprawled on the rocks. One gun tumbled down the slope; the other blasted, kicking up pebbles near Cummings's feet. Angus leaped the intervening distance, kicked the gun from Eastop's hand.

99.

With the Eastop brothers securely lashed to their own horses, Cummings took off for Muskogee and Angus headed back toward Okell.

To replenish his stock of corn meal, he walked over to the store.

"H'lo, iggerant," the girl said, her features twisted in what he correctly interpreted as a grin.

"Good evening, young lady," he said gently, elation burgeoning within him. The word must get around here as fast as on the prairie. Old Alleghany, it would seem, had given Angus his tentative approval.

It was a week or so later that McCord openly showed his acceptance. A towhead brought word that Angus was wanted at Seven Pines. The youngster was to "carry" preacher back. "Grampaw's afeared you'd get lost," he explained.

Angus swallowed his belly laugh, guessing that the boy

provided him safety. He was amused, too, at the old man's unceremonious summons. He shrugged. He'd wanted a chance to resume his duty to the Almighty, and here it was.

As they rode southwest from Okell, the wooded area gradually closed in around them. The boy led the way without hesitation, but after a time, Angus knew himself to be hopelessly lost. The woods were dense, and he again had the feeling that eyes were following him. The smell of sour mash permeated the air.

He drew a sigh of relief when they reached Seven Pines. Compared to Okell, this was a big town. A dozen shotgun houses, the ubiquitous general store, a combined smithy and livery stable and a small church. Angus looked that over with interest. It had never known paint, and the green wood had warped and silvered under the harsh sun. Its windows were broken, and altogether the building had a forlorn, neglected look.

He pondered as they rode the additional ten or fifteen minutes up into the hills. The house at which the boy reined in could have been any of a hundred others Angus had seen. Logs daubed with sod, no windows, a rickety stovepipe. This one, however, boasted a sagging front porch, on which sat a gargantuan bathtub with gilt legs and claw feet.

Alleghany sat on the edge of the porch, and as Angus rode up, lumbered to his feet. "Hello, preacher," he said, "got a marryin' job fer you."

Angus dismounted, nodding, and McCord said, "Mind the horses, Ted, then skedaddle over to the Yarbers' and tell Luke to get hisself over here."

"Just a minute," Angus intervened, "why not have it in church?"

Old Alleghany scowled. "Why?" he asked.

Angus thought fast. "Because a weddin' ain't hardly legal 'less there's a prayer. And I pray better in church."

"Oh." Alleghany considered this, rubbing his face with his hand.

"You got a key to the church?" Angus asked.

"Don't reckon it's locked."

"Any objections?" Angus demanded.

"You ain't fixin' to start any glory, hallelujah stuff?"

"Gave you my word, didn't I?" Angus's voice was harsh.

McCord studied him. Finally, he spoke again. "Tell Luke to be down to the church," he instructed Ted. "Come on in, preacher," he added, "meet my kin."

The house was small and dark and crowded and hot. Hams hung from the rafters, beside braids of onions, and the rooms were fragrant with the smell of baking.

"This-here's the preacher," Alleghany told the roomful of people. "You-all quit fidgetin' like maggots in hot ashes, 'til I tell him yore names." Obediently, they stilled, eyeing Angus covertly, without enthusiasm. "This-here's my son, Ben," McCord went on, and a dark-visaged younger man nodded shortly without meeting Angus's eyes. Angus took a step foward and stuck out his hand. Ben didn't stir.

"Goddammit, boy," Alleghany roared, "shake hands with the man! Want him to think you ain't had no raisin'?"

Ben flushed but grasped Angus's hand. "How-do," he muttered, and pulled back, shoving his hands in his pockets.

Alleghany proceeded around the circle. Most of the room's occupants were children, and Angus wondered how many there were, all told. "This-here's Lucy, Ben's woman," Alleghany went on, and Angus looked into the tired, lined but unexpectedly sweet-natured face of a woman old before her time.

"Hello, Lucy," he said, not offering his hand this time, lest Ben think it forward.

"These are their kids." By this time, Angus had counted nine, besides Ted.

A thin, sandy-haired girl sidled in from the other room. Her eyes were red, face puffy from crying.

"This is Sally," Alleghany told him flatly. "The bride." They all turned, even the kids, to glare at her. Sally sniffled, and tears filled her eyes. Angus guessed correctly that the slight curve of her belly bespoke a new life in the making. The girl herself, he judged, could be no more than thirteen.

"Hello, Sally," he said gently. "Is it all right with you if we hold the service in the church?"

The girl looked wildly at her father, then at her grandfather, as though fearful of expressing herself. When neither of them objected, she said thickly, "Don't make no difference to me."

"Come on out on the porch, preacher," Alleghany invited him, and they walked out with Ben, followed by the largest of the boys. The senior McCord produced a jug from behind the bathtub. Ben squatted, with his back against the wall.

"Have to wait 'til the old woman gets through with her cookin'," he mumbled. "Nothin' would do but she must fix up a spread." His eyes were on Alleghany, but Angus assumed that the explanation was for him.

"Women like to do things up nice," he said.

"Reckon."

The older man had finally got the corncob out of the mouth of the jug. "Here, preacher," he said, "have a snort."

Angus's mind worked rapidly. On the circuit, a preacher who "drank," no matter how little, would have invited strong disapproval. Here, the man who wouldn't take a drink would be equally suspect.

"Don't mind if I do," he said, and, holding the handle with one finger, tilted the jug over his right shoulder, opened his mouth and allowed a spurt to slide down his throat. He swallowed, lowered the jug.

"Good," he said judiciously, "but different from last time."

Alleghany slapped his knee and beamed. "See, Ben?" he crowed. Ben allowed a reluctant grin to cross his face. "Yeah," he admitted, and Angus gathered he had passed some unspoken test.

The gangling boy spoke to Angus, abruptly. "Do it again," he demanded.

"What, son?"

"Whomperjaw 'at jug 'thout spillin' none."

His father cuffed him lightly. "Yore too young, Pete."

"I wasn't fixin' to drink none," Pete protested. "I jes' want to see."

"I'll show you how, Pete," Angus said, "but I want a favor in return." The faces of the three McCords became immediately and identically suspicious.

"Whut?" Pete demanded.

"Go pick some black-eyed Susans."

"You want a bo-kay, preacher?" All three McCords guffawed.

"Not me." Angus grinned too, then sobered. "Girls like to carry a bouquet when they're marryin'. Gives 'em something nice to remember."

"Get one of the girls to do it," Pete muttered.

"Okay."

"Now show me how you hold the jug."

"When you've picked the flowers." Angus's voice was uninflected. He was scratching a design in the dust with the toe of his boot.

There was a curious silence. A quick glance showed Angus that the two older men were watching Pete quizzically. The boy shuffled his bare feet. Presently, with obvious reluctance, he moved off in the direction of the fields.

"Fine boy you've got there," Angus said.

"He'll do," Ben conceded. "Stubborn, though."

"You got around him pretty good, preacher," Alleghany added.

"Name's Angus," Angus told them. He sat down on the edge of the porch, fanning himself with his hat. The atmosphere had changed, he thought. At least Ben no longer looked so hostile.

The boy, Pete, was back in moments with a small bunch of the yellow-and-black flowers. He was eyeing the house furtively, and Angus correctly deduced that he didn't want the other kids to see him. He thrust the ragged bouquet at Angus.

"There," he said shortly. "Now show me that trick."

"No trick," Angus said; laying the flowers on the wood planks, he curled his forefinger through the handle and hoisted the jug so it tilted forward just over his right shoulder. He turned his head, tilted the jug a bit further and liquid spurted into his mouth. "No trick," he repeated, "practice."

Pete reached for the jug. His grandfather jammed the corncob back into it, and the boy began attempting to jockey the jug up on his shoulder. Angus turned to Ben.

"Would you want to give Sally the flowers?" he asked.

Ben gave a hoot of scornful laughter. "Me?" he asked.

Alleghany picked them up. They were already beginning to wilt in the heat. "I'll take 'em to her," he said. "Reckon that was a right nice thought." He went off into the house, and Ted returned to report that Luke would be on his way to the church as soon as he got cleaned up.

Ben slowly stood. "Reckon we may as well go on down. Though why that's any better'n the house . . ." He was grumbling half aloud. Angus found it interesting that, grown though Ben was, it was old Alleghany who still called the turn.

Thank you, Lord, Angus thought. With the patriarch on my side, I might get to do some preaching again, one of these days.

Within a few minutes, Lucy and the children came straggling out of the cabin. Better able to see them in the sunlight, Angus noted that though their clothes were shabby and patched, they were clean, and wondered how in the name of God the woman managed that. Sally was in the midst of the kids, clasping the black-eyed Susans tightly. She gave him a shy half-smile, then quickly ducked her head and blushed.

As Alleghany had predicted, the church was unlocked. It contained half a dozen benches and no rostrum, but there was a pulpit stand of raw wood. As they entered, a cloud of dust rose up to meet them, and there was a whirring of wings as a frantic wild turkey half-ran, half-flew through the door.

"Good thing we come down," Lucy said compassionately. "Poor thing'd never have made it out through the window. Wonder how he got in."

The Yarbers arrived then, a boy of sixteen or seventeen in the forefront. As the family trekked in, Angus judged that there must be as many of them as there were McCords. He knew a moment of terrible compassion. Sally, with the angularity of childhood still on her, heading into a lifetime that offered nothing but childbearing and backbreaking work.

Alleghany was at Angus's side. "That-there's Luke," he said, pointing at the young man who headed the clan. He wore clean overalls and a very sulky look. Sally was watching him, and Angus winced inwardly at the appeal written on her features. Had his child ever had to beg for kindness from some man? There was a knot in his throat, and he felt enraged by the gangling boy.

"Come stand in front of the pulpit," he told Luke and Sally. His voice was harsh, and he cleared his throat. He had performed marriages before, of course, and knew the service by heart. Today, he put it aside and talked in a stormy holy-roller style about how women were supposed to be treated by their husbands.

"When a man and woman sin," he thundered, "it is the man God holds responsible. Women are the weaker vessel. Their desire is to please the man they love. It is the man who must be strong, put temptation behind him until God has put his seal of approval on the union, through marriage.

"It is the man God holds responsible for seeing that the children are brought up fearing and knowing the Almighty. If God had meant the woman to carry the responsibility, he would have created her first."

He went on at some length, shouting himself hoarse and hoping all the things he was saying were in the Book.

Sweat was running down his sides by the time he finished.

"Let us pray," he concluded, and offered Luke's skewered heart up to the Lord, with the reminder that if a man mistreated any of these little ones, "and that means his wife too," he inserted parenthetically, it were better that a millstone be tied around his neck and he be cast into the sea. "Amen," he said, and looked up to meet Luke's dazed eyes. The boy was pale. Fear had replaced the sullenness.

Angus shook hands with him, reflecting that he himself did not like "God will get you" sermons, but perhaps they had their place. He shook hands with Sally, whose eyes were big as silver dollars.

"I never heerd it like that afore," she said.

"Y'all come on to the house 'fore the victuals get cold," Lucy said into the silence. The crowd stirred and began to file out. Alleghany waited for Angus.

"That-there didn't sound much like our agreement," he muttered.

"You didn't hear any shoutin' or yellin' glory, hallelujah, did you?" Angus asked. "I didn't say anything that would make a feller quit moonshinin', did I?"

The old man frowned. "Yore gonna have the women gittin' uppity," he complained.

"You got a woman?" Angus asked, and when Allegheny shook his head, added, "What do you care, then? Sally's your granddaughter, man. Reckon she could stand a little kindness."

Alleghany pondered so long, Angus was fearful he'd gone too far, too fast. But finally the old man ran a hand over the lower part of his face and nodded.

"Reckon she could," he agreed. "She shore caught hell from her pap. Let's go up and eat."

100.

For the next month, there was little activity in Okell. Evan Briscoe sent one of his hands down one afternoon to tell Angus he'd heard that a man named Truitt had broken out of jail in Oklahoma City and might be headed their way.

Angus thanked him and rode his territory the next four days, looking for indication of an alien presence. He found none, and later heard Truitt had been shot to death in Kansas.

As for the business of marrying and burying, Angus knew that if he attempted to push it, he'd lose out altogether. It was nearly six weeks from the time of Sally and Luke's wedding before he was sent for again. This time one of the Yarbers came for him. The boy sidled into the office, his hair so red, it looked like flames, and his face buried in freckles.

"Howdy," Angus greeted him, rising from his desk.

The boy swallowed a couple of times, and Angus realized he was overcome with an agonizing shyness.

"Sally and Luke getting along all right?" he asked.

The boy had been studying his bare feet. His head jerked up. "You 'member me?" he blurted out in surprise.

"Sure do. Want to sit a spell? I'll get you a drink. Pa send you in?" he asked as he handed the youngster the tin cup.

The boy shook his head. "Ma," he said. "Her pap's fixin' to die. She wants you should come and baptize him so he won't go to hell."

"Oh." Angus's belief was that baptism was symbolic, not a magic carpet to the hereafter. He didn't know what the mountaineers' belief was, but he'd cross that bridge when he got to it. He picked up his hat.

"All set," he said, and the red-headed sapling sped out the door and was on his horse like a streak of greased lightning. Attention caught by the boy's unusual speed and agility, Angus began to ponder. He'd heard of the Wild West show put together by Colonel George W. Miller, of the 101 Ranch.

"What's your name, son?" he asked as he swung into the saddle.

"Walt. You ready?"

Angus nodded and let the boy lead the way. Walt sat on the horse as if he'd been born there. The preacher continued to think of the possibilities, as they plunged into the woods.

When they reached the Yarbers', Laban, the father of the brood, was waiting in front of the house, half a dozen or so of the kids beside him or peeking around the corner. "Howdy, preacher," Laban greeted him as he dismounted. "Me'n the kids changed the water in the stock tank so's you and Gramper can use it."

"Just a minute," Angus said. "I have to talk to the old man first."

Laban's face tightened. "He ain't gonna last long," he warned. "And Dorie, she's dead set on him being dunked while there's still breath in him."

"Let's be about it, then," Angus said, and strode toward the house. There was a cot, of sorts, in a corner of the room, split logs hammered together to hold a straw mattress. But the mattress had been covered with a clean sheet of flour sacking. The woman who sat beside the cot was red-eyed; her hands were clasped together.

"Hold on, Pap," she was saying. "Jes' hold on a little longer, 'til that preacher gets here."

The emaciated old man, who lay with his head propped up, was struggling for breath. "I'm holdin', Dorie," he snapped, then noticed Angus. "Hurry up, preacher," he urged him. "Hope you warmed that water."

Angus grinned, liking his spunk, then turned to the family. "I need a few minutes alone with him," he told them. Dorie looked at her husband, tears dripping from her wrinkled face.

"They ain't no time, Labe," she whispered.

Laban turned to Angus. "You heerd her," he said. "Dorie, she knows about sich as this. Now, me'n the boys will make a pack saddle and get the old man into the tank. All you got to do is dip him."

Angus stiffened. "There'll be no baptism 'til I've talked with Mr. . . ."

"Lewellen," Dorie supplied.

"Lewellen," Angus repeated. "Now, you want to clear the room, or you want me to ride back home?"

In answer, Laban pulled out a gun that looked like a small cannon. "Baptize him!" he ordered.

In that minute, Angus knew his future with the mountain people hung in balance. He could baptize the old man and perhaps have other opportunities to be involved with these people, or he could hold out and risk not only the opportunity, but possibly his life. Still, he could not find it within himself to go through meaningless motions.

"No," he said, and folded his arms.

Laban clicked off the safety catch, and Angus felt the sweat trickle down his back. The kids scattered like a covey of quail. Dorie made a little whimpering sound. Then, in a surprisingly strong voice, Gramper shouted at his son-in-law.

"Goddammit, Labe," he roared, "you don't know nothin' 'bout religion! Get the hell out of here and let the man have his say."

For a breathless moment, Laban was motionless. Then, scowling, he shoved the weapon back into his belt and clumped toward the door, Dorie following him. When the room was quiet, Angus sat down. His knees were weak.

"Mr. Lewellen," he said, "God loves you."

"I know thet," the old man said testily.

"He has provided a way for you to reach heaven, through his Son. But you have to have faith. You have to believe that Christ is the Son of God, and that it is through his death that our sins are forgiven."

"Hell, preacher, I believe thet. Think I'm stupid? I allus knowed it'd take somethin' special to git an old sinner like me through them pearly gates. I jes' never got around to being baptized, and Dorie's in a taking."

He had raised himself on his elbow in his vehemence, but now sank back on the pillows, eyes closed. Momentarily, Angus was fearful, but the eyelids flickered open again, and the old man gave him a puckish grin.

Angus picked him up, coverlet and all, and carried him

outside. The family was milling uneasily around the front door.

"I'll take him," Laban growled, but Angus shook his head.

He hurried the fifty yards or so to the tank, the family trailing along behind them. When he reached the huge metal basin, he stopped and gently handed the old man over to Laban. Then he hoisted himself over the side, into the water. It was so cold, it took his breath away.

He turned and took Gramper into his arms. "Water's cold," he warned.

Mischievous old eyes twinkled at him. "That's all right," the old man whispered. "Jes' don't drown me."

Angus hesitated briefly in order to keep a straight face. "Now, my brother," he intoned, "upon profession of your faith in Jesus Christ, I baptize you in the name of the Father, Son and Holy Ghost."

He lowered the frail body into the water, felt the shiver of shock as the cold penetrated it. When he lifted him out, though, thank God, the old man was still alive.

Lewellen looked directly at his daughter. "Well, Dorie," he asked, "you satisfied?"

Angus had thought it likely the old man would die before they could get him back to bed, but he held on through another day and night. Angus stayed with the Yarbers. He and Dorie were at the man's side when he died. His breathing had grown steadily more labored, and at sundown of the second day, a kind of rasping could be heard.

"Death rattle," Dorie whispered, tears starting afresh. She took one of the withered hands. The old man opened his eyes, the spark still there.

"Dorie," he said, and they had to lean close to hear above the dreadful gargling sound, "wonder if yore ma is workin' her jaw up there as much as she did here."

He relaxed, a faint grin on the thin lips, and the stertorous sound faltered to a halt. Angus leaned forward, gently closing the old man's eyes. Dorie burst into a torrent of wails and ran outside.

Angus and the males of the family worked that night building a casket and digging a grave. It was considered bad luck to perform such tasks prior to death. In mid-morning, Laban hitched the mule to a cart and carried the box holding the old man, down to the church. Angus had insisted the service be held there. He wanted the mountain people to get accustomed to using the small building.

He marveled again at how news travelled. The church was crowded when they arrived. Angus went ahead of the family and pulled two benches together to form a trestle. The old man's grandsons carried in the box.

Angus's sermon was short. He stressed the old man's simple faith, and to comfort Dorie, he told of the baptism, saw her beaming through the tears. He concluded with a short prayer. Laban stepped up and removed the two rough planks that had been applied crosswise, so head and shoulders could be "viewed."

Someplace in the back of the room, a song was struck up, and Angus felt his throat tighten as he recognized the hymn that had been sung at Lexie's funeral.

The crowd began to file by the box, gazing at the peaceful old face. Everyone, even the men, was sobbing in an ecstasy of emotion. Some leaned over to kiss forehead or cheek. All the Yarbers were wailing at top volume, and Dorie fainted as she went forward to view the remains.

Though part of Angus empathized with their sorrow, part of him was dumbfounded at the display. These people had seemed so impassive. Inured as they were to the harshness of life, Angus had thought it left them drained. He was bemused as they filed by, began to leave the church. Finally, he began to realize this was the one outlet they were permitted, their catharsis.

If ever I get to hold a brush-arbor meeting here, he thought, I'll bet there'll be some shouting, no matter what Old Alleghany says.

101.

In New Orleans, Dude Malicote's preoccupation with Rowdy had become an obsession. His pride was scraped raw. Slut, he thought viciously, acts like she's the Queen of England, when she's no better than a whore. He resolved repeatedly not to think about her any more. His obsession was no longer sexual. He was so hate-filled, there remained no room for lust. He longed to smash his fist into her face, wipe off that inscrutable smile. He wanted to violate her repeatedly until she broke from pain. He could have taken her by force, but in some small remote part of his person, he was superstitiously afraid of her.

And, of course, she was his meal ticket. The time's coming, though, when I'll be through with her, he thought at times. Once he'd made his pile, he'd take a knife to that luscious flesh.

For her part, Miss Rowdy drifted, trying not to think. The brandy helped, although she sometimes complained to Dude that it was weaker than that in St. Louis and Kansas City.

"Hell, they ain't nothin' wrong with the brandy," he told her roughly. "Yore a boozer, that's all. More you drink, more it takes."

She smiled at him, that smile that still held the sweetness of a child, the beguilement of a coquette. "You're going to go buy me another bottle now, aren't you?" she asked.

Dude had to grit his teeth to keep from hitting her. Nothing would have pleased him more than to deprive her. He dared not. He had forgotten once to bring her a bottle, and she had thrown at him everything she could get her hands on, made a shambles of her room, almost gotten them ousted from the hotel. He wouldn't risk that again.

In St. Louis, a young reporter by the name of Eddy had

heard a rumor about the game and the velvet rosettes. The story tickled his funny bone, and he felt it might amuse the paper's readers, a surmise with which his editor concurred.

The young man nosed around for several days and found out which hotel Rowdy had stayed at. He reasoned that the security man would have to be privy to the scheme. When he finally ran the man to earth, the fellow looked like nothing so much as a bulldog. A five-dollar bill waved under his nose produced docility and a spate of conversation.

"I don't know nothin' about no velvet row-settes," he declaimed, "but yeah, there was this filly and this cheapjohn working the game." He sighed. "Gawd, she was pretty," he said. "You couldn't hardly credit she was a twister."

Eddy spent two hours with the security man. He went back to the paper and wrote a tongue-in-cheek denouncement of the political corruption that permitted such immorality to flourish. He dubbed the woman "The Velvet Rosette," and laughed the whole time he was writing.

A Chicago paper picked up the story and carried it under the headline, "Velvet Rosette Girl," causing some nervousness among certain of its readers. But when the story appeared in New York, greatly embellished along the way, there was one gentleman who, far from being nervous, came to a decision.

Lionel Sedgwick lived by his wits. He skimmed close to the wind but had never so much as been accused of malfeasance. He had had legal training, been a lobbyist in Washington and bragged that he carried half a dozen congressmen in his vest pocket.

Being a grifter himself, it had hurt his professional pride to be hoodwinked. However, because of another project on which he was working, it had been expedient, at the time, not to lodge a complaint. But now, reading the article, he tapped his teeth with a pencil.

Presently, he looked up the Pinkerton telephone number.

In New Orleans, Dude continued to brood, finally reached a conclusion that salvaged a measure of his pride. The bitch thought she was in love with some hick back in Oklahoma. That was why she cold-shouldered him.

371

His ego began to revive. Probably some sweaty plow-boy with whom she'd exchanged childish kisses and vowed undying love. Then they'd quarreled . . .

Sure, that was it. So it was just a matter of biding his time.

Over supper that night, he said, "I want to talk to you," and was surprised at the raggedness of his voice. Rowdy's delicate eyebrows lifted.

"Talk," she said.

"They's another man, ain't they?" he blurted out, though he'd meant to lead up to it gradually.

A chilly smile curved the girl's lips. She studied the amber liquid in the thin glass she held. Finally, she spoke. "Yes," she said, "another man. Did you think *you* were going to get into my bed?"

Dude's mind exploded with rage. His hands began to tremble and he thrust them into his pockets. He wanted to kill her.

He jumped to his feet and rushed out of the dining room.

Rowdy thought of one of Dove's phrases. "Poor white trash," she murmured, and for some reason, shivered. She composed herself, lowered her eyes demurely to her plate.

102.

In Okell, Alleghany McCord rode in from his mountain lair to see Angus. When they had shaken hands, had a snort from McCord's jug and commented on the weather, the old man divulged the reason for his trip.

"The women want you should come and hold a meet-in'," he said sourly.

Angus was startled but pleased. "How about you?" he asked bluntly.

The old man had another drink and wiped his mouth. "Told you you'd have the women gittin' uppity," he complained. By which Angus judged that the wedding and funeral services had set the women thinking they wanted their kids at least to know about the Almighty.

"How about you?" he repeated.

"Hell, I reckon it's all right, long's it don't interfere with business. Maybe it'll shut their traps, anyhow."

"I'll be there next Sunday," Angus promised, and the old man rose to go. There was a glint of amusement in his eyes as he bade the lawman goodbye. "Yore a sidewinder if ever I seen one," he accused the younger man, but his voice held reluctant admiration, and Angus laughed.

McCord's visit decided him. Until now, he'd been unsure whether he'd stay here. Now he knew he would. Tomorrow, he'd go back and pick up the rest of his belongings, in Oklahoma City. Not until he was on his horse jogging across the uneven countryside, did he admit to himself how lonely he'd been in the mountain country.

With that acknowledgment came an idea. By the time he reached Oklahoma City, he was in a fever of impatience to put it into operation.

Deliberately, he held back, though, first getting his business out of the way. Mizell and his wife were firmly entrenched in the Buffalo Creek House, and were keeping the land in good shape. No Johnson grass.

They welcomed him, and as the three of them had coffee, Mizell said he'd like to buy the place if ever the preacher decided to sell.

Angus shook his head. "The place is for Miss Rowdy. She'll be back one of these days." He hoped it was true.

He stopped briefly at the senior Smiths', the Tennysons', the Holtzworthys', but even as he visited with all of them, his thoughts were churning. This plan he had, would it work?

Finally, he headed toward the big, two-story white house. It was Dove herself who opened the back door, at his knock. Momentarily, he stared at her blankly.

"What's the matter, man?" Dove asked. "I so old you don't know me?"

Angus shook his head. "Same old sandpaper tongue," he said. "No, I think maybe I was expecting Auntie Po."

The mulatto face softened. "I know," she said. "Come on in, Angus. What brings you back to the big city?"

He followed her, tongue-tied. He couldn't just blurt out his plan. "I c—came," he stuttered, "t—to get the rest of my gear. I'm moving down there permanent. Dove!" She was leading the way to the parlor but turned at the urgency in his voice. "Dove . . ." No, dammit, he thought, it's too soon. He caught her hands. "I'm getting a chance to preach again," he said.

"I'm glad, Angus. I hope it'll go well for you. Come on and sit. I'll have the girls throw another bean in the pot."

"I don't want to interfere with your plans."

"You're not," she assured him. "I've about shut down. Got only two girls left. Soon's they find another place, I'm going to close up. Excuse me just a minute." He heard her run upstairs.

When she came back, she was carrying a newspaper, which pleased Angus. He hadn't seen one since he'd gone to Okell.

"Angus," Dove said slowly, "I got something wonderful to tell you. Then I—I'm afraid there's something—"

"What's wonderful?" he interrupted, hardly hearing the last part of her sentence.

"Samson's a lawyer! He's with a big firm in Philadelphia."

"Is that right?" he exclaimed. "A Philadelphia lawyer. That *is* wonderful. How'd you find out?"

There were tears in Dove's eyes. "One of my clients is in Congress. He did me the favor of checking on Samsy. He *passed*, Angus. He would always have been a nigger here. In Philadelphia, he's a white man."

Her voice rang with pride, and Angus said soberly, "You've got more guts than me, Dove. I'd have Miss Rowdy back with me in a minute, if I could. No matter what the consequences were."

Dove's face clouded. "The—the other thing I wanted to tell you . . . well, this paper's over two months old, but I think you ought to read it."

She handed him a *St. Louis Post-Dispatch*. "Down there, close to the bottom of the front page," she said. "Politicians allow vice to flourish," the headline cried. "What do the officials of this city do besides collect taxes and hand out patronage?" the article began.

What is the law-enforcement branch doing besides making gestures toward cleaning up the mess St. Louis has become? To cite one example: A young woman and her male accomplice operated for several months at a large downtown hotel without being questioned, much less arrested. Their confidence game is thought to have netted a tidy sum.

Posing as brother and sister, they called themselves Earl and Marie Dubois. The smooth-talking man would fall into conversation with a prosperous-looking gentleman at the bar. In the guise of being a businessman himself, he would spend some time discussing the cattle market, railroad stocks, grain futures or whatever was of interest to the older man.

Dubois, as he called himself, would insist on buying the drinks. When the other man was sufficiently befuddled, Dubois would suggest they adjourn to the dining room or lobby. There he would "discover" that his "sister" had recovered from her headache and was waiting for him. The young woman is said to be uncommonly beautiful.

After an hour or so at the table, the "brother" would "remember an appointment" and excuse himself. The game appears to vary a bit from that point. If the victim were bold enough and/or drunk enough to suggest a rendezvous, the young woman would pretend to be so influenced by the wine, that she would agree. If the man did not suggest it, she would become "faint" and ask that he assist her to her room.

Once there, it is theorized that he was offered a nightcap, and that when he accepted, certain drugs were slipped into the drink. The "brother" would reappear when the victim became unconscious. The man's valuables would then be taken, and he would be dumped unceremoniously in front of his room or, if he was not a guest at the hotel, would be left in the back alley.

The police insist they never received a complaint about this. Perhaps the victims did not want publicity. The young woman, it would appear, had a sense of humor. In an inconspicuous spot, she tacked a velvet rosette to the clothing of her "guests."

There was more, but Angus thrust the paper away blindly. The pain had begun in his chest as he read the second paragraph. When he read further, the pain spread through his belly and abdomen, so that he felt he was being consumed by flames.

Dove had watched the color drain from his face. "Angus," she whispered, twisting her hands, "I'm so sorry, but I thought you should know."

It was as though he had been stricken insensible. Her words didn't register. "I have to find her," he told himself. Tears, of which he was unaware, dampened his cheeks. "Miss Rowdy!" He wanted to howl his agony, but the sound came out hoarse and ragged.

He tried to get up and found he was shaking so, his legs would not hold him. "The bastard." His voice was choked. "The son of a bitch. I'll kill him!"

Dove's slap hurt. He put his hand to his cheek, blinking as sanity returned. "I've got to get to St. Louis," he said.

"Whoa!" Dove ordered. "You didn't read it all. They left St. Louis. Angus"—her voice was pitying—"you've got to realize no one's holding Rowdy against her will."

Rage sent hot color into his face. His hands were clenched. "You're so goddam smart!" he said thickly.

Dove forced herself to meet his glare and waited. It seemed hours before the color began to recede, his hands finally unknotted.

Unobtrusively, Dove wiped the sweat from her forehead. "I'll get us a brandy," she said.

When Dove came back with the bottle and glasses, Angus demanded harshly which way they would have gone.

"God knows," she answered. "Why do you suppose they took my name?"

It was Angus's turn to look baffled. He tossed the brandy down in one gulp and grimaced. "And why the—the . . . what was it . . . ribbons?"

"Rosettes. Velvet rosettes," Dove filled in. "You remember she loved velvet; those pants she made . . ." Her voice broke, and the two sat in silence with their ghosts.

After a time, Dove said thoughtfully, "Angus, I bet she's sending us a message. Deep inside herself, without even realizing it, she wants to be found."

Angus's brow was furrowed. "I'd go to hell and back for her," he said.

"I know." Dove rose to refill the brandy glasses. "Since you're a lawman," she said slowly, "can you telegraph messages?"

"Sure," he said; then, as he got her meaning: "Sure, that's it. To the sheriff in the big cities, or would it be the police? Hell, I don't know."

"Law-enforcement agency?"

"That ought to do it." He put the glass down and smacked his right fist into his other hand. "Dove!" he shouted, "you're—you're . . ."

"So goddam smart," Dove finished drily. "All right, git!"

Angus got. As he rode, he tried to think of the names of big cities. They wouldn't try their game in a small place. Chicago, New York, Atlanta—was Atlanta big enough? Damn, he didn't know much of the country except Texas, Oklahoma, Missouri, Kansas.

He reached the railroad station and got the same message off to as many places as he could think of. "Advise OK City if man and woman working any your hotels enticing men to woman's room, purpose robbery."

"Good golly, Angus," the telegrapher protested. "It'll take a week to get all those out."

"It's important, Jonas. Figure out how much I owe, and I'll be back." He left the man muttering and went off to find the sheriff, made arrangements for him to accept the replies and get them on to Okell.

He was tired by the time he finished. And it was not until then that he thought of the reason which had taken him to Dove's originally. He headed back toward the big white house.

Dove again opened the door. "Figured you'd gone on back to your mountains and trees," she said.

Angus shook his head. "Can I come in?" he asked. "I came to Oklahoma City special to ask you . . . in the parlor, maybe?"

Puzzled at the unevenness of his voice, Dove said, "All right," and led the way.

Angus remained standing though she gestured to a chair. "D—Dove," he stammered, "what are you going to do after you close the house?"

She shrugged, and for a moment her mouth drooped. "I'll think of something," she said finally.

He put a hand on her shoulder. "You're lonely; I'm lonely," he said. "Will you marry me?"

Dove caught her breath and jumped to her feet. "That ain't very funny," she snapped.

Angus took her hand. "It wasn't meant to be funny. I've never been more serious."

Moisture glinted suddenly on her lashes. "Oh, Angus,"

she said, caught between laughter and tears, "you purely are a fool. There's bound to be a law says no white man can marry wif no nigger woman."

"If we can't get married here, we'll find a state where we can."

Her face fell into lines of sadness. "You have a chance to start preaching again, Angus. A black woman? Your mountain people would be just as horrified as your friends around here."

"It's none of their business," he said harshly.

She sighed. "I'm honored, Angus. I am for sure, but no. People make such matters their business."

Angus scowled. He could give up preaching entirely. No, he could not. It was his duty.

"We'd manage somehow," he said. "And it would . . . we're not crazy kids expecting the moon . . . but we've known each other a long time . . . we get along pretty well—" He broke off when she grinned derisively. "—most of the time," he finished. "It would pleasure me, honor me, to make you my wife. We'd be company for each other."

Dove was trembling; her cheeks were wet. "Damn you, Angus Scofield," she whispered. "It—it would never work."

He heard the indecision in her voice and waited. She looked up at him towering over her, and the questioning wistfulness in her scrutiny touched his heart as nothing else could have. He longed to take her in his arms, comfort her as he would have comforted Miss Rowdy. He thought in that moment that an embrace would have swayed her. But he wanted the decision to be hers.

"It would work, Dove," he said softly. "I know it would. Think on it. I'll be back in a month." He smiled, that lucent smile that transformed his whole face. "Or sooner," he said.

103.

The Pinkerton man's name was Cook. He stood five foot eight, had thin sandy hair and the invaluable quality of being inconspicious.

He went to St. Louis first, called on the reporter who had written the story but learned nothing new other than the name of the hotel detective.

Feeling no compunction, he roused the security man from his afternoon's sleep. The door to the man's office was opened a crack, and the detective was greeted with a snarl. Knowing the breed, Cook produced a ten-dollar bill. A hand with dirty nails reached for the money. Cook drew it back.

"Looking for information," he said.

The door opened wider, and he entered the stuffy room. Sat down without invitation. "This man and woman who were working the game at the hotel a while back . . ." he began.

"You a newspaper reporter?" The hotel manager had nearly had apoplexy about that story.

Cook shook his head. "We're looking for a missing heiress," he improvised. "There's a possibility she's the young lady."

"Purty little thing, she was."

"Any idea which way they headed?"

"Nope."

"Thought they might be in some other hotel here."

"Naw, I'd know about it if they was. The other hotel detectives and me, we sort of exchange notes, so to speak."

"Makes sense. One more question. How'd they travel?"

"Horseback. I 'member 'cause the stable boy was plumb scandlized. The gal was wearing britches."

Cook thanked the hotel man, the bill changed hands and he left. He thought of going to the police, but that was chancy. Some places cooperated with the Pinkertons. Some places didn't.

He had another lead, though. The couple couldn't have carried their traps on horses. He began systematically, with the drayage firms, and spent the entire day without so much as a clue.

The next morning, he went to the office of the coach company that operated in a three-state area. Fruitless. That left only the railroad. He was less than sanguine about that. In a city the size of St. Louis, the baggage agent would be unlikely to recall one transaction months back. But he had reckoned without the impression Rowdy made.

The railroad man tilted his cap back and said, sure, he remembered a couple like that. The girl was pretty as a spotted pup. He couldn't figure out, though, why she wanted to dress like a man. It wasn't fitting. But when Cook asked where the baggage had been sent, the garrulousness came to an abrupt stop.

"Sorry," he said, "that'd be confidential information."

Cook sized him up, decided an attempt at bribery would be resented. Wondering if there were a patron saint of liars, he again produced the story about an inheritance. The baggage man squinted at him thoughtfully, rubbed his jaw.

Cook sensed the man's hesitation and pushed his luck. "Reckon you might have daughters of your own," he suggested. "It's nice to see folks made happy."

The baggage man glanced to either side. "Kansas City," he muttered, and turned his back, suddenly very busy.

Kansas City was a repetition of St. Louis except that it took three days instead of two. Information finally in hand, he sent a report to New York and headed for New Orleans.

In New Orleans, Dude's hatred of Rowdy had reached such proportions that he could scarcely look at her. It wasn't that he minded her admitting there was another man, though he'd like to put a bullet through that one; what he couldn't stand was that she continued to treat him with contempt. Like he was dirt. He'd treated her right. Whatever happened to her now, she'd brought it on herself. He began to dream of ways of killing her.

Hands tight around her throat, throttling her until she

380

turned blue and begged for mercy. Taking his Bowie knife to her, starting with one of her breasts. He dreamed one night that he'd shot her, and woke sobbing with rage and frustration. Killing her wasn't enough. He wanted her to suffer. And beg for mercy.

Yet, he could not walk away. He told himself it was because she was profitable to him. The truth was that he wanted her to be sexually obsessed with him. Then he'd turn her down, sneer at her and give her the boot.

He had never been a lush, but now he began taking a glass or two of absinthe, liking its licorice taste. He went whoring regularly, beat one crib girl into insensibility because she reminded him vaguely of Rowdy. He found a poker game in the French Quarter that ran continuously, and sat in. He lost with unfailing regularity, but it took his mind off his torment. The absinthe helped too.

Rowdy was indifferent to his demoralization. The nights he was sprawled out drunk on his bed or was out gambling, she ate in her room and spent the evening reading or sewing. So long as the apricot brandy was there, she was insulated.

Cook knew he was not far behind the pair when he reached New Orleans. They had stayed for several months in both St. Louis and Kansas City. He felt sure they would follow the same pattern here. He booked a room at the Arcadian and spent the first evening waiting around the lobby. He was not disappointed when he saw nothing of them; it would have been too much to expect on his first night.

Cook was a patient man. He checked the hotels, one by one. On the sixth night, he hit pay dirt.

104.

Dude's eyes were bloodshot, his hands unsteady when he knocked at Rowdy's door. When she opened it, he told her curtly to be ready at seven. Rowdy nodded without speaking. He felt her contempt and turned away abruptly lest he hit her.

He needed her tonight. And for several other nights as well, damn it. The last poker game had cleaned him out. He'd build up the roll again. Then he'd walk out on her.

He was having trouble thinking straight and felt that she had somehow caused him to lose at cards. He had no idea the wormwood was wrecking his mind, that he was in the throes of an irreversible nervous disorder. His world had become a place of fog, fury and increasingly frequent blackouts.

His hands shook so, he could hardly dress, but finally he managed and went along the corridor to pick up the girl. She joined him, looking demure and innocent in a full-skirted dress of emerald velvet.

From his vantage point at the bar, Cook spotted them while they were on the stairs, and his heart gave an unaccustomed thump. He had been told the girl was pretty, but the descriptions he'd been given had not done her justice. Face impassive, he asked for a second beer.

Though his back was to Dude and Rowdy, he watched their every move in the mirror behind the bar. He saw the girl settled into an easy chair in the lobby, with every appearance of deference by the man. Was it possible she was in love with this cheap-john? Cook had seen some funny combinations of male and female, but somehow could not believe these two were romantically involved. Nor could they be brother and sister. It would have been impossible for them to have come from the same background.

He sipped his beer and engaged in desultory conversation with the bartender. Dude drifted into the bar and ordered a drink. Cook became even more thoughtful when he saw the glass of absinthe appear. When he'd been with the police department, he'd once been assigned to take an absinthe drinker to the upstate insane asylum. It had taken six men to get the prisoner into a straight-jacket.

Unobtrusively, Dude surveyed the assortment of men lining the long bar. They looked like a bunch of penny-pinching drummers, he thought irritably—more of the bad luck that slut brought him. He drew a deep breath and gulped down the absinthe.

Cook shuddered. He shrugged to himself, held hs glass up to the bartender so that the diamond on his pinky sparkled, fake but flashy. Dude caught its glitter in the mirror, gave Cook a second look. The man didn't have that moneyed aura Dude preferred, but he had another larger diamond in his stickpin, and a heavy gold watch chain lay across his vest.

Dude ordered a second absinthe and waited, hoping a more prepossessing prospect would appear. His wary animal sense was alert to the smell of danger. He sipped slowly this time. The sandy little man didn't look like he had wealth, but you could never tell. It was said John D. himself looked at times as if he didn't have a dime.

Presently, the men standing between Cook and Dude left in search of dinner, and Cook moved down the bar.

"Could I trouble you for the salt?" he asked. "Put a bit of a head back on this beer."

"Certainly." Dude's voice was as cordial as he could make it. He had been torn between approaching Cook or writing off the whole evening. He took the fact that Cook had initiated the contact as a good omen. Maybe Lady Luck was finally getting ready to smile on him again.

"The New Orleans humidity must be a hundred percent," Cook ventured.

Dude nodded. "Guess I'm so used to it, I don't notice. But you, now, you sound like a Yankee. Reckon you don't get the heat up there like we do."

"That's right. We get hot weather in New York, but not like this sizzler." He wiped his brow theatrically. "Lord help us, what we do to keep up with our invest—" He broke off with a cagey glance at his companion.

Dude was cheered. Investments? "I'm in real estate myself," he improvised, "so I have to be out and around a good deal. Home's in Galveston."

"Galveston?" Cook sounded impressed. "I've heard that's one of the prettiest spots in the county. Palm trees and all that?"

"Sure. Palms. Ocean breeze. And not too much riffraff." He chuckled richly. "They can't afford it."

"Fellow has to be careful." Cook nodded sagely. "There are always tricksters out, trying to take advantage of a well-to-do—" He broke off again.

Dude beamed at him. "Name's Dubois," he said, making up his mind. "Here, a man needs more than beer to get the dust out of his throat. Let me order you a real drink. Bartender!"

"Obliged to you," Cook said hastily, "but I have a

cranky stomach. It won't tolerate anything stronger than beer." He giggled foolishly. "I can put away my share of that, though."

"Another beer for my friend—I didn't catch your name."

"Cook."

"My friend Cook," Dude concluded, speaking again to the bartender.

The two men chatted and drank for a time. Then, with a theatrical start, Dude pulled out his watch. "I'm in trouble," he said sheepishly. "Company's so pleasant, I forgot my sister. She's waiting to go in to supper." He hesitated; then, as though on impulse: "Come eat with us, Mr. Cook." He laughed. "You might save me a dressing down. She's pretty but fractious."

Cook laughed with him, turned away from the bar and appeared to be unsteady on his feet. "Guess I should get some food under my belt at that," he agreed. "Where is this pretty lady?"

Both men were well pleased with the exchange. They collected Rowdy, who, when they were introduced, gave Cook such an enchanting smile, he straightened his tie and wished they had met under different circumstances.

A portion of him watched with mixed admiration and dismay as the playacting unfolded. Dude ate little but had carried his absinthe to the table with him, and continued to sip it. When Cook had all but finished his meal, Dude suddenly put his hands to his head and squeezed his eyes shut, as though in severe pain.

"Mr. Cook . . . could I impose . . . sister . . . room . . ."

"My dear fellow," Cook cried, "are you ill?"

"Pain!" Dude appeared to stagger as he got to his feet, and Cook wondered cynically why the man hadn't turned to the stage as a livelihood. "I'm . . . all right," Dude finished.

Rowdy had risen too. "I'll help you," she cried.

"Our guest . . . finish your meal . . ." Dubois, or whoever he was, stumbled out of the room. Cook had gotten up when Rowdy rose. He stood watching as Dude zigzagged across the lobby, to the staircase. When he turned around again, Rowdy had reseated herself.

"Please finish your supper, Mr. Cook," she said shyly. "My brother suffers from migraine, which often comes on

384

without warning." She lowered her head. "You—you musn't feel it necessary to—to see me to my room. I shall be quite all right."

Smooth, very smooth, Cook said admiringly to himself. Aloud, he said, "I wouldn't think of permitting you to go up those stairs alone, the crime situation being what it is."

Rowdy allowed herself to be persuaded. At the door to her room, she said, sounding impulsive, "Won't you come in for a nightcap?" Then, with an appearance of confusion, she added quickly, "I'm sorry, Mr. C—Cook, my brother and I have traveled so extensively on the Continent, I forget a lady does not invite a gentleman to her room, here in the States. Even for anything so innocent as a nightcap."

Cook felt sick. Every instinct told him the girl was no brazen adventuress. Even while rattling off the glib speech, there was something sad and lost about her. Then he silently scoffed at himself for letting a pretty face cloud his judgment.

"No one could mistake your motives, Miss Dubois," he assured her. "I would be delighted to have a nightcap if you feel I am to be trusted in the company of such loveliness."

For the space of a second or two, she hesitated, and he wondered if the irony of his words had tinged her voice. Then she laughed lightly. "I'm sure you are to be trusted," she said, "though I declare you are a flatterer. Do come in."

She stepped back, and he entered the room. She asked him to be seated. While she busied herself with the drinks, he glanced around, looking for something that would explain her part in this farce.

Although she had been there for some time, he knew, the room was as impersonal as though it had no occupant at all. Even the dresser held no comb and brush, or rice powder. It was as though she wished to negate even her existence.

He patted the "knucks" derringer stuck in the back of his belt. His suit coat covered the small bulge it made. It was, as he had acknowledged when twitted about it, an odd-looking contraption. Half pistol, half brass knuckles, it looked more like a wrench than a gun. But it had never failed him.

Rowdy came back, put the glasses on the dresser and poured the amber liquid. Her back was to him.

Cook sighed, suddenly weary of the shabby world in which he operated. Rowdy brought his drink and her own and seated herself.

"You must find New Orleans slow-paced after the bustle of New York," she said.

"I find New Orleans charming," Cook replied. "Especially on this trip."

Rowdy glanced down at her hands, holding the fragile-stemmed glass. "I declare, you're so gallant, a girl would think you a Frenchman," she murmured. Their eyes met, and something in those amethyst depths—despair?—shook the man to the core.

"Why do you—" he blurted out, caught himself. "Why do you drink sweet liqueurs?" he hastily concluded. "I thought southern ladies were raised on sippin' whiskey."

Her laugh tinkled, and he shivered. The sound was a desolate one, containing no mirth. "Here," she said, "let me freshen your drink."

"I'm still fine," Cook said, touching the glass to his lips. When Rowdy went to refill her own glass, Cook rose and walked over to the window, ostensibly to look down at the busy street. He had not seen so much as a vase or a spittoon, into which to empty his glass, so he poured most of the liquid onto the carpet behind the drapes.

Rowdy had reseated herself, and Cook made his steps seem unsteady as he moved across the room, sat down. He put the palm of his hand to his forehead. "I'm beginning to wonder if that chicken at supper wasn't kept a little overlong." He slurred the words, allowing them to run together, seemed to make a tremendous effort to speak. "Maybe you should call . . . Please ask someone to help . . ." He broke off, letting his head fall on his chest.

He heard the sibilance of her garments as she rose, and waited for the next move. He had let his fingers go lax, and the glass fell. Through slitted eyelids, he saw her pick it up, heard the breath she drew. It was close to a sob.

As he had never wanted to know anything before, he wanted to know this girl's story. Never let yourself get personally involved. That instruction had been drilled into him from the first moment he entered police work, even more so when he went to work for the Pinkertons.

He tried to set his feelings aside, telling himself once

more not to be taken in by a pretty face. He felt her touch on his lapel. That would be the velvet rosette. He heard the small snap as she broke the thread, felt the lapel being turned back to its original position.

He risked a peek again and saw her cross the floor, open the door and go out. He sat unmoving except to permit his body to slump as though he were about to fall out of the chair. But in that movement, he managed to move his arm against the gun, reassure himself it was in place.

When the door reopened, the "brother" was with her. "You're sure he's out?" the man asked.

"Yes."

The man gave an ugly laugh. "I've got my little Jim Dandy friend ready, just in case." Cook was suddenly uneasy, but he forced himself to remain relaxed.

Dude patted him all over, sides and legs. "No shootin' iron," he grunted, and Cook was once more thankful to the ancient felon who had advised him to wear his gun in back. Dude was turning out his pockets. His wallet was lifted, the watch and chain, the stickpin; the ring was roughly jerked from his finger. Dude even removed his handkerchief, but then shoved it back into his pocket. Cook heard the wallet being opened.

"That ain't bad," Dude muttered. "OK, gimme a hand and we'll get this bugger down to his room."

As Dude started to straighten him up, Cook's Puckish humor got the best of him. "Let me help," he said, and leaped to his feet, gun appearing as though by magic.

Dude froze. The color drained from his face; the pupils of his eyes expanded until the iris was all but blacked out. Rowdy, the operative saw, was on her feet but unmoving, her face a mask.

Cook spoke. "Hands on top your head, both of you," he ordered. "We're going downstairs, have the desk clerk call the police."

The Pinkerton man had correctly sized up Dude's cowardice. He had reckoned without the desperation born of terror. Dude panicked. He snatched his Bowie knife and lunged. Cook pulled the trigger.

The hammer clicked against a dud shell.

The next instant, Dude was on him. It took Cook not more than two seconds to slide his fingers into the metal loops that transformed the gun into knuckles. But those seconds were costly. Sobbing with fright and rage, Dude slashed at him.

Cook struck at the man's eyes, cut his cheek open, but Dude's second thrust got the Pinkerton man in the throat. A great freshet of blood spurted out like a fountain.

Cook's face mirrored his astonishment, then went slack. He stood for an instant, arms hanging, knees buckling. "I'll be damned," he tried to say. And fell.

Rowdy felt faintness wash over her, felt the nausea in her stomach rise to her throat. Dude was shaking so badly, he could hardly stand.

"Get a doctor!" she ordered, and ran to the bath for towels. When she returned, Dude was standing where she'd left him.

"It's all yore fault!" he hissed at her while she knelt and tried to staunch the blood. "You told me he was out. You didn't even use the drops. Was he that other man you told me about? Was he?" He grabbed her shoulders and shook her.

"Damn you!" Rowdy shouted at him. "Get a doctor!"

"They'll hang us." Dude whimpered. Then, viciously: "They hang women too, you know."

Rowdy looked up at him with such loathing that it penetrated his panic. "I ain't goin' for no doctor," he snarled at her. "I'm goin' for the horses. I'll be in back of the hotel in five minutes."

He turned jerkily, got the door open and fled.

Rowdy's legs were unsteady as she stood up. She forced herself forward, hurried shakily across the hall, down the stairs. "I need a doctor!" She had meant to whisper to the clerk, but her teeth were chattering, and the words came out in a hysterical scream.

The clerk gaped at her. "Hurry!" she shouted, and took hold of his arm to shake him out of his daze. She saw that he was looking at her hand with horror, and followed his gaze. Her fingers were encrusted with blood.

The clerk's mouth was opening and closing, but he was making no sound. "A doctor!" Rowdy said again, fighting tears.

A man strode through the dumbstruck crowd. "I'm a doctor, Miss," he said quietly.

She raced back to the stairs, the doctor at her heels. In the brief moments it took to reach her room, she fantasized that it was all a nightmare. There would be no body, no widening bloodstain.

She opened the door. Cook lay as she had left him. Without a word, the doctor knelt, grimaced when he saw the blood.

For a second, Rowdy stood, hoping, praying. Then, with a sob, she snatched up her reticule and fled.

She was struggling for breath as she shoved open the heavy employees' door. Dude was already mounted, holding her horse. "Where the hell you been?" he snarled. Without answering, Rowdy swung up into the saddle.

"We'll head for the Ouachitas," Dude said hoarsely. "Don't do no runnin' 'til we get out of town." They moved out of the hotel grounds at a sedate pace.

They reached the outskirts of New Orleans without encountering any problem, and Dude said harshly, "Ride at night, lay low in daylight," and took off at a gallop. Rowdy followed.

As they rode, she had a sense of unreality. She would wake presently, at home, with Uncle Jim telling her to bestir herself, with Samsy suggesting they play church, with Papa coming home to swoop her up in his arms.

They were riding northwest, and her heart gave a sudden leap. At least they were riding in the *direction* of Oklahoma. Suddenly exhaustion overwhelmed her. She clung to the horse to keep from falling.

When, after a lifetime, streaks of light began to appear in the eastern sky, Rowdy scarcely noticed.

"Next woods we come to, we'll stop," Dude growled, and less than an hour later found a wooded section to his liking. They turned in, dismounted, found a stream and watered the horses. Then they lay on their bellies, washed their faces and scooped water into their hands to drink.

"I want some absinthe," Dude grumbled, wiping his mouth with the back of his hand. "Water tastes like hogs been trompin' in it."

Rowdy could understand his thirst. She herself would have given much for a dollop of brandy.

They got their saddle blankets, and within minutes, Dude's snores sounded, like the rumble of thunder. Rowdy was wide-eyed, too exhausted to relax.

Once again she experienced a sense of bewilderment at the circumstances that had brought her to this point.

True, she had been headstrong and rebellious, but other girls had been too, without suffering disaster.

Still, she knew the proprieties and had defied them. "Good" women did not associate with "bad" men. Thus if you were seen in the company of "bad" men, you were a "bad" woman. It was hours before she slept.

Dude woke her at dusk by shoving a foot against her backside. "You gonna sleep forever?" he complained, then: "Dammit, I'm hungry and I want a drink."

"You're not the only one," Rowdy snapped. Groggily, she got up, stumbled down to the stream, drank thirstily and scrubbed herself as best she could.

Dude was sitting on a log, staring glumly at the ground, when she went back to the clearing. She saw that a tic had developed at the right side of his mouth. She heard a cow bawl somewhere in the distance.

"Maybe I can get some milk," she told him. "Let me have your hat."

"Yore not puttin' that stuff in my Stetson."

She shrugged. "All right, you figure out something," she said. "I'm going to look around for some nuts or berries."

As she struck out through the trees, she heard him cursing furiously, and presently heard the soft susurrus of hooves as he rode off. She wondered indifferently whether he would be back.

She found a few acorns, but nothing else that was remotely edible. She was beginning to feel light-headed from lack of food, shaky for want of the brandy to which her system was accustomed.

She sat down on a log, thought on Dude's peculiar condition. She had heard somewhere that absinthe not only affected the body, but caused severe nervous disorders. She knew a moment of compunction for him. Her own need for brandy was bad enough, but at least it affected only her body. If his mind were undergoing the rigors of denial, he must be in agony.

Dude was surly when he returned. He had bought some food but was livid because there was no saloon in town. He had also stolen a calico dress from a clothesline "so you won't stand out like a sore thumb, in yore gaudery," he gibed. Rowdy refused to respond. She found a shelter of trees away from the clearing and changed clothes. The calico hung on her like a bed sheet, but certainly it was less conspicious than the velvet dress.

390

As they ate, her head began to clear. A measure of strength returned to her legs. Dude was making heavier weather of it. He ate a few bites, began to vomit and could not seem to stop. Rowdy wetted her handkerchief in the stream and wiped his face. He had begun to shiver, then he fell to the ground, shuddering as though he were having convulsions. "No, Pa!" he screamed. "I didn't do it, honest I didn't! Don't hit me no more! Thet buckle c— cut my lip! No, no, I won't do it no more!" He went on, alternately shaking, cursing and screaming for mercy.

Rowdy felt her stomach contract. She had never thought of Dude as being anything but a weak excuse for a man. Pity came to her now as she knelt beside him, continuing to dampen his face, holding him tightly when the awful ague rocked him.

She had never seen a man in the agony of withdrawal from absinthe. She thought he was dying.

It seemed to her that years had passed before the shudders subsided and he lay spent. "Duke," she whispered, "can you ride?"

He cursed her then, accused her of wanting to ride off and meet that other man. Rowdy maintained a grim silence, disgusted yet pitying. She waited until he ran down, then said gently, "We have to leave."

Again, he became agitated. "Don't go off and leave me, Rowdy," he whimpered. "Yore the only good thing that ever happened to me. I love you; I want you."

Rowdy tried to ignore her revulsion. "I'm right here, Dude," she said soothingly.

"You won't leave me?"

"No."

"Not ever?"

Rowdy hesitated. She did not make promises lightly.

"Say it!" Dude screamed. "Say you won't ever leave me!" He was hysterical, beginning to thresh about again. Rowdy drew a long, painful breath, knowing she was saying farewell to even the possibility of going back home.

"I won't ever leave you," she promised.

105.

It was five hundred miles from New Orleans to the Ouachita Mountains, straddling Oklahoma and Arkansas. Rowdy and Dude rode at night, slept during the day. The stubble on Dude's face grew into a patchy beard. His face was gaunt, his eyes lusterless. At times he was lethargic, at other times almost frenzied.

He was eating practically nothing, and Rowdy, dismayed and uncertain as to how to help him, realized that his deterioration had speeded up.

"You have to eat, Dude," she would repeat patiently. "Here, try a little of the cheese, a bite of apple."

Occasionally, he took a few bites, looking at her with mournful eyes. Other times he knocked the food from her hands and cursed her.

Time lost all meaning. Somewhere during that nightmarish flight, Dude said weakly, "Why are you so good to me? I'm no 'count. Pa said I'd never amount to nothin'. He was mean, Pa was, hurtful . . ." He drifted into incoherence, then began to scream for absinthe.

She never knew how many days they traveled. She did know that Dude grew more and more disoriented, the farther they went, his periods of lucidity less frequent.

Rowdy had an additional worry. Dude had never trusted her with much money, and it hadn't seemed important. Now it did, for what she'd had in her reticule when they left New Orleans was almost gone. And that last poker game had left Dude virtually penniless.

She had to have money to buy food.

She had taken over the direction of the trip; Dude was too muddled. On those occasions when he roused himself out of his confusion, he was abusive and threatening. The "other man" preyed on his mind, and he accused her of every indecency he could fantasize.

Rowdy tried to ignore him. Her revulsion grew. Her pity, and her promise, would not let her desert him.

In one of his more rational moments, he had told her to head due north, into Arkansas. But there was a hunger for home within her, so, with the sun as her compass, she guided them northwest.

Her spirits lifted when she rode into town one evening, for provisions. The post office sign said Buford, Texas. She swallowed past the lump in her throat and turned her thoughts to the problem of money. After purchasing her few supplies, she was literally down to her last dime. They had to have some cash. I'll pay it back, she thought. I just need enough to get home.

As she rode back to Dude, she decided she would have to rob a bank. Even ten dollars would get them to Oklahoma City. And it had seemed easy enough when Dude got that money in Lincoln.

She fixed him a meal, told him her plan while she helped him eat. When she had finished, he said viciously, "I want a drink. Why won't you get me some absinthe?"

She stood up when he staggered to his feet. "I want a woman," he whined; "I want you," and began to make rutting motions, fumbling with his pants buttons.

Her innermost being recoiled with shock and disgust; sickness rose in her throat. She forced herself to stand absolutely immobile, even when he thrust himself at her, holding her shoulders and rubbing his body obscenely against her.

"I'll kill you," she said, and her voice was at once both so level and so deadly, it cut through his fog. His hands dropped, the gyrating movement ceased and he moved backward, giggling foolishly. "I was funnin'," he said.

She turned away lest he see her trembling. "Get some rest," she said in a carefully matter-of-fact voice, and swung up into the saddle.

Tears were streaming down her face, sobs made her throat ache and she was sick to her stomach, as she rode away. The scene had demoralized her. I can't take any more, she thought. I won't go back to him. I'll keep on riding.

"You promised," an inner voice reminded her.

Finally, the shaking lessened, the storm of tears stopped.

Lamps were glowing in windows when Rowdy reached

the town. She saw no one on the street, but light spilled from the saloon. A tinny piano was being thumped, and occasional raucous shouts could be heard. It must have been payday for the ranch hands.

She glanced around nervously. She had hoped the town would be sound asleep. She tied her horse at the hitching rack in front of the store and, keeping to the shadows, walked down the street on the opposite side of the saloon.

The sheriff's office showed a light but no activity. The livery stable was dark. Close by, a dog barked, and Rowdy froze. An angry human voice shouted threats, and the barking stopped.

The bank was near the general store. It was a frame building with no windows in front, mullioned glass in the top half of the door. Too small to afford entry. Still keeping to the shadows, she walked silently around the building. A door here too. Solid wood, this one. No windows.

I'm not cut out to be a robber, Rowdy thought, frustrated and angry. I don't even know how to start. Even the side windows have bars on them. She felt tears come into her eyes again, snapped at herself to forget the self-pity and *think*.

Dude had used a small metal tool to force the lock in Lincoln. . . . Chest tight with fear, trying to keep watch, she dropped to her knees and scrabbled around in the dirt for a piece of sharp metal. A cocklebur pierced her finger, and the tears threatened again. A person would think you're two years old, she scolded herself.

Groping on the ground again, she found a tenpenny nail and thrust it into the lock, twisting it first one way, then another. It simply would not work.

You are not going to start bawling again, she instructed herself, not knowing what to do next. She thought she heard a rustling sound and fled around the corner of the bank to the street. Fearfully, she glanced back but saw no one. She'd better get out of here while her luck held.

She reached her horse at the same moment the louvered doors of the saloon swung open. Two crowing cowpokes wobbled out, leaning on one another.

"I won! Damn their crooked hearts, I won once! I'm gonna find me the prettiest girl in three counties and . . ." He maundered on, and when he was silent, his companion took up the slack. They headed toward the stable.

Briefly, Rowdy stood unmoving while her mind worked.

Her hands were unsteady as she slid the gun from her purse. Then she went after the men, silent as a moth. They had passed beyond the glow of the saloon lights by the time she caught up with them. She pressed the gun into one back, her finger into the other.

"I'll take that roll," she growled, trying to make her voice low and menacing.

The cowpokes were drunk, but not so drunk that they didn't recognize danger.

"Hell's katoot," one complained, "first time I ever won."

"Quiet!" Rowdy hissed. "Get them guns out—careful. Throw 'em like you was pitching horseshoes." She jabbed with both finger and gun, to emphasize the words.

The men obeyed.

"Now, real careful, get them greenbacks out." She didn't have to try, now, to make her voice sound unnatural. She was so frightened, her throat so dry, the words came out in a croak.

The cowpoke who had won, reached in his pocket, pulled out a Bull Durham sack. "It's in there," he grumbled, holding it behind him.

"I'm gonna move one of my hands," she told them. "But the other one's fast enough for two." She grabbed the sack, felt the crinkle of money, had her finger again in the second man's back with the speed of lightning.

"You pokes keep a-walkin' west," she instructed. "Count to fifty real slow afore you turn around. I got a rifle handy that don't take no sass."

The two started on their walk. Rowdy whirled and ran, swung up into the saddle, spurred the horse and headed north at a gallop. Her teeth were chattering, and there was a frozen sickness within her. Yet, she also felt a strange desire to mark her work.

Fumbling, she pulled the roll of bills out of the tobacco sack, found one of the velvet bows in her reticule, fastened it to the bag with a hairpin. Judging she had gone half a mile or so, she dropped it.

When she got back to the woods, Dude was stomping up and down, cursing and crying. He began screaming at her, the moment she appeared.

"Be quiet," she snapped. "I got us some money. There'll likely be a posse out. Let's ride."

At the word "posse" he quieted, got on his horse and they took off.

They reached Red River well before dawn. "I'm skeered," Dude whined. "I ain't never swum a river. I'll drown."

"No you won't." Rowdy contradicted him with more confidence than she felt. "Walk your horse out as far as he can go. Then let him have his head. He'll swim it."

She glanced back. So far, there was no sign of a posse. It might take time for them to pick up the trail, but sooner or later they would. She and Dude could either cross the river and find refuge in the wilds of the Kiamichis or be captured.

Rowdy herself was terrified of the water but urged Biscuit forward. The mare whinnied, throwing up her head as though to bolt. Rowdy held firm. With her other hand, she grasped the bridle of Dude's horse. Biscuit went into the deeper water reluctantly, sliding now and then as she tried to keep her footing.

Rowdy gasped in shock at the cold water. The current was pulling at them. Without warning, her horse stepped into what was apparently a drop-off, and Rowdy felt the water close over her head. Dude's horse carried him down, and the man panicked, tugging at the reins, jerking the strap from Rowdy's hand.

Instinctively, the horses began to swim, fighting their way back to the surface. Dude emerged, screeching. When Rowdy came up, fighting for breath, she was almost tempted to join him in yelping. The current was swifter here, and she could feel that they were being swept down river.

She bit down hard on her lip, knowing that if she gave way to hysteria, they would both be lost. She grasped the reins more tightly, forcing Biscuit to fight the current. Dude was already a quarter of a mile downstream and out of his senses with fear.

"Damn you!" she shouted. "Hold that horse's head. Turn him, you fool!" When Dude continued to swirl with the current, she shouted again. "Dude, I'm leaving you!" and forced her horse toward the north bank.

Dude shook his head as though trying to shake off the haze that enveloped him. "Leaving . . . leaving you . . ." The words hung in the air, undercutting his whimpering. The bitch! She'd brought him here to let him drown! She was headed for that other man. Adrenaline flooded his veins. He snatched the reins, kicked the horse viciously with his heels, turned the animal's head to the north, felt the struggle as the animal began to fight the current.

Rowdy reached the north bank and slid off her horse, weeping, hysterical with relief. Unaware of the chill creeping through her, she watched as Dude fought his way forward.

His horse slid as it came onto the bank, and the man cursed him. He dismounted, leading the animal to where Rowdy stood. "I'm gonna kill you," he said.

"Not now, Dude," she murmured, scarcely aware of his words. "There's no time. We have to make the Kiamichis before the sun comes up."

Her voice was so authoritative that he hesitated, then climbed back on his horse.

As they rode north, Rowdy was more and more conscious of the cold. Then she fell to thinking about her answer to Dude. "Not now; there's no time." We don't have time for you to kill me here, Dude. Wait 'til we get to the mountains. It was so absurd, she felt hysterical giggles pushing their way into her throat. Somehow, she managed to stifle them.

Rowdy did not know how to gauge distances. They could not possibly have reached their goal that morning, but they did come into the foothills—rolling, heavily wooded country—shortly after dawn. They rode until they were too exhausted even to hold up their heads. When her chin dropped to her chest a second time, Rowdy called a halt.

"We'll have to stay here today," she said.

"Thought you was leadin' us into the Promised Land," Dude said, sneering.

"Tonight, Dude, for sure." She hoped it was true.

The man slid from his horse. "I'm hungry," he complained.

"So am I. But I'm too tired to hunt for a town. We'll just have to do without."

"I'm hungry," he repeated obdurately, as though she had not spoken. "I'm gonna hunt me a rabbit."

"Fine," Rowdy snapped. "First shot, there'll be a sheriff after you."

"Rifle don't make much noise," he answered, sulking.

"Wait a minute. Right over there. Acorns. We can ea those."

She gathered up a handful, began to crack them and handed one kernel to Dude.

"You tryin' to poison me?"

Too weary to answer, she put one in her own mouth, chewed and swallowed. Dude watched her suspiciously but finally ate his. They walked a way, found some possum grapes and ate them, came on some wild blackberries, stripped the bushes, ate all they could.

Then they slept.

It was full dark when Rowdy woke. She heard Dude still snoring. There was a new moon in the sky, close to the horizon, as was the evening star, so she judged it was early night.

She woke Dude. They ate the rest of the berries and set out once more. In the distance, they heard the cry of a panther, and Dude whimpered. "Good Gawd, what's thet?"

"Oh, some kind of animal," Rowdy said carelessly, though a chill ran up her own spine. "Nothing to worry about."

"I'm hungry," he complained.

"Maybe I can find a store tomorrow."

"I want some absinthe."

"They don't sell absinthe in this part of the country. But I'll try to find you something to drink."

"Moonshine." He sneered.

"It's better than nothing. Hush, now, and ride."

They found an old cave in one of the higher foothills that morning. Fallen branches and underbrush hid the opening, but Rowdy had gone off through the trees to relieve herself, when she came across it. It was dark inside the cave and smelled musky, as though animals had used it as a lair. But when she sailed a rock into the depths, nothing moved.

"We'll be safe for today," she said. "Tonight we'll find a better hiding place." Dude was twitching again, and she knew his nerves were raw.

"Why don't you try to sleep?" she asked gently. "I'll see if I can find a town, buy some food."

"Yore goin' off to that other man."

She didn't bother to answer, but as she rode, she was uneasy. She knew Dude was on the verge of complete collapse, and he seemed obsessed with "that other man." She wondered whether it would help if she told him the other man was long since dead.

"Johnny," she whispered, and wept. For her lost love, her shattered life, for home and Papa, Uncle Jim, Dove and Samsy. She was still crying when she came on the small store sitting in the middle of nowhere.

Drying her eyes, she tied Biscuit to a tree and went in. She had tied a scarf over her head, and the ill-fitting dress functioned as a kind of disguise. Probably, she could be taken for a mountain woman. The man who waited on her didn't appear to be interested anyhow. He brought the items she asked for, and never looked up.

"I need some mountain dew." The squinty eyes finally did peer up at her. "For my man," she added.

"Ain't got none."

"Could you get some?" she asked. "I'd—give you a—a dollar for a jug." She knew it was an outrageous price.

The impassive face didn't change, but the squinty eyes blinked.

"Come back tomorrow," he said, and turned to his shelves.

As she rode toward the cave, she debated with herself. She was sure he'd have the liquor for her the following morning, but it would mean staying here tonight. She'd planned for them to push on to Robber's Cave. It was, she had heard, the safest place to hide out.

Still, maybe the alcohol would help Dude. And this cave seemed safe enough. They'd stay, she decided. She'd get some warm food and coffee inside him.

When she reached the cave, Dude was sitting on the ground, at its opening. He looked up at her dully but didn't speak. He was shaking as if he had palsy.

"Got some victuals," she said briefly, and gathered sticks, made a small fire. Dude sat like some great glum animal. She carried coffee to him, jerky, cornpone.

He ate, retched, complained she was trying to poison him.

"It's all that absinthe you put away," she said, trying to reason with him. "You've wrecked your body. Once you get that out of your system—" He interrupted with an obscenity, scrambled farther into the cave.

He offered no objection when, late in the evening, she told him they would stay there that night.

She fixed breakfast the following morning, then rode back to the store. Without looking at her, the man handed her a fruit jar filled with a cloudy white liquid.

She bought salt and some cheese, put the fruit jar in her saddlebag and rode back to the cave. Dude seemed somewhat rejuvenated. He talked without reviling her, nodded when she said they'd ride on that night to Robber's Cave.

106.

The Oklahoma City paper picked up the item about the "rosette outlaw" because Buford, Texas, was near the border of the two states. It stood to reason that the pair was headed for the Kiamichis. The paper also printed the story because Pinkerton's had offered the unheard-of amount of a thousand dollars for taking the two, dead or alive. Lawmen, private citizens, other outlaws, bounty hunters—the Pinkerton agency would pay any of them.

That was going to put an awful lot of people on their trail, the editor thought grimly as he reread the column. Someone was likely to get killed, and not necessarily the outlaws. He crossed out the mention of the reward, then marked it "stet," upon reconsideration.

Dove read the paper that afternoon, and her stomach lurched. "Oh, you fool," she whispered. "Rowdy, you fool! My God, Angus!" She whirled into action. She was shivering as she saddled the horse. This will kill him, she thought.

She rode as she had never ridden before. When the horse came up lame she found a farmer who was willing to sell her another.

In the meantime, the telegraph had flashed the news, and lawmen throughout the southwest gave some thought to heading in the direction of the Kiamichis. Others thought the fugitives might be heading for the barren wastes of West Texas, and struck out that way.

Angus got the news, though, from one of the McCord tribe, who rode in "special" to tell him there were strangers in the mountains.

"The woman was at Sam's store twice, yestiddy and the day 'afore. Sam said she had funny hair, kinda moon color."

Angus's heart thumped, hesitated so long, he thought it had stopped. Laboriously, it resumed beating.

"Sam's," he said, and got out a map he had drawn of his territory. "That'd be about here, near Nanshona."

McCord nodded. "That's where it be, all right." Then, almost shyly: "When you comin' back our way, preacher?"

Angus managed a laugh that sounded almost natural. "When you send someone to fetch me," he said. "That is, after we find what these strangers are—up to."

"Maybe next week," McCord suggested. "My old woman's been jawin' me. She thinks them kids ort to be in church."

Angus agreed to come and was on his way the minute the man left, heading south and east. It was rough going, mountainous and heavily wooded. He had the curious feeling that he would somehow sense Rowdy's nearness when he was on the right track.

He spent the entire day combing the district, checking out caves, once coming on a dozing bobcat. The cat snarled but apparently had fed recently, so it bounded past him and fled.

When night approached, Angus considered spending the night where he was, but could intuit no trace of her there. He scoffed at his feelings, yet they persisted. At last he turned back toward Okell.

Dove reached Okell, exhausted, and wept when she found the sheriff's office empty. Then she dried her eyes and went to the store, seeking information.

The girl gabbled at her willingly enough, and Dove finally interpreted her words to mean that Angus had been gone all day, "huntin' them outlaws." She wondered if he knew who "them outlaws" were. She took care of her horse, went into the unlocked office and within two minutes was sound asleep on Angus's cot.

Angus noted the strange horse in front of his office when he arrived, figured the deputy from Muskogee had ridden down to bring him news again. When he lighted the lamp in his office and saw Dove, he rubbed his eyes, thinking he was seeing things.

Dove sat up, blinking. She said, "Angus," and began to cry.

Astonished, Angus went to sit beside her, put an arm around her shoulders. "For the Lord's sake, Dove, what are you doing here? And what are you bawling about?" Then, thinking he understood and that she was embarrassed, he said more gently, "You've decided to marry me."

Dove shook her head, wiped her eyes. "Angus, I— I've got terrible news. I—had to come."

The light went out of Angus's face. His voice was thick. "Miss Rowdy," he said, and Dove nodded. He got to his feet, lumbering around the small enclosure as though blind. "I figured it had to be her," he said.

His sorrow nearly broke the woman's heart. She went to him, put her arms around him, pulled his head down to her shoulder. "I know, Angus," she said, "I know."

"H'lo the sheriff!" a man's voice called from outside, and Angus lifted his head. The room blurred before his eyes, and he found it difficult to speak. He went to the door.

"Overbrook, from the Brushy area," the man greeted them, swinging himself down from his horse. Angus saw that he wore a badge and invited him in. "This is my— my wife," Angus said, and the big man took off his hat. "Pleasure, ma'am." Dove murmured, "Good evening."

"I'm huntin' them killers," Overbrook said. "Reckon there's plenty others doin' the same, with that thousand-dollar price tag on their heads."

A cold hand seemed to close around Angus's insides, drawing them into a knot. "Thousand dollars," he repeated. Overbrook appeared not to notice the other man's sudden pallor, but Dove saw and was sick with pity.

"I come by Robber's Cave," Overbrook went on. "No sign of 'em."

"I went southeast." Angus's voice was devoid of expression.

"We'll find 'em." Overbrook was confident. "Think I'll ride on down a ways tonight. Likely they're travelin' at night, holin' up by day."

Angus nodded. His mind seemed to have deserted him.

He simply felt in his guts that he must find his child, carry her away to safety.

When Overbrook left, Angus's face was working. "Dove," he said hoarsely, "I've got to pray on this."

"All right, Angus." When he knelt beside the cot, she knelt with him. Angus lifted his face to heaven.

"Lord," he said, his voice choked, "I'm begging you. Help me find Miss Rowdy. She's—You know it's not her fault. If I hadn't been so—so hate-filled, none of this would have happened. It's my sin, Lord. Don't punish her!"

His voice broke. He cleared his throat and went on. "Lord, I'll do anything You want. I'll—I'll even go preach to the Injuns! Amen."

"Amen," Dove echoed, her cheeks wet.

When they stood up, Angus said, "I'll be goin' now." Dove nodded and kissed him on the cheek.

Angus spent the next three or four hours riding, hunting for a trace of them. Overbrook was right; they would be traveling by night. And since the other man had gone past Robber's Cave, they were obviously not there. Yet Angus was sure Robber's Cave was their objective.

By midnight, he'd found no sign of them. He was still determined to continue, but when the horse stepped in a hole and went down, he had to give up. With gentle fingers, he examined the area around the fetlock. There seemed to be no break. Leading the limping animal, Angus walked back to Okell. He'd get a short rest, borrow Dove's mare when daylight came.

Dove opened the door when she heard his steps; she asked no questions. He went inside, realized suddenly he was bone-weary.

"You're gonna lie down, get yourself some rest," Dove instructed.

"You can have the cot. The floor will do fine for me."

"Damn it, Angus, don't *argue!*" Dove shouted. "Just once, do what you're told."

He would have laughed, had he had the energy. He threw himself down on the cot, groaning with relief, heard the rustle of Dove's dress, felt the tug as she removed his heavy boots. He ought to thank her. But she'd probably swear at him.

He saw her blow out the lamp, heard the creak of the chair as she sat down. His mind was jumpy, skittering now this way, now that. He could not shut it off. He tried to force his muscles to relax. They responded by tightening further. He closed his eyes. They flew open again. He stared into the darkness.

After what seemed an age, he said, "Dove, I can't sleep. You might as well have the bed. I'm going to get up."

"You're going to do no such thing." He heard the swish of her skirt, felt the cot give as she lay down beside him. He made as if to roll off on the other side, but she held him.

"Relax," she said tartly, "I'm not going to seduce you."

She put her arms around him, drew him even closer than the narrowness of the cot demanded. "My poor love," she whispered. "Relax. Rest." She coaxed his head over to her shoulder. "We'll find her," she told him. "We'll get married and go home and live on Buffalo Creek. Miss Rowdy will live there too. She'll get married and have children. Samsy will come home for visits . . ."

She went on murmuring, dreaming unattainable dreams for both of them until she felt Angus's body lose its tension. He slept, and she held him, until the sun appeared.

"They'll be at Robber's Cave by now," he said as soon as he opened his eyes. His voice was as certain as though the pair was visible.

Dove said, "Yes."

By the time he'd washed and gotten his boots on, she had breakfast ready.

"I'll have your horse back by evening," he promised.

"Don't—do anything—stupid," she said, trying to scold him, but her voice broke.

Already at the door, Angus paused. He put a finger on her cheek, drew it down to the curve of her mouth. "You know what you are?" he asked. "You're a big humbug."

Then he was gone. Dove put a hand to her cheek where he had touched her, and tears stung her eyes. "Take care of him, Lord," she whispered; and then, in her normal manner: "He's such an idiot!"

107

When Rowdy brought the jar of moonshine to him, Dude tilted it and drank thirstily. He grimaced as he lowered the jar. "Tastes like coal oil and lye water," he complained. But in minutes he was dead to the world.

No wonder, the girl thought. He'd been able to keep barely any food down since they'd left New Orleans. That kind of whiskey on an empty stomach . . . She hoped that now he could sleep the day through.

Feeling that they were safe for the moment, she led the horses back into the cave. Then, she too slept.

The sun was going down when she woke. Dude was still asleep. She went outside. Sunset. She watched the sun, draped with blue and pink and violet and gray, and thought surely this must be the most beautiful place on earth. There was a knot in her throat.

Dude got up, unsteady on his feet, and began to complain. In silence, she handed him some cheese. He ate a few bites, threw it petulantly aside, reached for the jar of liquor.

They rode cautiously through the darkness. The night was cool, the sky dimly lit. The breeze felt good on Rowdy's face. If they got out of this alive, she'd find a new place, start a new life. In the East, maybe.

With a thud, her dreams crashed. Her promise to Dude . . . She tried not to think at all during the rest of the ride.

It was, she estimated, a couple of hours before sunup when they reached Robber's Cave. She'd heard enough about it to recognize it on sight. The enormous rocks guarding it like sentinels . . .

"This is it, Dude," she said. "I've heard it runs far back. We'll be safe."

There was no answer. He was trying to get off his horse, swearing constantly. He grabbed the empty fruit jar and smashed it against a tree. Rowdy grimaced. Whether he was too drunk to negotiate the descent or too debilitated physically, she didn't know.

She went to help him. Maybe she shouldn't have gotten the moonshine, she thought, but it had seemed to soothe him a bit.

He finally got his foot out of the stirrup, staggered as he touched ground. His eyes were those of a madman. Fright chilled her. She touched the reassuring bulge in her reticule. The .38 was there.

"Careful, Dude. Here, I'll help you. The footing's uneven."

He lurched toward her, and before she could anticipate it, Dude dropped his arms around her and gave her a slobbery kiss. "Let's you and me go after it." He was panting. "I'll show you a goo' time . . . you ain't never seen the good time . . ." His words were slurred, all but unintelligible. Rowdy felt herself tensing. Don't struggle, she kept reminding herself. Don't make a move.

But his breath, the feral smell of him, the groping hands and the revolting body thrust against hers, made her want to gag, to strike out.

"Dude"—she forced calmness into her voice—"if you don't behave, I'm going off and leave you."

"Don't leave me!" Suddenly, he was whining. His arms dropped, and the girl drew a long breath. "Yore not gonna leave me," he whimpered. "I know what it is—that other man! But you promised. You promised!" His voice was rising hysterically.

"If you want to get strung up, you keep right on hollering," Rowdy told him in a voice so cold and hard, it cut through his howls. He hushed, and when she cautiously edged into the cave, he followed.

She made her way as deep into the cave as possible. The darkness was complete. For an instant, she had the sensation of being unable to breathe. She dug her fingernails into her palms and continued to walk. There were, thank God, no sounds of animals.

She came, finally, to the end of the cave, Dude mumbling behind her. "This is it," she said. "Get some rest."

She dropped her gear where she stood, spread the saddle blanket and was asleep immediately. Dude fumbled with his belongings, then kicked them petulantly aside and lay down on the floor of the cave.

He couldn't sleep. His thoughts muddled, he felt deeply resentful. Where did she get off, ordering him around?

He didn't have to take that from any female. What she needed was a good man to break her spirit. Give her a good goin' over. He should have realized it sooner. Women always pretended they didn't want to be taken by a man, but once you opened 'em up . . . Hell, yes, that was the answer. It would change the whole situation.

He inched his way toward her.

Rowdy awoke to the feel of his body heavy on hers, his hands biting into her shoulders.

"Now, damn you"—his voice was thick—"we'll see if yore so high and mighty. Think yore too good . . ." He continued to mumble while his hands left her shoulders and clamped onto her breasts, clawing and ripping at them.

"Hellcat! Slut! Whore!"

I must not move. I must not make a sound. The words circled in her mind as though painted with fire. Her shoulders throbbed where he had held her; the pain in her breasts threatened to cause her to faint. Dude lifted himself slightly, jerked at her skirt, ran a hand up the inside of her thigh and pinched her viciously.

Rowdy bit hard into her lip, felt the saltiness of blood on her tongue.

Finally, her mind ceased its stunned whirling. Her hand snaked out, found her reticule. The next moment, the .38 was pressed into the man's side. With a tremendous effort, she made her voice calm.

"My finger's on the trigger," she said with deadly gentleness. "I'll give you three. Then I'm going to kill you. One . . . two . . ."

He flung himself away from her, mouthing obscenities.

Within a minute or two, she heard his steady snoring.

She lay awake in the darkness, sobbing as though her heart would break, but soundlessly, lest he wake and come at her again. She would have been too sick and weak and despairing to fight him off again. She cried until there were no more tears. Then, exhausted, she crept nearer the mouth of the cave.

She could not sleep. The revulsion within her was like the gnawing of a deadly illness.

108

Angus reached Robber's Cave at around ten. The sun was bright; the morning would have been perfect, were it not for the hideous chore facing him. His certainty had increased as he rode toward the cave. Rowdy would be there. He would somehow get her away from this part of the country. Head west, maybe.

But how to get her out? That tinhorn was probably still with her. Angus didn't want a bullet in his gut before he could explain himself to her.

With his child so close, he was wild with impatience. He tried to reason, think sensibly about how to draw them out. Suddenly, yearning overcame caution. In the shelter of a huge oak, he cupped his hands around his mouth and shouted.

"Miss Rowdy!"

After dawn, Rowdy had fallen into uneasy sleep. When she heard her name being called, she thought it was Dude. The sound came again, and she sat up, groggy, trying to rub the sleep from her eyes.

"Miss Rowdy!"

From deep in the cave, she heard Dude stir and curse, heard his unsteady feet dislodge small stones as he walked toward her.

And the voice came again. From outside! "Miss Rowdy! Love!"

She sprang up, torn between tears and laughter, disbelief and hope. The next moment, a slight form was hurtling toward Angus. The pale hair floated out behind her like a shimmering cape. Angus thrust his gun into its holster and raced to meet her.

Dude was forgotten by both of them. As Rowdy ran from the cave, he reached its mouth. He saw them come together, throw their arms around each other, and rage rose in his sick mind. He hurried back to his saddle pack, put the rifle together with trembling hands.

That was that other man, damn him! The one who kept him from having Rowdy. His mouth was jerking as he rushed back to the cave's opening.

In the shelter of Angus's arms, Rowdy was whispering, "Papa, I knew you'd come," while tears ran down her cheeks. And Angus was saying, "Don't cry, Miss Rowdy. It's all right. Papa's here . . ."

Somehow, despite the depth of his fury, Dude managed to still the shaking of his hands.

Facing the cave, Angus caught the glint of sun on metal. Instinctively, he shoved Rowdy to the gound as he snatched his gun. The .45 and Dude's rifle barked at precisely the same moment. As though in slow motion, Angus saw the other man go down, saw the reflexive jerk of musculature that spoke of death. But even as he took in the scene, he himself was falling, spasms of pain radiating from his shoulder.

He was conscious of the pebbly roughness scraping his face, saw Miss Rowdy rushing to him.

"Papa!" she whispered. "Oh, God, Papa, don't die!" She tore off a piece of her petticoat to staunch the blood.

Angus fought against the pain. By sheer force of will, he banished it. "Ride out, girl!" he commanded; "I'll be all right. You go. They're huntin' you. . . ."

Shaking her head, Rowdy held the cloth tightly against the wound. "No, Papa," she said gently. "I'm going to get you taken care of; then I'll face the music. I'm through running, Papa. I'm home. We're together again. That's all that matters."

"A rich, stirring novel of the westward
thrust of America, and of a dynamic woman
who went West to tame the wilderness within her."
The Literary Guild

PASTORA

JOANNA BARNES

The passions of two generations, and the rich,
colorful history of 19th-century California, are
woven into this 768-page epic of adventure and
romance! It follows one strong and courageous
woman through tragedy and triumph, public scandal
and private struggle, as she strives to seize a golden
destiny for herself and those she loves!

"Blockbuster historical romance!"
Los Angeles Times

"Readers who like romantic sagas with historical
backgrounds will enjoy this."
Library Journal

AVON Paperback   56184 • $3.50

Available wherever paperbacks are sold, or directly from the
publisher. Include 50¢ per copy for postage and handling: allow
6-8 weeks for delivery. Avon Books, Mail Order Dept., 224 West
57th St., N.Y., N.Y. 10019.

Pastora 12-81